Praise for John Brady's
MATT MINOGUE series:

Unholy Ground

"Riveting . . . The suspense builds to barely bearable intensity . . . crackles with pungent Irish idiom and its vignettes of the country's everyday life."
– Toronto Star

"Excellent Sergeant Matt Minogue . . . marvellous dialogue, as nearly surreal as a Magritte postcard the sergeant likes, and a twisting treacherous tale."
– Sunday Times

Kaddish in Dublin

"Matt Minogue, the magnetic centre of this superb series . . . and Brady's tone of battered lyricism are the music which keep drawing us back to this haunting series." – New York Times

"Culchie Colombo with a liberal and urbane heart . . . like all the best detective stories it casts its net widely over its setting . . .[Minogue is] a character who should run and run." – Irish Times

A Stone of the Heart

"Towers above the mystery category as an eloquent, compelling novel . . . a tragic drama involving many characters, each so skillfully realized that one virtually sees and hears them in this extraordinary novel . . ." – PUBLISHERS WEEKLY

"A masterfully crafted work of plot, atmosphere and especially characterization . . . Minogue, thoughtful, clear-eyed and perhaps too sensitive . . . is a full-blooded character built for the long haul of a series . . ." – MACLEAN'S

ALL SOULS

"As lyrical and elegantly styled as the last three . . . a first-rate story with marvellous characters . . . Another masterful tale from a superior author."
– GLOBE AND MAIL

"Nothing gets in the way of pace, narrative thrust or intricate story-telling." – IRISH TIMES

"A knockout." – KIRKUS REVIEWS

THE GOOD LIFE

"Brilliant craftsmanship."
– LIBRARY JOURNAL

"Brady, like Chandler, has a poet's eye for place . . . [he] is emerging as one of the supreme storytellers of Canadian crime fiction." – GLOBE AND MAIL

Wonderland

A MATT MINOGUE MYSTERY

JOHN BRADY

Wonderland

A MATT MINOGUE MYSTERY

McArthur & Company
Toronto

This McArthur & Company paperback edition published in 2003.

First published in Canada in 2002 by
McArthur & Company
322 King Street West, Suite 402
Toronto, ON M5V 1J2

National Library of Canada Cataloguing in Publication

Brady, John, 1955-
        Wonderland : a Matt Minogue mystery / John Brady.

ISBN 1-55278-387-1

I. Title.

PS8553.R245W65 2003   C813'.54   C2003-903781-9

Composition / Cover & f/x: *Mad Dog Design Inc.*
Printed in Canada by *Transcontinental Printing Inc.*

The publisher would like to acknowledge the financial support of
the Government of Canada through the Book Publishing Industry
Development Program (BPIDP) for our publishing activities.
The publisher further wishes to acknowledge the financial
support of the Ontario Arts Council for our publishing program.

10 9 8 7 6 5 4 3 2 1

For Hanna, Julia and Michael,
and for Chris and Mary Brady

TWO BIRDS, ONE STONE

There wasn't much talk when they decided about the Albanians. It was the main order of business, and everyone around the table knew it was coming. Gallagher stuck to what he'd started with, to take care of it out in the street. Liam Grogan wasn't surprised really.

The Albanians had shown up in March, on the asylum run from France. Their papers said they were from someplace you couldn't pronounce in Yugoslavia, or, as Gallagher liked to say, the *former* Yugoslavia. Nobody really knew. Everything over there was forged or robbed. The fact was that these two were putting stuff out on the street for months now. There was talk too of them trying to get girls in from Bulgaria or Russia. Trying their hand at everything, according to Gallagher; mooching about.

Grogan shifted in his seat, and gave up trying to mentally place Albania on a map of Europe. He eyed Gallagher's mop of white hair. The Professor he was called inside, right, with the Einstein do and all. It always looked so peculiar over his black beard. Well, he did take himself a bit seriously. But he'd always been that way in the however many years he'd been Warrant Officer for the West Belfast brigade too. Thanks to Her Majesty, he had two degrees from the Open University under his belt.

"Anything else from the Guards," Gallagher said. Specifically, in relation to the Russian thing, or where did they get their heroin from?

"No," said Kelly. "Nothing new."

Grogan watched Gallagher's fingers move around the rim of his glass. Arms on him the size of another man's legs. His rig was one of those you saw on the wheelchair athlete races. But for all the free sociology lessons, Gallagher was a savage.

"Liam?"

Grogan had to make an effort to take his eyes off Gallagher's hands.

"We're game ball with your Dublin friend?"

Grogan felt the other eyes settle on him now.

"Ready, willing, and able?" Gallagher asked.

"No change," Grogan said. "He's sound."

"Since when?"

"Well, I was talking to him last night."

Gallagher kept his gaze on him.

"Even with the additional item?"

"He's okay with it. He understands."

"He's not entirely happy with it though, is he."

"He'll do his bit. The follow-up and everything."

Gallagher sat back and he rested his hands on the table. Grogan wondered if this would be enough to finally convince them about Bobby Quinn. Maybe then, Gallagher would cut the sarcasm and finally call "your friend in Dublin" by his proper name.

They went around the table. When his turn came, Grogan nodded. He didn't feel badly about it, he realized. He didn't feel anything at all really.

He lit another cigarette, and he listened to Frank Nevins begin to explain to the meeting how the laboratory effort was going. Nevins had done a lot of reading about chemicals and equipment. He loved talking about the technical stuff, the gear. Bore the arse off you.

Grogan didn't try very hard to stop his mind wandering. *Item.* In his mind he heard how Gallagher hit the *t* hard when he said it. *Additional eye-tehmm.* Was it because they were from Dublin that Gallagher could talk like that?

He'd heard it all over the years, about the crowd down South, the crowd in Dublin. He'd heard it from the men who now sat around this table, he'd heard it from the others who were dead now, he'd even heard it from his own family. Oh, a different mob down South, so they are. You can't trust them, even the politicals. Not a one of them can you trust. They'd turn on you without warning.

No. It was probably because Quinn himself hadn't even been aware of how bad it had gotten. Their insider in the Guards had tipped them off. It was Grogan who had to drive down and tell Quinn. That was just one more thing for Gallagher, of course, one more excuse to be the way he was.

The "item" was all over the place, trying to start up his own jobs. Wouldn't listen to anyone. He'd even tried to talk Quinn into letting him try to bend some of the Drug Squad cops. Quinn had found out a fortnight ago that he was selling drugs, or trying to sell them, in clubs and out in the suburbs. The story was that the drugs were coming from the Albanians, too. Right under Quinn's nose, type of thing.

Nevins went off into something about a chemical formula.

Last month, Gallagher had asked him about Quinn again. Was he on the ball. Was he really aware of the situation down there. Had he still got contacts. Did he have the brains for this. Finally, after the digs about incompetence, was Quinn above board.

It was almost an exact replay of Gallagher trying to sound

him out about Quinn after the first meeting in Newry last year.

What bothered Gallagher about Bobby Quinn back then was his lack of blather. Quinn wasn't a yapper, especially in that Dublin way. It was only poor choice of associates got him the five years. In the eighteen months he and Grogan had in Portlaoise, he couldn't remember Quinn losing it, or being stupid, or complaining.

"Not much to say for himself, has he," was Gallagher's take then.

"Not such a bad thing, is it."

"What, a fella from Dublin who doesn't talk his head off?"

"Well, how many have you known?"

It was true, and Gallagher knew it. They were very parochial here. They were paranoid actually, if you wanted to be frank about it. How else would you be after thirty years of this? The people in the South were just like anyone else these days. They went shopping, they went to Disney World, they put in new kitchens and all the rest of it. Sure, it was only a hundred miles to Dublin. It might as well be a thousand.

The money to be made had nothing to do with the border, or the Brits, or what you did for Ireland's freedom, or even what happened a year, or a week ago. What it was about was waking up, and realizing that you didn't go through thirty years of war here just to sit on the sidelines while a pack of jackals landed here and started taking things from under your nose. Someone needed to get the message in right short order.

Nevins finished up with something to do with volatility and disposal, how he'd found a good way. It went to Kelly then. He made a joke about mice eating the stuff and going wild. Then he started in on what had gotten done in Velsen, the place they'd been recommended near Amsterdam, and the new shipping agent.

Grogan stretched out one leg and then the other. The ache

had turned into pain now. The cortisone had been Tuesday. His hip was taking too much weight; he just had to get up. No one paid attention to his slow patrol around the room.

His turn came sooner than he expected. He told them about the Dublin trade and the routes to Galway and up to Sligo. Kelly tried more wit but it didn't take this time either, something to do with the time he asked the fella in Sligo with no kneecaps if he wanted to buy painkillers.

Grogan said he hadn't thought of that. Having a dealer kneecapped over a late payment wouldn't have been his first choice. Kelly didn't like being deadpanned.

"We'll see how these Albanian fellas take to it then," he said. Nobody laughed.

And that was it. Kelly reminded them that his daughter would be on the telly tonight. They'd interviewed her on account of she was the head of the residents' association on the estate. It was a thing about Orange marching routes and would the riots last year be repeated again this year.

"Well, at least we know we can depend on somebody," Kelly said.

Grogan almost felt sorry for some of the Orangemen, the ancient ones anyway, with their bowler hats and their union jacks. Frozen in time, they were, and the smart ones knew it. Their gangs he'd have no trouble with. That hadn't changed: one in the back of the head for every man jack of them. One dozen, if that's what it took.

He let himself down into a chair again. Gallagher wheeled over.

"Well, Liam. Getting any easier?"

"Wait and see, says the surgeon."

"They always say that, don't they."

Gallagher rolled his wheels back and forward. Kelly was still holding the door.

"No second thoughts from Mr. Quinn?"

Grogan had known it was coming. Still he replied a little quicker than he liked to hear from himself.

"No. Like I was saying, he's on board."

"We're doing his housecleaning for him too. He understands that, doesn't he."

Grogan nodded. Kelly let the door close, and he made his way over.

"Our fella's there already," Gallagher said. "He went down this morning."

"It might take time to do it right."

"They have to sign in at some office there before the end of the week?"

"The Aliens' Office."

"He'll be quick when the time comes," Kelly said.

Roe, Johnnie Roe, Grogan thought. He'd never actually met him. The fact was that Roe was a header, a header in more ways than one. It was some disease or condition. He'd heard someone give it a name once, a word that sounded like one of those mountain goats in South America they got wool from. A stress thing from prison, maybe. Roe had been working steady on contract since he got out. Gallagher let slip one night that he figured Roe had done a dozen or so jobs in the past three years. You could tell from the descriptions in the papers anyway.

Grogan planted his stick in the carpet, and shifted to his right. Kelly bent to him.

"Are you okay there, Liam."

He wanted to yank Kelly's hand from under his arm, throw him across the room.

"Grand."

They weren't a year apart, Kelly and himself. They'd been amongst the first out in 1971, the time they'd gotten the

American guns into the Ardoyne. The joke for years had been how Kelly's mother had beaten the ears off him that night when she'd found out. It was Kelly's luck not to have been in that car nine years ago when it was riddled at a checkpoint. Kelly's younger brother Jude had twenty-seven bullets in him.

Grogan followed Gallagher's wheels to the door.

He'd need to use a second stick in the not too distant future. But he'd always have Kelly's pity, wouldn't he.

Gallagher turned and looked up.

"Mind yourself, Liam."

WILD BORNEO

Eileen Magee wasn't one for waiting, especially when she could see the traffic stopped ahead on the Goatstown Road. She made her way to the front of the bus and rearranged her shopping bags on her hands. It was good to be out of town before eleven. The traffic—Holy God!

"I'll race you, missus."

She looked over at the driver. The bags slid down and pinched her fingers.

"My racing days are over, let me tell you."

He stretched and pretended to laugh and then he opened the door.

"Mind yourself crossing."

The traffic was stopped in both directions now. She heard car horns in the distance, a pneumatic drill. She stepped into the park and headed down the long, curving tarmacadam path that followed the river Dodder upstream toward Milltown. The grass was spotted with daisies. She wondered if kids made daisy chains anymore.

Just to be alive, she almost said aloud, even to be sixty-three years old. How lucky she was, how very lucky. She had her place bought and paid for, long before the property madness had hit Dublin. Tonight was bridge. There'd be Maddie Rowan and her husband, Tom, with the laugh like a horse.

Saturday they'd drive up the mountains.

Maybe the nicest thing about Dublin—if you weren't worried about getting mugged or that class of thing—was that the city was teeming with young people. She liked that, even the madness down Henry Street. Still, she found herself wondering where her own places had gone over the years, her landmarks, her own Dublin.

A scent of lilac came to her. She stopped and moved one of her bags to her other hand. She looked across to the garden walls backing onto the park. A lot of the houses there on Whitebeam Road had had their attics converted. It wasn't for having bigger families though, was it. She rarely saw kids around here. They were in care, she supposed, what with both parents having careers these days.

The grass gave way to shrubs and trees as the park narrowed, and the path drew closer to the riverbank. She knew she'd never get used to the overgrown look to the parks now. There was a plan behind it, she'd learned, the way they wanted to naturalize the park. It was the new way, ecology.

Eileen wouldn't walk down here at night. Years ago, the kids from the flats in Donnybrook would give you pause, but those gurriers flinging rocks into the river or fishing for pinkeens were long gone. She sort of missed them.

Well, maybe not all of them were gone. Here were two kids, two boys, half-walking and swinging their sticks across the grass. A little wave of gladness for lost times came over her. They must be from an old style family, she decided. It was the way it should be, if truth be told, even nowadays. Kids should be playing and wandering, carefree, with a mammy waiting at home for them.

"A great day for exploring, lads, isn't it?"

One of them, he couldn't be more than nine or ten, stopped swinging and looked at her. She felt her smile slip.

Did no one talk to kids, bid them good day anymore?

The other continued his swinging. He lopped a dandelion and he examined the tip of his stick. She liked the grass-stained knees, the unruly hair, the freckles.

"It's like wild Borneo, isn't it?"

One glanced at her, looked away. Maybe they hadn't done that in geography.

"On an adventure, are you?"

The tall boy sort of nodded and he began to walk away. The whir of his stick on the grass reminded her of something. She smiled at the younger one. He had curly hair. His socks balled at his ankles, and his shoes were caked with mud. He looked at her.

"There's a girl," he said.

She smiled, waited. He wanted her to say something, though.

"A girl, is there?"

The taller boy had turned now. He eyed Eileen.

"Sleeping," said the curly one.

Eileen studied the face. God knows all the warnings they must get about strangers these days anyway.

"Eoin," said the tall one. "Come on."

"Yes," he said. "Sleeping, so she is."

She watched him trudge after his pal. He looked back at her once.

She turned toward the shrubs and the trees beyond. The river was shallow down there, she remembered. She couldn't hear it.

Someone gave a long beep in the traffic jam back out on the Goatstown Road. She sighed and she headed up the path toward Milltown.

The shopping bags had slid from her palm down her fingers again. She slowed near the shrubs and listened. A couple courting in the bushes on a summer's day wasn't news, was it. Maybe the girl pretended she was asleep. The fella might've been quick enough to make himself scarce when the two explorers showed up. As fellas will do.

The hush of the traffic still hung over the park, but now she could hear the low mutter of the river. She looked in through the leaves. Wild Borneo, was right. A jungle. She sighed, and she thought of Sister Brophy, that battleaxe from Leitrim, running the wards all those years ago. Those expressions barked out used to drive them up the walls, but they'd lodged, as Brophy had of course intended, and they'd stayed.

Things are not what they may seem, nurse. Examine. Ask. Report.

And how could she not remember the other great Brophyism, the same one that hundreds, thousands would know?

Look to the girls, nurses. The boys will turn up in their own good time.

Eileen stopped and looked up and down the path. There was only herself and the birds. The look on the little lad's face came back to her again, his bafflement, the unknowing that he couldn't help himself passing on to someone else. God Almighty, it wasn't her place to be telling girls how to conduct themselves, like parish priests beating the bushes years ago.

She stepped off the path and she laid her bags under a shrub.

"Hello. Hello in there?"

The rustling she half-expected didn't happen. More birds she heard, the river, and still the soft hum of the city. She pulled a branch aside.

"Is anyone there?"

There were briars at her ankle. Faded, half-crushed cans

lay in the undergrowth. Nothing much romantic about this place, was there.

Well, they were gone. At least no one was around to see her making an iijit of herself.

Someone had dumped bags of rubbish or grass cuttings near the foot of a fir tree. Tinkers, she thought—*travellers*, she should say—that was it. So that was how they valued what was given to them. They'd be given a bag of clothes when they'd come begging, then they'd sort out what they wanted and pitch everything else. By God, it was hard to be charitable to people who did that sort of thing.

Sunlight flared in small patches. Her eyes were giving out on her here in the gloom. She rubbed at them and looked again. These bags were still bundled up, maybe even unopened. Her eyes ran along the bag half hidden by the bottom of the tree.

Something didn't fit. There was a shape to this bag, or bundle.

The stillness in here felt like a weight on her now. She heard herself swallow.

Something moved in the bushes. Eileen started, felt the jolt work its way down from her scalp. There was a blond or red tint between some leaves and it moved. She took a step back and it moved again. She saw the face then, if that's what it was, the snout more like it, and the eyes watching her.

It was a dog, but not really a dog. There was interest, but then indifference, in those amber eyes. Did a fox really have such a pointed nose? Its eyes flickered over to some place near. Then it was gone. She didn't even see the tail, the brush.

Her legs had gone rubbery. Eileen felt the pounding, and she put her hand under her arm. She tried to ignore the pops of light in front of her. Her mouth had gone dry.

She stared at the bundle again. If only she had something,

a stick or a cane.

She didn't want to go over. She'd have to go over.

"Hello?"

It was a head of hair she'd been looking at. People didn't, shouldn't, lie like that. She took three steps and stopped. Those were fingers. At least the girl was dressed. She still couldn't see a face.

Her next step broke a twig.

There were spots moving along the fingers.

"Oh," she heard herself say. Now she couldn't move. She wondered if she'd fall. The chatter in her head had stopped. The river had a tinkling sound. She stared at the ants on the fingers, the jeans, the hair tossed over the head.

Eileen was talking to herself now.

"I know what to do," she said. "I'm a nurse, so I am, and I can do this. I can go over and I can look and I can walk back to the path too."

She tiptoed to the dead girl, thinking all the while of her own heart, of Sister Brophy, of the two boys, of the bus driver and the city and the fine summer's day, of buying one of those mobile phones, of God, of the Guards, and many other things.

MUTINY

Things had started to fall apart for Minogue early in the week. He'd sensed it, like a listing or a yaw, but he couldn't put his finger on one thing. There'd been that look from Kathleen when he'd snorted about house prices or something. It was the way things went quiet when he came into the Fraud office each morning too. Everyone polite, but a brittleness. He had a feeling early on that this descent would pick up speed.

Today wasn't a great start, even at home. He was thick-headed from staying late at a session in the Garda Club last night. He was more annoyed than embarrassed that he hadn't left before the rounds of drinks started coming in fast. It had turned into pretty well industrial drinking by closing time.

A ten-minute shower hadn't helped much. He plugged in the kettle and brooded. There were more brochures for new apartments under yesterday's paper. These ones were in Bray: two bedrooms, generous balcony, unparalleled view of the sea. They had started calling these new apartment places by names. *Bountiful*. Make the change to *Bountiful*. Bray, he wondered, sourly, a town he'd never liked. An apartment that'd cost only sixteen times what they had paid for their house. Bray: full of tinkers, years back, bottle fights at closing time. Hadn't there been tons of banks robbed there?

He stuffed the brochures into the bin too hard, slicing open the plastic bag. He did nothing about that but stared at the kettle instead. Kathleen's footsteps moved from room to room upstairs. Humming, she was too. "I Will Survive," it sounded like.

The coffee didn't make much headway against the dull, familiar resentment that was settling on him.

Kathleen arrived downstairs in top gear. She moved through the kitchen at speed. He eyed her over the rim of his cup.

"Will you think about phoning Pat then?"

"I will," he said.

"He needs to talk to someone. And you used to have great chats, the pair of you."

Minogue didn't want to phone his son-in-law. He liked Pat well enough, but he had no advice to offer him. He didn't want to tell Kathleen to stop pretending she wasn't worried sick about their daughter's marriage falling apart either.

"Always walked to his own drummer, Pat. Have you his work number?"

"I do. 'Marched,' by the way."

She stopped pushing something into the cupboard.

"'To the beat of a different drummer,'" he added.

"A bit of a session last night, was it?"

"A bit unexpected."

"The usual suspects, I take it."

He nodded. She made to say something but turned away instead. He edged into the table and looked through yesterday's paper. His eyes were hurting even more.

"I was on the phone to Maura Kilmartin the other day, you know."

"Were you," he said.

"I was. Says she . . . you wouldn't know Jimmy these days. Since the move, like."

He remembered standing outside the Garda Club about midnight, Kilmartin trying to light a cigar all the while rabbiting on about helicopter costs, the percentage of staff attending court, money laundering, the disgrace of not having up-to-date surveillance gizmos for Serious Crimes, his son in the US who didn't phone much.

"The best thing ever happened to Jim," says she to me. "From a personal point of view, of course. He loves it."

It was seven months since the Murder Squad had been folded up. Jim Kilmartin had been parachuted to Support Services up in the Park. Meetings, travel, conferences.

"Sleeps properly," says she. "And he's cut down on the gargle."

Not last night he hadn't, Minogue thought. Along with half-remembered bits of dreams, he still had some of Kilmartin's antics and soliloquies replaying. But, for all the nine to five, the desk and the office and the suits, Kilmartin wasn't ready to admit that Garda Commissioner Tynan had done them all a favour with the shuffle.

Minogue waited for her to look over.

"Will you come up to Glencree with me this afternoon?"

She closed the dishwasher with her heel.

"Glencree? Glencree way up the mountains?"

"Is it that far?"

"It is that far."

"Well, that Glencree, yes."

"This afternoon?"

"I can pick you up handy enough."

She made a smile that he hoped he was wrong about.

"I'll be at work," she said. "So will you."

Behind her, the pear and the apple trees, planted one for Daithi and one for Iseult, were in full leaf. He remembered the showers of blossoms, the most in years.

"Let's get going," she said. "It's just that I have to be there."

He had been planning his second cup of coffee.

She stopped him in the doorway, settled his tie, pushed strands of hair behind his ears. He studied the job she had done on her hair. The fruity perfume with the herbal afterthought he had sworn he'd say nothing about.

"Cheer up," she said. "It might never happen."

He got into his jacket in the hall, took the phone out of the charger. His briefcase was by the stairs. A truce was in order. He winked at her. She smiled, and she grabbed him. He held her tight.

"It takes time," she said. "I know. But change is good."

Phrases like that seemed to be cropping up a lot lately, he thought. He held her tighter. Yes, there was spray something in her hair.

"You've still got the moves," he said to her.

"Play your cards right and you never know."

"Do you think you'll have the time?"

That was as far as he got. She pushed him to arms' length, but held his shoulders.

"Aren't we gone beyond that? I mean to say, haven't we?"

She was right. He knew now was a good time, a very good time, to say nothing.

"I have a career," she said. "Just like you do. I'm in property appraisal, which you give speeches about every now and then, as being a shady effort, of huckstering."

"I only said hooks. I think."

"It's your whole approach."

"We could talk about it up in Glencree."

"Is it my fault that the property market keeps going through the roof? Or that I took courses so's I could get back into the working world?"

He looked through the front window to the cars lining the road outside. There'd been no more than a few cars parked there when he'd walked Daithi down to the shops years ago. Now there were a dozen, and pricey motors they were, a lot of them. Some of them were owned by grown-up kids who hadn't left home.

"It's like you'd prefer all this never happened, is it? Poverty is good for you?"

"I'm not exactly hankering after the Famine."

"You're not, are you? Wake up, then. Look where we are, the both of us. I'm lucky to be able to work again, so I am, and not be sitting at home in this empty house. And you, you're on the up and up. But it's like you don't *want* to do well at all."

The hangover came to him as a muffled ache now, bone tiredness.

"You've moved on," she went on. "Moved up. They're grooming you for something. Cop on, can't you. I mean to say, you're supposed to be the detective here."

She went to the mirror, moved her head around, patted the tips of her hair.

"'International Liaison,'" she added. "Ask yourself, would they give the job to any gom in there? No they wouldn't, and well you know it."

He watched her tug on the hems of her jacket. Now wasn't the time to tell her he knew plenty of goms in the Gardai. Some he liked a lot.

"What I think is," she said while she paused to clamp her lips together and study the coverage of the lipstick, ". . . is that you need to work on something."

"I am working. I'm learning all about Fraud."

"Not work work. The other thing."

"Give me a clue."

"Your goals, is what I mean."

"Goals."

For a moment all he could think of was evening by the ruins at Tully, the birds calling out from the darkness in the hedges. Or by the sea at Killiney, the waves running, drawing back, and pebbles whispering. Were these goals?

She turned from the mirror.

"This is July," she said. "It's been seven months. Count them."

"All right, I get it. All right."

"But do you? The phone ringing two in the morning, falling out of bed? Prowling around in ditches and alleys? Working thirty hours straight? Who in their right mind would miss that?"

"You're right."

He hoped she wouldn't say something like the self-sabotage thing she had said to him one night last week.

"Will you check the front window upstairs," she said. "I'm always forgetting."

He checked Daithi's bedroom last. The model aircraft were still there, the bits of computer parts, the photos. He stood by the window and looked out over the driveway. Kathleen was rummaging in a briefcase that she held on the bonnet of the car. There were clouds building up toward the east.

He turned back to the window. The Nissan was still there by the laburnum at the Costigans'. There was a proper antenna on the roof. It was an unmarked car for sure.

He went down the stairs one at a time. He set the alarm in the hall and pulled the door shut.

"That blue is nice on you," Kathleen said. "It says something."

He cooked up a smile. He started the Citroën. The Oul French Tart, Kilmartin still called it. The brakes needed doing and the sunroof was leaking again. He let it roll out onto the road and put on the handbrake. He slipped out and pulled the gate shut.

The window on the Nissan was half-open. The driver's head rested low against the headrest. Minogue wondered about the trouble the Costigans' oldest son had gotten into last year, the drugs. Maybe they were keeping an eye out for something here again.

"The poor parents," Kathleen was saying. "God, can you imagine!"

"Whose parents?"

She tapped at the newspaper.

"That poor girl. The one they found in the park there Monday. The Dodder?"

He looked down at the paper.

"Sixteen, she was," Kathleen said.

He shook his head. He steered around the neighbour's new four-wheeler.

"An end of the year thing it was," she said. "A rave or something."

The driver of the Nissan stirred and sat up. Minogue forgot about his lurchy stomach, the spacey feeling he had when he turned his head, his alien wife.

He let the Citroën coast in second. He looked at the driver's profile, the slowly turning head framed by the window. There was that nose that had changed direction, all right, the right ear that had been squashed too often, the military cut.

Kathleen had spotted him now.

"Is that who I think it is?" she said.

He pulled in, in front of the Nissan. Kathleen looked around the headrest.

"What in the name of God is he doing here?"

The fact that Garda Thomas Malone wasn't getting out of his car told Minogue something. He turned off the ignition and studied Malone in the wing mirror. Then he opened the door. Kathleen grabbed his arm.

"No," he said to her. "I mean, I don't know why he's here."

WAITING

The fella in the back seat seemed to be dozing. Doyle wasn't fooled. He stole another glance at the cap. It was like a cap you'd see on a farmer or something, and it was definitely a wig of some sort under it. This was a disguise? It had taken a while for him to realize that the guy had no actual eyebrows either. Like a fish or something, he was, maybe a lizard. Lizard-man, that'd do.

He didn't know the man's name. All he knew was that he had a Northern accent, that he was a weirdo, and that he was going to blow the kneecaps off two Albanians.

The thin liquid line where the eyelids met glittered for a moment. You're not codding anyone with that move, Doyle wanted to tell him. He himself had played that one before since he was a child, pretending to have dozed off, but seeing plenty, all he needed to see, between his eyelashes.

He touched the swelling on his cheekbone by his eye. It felt watery under it now, but it wasn't as sore. He hadn't expected the belt from the left. Lucky he had a few drinks in him, then. Malone would be feeling the pain soon enough after this, and he knew it too. Right after he'd taken the first dig off Malone, he remembered seeing it dawn on his face: end up in court, lose the job over this. And if he couldn't remember what he'd dug himself into, that Chinese-looking girlfriend of his would remind him soon enough. She was none too impressed, was she.

The eye would go black, but that didn't matter. His eye was a bit bloodshot.

What was a cop like Malone doing with a girlfriend like that anyway? There was plenty out there; you could have it off any night of the week you wanted to. With anyone, basically. All you had to do was have your eyes open. Even the snotty ones in the clubs wanted a bit of danger, the glamour, well, what they thought they knew from their music and their magazines and films and that. Hooligans were in, yes, thug love. Who'd have guessed that years ago. Schoolgirls, even. What a joke.

The man in the back stirred and settled himself in the seat. Yeah, it was getting hot in the car already. Doyle wondered what he was getting paid, what he'd use on the two Albanians. He hadn't seen any gun. They used .22s in the punishment jobs up in the North he'd heard. If it was going to be Six Packs, shots behind the kneecaps, they were out to keep the guy in a chair for life. Savages, up there.

Well, it was all relative, wasn't it. After all, here he was, driving this maniac for a job here in Dublin. With his gym bag there beside him, the fancy Adidas bag. Like he was an athlete or something. Right.

He'd been leery about this from the first time Bobby Quinn had asked him. All it was was driving, sure. Bobby looking at him, waiting, like he knew what he was thinking, what he was going to say. He remembered stumbling and fumbling his way through. "Well, Bobby, I'd like to help out, you know, and prove I can do stuff and all, but kneecapping people out in the street was kind of the deep end, wasn't it? Even though I appreciate how much it means to be asked in on this, and all?" Quinn had just nodded, said he understood. Said he appreciated him telling him straight out.

Later, when Bobby Quinn put ten fifties on the counter right there in front of him that afternoon, Doyle's biggest job right then became pretending that he still needed to think about it. The other five hundred after. A chance to get steady work, Bobby told him then. He needed someone to rely on, to help out every now and then. But were there going to be other lads on this job, like wouldn't it take a few to get hold of these two Albanian fellas . . . ? "No, no," Quinn told him. It wouldn't be a problem. The fella they were sending had lots of experience. He'd take care of things.

"Turn on the engine, there."

"What?"

"There's air conditioning in this."

"What, are you sweating?"

He waited for Doyle's eyes to meet his in the mirror.

"Well, I know you are."

"Save your smart aleck stuff for them that likes it."

The man didn't reply. He rolled down his windows as far as he could and began humming very low.

"They said ten," Doyle said. The man ignored him.

"So is it gone ten or not?"

"What, your girlfriend take your watch? After she walloped you?"

Doyle turned and looked around the headrest. It was the smile that wasn't a smile at all that got to him, even more than the mockery he could hear in the accent.

"You'll be fucking walking, if you carry on like that."

"Turn the key. There's a clock on the dashboard."

Doyle put on his mime act, and turned the ignition.

"Look," he said. "What did I tell you? It's ten. Game over. Let's get out of here."

"The clock is fast. I'm three minutes to. Give it a wee while yet."

"Forget your 'wee while.' No way. Ten, it is. Orders is orders."

Doyle looked down at the Adidas bag.

"After all, you have to go off and train for the Olympics and that, don't you?"

"Give it two more minutes."

"Fuck you," said Doyle. "You're a tourist here. Me, I've got things to do."

The man in the back looked down at his mobile again. Doyle turned the vents toward the roof. Then he looked down the street toward the Aliens' Office. People had been lining up there overnight since last year. He watched the traffic in the mirror.

The man in the back was watching him.

"What?"

"Nothing."

"Well, what are you staring at?"

"Am I staring?"

"Yeah, you're staring."

"Well, I was wondering about your tattoo."

"Well, go and wonder about something else. What is it to you?"

"Oh, nothing, I suppose. I was just curious."

"You were, were you? You don't like them or something?"

"I don't have an opinion on tattoos."

That schoolteacher tone too, Doyle remembered, full of sly sarcasm, for sure.

"Well, don't look at it if you don't like it."

"Hard to miss it."

"Well, find something else to do, right? Instead of annoying people."

"Why did you get it there, on the back of your hand?"

"None a your fucking business. Look, are you trying to be smart with me?"

"Smart?"

"Yeah, smart. It's what we say here if someone's looking for trouble."

He closed his eyes and laid his head back. The cap moved down his forehead.

"Like, what exactly is your problem?"

He opened his eyes again and rubbed them. Doyle thought he heard a faint sigh.

"Me?"

"Yeah, you. Is there something wrong with you?"

"Oh no, thank you very much. I'm as right as can be. But now, you look a bit tense, I would have to suggest."

"You're a needler, aren't you. Well you can go needle yourself now, cause I'm going. It's ten o clock."

"We should give it a while longer."

"No way. Ten's the limit. The traffic'll build up and we won't be able to move."

"Well these two have come a long way to meet us. The least we could do is give them a bit more time."

"What, they've only got to go a few miles from where—"

"From Albania, I meant."

"What, do you actually think they came all the way here to *meet* us, to meet *you?*"

"Do you know where Albania is? What it is?"

"Just shut up, will you. Enough of you. We're going, and that's all there is to it."

Doyle put it in first and turned the wheel. The beeps from the mobile stopped him from taking a gap in the traffic. He let the car roll back to the curb.

"Well," the man in the back said. "A taxi. How about that."

The phone beeped once as it was powered off. Doyle noticed that the man in the back was wiping it with a cloth too now.

"Well?"

"Some refugees, with their taxi."

"Tell me what you heard, will you?"

"All right. They're on their way, the both of them. They just got out of a taxi, and they're heading our way."

Is There Anything
You'd Like to Add to That?

It had gone quiet now in the interview room. Minogue could hear his stomach at work. This would be a daylong recovery from the Garda Club last night, then. But if he could hear it, so could they. He shifted a little in his chair. It was little enough to get over, compared to what Tommy Malone had told him in the few minutes' awkward conversation with him at the side of the road.

He took a glance at the notes that Detective Garda Fiona Hegarty was writing. He'd made cursory notes himself earlier on but he had soon tired of pretending. It was ten o'clock on the dot. One hour that felt like a day's work already.

Fiona Hegarty's writing was regular and readable and spaced and uniform. She was studying Spanish and Computer Science. Minogue had later heard that her husband, a Garda Sergeant, also a night-course cop, was on track to becoming the youngest Garda Inspector in the history of the force. He thought he had heard her say MBA a few days back, but he didn't want to ask her about that.

Her Biro stopped. She stared at where the tip poised over the page. Then she looked up at Jennifer Halloran. A hefty class of a woman. You couldn't use that word anymore of course.

It had been a half-hour since the same Jennifer Halloran couldn't stop herself— or at least Minogue supposed she had no control in the matter—from sliding off her chair onto the floor in some kind of fainting panic, hysterical, breakdown type of thing. She'd ended up on her knees. It was like she'd started praying, after an apparition or something, her forehead resting and shaking gently on the table.

"I knew I'd end up here," she'd said. "I knew right from the start. Yes, I did."

She had refused attention from a doctor. Fiona Hegarty was for pushing on with the interview, and she'd gotten her way. Minogue wasn't up to the task of trying to understand why it was he expected women to be good to one another. A lifetime of illusion he'd had then, a bone-headed chivalry thing, or just ignorance? The tight-lipped responses he'd gotten from Fiona Hegarty outside in the hall. This was equality.

"She's not pregnant. And no condition that she knows of."

"That's on tape, is it?" he asked her.

"It is."

"It's not her time or anything?"

"Do you mean her period?"

"That's what I mean, yes."

"I don't know. Ask her."

He didn't. Jennifer Halloran looked okay now. He wondered if he should make a note of that. "Composed" maybe. "Relieved"? Gone limp, would be more like it.

He wondered where in Spain Jennifer Halloran had gone. Which particular spot would attract a forty-two-year-old bookkeeper living at home with her mother and a Down's

Syndrome brother. Had she maybe met a fella there, a local gigolo, and had a fling. Maybe not. Had she thought of never coming back. Had she wondered if or when she'd be caught.

Right: the subconscious. There was always that, wasn't there.

Immediately he saw Kilmartin's face curled up in disdain: *Don't even start on that subconscious shite with me.*

Maybe a Catholic thing then, a wish for punishment? Not this day and age.

Ms. Halloran had hardly anticipated being in this claustrophobic room with three chairs and a table and two other microphones in the ceiling that no one got told about, and a detective laying into her while a middle-aged hungover detective on trainee assignment in the Garda Fraud Squad watched. Hardly.

Minogue rubbed at his eyes. It's trying to help sort out Tommy Malone's damned mess he should be doing. Malone had made up his mind that wouldn't turn himself in until they'd had a proper chat later on.

The basics: at one o'clock in the morning, after a skinful of drink with Minogue and Kilmartin and Co., Malone had ended up at a chipper with his girlfriend. In came some lowlife who knew him, half-knew him, a gouger. Doyle, he thought his name was. Worse, this Doyle knew about Malone's brother Terry, and that Terry had OD-ed in his cell last week. With as much drink in him as Minogue had had, and the pressure of his new job at Drugs Central, Tommy Malone was never more likely to lose it.

Minogue had tried seeing the ways around this while he listened to Kathleen's ideas about an apartment and for Iseult finding teaching work, say, and maybe even moving into an apartment they could get the mortgage for or maybe Iseult moving in and paying a lower rent to them and then maybe

Pat might think that they could afford Dublin so that would take some of the pressure off.

All the while they inched through Ranelagh, jammed unnecessarily at new road works no one had told him about, the temperature needle a hair away from red, the heat that some people said couldn't be global warming crushing his dehydrated brain, itself already a mess of irritation and fragility and remorse. A fine state in which to arrive at the office, the white-haired boy, the trainee headed for a big Europolice job.

Only an hour ago, too. Minogue eyed the statement that Fiona Hegarty had drawn up. Where could you learn to hand-write like that, was all he could think of. Across the table, Jennifer Halloran, shortly to be the official accused, was examining the ends of her hair. Thirty something thousand pounds over six years. How many Euro was that? Her employer of twenty years had been shocked. He'd tried to get a condition that she not go to prison. Well, that was consideration of a sort.

"Miss Halloran?"

Minogue waited for her to look up.

"Is there anything you'd like to add to that?"

She found something about the tabletop that seemed to surprise her. Her voice was low when she spoke, and she didn't look up at him.

"Only that, like I said, I didn't mean to hurt anyone."

Her lower lip began to tremble.

"And I'd just like to say, well, thanks, I mean thank you. For waiting till I got around the corner and all before, you know, bringing me here. I appreciate that, yes."

The arrest, he realized. She's deranged now, exhausted. She'd say anything.

He turned to Fiona Hegarty. She finished writing something, dictated a break on tape, and rose from the chair. He followed her, trying not to look at her. He closed the door slowly and stared at the door handle a moment. Well, at least Malone hadn't shot this Doyle fella.

In the Blink of an Eye

The man in the back hadn't moved since hanging up. Doyle had to clear his throat to get the words out. There was a shrinking somewhere in his gut, like a vacuum at work in there.

"Is this it?"

"It is."

"What if they make a run for it, cross the street or something? Or split up?"

"Don't worry about it."

"Well, they'll cop on to something, they're not stupid."

Even now there was that slight little curl to the lip, the skins where his eyebrows should be up in an arch. Looking at him like he was a specimen or lower form of life.

"Have you your bally there."

"Me what?"

"Your balaclava."

"I do, I'm ready."

"Go down to that laneway there. So's you can turn in right away afterward."

"You don't have to tell me, you know. I know the plan. I'll do the driving, okay."

Wrestling with the wheel while he hung onto the headrest brought up the BO worse. So that's what lizard-man was saying with the air conditioning.

He thought back to when he'd left after meeting Quinn at the pub. It was like floating really. And Bobby'd said he'd think it over, the idea of getting Malone in a spot, that there might be a future to that. He hadn't just given the idea the eff-off.

"You're not going to follow them down to the Aliens' place, are you? In front of those people, the refugee crowd or whatever?"

"You think they're refugees, do you."

He turned around. His palms were wet now. The man kept staring down the street. He had opened his jacket. Doyle didn't want to stare but he thought there was some kind of a strap up next to his collar now.

"Can you answer a simple question without being a sarcastic gobshite for once?"

The man in the back sniffed.

"A bit of soap wouldn't go astray," he said.

"Just shut up."

"What, are you a wee bit nervous, or something?"

"You're asking for it, I'm telling you."

"Might even wash off that borstal tattoo. Two birds with one stone."

"Look, you stupid Northern fucker, who do you think you're dealing with here?"

"Here we go," the man whispered. "That's them."

Doyle looked back up the street. One of the men had a jet-black beard, the other a tight cut, almost a skin really, and a moustache. They were smiling about something. He wondered if they were really Arabs or something.

"Move the car over to the lane, now. And leave it running. That's where I'll be."

Before Doyle had put it in gear, lizard-man had somehow stepped out and closed his door. Doyle stared at his back: how had he slid out like that, so quick? He thought about just driving off, getting the hell out of the city, and to hell with them all. He pulled on the balaclava instead, and tried not to panic.

The two Albanians reached the laneway and stepped off the curb.

The one with the beard was doing all the talking. Was there an Albanian language, Doyle wondered. There must be.

The man walking out of the laneway had a black balaclava. Doyle saw the two guns, and for a moment tried not to believe it.

The one with the moustache spun around as the shotgun went off. He fell against the railings, with something on his face and his chest, and he tried to hold on to them. He couldn't stop himself sliding down, sitting down heavily, sagging sideways. The one with the beard had tried to head out on the street. The shotgun went off again, and the running man hit off the boot of a parked car and fell behind it.

The one by the railings had curled up and he was trying to say something. Doyle saw the blood then on the cement. The man with the shotgun stepped over, put the barrel to the man's head, and fired.

Doyle wanted to shut his eyes, but he couldn't. There was the sound of tires squealing on the street behind. Across the street he watched two women crouch, their hands at their mouths. This is actually happening, he thought.

The man with the shotgun skipped across the footpath. He stopped and pointed an automatic down between the parked cars. The arm jerked and then he leaned down and fired again.

It was himself who was talking, shouting, Doyle realized. There was a scream somewhere, a woman's. Then the man with the gun was pulling open the door behind him. Where had he put the shotgun, Doyle wondered.

"Go, get a move on. Go!"

Doyle hit the accelerator hard. His stomach was giving way on him now. He had to find a jack, and now.

The man in the back was breathing through his nose.

"Jesus Christ, Jesus Christ," Doyle muttered.

"Watch the road. Stop looking in the mirror."

Doyle thought about slowing, fitting in with the traffic, just getting the two miles to the garage. But they'd have a description of the car.

"You knew all along," he said. "It was all decided, wasn't it?"

The man didn't answer him. He looked in the mirror again. He had taken off his balaclava too. No cap now, and he'd been right about the wig. Completely bald, with weird little shadows and bumps all around. He held the handle tight overhead as Doyle accelerated through the laneway toward the canal.

Doyle got around two people on bicycles with a foot to spare. He heard one yell at him. He made the amber light by the bridge.

"Talk to me! Answer me question, will you?"

"Give over, will you, and just shut it a minute."

"No I won't! The job said kneecap, that was the worst it would get, that's all! No one said anything about topping anyone! But you knew all along, didn't you?"

"Calm down."

"Don't tell me to calm down! I'm on the hook for this too, you bastard! If I'd a known this was going to happen, well I wouldn't be here, would I."

He dodged a van coming out from the curb.

"Slow down. You'll just get us noticed."

"You're an animal, that's what you are. An animal . . . ! Jesus! You come down here and you're doing something like this—I mean, who said for you to do that? Who?"

Doyle heard the sirens now, far behind. He took his place behind a bus. They were almost within sight of the turn for the garage.

"This isn't frigging West Belfast here pal, you don't just pull something like that!"

"Oh. I'm not welcome here anymore. Is that it?"

"We'll see how welcome you are when we get to the garage and Bobby hears what you done."

For a moment the man met his eyes in the mirror.

"You've got some explaining to do, you hear me? You *animal*, you."

The eyes turned back toward the passing traffic.

"I do believe that you're losing it a wee bit," the man murmured. "And you know it."

SHE'S NOT A CRIME WAVE

Minogue just didn't know where to begin with Garda Hegarty. She stood in the middle of the hallway and pretended to study the names on the doors. She wasn't going to make this one bit easier. Why would she, it was her job. He was out of order. Basically, he'd pulled rank. He should have kept his big mouth shut.

He tried to find a pattern to the grime that was collected on the window. Malone was out there somewhere, waiting for his call. One disaster at a time, thank you.

"Can we move on so," he said.

Her delay registered with him. She spoke in a thin voice, slowly.

"I think there'll be more," she said.

He remembered a ditty that Kilmartin had sung one night late, after getting an admission from a woman who killed her friend.

'Tis true that the women are worse than the men,
Right fol tight fol, ditty aye day
They go down to hell and come right back again . . .
With your right fol die, ditty fol die, right fol tight fol,
ditty aye daaay

He waited for her to break her stare down the hall, to say

something. Two sirens came faintly to him from somewhere in the south city, losing and then regaining their synchronic yowling. He saw a squad car tearing by a gap between buildings.

A detective with a hippie moustache under which he had tucked two desserts last week in the cafeteria while Minogue and Fiona Hegarty had a getting-to-know-you lunch came around the corner wrestling with his jacket.

"Did you hear," he said. "Someone's after shooting people by the Aliens' Office there on Mount Street."

"The Aliens' Office?"

"A few minutes ago. Some fellas went all out. Shotguns, the whole bit."

He squeezed past and he was gone, his jacket still half on.

"Look," Minogue said. "She'll sign, we get her solicitor. Are you okay with that?"

"But she waived, Cig."

Cig: that had only started a few years ago. *Cig* for Cigire, the Irish for Inspector, used to be something only a Sergeant would try.

"Fair enough," he said. "But she's not the full shilling in there, I'm thinking."

"How do you mean?"

"Stress, duress, whatever we can call it."

"She could flip that handy enough, Cig."

"She's ready to confess to the Kennedy assassination, to my way of thinking."

"It's a cod. She's playing for sympathy. That'll change."

"Change her statement is it? Or her solicitor could?"

She nodded.

"It's happened."

"What, now?"

"Come on. A barrister pumps that up. Suddenly we get

hit with Improper Caution to the Suspect or it's a constitutional case. She walks. We bang our heads off the nearest wall for an hour."

Minogue listened to the sirens fading, joining, separating in the distance. He wanted out then and there. He thought about the resignation letter it had taken him a week to word-process on the sly.

"You really see her doing that, do you."

"It's possible. She's no daw, is she. She knows she's a goner. She might be trying to get ahead of us already. Mitigation at least."

Minogue strained to listen to another siren. Mongoloid, that was the word they used for Down's, he remembered. Jennifer Halloran's brother was thirty-seven. They lived that long now? Malone must have been drunk when he left the Garda Club, must have. He'd better phone Pat.

Fiona Hegarty was saying something to him.

"I still say we go ahead. We get what we can. We can reasonably assume she's a bit of an operator. I mean, five years, she kept at it, yeah?"

He looked away from the closed door of the interview room. The "yeah?" had annoyed him mightily.

"Well," he said. "I still say we have enough."

"She stole thirty something thousand quid that we know of. More, maybe."

"It took her five years. She's not a crime wave."

Fiona Hegarty took a step back, and leaned against the wall. She rubbed her nose in a way that Minogue knew wasn't the thoughtful way she tried to affect.

"I'll call the duty counsel," he said.

She pushed off from the wall and she turned the door handle in one motion. He'd expected a glare at least.

He followed her in. Jennifer Halloran, bookkeeper and soon to be felon, gave him a blank look.

"I'm phoning your counsel, Miss," he said.

She didn't get it. Detective Garda Fiona Hegarty was turning a page on her clipboard. Squash league, Minogue was thinking, marathons, computers, career goals. An MBA was the way to go.

"It's someone to advise you," he said. "To represent you."

"But I don't need one, do I?"

Jennifer Halloran looked to Garda Hegarty for a signal but none came. For all the wrong reasons, a bright spot was starting in Minogue's day.

"You might consider phoning your mother soon too," he said.

WHAT SHAPES SHE HAD SEEN

Eileen Magee felt well able for the two detectives. They had gotten her dander up about the fox.

"I was reared in the country," she told the skinny one. Collins was his name, she remembered. He was the one she'd taken a liking to. He had those doe eyes that reminded her of the kids in intensive care.

"My father, God rest him, said they were vermin, the foxes."

"You didn't see it do anything to the body, did you."

She turned to the Sergeant, Tunney. Maybe he took his cue from Gene Tunney the boxer. The shiny baldness pushed through the few hairs at the front. Impatient wasn't the worst of it with him.

"I saw it standing there," she said, "and it looking at me. But I didn't see it do anything."

"To the 'bundle,'" Tunney said. "Your first thought, right."

"I knew it was the girl. It was in the paper, when she was missing."

Tunney made a note of something. Eileen looked around the room. She had fairly trotted up the laneway to the road, out onto Whitebeam Road. The heart had been leaping out of her chest, imagining the fox might be following her. Not wanting to think what it would have done to the girl. The relief she'd felt when she spotted the woman of the house, gardening. Sat her down here in this lovely conservatory, and believed her, right away. The calm voice making the phone calls, the first Garda car pulling into the driveway within minutes.

It was Collins who had just spoken to her.

"Pardon?"

"I said, are you all right going ahead now with us here?"

"I'm grand. I mean, I'm not going to, you know."

Collins gave her a wan smile.

"Fold up on you, or that."

"You think one of the boys was a Sean, was it," Tunney said.

"The bigger lad, the taller lad called him some name, I think it was Sean."

But it was the little lad who told me. A girl was sleeping over there, or words to that effect.

Tunney read something he had written and then he closed his notebook.

"If you're able, Miss Magee, would you come out with us and show us the way you came to here."

"To this house?"

"From the time you got off the bus. Could you maybe do that for us."

Eileen had forgotten that Noirin, the woman of the house, was sitting in the television room with the doors open. Noirin looked over at her with a strained smile.

Eileen thought of the shopping bags she'd left down near the bushes. There was cheese that'd go bad for certain.

The Guards stood up and went into the hall. Noirin came over and knelt down beside her. Eileen studied the face. She had a country accent, her kids reared and out at uni. The roots of her hair were still red. Eileen managed a smile. Why did it take a situation like this to bring you into the company of someone nice. It was that thought that made her sob.

Noirin gave her another hanky. She asked her if she would like to go to the toilet before they headed out. Eileen said she didn't. She stood up and took a deep breath. She had overheard one of the detectives earlier, and words she'd taken to be about her, "a great oul warrior." She didn't know if she could go back down there to the park though.

"Would you come down with me?"

"I will."

Eileen felt the hand under her elbow. She grasped it, wrapped it inside her arm, and held it. It was like school friends years ago.

The Guards were waiting in the hall.

"I want to know something," Eileen said to Collins. "Is it the girl went missing?"

"It could well be," Tunney said. "But we need to find out for sure."

"And is she still there below?"

Tunney nodded.

"It takes time," he said. "Certain things have to be done."

There were small groups standing by the top of the laneway. Eileen stepped out smartly. She felt Noirin's hand tighten on her arm. There was that yellow strip of tape at the top of the laneway, a Guard watching not far behind.

A priest stepped out of a car across the road. He reached the tape before the two women. The Guard lifted the tape and the priest stepped in. He reached into a box he had carried and took out a pyx; he kissed it and put it around his neck. The Guard at the tape took off his hat and blessed himself.

Eileen was full of questions. What if the girl wasn't Catholic, who had called the priest, how long would she be lying here?

Tunney held up the tape for her.

"This is where you came up?"

"It is," she said. "Right here. Can I ask you something?"

There it was again, she saw, the irritation. He nodded.

"Nothing happened there on account of the fox, did it? I couldn't bear to think."

Tunney glanced at Noirin. She whispered something Eileen didn't catch.

He looked back at her. As if he hadn't a mother of his own, this fella. He might have a soft spot, a tiny one, but enough, she thought.

"No," he said. "It doesn't look like it."

Eileen looked down the lane. There was blue sky and fluffy white clouds now behind the spread branches that hung over the glade where the dead girl was. What shapes she had seen when she was a child herself all those years ago. These billows looked like nothing now.

A SPOT OF BOTHER

Minogue watched Malone horsing down the full breakfast. He had a scratch near his right eyebrow. Yes, he'd slept in the car last night. No, he hadn't checked for messages.

"So," Minogue said finally. "You were out on manoeuvres last night. Go on."

Malone glanced up from the table at him.

"I wasn't exactly drinking me way into Bolivia, boss. No more than you were."

"But I went home, Tommy, like the honest culchie that I am. I didn't go out on the town and get into a row in a chipper."

"Wait a minute. Did I leave a message on your machine that said, 'Give me a fu— give me a lecture.' Did I?"

"No," Minogue said. "It said 'I had a massive big feed of drink with the fellas I work with, who are Guards, by the way, and shouldn't even consider trying to cover up for me. Then I went around to my girlfriend's place, decided I needed fish and chips. Being as it was only one o'clock in the morning, which is exactly when all the headers in Dublin are spilling out of the pubs looking for trouble. Yours Sincerely, Perplexed, Dublin 12.'"

Malone gave him a blank stare.

"Well, it could have been worse," he said. "I could have lost the head entirely."

Minogue raised an eyebrow.

"You don't understand," Malone said. "I was managing grand, so I was. Sonia was working late at her parents' place last night, the restaurant."

Minogue began to think of the new travel agent in Abbey Street again, the one who'd told him he could get him and his missus to Paris for a weekend, two hundred and fifty Euro all-in. No, he remembered, he wouldn't go back there: he had almost forgotten the wink, the "how would the, uh, missus like that, then?"

"And for another thing," Malone said. "She's not like that. You make it sound, well, you know what I'm saying?"

Minogue gave him the eye. *Knowharamsane?*

"You're jealous in anyhow," Malone murmured.

"Am I now."

Minogue thought of Sonia's way of laughing, how she always turned away. An Asian mannerism? Soon he'd ask though, why a woman from Macau studying for a degree, and working nights at her parents' take-out, would want to be with the likes of Tommy Malone, a working-class Dublin git who worked in the Garda Drug Squad Central.

"It's obvious," Malone said. "All the questions you were firing at her there that time, remember we bumped into you and Kathleen in Bewley's that night?"

"Polite conversation, you gurrier. Something you wouldn't know about being reared here in this place. In this infernal city."

Malone sat back and looked around the restaurant.

"Oh Jasus, will you listen to the tough talk here," he said. Minogue felt the smile start. He had almost forgotten how much he missed Kilmartin sparring with Malone, how sly Malone's digs could be.

"I'm not Kilmartin you know," Minogue tried. "They'll be carrying you out of here on a stretcher in the finish-up, if I get going on you."

Malone yawned. The tension had ebbed already.

"Suddenly you're Jackie Chan or something, are you."

Minogue watched someone spill a handful of coins on the floor by the cashier. Pablo was on cash this morning, according to his name tag anyway. It had been a Polish fella the other day. Dublin: capital of Europe, by God. And now, two refugees were shot dead?

Malone sat up and rested his elbows on the table between them.

"Maybe he phoned another station," he said.

"We'd know by now, Tommy. They're all redirected."

Malone looked down at the remains of a bun. Minogue took another sip of coffee and tried to hear more of the French coming from a group of students who'd just come off the escalator.

"Anyway," Malone said. "The point is, well, what I said to you this morning."

"Is there a warrant out on you?"

"Well, yeah."

"There isn't. And I didn't find any incident report at the station either."

"So far."

"So far."

"You're sure."

"I'm sure."

"Yeah, well I'd like to stay kind of paranoid. I find that works for me."

Minogue felt his annoyance return. Sure, Malone was

under pressure. Since coming into Drugs Central he'd had a gun pointed at him. There was a lot of night work. He'd found two addicts who'd been dead nearly a week in a flat.

"How'd Sonia take all this anyway?"

Malone stopped running his hand through his hair.

"She's upset," he said. "Can't say as you'd blame her, can you."

Minogue watched one of the students fumbling for change at the cash.

"Says I have issues."

"That sounds about right, I'm thinking."

"She says, well, I have to get more, you know, evolved. That sort of thing."

Minogue watched him push a cuticle down hard. Then Malone looked up.

"This guy last night, he does odd jobs for Bobby Quinn. You know that name?"

"Only what I read in the papers. Who's the fella you clattered? You never told me."

"Doyle."

"You know him from before?"

"Sort of, but not really. His mug is on the wall of a task force thing going on, I pass by them every day. That's how I remember."

"A big thing, is he."

"Ah, he's a fucking iijit. A wannabe. Really from planet arsehole, I'm telling you. Fancies himself. But he's got form. Dealing, robbing houses. He got two years for assault on a barman, went after him with a bottle, man nearly bled to death. Then he shows up trying to start up rackets and his own gigs locally."

"Was he high last night?"

"Well, he was on a tilt for sure."

"More than that?"

"There was a smell of booze off him. But he wasn't falling around the place."

"Before you gave him the hiding, you mean."

"Ah, Christ you have the same look I got from Sonia. Give over, will you."

Minogue rested his chin on his knuckles. Malone took up a sugar packet, twisted it, and studied the spilled granules.

"I think maybe there's something else going on."

"What something else?"

"He knew more than a scut should. He knew about the brother, Terry. He knew stuff that happened very recently, when Terry OD-ed and that. So. What am I thinking? I don't know. But what I'm wondering is, maybe Doyle came on to me on purpose. Maybe someone sent him."

Minogue looked at the sugar.

"He's not the first," Malone said. "You sort of getting the picture?"

"Hardly. I'm after being fierce confused by the cleverality of ye Dublin jackeens."

"Look, there's stuff we keep to ourselves. Just think: how does the Drug Squad get insider information and make busts and that? I mean it's not high-tech, is it. We turn fellas, we get inside. We pay. We threaten. Okay?"

"Well, what are you saying about this Doyle fella then?"

"It's a two-way thing, is what I'm trying to say. They try the same on us. It's how they work. I got word last month something was going to happen to Terry. That it'd give me something to think about. Just a little phone call, a few words, from one of our ears. 'Informants' if you like the words that go on the receipts. Yeah."

"What's Terry's situation, if you don't mind me asking."

Malone stared at what he'd done to the sugar pack.

"Poxy," he said. "Just poxy. Couldn't be worse."

He glanced up at Minogue.

"Me ma's sure he won't come out alive this time. She had to go back on sedatives, she's in such a state. Me, I don't know. I just don't. He's gone right down."

"How long is he in for?"

"He's done two years out of a five to seven. He had a knife in the break-in. They threw everything at him. He has eighteen months before he can apply."

"And he's . . ."

"Yeah. There's no bother getting stuff in there."

"They can't stop it at the prison?"

Malone shook his head.

"Someone gave him bad stuff. Or at least they got to his supplier . . ."

Minogue waited.

"Terry has, well, no will power really. He doesn't want, well, you know what I'm saying. There's damage done to the part of the brain that—ah, fuck it, what am I talking about? It only makes me mad. I'm not a frigging doctor. It's just bad. Bad."

Malone was studying the ceiling now. Minogue heard his breathing slow again.

"That's fierce pressure, Tommy. Fierce."

"The way it works," Malone began, "is, you just get a hint. Okay, picture this: there you are in your own local. You're having a pint, life is good, and all that. Then a fella walks up to you, orders a pint. Stands there, waiting. 'How's it going,' says he. And you say nothing 'cause you know he's a gouger. Then he says to you, you know, something like this: 'So-and-so has a lot of respect for you.' Or 'So-and-so'd like to help out.' 'You should get in touch with so-and-so, he'd like to hear your opinion.'"

"Money?"

"They never say. I keep track of them, file them with the Squad. Nothing much happens, but we're aware of it. It's part of the job, know what I'm saying? But this Doyle, he went over the top. The cheek, see? Right in me face. That's why I'm thinking he got sent."

"You were in the chipper first, were you."

"Yeah."

"He started the thing?"

"Well, what do you think? I'm there with me girlfriend, and I'm going to get into a barney with some head? What, to impress her or something? Come on, boss."

Minogue stared back. Then Malone shook his head, and looked away.

"Okay," he said. "I lost it. I wanted him hurt."

"Were you, are you, carrying?"

"Course I was. I have to. But that was never in the picture."

"You said you wanted him hurt, but . . ."

Malone shook his head, he smiled grimly, and he sat back.

"Come on, boss, for Jasus' sake. I mean a tune-up. You know, just to park him, good him proper. Maybe even give him some plaster to carry around awhile. But I'd never pull a gun on a fella. No way."

Minogue took in the mind-made-up look. He remembered Kilmartin telling him that that very look would stop Malone ever getting Sergeant.

"He starts out with some guff," Malone murmured. "Some slagging, you know, cops guarding fish and chip shops. I ignore him. But he starts trying to get the fella behind the counter in on it, Tony."

"Tony."

"Yeah. Tony's the son there. He's not the smartest. Seriously, he's a bit simple, like. But Tony wasn't having any of it. I should have left, I know, I know. So Doyle really starts getting aggravating. What, do I have to be Russian to get taken seriously around here? That sort of thing. You get the Russian thing?"

"No."

"Well, it's a thing over at Central. There's a lot going on in that line, how there's a Russian connection showing up all over the kip. Or fellas fronting for them—Eastern Europe. I'll bet you ten pints you'll be getting the tour of that section when they send you over, when is it?"

"The end of September, as it stands now."

Malone gave Minogue a moment but the Inspector wasn't biting.

"What," Malone said. "You're not excited about Fraud? Come on. Criminal Asset Bureau? Getting together with coppers on the continent and all that?"

"I don't get that level, no. Anyway, finish with this thing. Your man's needling away at you."

"Right. 'The Russians' thing. There was quite the smash last month when two fellas started up their own racket or tried to. It was over in Dorset Street. Two Russians in actual fact, just in off the plane. They try to put the heavy word on two pubs there. Like one pub wasn't enough for them. One of them's The Rambler's Rest. Came in with the proposition, you know, show us some money every week or call the fire brigade. No translation needed there. Trouble was, the IRA had a connection to a partner owns the pub. The got a hold of the two Russians the next and them coming back to collect, or so they thought. You saw that, right?"

Minogue nodded. It had been in the papers. One of the Russians lost an eye.

"So there I am in the chipper. Tony has me money, and I'm just waiting for the chips. But this bastard, this fu—, this bollocks, he won't take a hint. I'm thinking, yeah, I should walk. Here I am, half-jarred, beginning to get very *annoyed*, know what I'm saying, and I'm on the 24-hour detail carrying a gun. But no, I says to myself. It's my town. I live here. Me and Terry never got handed anything. I made it, see? I didn't turn out like this creeping Jesus in front of me."

"You mean Doyle, I take it."

"Right. But even after all this I'm holding up not so bad. I even get me chips and I'm heading out. But Doyle wants to stick it to me, says in my ear and going by, he says 'You're letting your own brother die, 'cause you won't play ball.'"

Malone's eyes slipped out of focus.

"What did he mean, in your mind at the time?"

"Ah come on. What are you, Alice in Wonderland, or what?"

"Spell it out for me. Someone else might be asking, so get used to it."

"Okay. That if I got on board, you know, that if I would make the odd phone call, get on the payroll, Terry wouldn't be going downhill the way he is."

"Did you believe him?"

"Did I think he knew what he was talking about?"

"Did you believe him, right then and there—not thinking it over later now?"

"Well yeah, I believed him."

"What happened then, after that. In the chipper."

"Well, I stopped. And I turned round. And I looked at him. He's smiling. He knows he's gotten to me. And he's shifting around on his feet 'cause he thinks he's something too. Like, he's heavy enough and he's got reach, and he's made a few bob hurting people. But even then, you know, I would've walked. I really would have. Maybe he knew too, so he just had to go over the top, right."

"Did he take a poke at you?"

"No he didn't. What he said was, 'Phone Bobby. He can stop what they're doing to your brother. If you don't lift the phone, you're killing your own brother.'"

A sudden screech from one went right into Minogue's fillings. A mother with two children in the one collapsible buggy was going through the wars near the cashier.

"Anyway," Malone said. "The arse fairly fell out of things then at that stage. But I do remember holding one back, I do."

Minogue looked at him.

"A lights-out, is what I'm saying. You know? He was wide open."

"Mother Teresa, you are."

"Easy for you to say. Fact is, I knew it looked bad in front of herself. I mean, you don't know her. She's a very kind of, well what's the point of talking. I just didn't want to hurt her, if you can believe that. Her feelings."

"Shy."

"As a matter of fact she is," said Malone. "She's fierce shy."

"So. What then?"

"Nothing much. The bastard picks himself up, dusts himself off. I think he only cut his hand. As well as maybe a shiner and a good-sized headache. He heads off under his own steam, a bit shaky, fair enough, but he gives me this look. And you know what? And he's *smiling*. I told them I'd pay the damage. The table . . . ?"

"Smiling, you say."

"Yeah. Like he got me. Like I fell for it. Whatever it is."

UNBELIEVABLE

The man in the back had gone limp, like he was completely shagged, his head resting against the top of the seat where it met the pillar. Doyle could still hear sirens in the distance. The air conditioning was giving him the shivers now. He guessed that it had probably kept him from puking. But if everything was so sharp and bright, why was he still wondering if this had really happened. No, he decided, he wasn't tripping.

Doyle took the turn into the back of the garage hard. The front end of the Opel bottomed on the bump and the man sat forward.

The door was closed.

"For fuck's sakes, open the door, whoever you are."

The man in the back was rearranging his jacket.

"Come on, come on—"

The door began to rise. It was Quinn himself pulling on the chain inside the garage.

"Jasus! Where am I supposed to put it? There's no room there."

He rolled down the window. The smell of paint stung in his nostrils. He saw that the plastic curtains had been used a lot already. He looked out at Quinn.

"Put it tight to the wall," Quinn said. "Climb out the passenger side."

Doyle turned the wheel full, corrected it as he got the Opel by the doorway and he brought it up toward the bench near the compressors.

The door was already closing behind them. The gloom felt like shelter. The door hit the cement and Quinn tied up the chain. Doyle turned off the engine. The man in the back was stuffing his cap and wig into a plastic bag.

Doyle was swearing, slapping the steering wheel. He stopped and he ran his hands down his face and he shook his head.

"Bobby," he called out. "Do you know what he went and did? Do you?"

Quinn cupped his hand around his ear.

"This guy," Doyle said. "He went mental. Did you know he was going to do that?"

Quinn watched the man in the back seat open the door and toss a sports bag out onto the floor.

"We have to sort this out, Bobby," Doyle said. "No way I'd a gone along if this was the plan, no way, you hear me?"

Quinn heard the creaking of the suspension as Doyle began to heave himself over the handbrake toward the passenger seat.

"I mean, you never said . . . ," Doyle called out. "I mean this is fucking nuts what happened. I'm in up to me neck here. You have to look after me for this, Bobby. This isn't some little barney you got me into. I've got to go somewhere, to lie low or something."

Doyle stopped shouting then, his hand on the dashboard. For a moment he seemed to be curious about how quiet it was now, or how the man in the back hadn't gotten out.

Doyle instinctively turned his head away, even managed

to shout and to raise his hand, but the bullet tore through that on its way to shattering the bone behind his ear.

MIGHTY QUINN

The Nissan car company needn't have bothered putting in any gears after third: Malone was as bad a gearbox mangler as ever.

Minogue switched off his mobile. There had been no messages. Somehow, the Fraud Squad had been managing without him for an hour now. Right about now, Fiona Hegarty would be going upstairs on him for shoving counsel at the Halloran woman.

Minogue tried the radio presets. Malone had none for RTE.

"What," said Malone.

"I want to hear the news," Minogue said. "About that shooting."

He found it just in time to hear that Connolly, a tireless bore of a Chief Super to judge by off-duty shindigs where he'd met him in company with Kilmartin, was "in charge of the investigation." Connolly went into the routine code: ascertain information regarding, liaise with agencies both at home and abroad, some difficulty in verifying documentation regarding the identity of the victims. He mauled the names, Minogue was sure, and then regretted the judgement on Connolly's command of Albanian. He threw in plenty of extras, many of which Minogue didn't doubt were sincere: unprecedented, callous.

"Did you ever think you'd see the day? That kind of thing? Here, like?"

Minogue shook his head.

"Ahh-med," Malone murmured. "That's Arabian I'd swear."

"Arabic."

"Right. Coming of age, we are, is that the expression?"

Minogue had seen the road signs against the hostels for refugees in Wexford, heard the querulous voices on the radio phoning in to say that they were not in any way prejudiced toward foreigners, but . . . The hardest to take had been the whinging from people on waiting lists for County Council and Dublin Corporation houses about refugees jumping the queue, and what about people born here, the real Irish people.

"Well, what do you think?"

"About what?"

"I mean, do you think those two were above board?"

"Kilmartin had been talking about budgets for detectives going to places like Moscow and Sofia where they'd better learn in a hurry how to deal with what was coming."

"I don't know who's above board these days, Tommy."

Malone managed to hit every pothole coming through Terenure. Minogue opened his eyes after a particularly jolting one.

"Sure I'm not keeping you from the job," Malone said.

"I was working on a mission statement, so I was."

"You were on your hole."

Minogue looked over at him.

"Well, I mean is I don't want you getting your arse in the wringer over this thing."

"Were you ever in Spain?" Minogue asked.

"Spain? To do with work, gangsters from here, you mean?"

"No. Recreating."

"Well, yeah. A few years back. I went with a crowd."

"Was it nice there?"

"It was all right. It got a bit wild. The clubs and that. I don't like that class of thing."

"You don't."

"Yeah. That's for the Brits, you know, the soccer crowd to do. I had to come home for a rest from me holidays. Why, you thinking of heading over?"

"No. I was just trying to think what it would be like."

"Kathleen maybe?"

Minogue eyed him.

"I'm only asking. People nowadays, you know."

Malone got through Terenure finally and turned up for Tempelogue. Minogue wondered if Jennifer Halloran would phone her ma. Maybe she'd just find her own way home and tell her later on. Ma, don't wait up for me, I'm going to jail.

"I'm going to stay out of it, you're going to talk, right?"

"That's it, Tommy. You're not going to give him a puck or the like."

"Well, as long as you're happy with your slagging, I'm happy."

"You can stare at him a lot though."

"All we're doing is going to see Quinn so's you can let him there's no dice," Malone said. "To be absolutely straight. Right?"

Minogue nodded.

Malone parked beside a row of shops. Quinn's haulage office was upstairs. Malone looked around the houses across the street.

"There could be surveillance on here," he said. "Not just

ours, there's joint task force stuff we don't get told about."

"No matter," said Minogue.

Minogue followed Malone up the stairs. They passed a tanning studio cum manicurist. An impossibly tanned woman passed them in the hall.

Mighty Haulage was easy to miss, a door only. There was carpet inside, a receptionist, with a glass door to the side of her desk.

Not too many lorry drivers tramping through here, Minogue decided.

The long blinks from the woman at the desk told Minogue she had made them for Guards. Mr. Quinn was not in the office at the moment. Could she take a message?

"When'll he be back?" Minogue asked her.

"I'm not sure," she said.

The eyelashes batting again. A Princess Diana move, God rest the poor woman.

"Can I trouble you for his mobile phone number, so?"

"I don't know if he has one."

"Are you the secretary here, Miss?"

"I'm the office manager."

"But you don't know how to reach your boss? And you don't know if he has a cell phone? The head of a haulage company. . . . That beggars belief, to be sure."

"Beggars," she said. "What are you getting at?"

"Can we try again? See if maybe you can find a number written somewhere."

Her eyes took on a glazed look that Minogue recognized from time in court.

"Who are you?"

Minogue flipped his photocard.

"As is my colleague here."

"What's this concerning?"

"We'll be working that out with Mr. Quinn."

"I have to know," she began.

Minogue pulled open the door. She was up and after them fairly quickly.

"You can't just barge in there," she said.

Someone was smoking a cigarette hereabouts.

"Mr. Quinn?"

There was a sound of a chair rolling across the floor from a room to his left. "Manager" was inscribed on a plaque, next to a shiny, embossed picture of a truck. Minogue turned the handle. A short man in a leather jacket was standing by a desk. Minogue looked around. The fittings were actually pricey, real oak furniture, brassy stuff. A television was on. It was some kind of motorbike racing from a satellite channel.

"Who are yous?"

Minogue looked over the barrel chest. The necklace and the ring matched.

"Well, who are you?" Minogue said.

The secretary was in behind them now.

"They just barged in, so they did," she said. "These Guards. I told them Mr. Quinn wasn't here but they just went in anyway."

The man frowned and he looked at Malone.

"You, you fucker," he said.

"And yourself," Malone said. "How is it going?"

"It was going not so bad, until yous two started trespassing. Show us a warrant."

Minogue tried his father confessor smile.

"Ah sure, what would we need a warrant for?"

"Oh here you go, like you can't think of anything new."

He came around the desk and stood with his hands on his hips. The bracelet slipped down over his left wrist. He lifted his arm to shake it back down. He stopped twisting it when he saw Minogue was watching.

"I have nothing to tell yous. Nothing. Yous're trespassing and that is an offence."

"Look it, Beans," Malone began.

"Mr. Canning to you, dickhead."

"We want to see Quinn."

"Yous must be deaf as well as stupid. Didn't Julie just tell you he's not here?"

"What's the number for his mobile?"

Canning picked up his cigarette from the ashtray and took a long drag.

"Call the Guards," he said to Julie. "We have some kind of break and enter or something going on here. Trespassers, robbers, I don't know what. And Julie, tell them they're deaf too—and kind of thick."

He rounded the desk again and sat heavily into the leather swivel. He took the remote control and turned up the volume. The race was tight apparently, the high-pitched whine keening as the bikes passed a commentator.

Minogue found the power switch at the bottom of the set. Canning kept stabbing the remote.

"You're too busy for that now," Minogue said to him. The boss hardly pays you to hang around his, well, his office watching the telly all day, now does he."

"Fuck off."

"Well, now we have your attention. We want Quinn to help us with our enquiries."

"See yous in court, fuckers. It'll look good on you. What's your name again."

"But you'll do," Minogue said. "To pass on our request."

"Do your own dirty work."

"That's your forte, I'd be thinking."

"What're you insinuating?"

"Lorryloads going out every night to landfills in Wicklow."

Canning shook his head.

"Why bother paying into a circus, I say."

Minogue looked around for close-circuit cameras. Then he leaned on the desk. Canning blew smoke out and reached for the remote. Malone swept it off the desk.

"That's broken," Canning said. "And you're fucked. Like your brother."

Minogue studied the lop-sided grin, the way Canning drew on his cigarette.

"Tell the boss something," he said. "Tell him it better not be true what a fella said."

Minogue waited but Canning continued with his smoke rings.

"Doyle," Malone said. "You'd know him. The usual, just like you. You know, big mouth, in and out of jail. Thinks he's a hard man."

"Tell Quinn we'll be following up on this," Minogue said.

Julie was busy pretending she was on hold. Minogue waited by her desk until she glanced up.

"Tell Quinn they're cheap," he said. "Cell phones. But you have to remember to switch them on."

GET ON BOARD

It was all finished by half twelve. Quinn had sprayed the Renault and done the seats the best he could. The bullet had come out Doyle's eye and gone into the dash. There were bits of brain and other stuff, maybe his eye, Quinn decided, even on the windscreen.

He'd asked Roe why he'd shot him inside the car.

"Well, he was becoming unstable."

"What do you mean unstable?"

"Unpredictable."

"Look at what we have to do now though."

Roe had pulled Doyle across the floor by then.

"What odds," he said. "It's going in the crusher."

"It's a loose end," Quinn said. "The idea was to do the job out here."

He remembered Roe looking down at the drains, back at the car and then at Quinn.

"Well, I have to concede that he was very, well, irritating."

"Irritating? That was the reason?"

"Indeed it was. He was coming up with a lot of slurs."

"Slurs? What are slurs?"

"Remarks about people from Northern Ireland. People like myself."

Quinn didn't know if he was trying to be funny.

"Totally uncalled for. I was doing my job. All he had to do was do his."

It was then that Quinn for the first time didn't feel immune. And maybe that was why they had sent Roe, maybe even encouraged him to be as freaky as he wanted.

He taped the windows in a rush just to get the compressor started so he wouldn't hear what Roe was up to with the body. Even with the sprayer going he'd heard thumps every now and then, and twice some power tool. He kept going, the sweat and nausea building behind the face mask.

There were a few times when he thought he wouldn't make it. A few times the bile was right at the back of his mouth, stabbing at his throat. Once he had actually yanked off the mask and crouched over the bin with a spasm, but nothing had come.

Philpott was at the door with the lorry right on time. Quinn tore a hole in the paper on the back window and reversed the Renault up the ramp. He had tried the propane torch on the dashboard after he had run it over the vinyl and the seats. It hadn't taken, but the damage from the bullet didn't look so obvious now. No way was he going to get the oxyacetylene for it.

He didn't try to clean the sprayer afterwards, but he took down the plastic right away and put it into the drum on top of the clothes. There had been patches and spots on the plastic to the driver's side. Doyle must have rolled down his window all the way. He was halfway finished with the floor when he noticed that Roe was standing in the machine-room doorway watching.

He stopped sweeping. Roe nodded at him.

The drums weren't as heavy as Quinn had expected. He didn't want to say a word to Roe, to ask when he'd be filling them with the acid. Roe had thick polytarp ready in the van, and they slid the drums along the bed of the van with it. Quinn stood back and watched Roe bracing the drums with pieces of two by four, checking the seals, and doing something with gaffer tape. He sprang out then and locked the van doors.

Light on his feet, Quinn noticed.

"You have the drum there with the clothes and stuff?" Roe asked. Quinn pointed the brush toward the corner by the door.

Roe shrugged and sighed, and went off to change.

Quinn sluiced more of the detergent across the concrete and went harder with the brush. Acid, he thought. He supposed it'd take days for bones. Roe would know, no doubt. He'd been working with them on and off for two years, Grogan had told him, ever since they'd let him out. No politics, no religion. Yes, Roe'd be back behind the counter in the shop in Newry before the day was out. He'd be smiling at an oul wan, maybe while he held up a chop or a roast. *Lean enough for you, Missus?*

The time must have passed: Roe was back. Quinn finished by the drain. Roe pushed the clothes deeper into the drum and walked back. Quinn leaned the brush against the wall and rolled the drum over to the van. His painting gear he could leave here for Chipper to use again anyway. Roe watched him pound the lid onto the drum. He balanced it on the van's bumper before sliding it in behind the others. Roe gave it a shove or two and then closed the door.

"That'll do it, then," he said. He adjusted his cap and then fixed Quinn with a look.

"As a matter of interest, Mr. Quinn."

It was the way he said it, Quinn was sure. Somehow every word felt like a taunt. Like a schoolteacher nagging you in that quiet way, annoying you, getting under your skin more than if he just gave you a belt and got it over with.

"We were correct in our estimation."

Quinn didn't get it for a moment.

"He had track marks all right," Roe said. "As we antici-pated. Just a matter of time."

Quinn said nothing. Roe was rubbing it in. He counted the hours since he'd last slept, thought about what paint did to your brain, fast dry undercoat or not.

"Yes indeed," Roe said. "Oh, but you could tell from his demeanour, at any rate."

Quinn let the words roll around in his mind. Demeanour, estimation. This man with the liking for big words had just killed three people. Then he'd calmly separated one of them into bits and dropped the pieces into oil drums. In a few min-utes, he'd be heading out through the streets of Dublin. He'd be leaving the van in Dundalk then, and driving home to Newry, carrying on as though nothing had happened.

"I'll be away now," Roe said. "See you around, maybe?"

Quinn nodded. He glanced at the ironed shirt and trousers that Roe had changed into now. How could a fella look dap-per after that. He tried not to stare at the man's hands. He had heard the water running, smelled the solvent still over the soap that Quinn had used.

He watched as Roe swung the Adidas bag into the van's seat ahead of him. What else had he got in there, he won-dered again.

"You like it, do you?" Roe asked.

"What? Like what?"

"You go to the gym too, do you?"

It was some kind of a warped smile on Roe's face all right, Quinn decided.

He watched the Toyota move off sedately down the lane. No wave from Roe.

He closed the door and looked around the garage. He

checked the drains by the door again. There was hardly any water in them now. He thought about Roe, taking his time motoring across the city, headed north. Bizarre wasn't enough of a word. Monster, was more like it. How many more of the likes of Roe were they producing up there?

Maybe as many Doyles as were turning up here, you could say in all fairness.

The old days were gone. Were there ever any? It had been make your own arrangements here for a while before that. A lot of it had to do with the Guards, in actual fact. Their Criminal Assent crowd had done a lot, and with the new laws, and all this new money in the country, things had gone haywire pretty fast.

Quinn blinked and shook his head. He had to get out of here.

He stepped out of the suit and hung it near the compressor next to the masks. He'd leave the fan on. Not that it had helped him much, with the lightheaded half-stupid feeling he had. He stopped and thought about that. Well, what did he expect? Hadn't slept a wink really; couldn't eat; living on smokes and tea since yesterday. And any normal person would be reacting, no matter how you tried to get ready for something like what had just happened. No wonder he felt shagged.

There was no one in the laneway. He pulled the steel door shut and tested it. The noise of the city traffic came from all around, and seemed to hover just over the rooftops. He wasn't just imagining that steady sound of banging, a piledriver, he guessed, for the foundations on the new places down the canal. The bleeping of a lorry reversing somewhere sort of calmed him. The normal world, people going about their business.

He patted his jacket for his mobile, wondered if Grogan'd

phone him. For a moment he thought about the men sitting around the table there in the Chineser in the centre of Belfast, a city he'd never known in all his life growing up here. Gallagher—the one who ran West Belfast from a wheelchair—it was Gallagher who'd have given Roe his orders.

He let out his breath and breathed in deep three times, concentrating. The ache in his stomach was still there. He headed down toward the canal end of the lane. There was a bakery somewhere near, but the smell of the bread was nearly giving him the heaves. He kept his eye on the walls, trying to spot any cameras. There were enough barbed wire and glass and signs about alarms.

Maybe he could manage a cup of something. He should head out to the office, do something that looked normal. Get hold of Canning and go out to Clondalkin about the lorry that had been towed there Monday.

He crossed at the light and looked down the row of cars to find his own. A six-year-old Astra, for the love of God. Even the Guards slagged him, the night two of them came to the house after the bank job. But a six-year-old pile of crap on wheels was part of the plan. He had the Volvo waiting anytime in Portugal, the car that Catherine picked and just liked to sit in. There was no point in even renting a car for Amsterdam.

He looked for people sitting in cars. He wondered if it would ever get to him having to run a mirror under his car. He opened the boot to get a chance to watch for movement on the street. Nothing. He pushed the spare wheel around and rearranged the toolbox before he slammed the lid shut.

He switched on his phone after he got in behind the wheel. The missed call was Beans' mobile. What the hell could Canning want that he was annoying him on a day like today? Know when to shut up, Beans. Back to driving lorries is what he'd end up doing if he didn't cop on. He didn't need a straight man that badly.

Then he held his hand out and watched his fingers. Yes, they were moving. What was the point of trying to cod yourself that you hadn't been out of your mind a half an hour ago? That you probably still were?

From What We Saw

Sergeant Lorcan Tunney wasn't ready to give the girl's father a wake-up word in the ear. Especially not here, with the hysterics going on in the next room.

Nothing would do the man. The missus was out of the picture. She had pretty well exploded, and then fallen over, but not unconscious. For a while they thought she'd have to go in an ambulance. Tunney had last seen her writhing on the floor, with two other women trying to get her to stop screaming.

Now he was watching Kenny stalking around, going mental. The last few minutes he had begun throwing his arms out every now and then, like a speech. The desperation in his voice that was too often a stifled cry or then a kind of a growling hiss. Maybe Kenny's business was a sort of performance, Tunney thought. Events management was what he called it. Tunney remembered something about the Pope's visit years ago, where Kenny said he'd got started in the business. Now it was rock stars flying in to get married in Slane Castle, that sort of thing.

He'd seen the photos in the hall and wondered about them. Mick Jagger looking a bit younger, and Kenny fairly delighted with himself, his arm around the star and a not-happy other fella looking on. "Cheers, and thanks a million, Mick" in recognizable scrawl. Next to that was the picture of the archbishop who'd died last year, with a much younger Kenny standing next to him, less delighted, and a "Many thanks for a job well done, Colm." The unreadable signature that Tunney assumed was the hallmark of important people was followed by a cross.

Kenny stopped in the middle of the floor, frozen. Then he turned on his heel and locked eyes with Tunney.

Tunney tried a sympathetic smile. Offer it up, his mother used to say. Their daughter, their only daughter, is dead. Niamh, sixteen years old.

Collins cleared his throat. I hear you, Tunney wanted to tell him.

Kenny sat down and placed his hands on his knees. Some kind of breathing exercise, Tunney wondered. There was a new fit of crying, a muffled shout from next door. Kenny darted a look at the door to the hall. A look of panic suddenly came over him. He held his hands over his face, and he shook while he cried.

He'd done this before, Tunney remembered, and he'd thought it was a seizure or something. It was right after he'd told them that he'd given the daughter a lecture on account of her using up all her time on the mobile she'd been given as a present to replace the one she'd lost, and that she'd have to learn to pay for her own. If only she'd have had . . .

Collins shifted to the edge of the chair. Tunney took in the paintings, real ones, the fireplace that looked two ways, the cherrywood or mahogany trim here and there. They could almost be sitting in one of those American houses he'd seen on the telly, he decided, not in Dublin.

Kenny heard the two policemen stand. He jerked his head up.

"But," he said. "But someone did this, someone."

Tunney stretched his toes, watched the light catch the leather.

"It's not some accident you know. Not some *misadventure*."

A new light came into Kenny's eye and he began talking about the Culligan case that had been all over the papers before Christmas. Tunney forgot whether it was five years or ten years the case had been put away as a misadventure. A lug facing life for a murder had coughed up enough to reopen it as a murder case. Tunney had heard that there were twenty something other cases being reopened because of the publicity.

Tunney couldn't walk off. Instead, he studied how Kenny looked to Collins while he went on about how the Culligan family had gone through hell, then back to him, taking turns with the lecture. Colm Kenny was sliding into hysteria and panic and anguish, and Tunney would not stop feeling sorry for him.

He thought of what he wouldn't, couldn't, say to this dead girl's father: There were no signs of trauma, were there. Be thankful she wasn't assaulted. Her hands showed nothing unusual. She shouldn't have been walking around on her own that hour of the night, should she. It looks like your daughter was drunk or disorientated. People do die of alcohol poisoning, adolescents most of them, did you know that, Mr. Kenny, I'll bet you didn't, no. You told us Niamh had friends you were not sure of, friends you'd never met, people she knew. So you were suspicious, weren't you. But that didn't go far enough, did it. So it's yourself you're raging against here, isn't it. We're just your punch bags for now. This kind of thing is not supposed to happen, is it. And you probably think we despise you because you're rich. Maybe we do, you

know. But rich as you were, you wouldn't pay for more air-
time on her mobile sitting up there on her dresser. Oh she
learned her lesson all right, she sure did. Now you'll be learning yours.

He had to stop thinking like this. Kenny was staring at
him.

"Why does it take so long? Why?"

"I'm not sure," Tunney said. "But people are busy. They'll
put priority though at the State Lab, that I know."

"How do you know that? Have you done work like this
before?"

Collins cleared his throat again. Tunney did his notebook-
closing routine.

"Well, have you?"

"Laboratory and Forensic's involved in a lot of Garda
work."

"What I mean is, have you ever worked on a murder case,
solved one, Garda."

Sergeant to you, Tunney said to himself. And don't push
it. Stay onside here.

"Mr. Kenny . . . ?"

"But isn't there supposed to be a Murder Squad or something?"

Kenny made no efforts to wipe the tears and snot coursing
down now.

"There was, but cases are done now local to the district.
Guards are trained in it."

Kenny made to say something but stopped, his mouth
half-open. He looked up from whatever he had been concentrating on to help him make some point.

This is it, Tunney guessed: it's dawned on him, he just
saw it.

"What am I saying," Kenny whispered. "What?"

He pushed the palm of his hand hard into his forehead and turned away.

Tunney nodded at the door. Collins was back in no time with a couple. The man looked a bit like Kenny. They went to him, the brother on one knee by Kenny's chair grabbing him, holding him as he sobbed.

Tunney passed the man he'd been introduced to as a doctor in the hall.

"Mrs. Kenny," he said. "Do you think she'd be able to talk?"

The man tightened his lips and shook his head.

"I gave her a sedative," he said. "She may look a bit settled but she's phased now."

Collins followed Tunney into the kitchen. There was tea left. They leaned against the counter. Tunney made notes in the book, put "murder" beside Colm Kenny's conversation. He checked his watch and wrote in the time.

"Is the girl's room locked up now?"

Collins nodded and blew on the tea. There was a long, descending moan coming from the other room, muffled talk, entreaties. Collins placed the cup down carefully on the marble top. He rubbed it with his thumb to the edge.

"We'll head back down," Tunney said. "Look in on any finds. Get a door-to-door going before he asks us why the hell we haven't started. Jesus, huh."

Collins nibbled on the ends of his moustache.

"My guess is the removal will be pretty quick."

"They have a boy too, don't they, the Kennys?"

"In the States. Training to be something there, finance or something."

Collins carefully poured the leftovers of his tea into the sink.

"I don't know," he said. "You have to wonder."

"Wonder what?"

"Ah, come on now."

"What are you thinking?"

"Well, how it could happen. These people, you know, they're not iijits. I mean they have everything going for them, it looks to me. The edumacation, the money, all that. Right?"

Tunney thought of the work ahead, the phone calls, the interviews.

"Jesus," said Collins. "The poor mother. God!"

Tunney threw his leftovers into the sink and he ran the tap.

"They're clued in, is what I'm saying," he said to Collins. "You heard the da earlier on, didn't you? 'Club drugs' and 'kids drinking.' They'd be on the ball, I'd say. They'd notice things."

"So it's not Red Bull," Collins said.

"What?"

"Ah, the drink they get."

"Oh, that. Right, the teenagers. Full of caffeine and that? Dance all night?"

Tunney studied Collins' eyes for a moment.

"Just a joke," Collins said. "Okay?"

A middle-aged couple with white faces and red-rimmed eyes stepped out of a parked car. They checked with the Guard assigned to the house.

"You're getting every name?" Tunney asked him.

"I am," the Guard said. "I got a driving licence too. No bother so far."

"We're going down in the park," Tunney told him.

"'Murder Squad' he wants," Collins said as they walked down the lane. The white-suited Technicals were in plain view now.

"Ah, sure, people don't know what they're saying at a time like this."

PRIORITIES

It was midafternoon, the dead part, before the roof came in on Minogue. He had been working alternately on Jennifer Halloran's statement, and on his list. He'd changed the names of his list several times. He'd started calling it The Now or Never List, but that had an edge of panic, he began to think. It was as though he was afraid he'd never get around to the things he wanted to do. Unconscious desire to fail, no doubt. He had settled on The Forbidden List.

The remains of a mediocre sandwich returned to the back of his throat as a burn. He returned to the list and began changing the numbers. Then he drew arrows to the new locations. 2 was now 1:

1. Letter resgn.

That he had word-processed a fortnight ago. Sullivan, the other new horse in Fraud, had shown him how to save it on a diskette. Minogue had been through probably ten starts. *It is with regret that I must request . . . It is with deep regret that I am putting in . . . It is with some regret that I am tendering my . . .*

He looked at the blinking cursor for a clue. MS Word supplied no templates for Resignation Letters from Former Inspectors in the Disbanded Murder Squad of the Gardai. He checked his list again.

2. Pat—29734218—after 3 pm.

Maybe he should drive down to Limerick and have a cup of tea with his son-in-law. Cup of tea? Dull enough. How about a few pints, maybe a jaunt up into Clare, and a stay-over? Pat would never admit that he found his father-in-law a bit intimidating still. Little enough use it was trying to be a normal father-in-law, inquiring about the job and the students and the holiday plans and all that. Iseult and Pat weren't going to Italy anymore. Minogue wasn't sure who had cancelled that. It could be the baby, simple enough.

Pat—Pat the Brain he no longer referred to him because he sensed Iseult didn't like it—had gone quiet this last while. Shuttling between lecturing in Limerick and a home in Dublin that was now on the skids wasn't any help. Iseult had more or less given up on any hope of buying a house in Dublin. Sometimes there are no solutions.

Number 5 had become Number 3.

Apartment.

As if he hadn't, as if Kathleen hadn't heard. He'd sooner leave Dublin than live in a place with no garden.

A wave of longing washed over him. He sat back and let the memories flood over him. Pathetic, it was, to be thinking of the kids all those years ago, chasing them in the garden. It was the late evening that they had liked the most, giddy and breathless and screeching with fright, the lights from the kitchen window flaring over the patch of lawn and turning the shrubs into dark jungle. It had gotten them all wound up, of course, and sometimes the laughter had turned to tears. Oh, but how Daithi had loved to run to him and be swept up, then to sit in his lap even in the dark. Sometimes to have him fall asleep then and there. It wouldn't come back, would it, ever.

Number 4 had stayed steady: Early Irish TCD.

And why would he only go to Trinity? It wasn't as though they were more biddable to mature student applications.

The Forbidden List from then on got more air-headed. It was impossible to put them in order: 6. Santorini 2 wks; 8. Lough Derg, ask Kilmartin (!!!); 9. Concern—Africa work?; 10. *Experience* Amis—buy; 11. Freesia bulbs; 12. Piano (a) Pavane (b) *The Lily of the West* . . .

He looked around the office. There was no sign of Fiona Hegarty since he'd come back from his excursion with Malone. He didn't want to read anything into her absence. But what was Jennifer Halloran doing at the minute? Would she stay away until five and then go home on the bus as usual, try to break the news gently to the mother? But neighbours would have seen her stepping into the squad car.

"Cup a tea," Sullivan said and he slid it across the desk.

"You're a doll, Paul."

"Before you start to snore entirely."

Minogue gave him a serious scrutiny. It wasn't the first time Sullivan had pushed it to see how far he could go with a veteran.

"You're coming over to us tomorrow still, are you?"

"I am," Minogue said.

Sullivan's case was petrol station receipts falsified by a fella used to work with computers and cash registers, he remembered.

Sullivan perched on the edge of the desk.

"Well. How do you like it, so far?"

Minogue sat back. Sullivan wouldn't be asking if it wasn't so obvious. He had grilled Minogue solid over lunch last week on where the rest of the training was taking him. Foreign language? Miserable French, self-taught, Minogue had conceded. There was hope for us all in the foreign language end of things then, if a Clareman could speak French.

Minogue, long a convert to the give-them-an-inch-etc. field guide entry under "Kerrymen," wasn't about to let that one go. Sullivan's own Kerry accent was enough to qualify as a foreign language, he had told him. Maybe that's when the cheeky guff started.

"I'll tell you soon's I have the paperwork done on this one," he said.

"Oh," said Sullivan and he nodded in the direction of Hegarty's empty chair. "Herself is after giving you the reins, is she?"

Minogue sipped at the tea. Sullivan must have put the whole bag of sugar in.

"But come on now," Sullivan said. "You'd have to miss the other work now. Grim enough, to be sure, was it? The murder business?"

Sullivan had told him that he knew Plateglass Sheehy well. His old brother had played hurling with Sheehy on a team out of Tralee a good number of years ago. Yes, Sergeant Fergal Sheehy had gone back to plainclothes out of Cork City. Sheehy had told Sullivan that the four cases he'd worked with the Murder Squad had been anything but plain sailing. He'd also told Sullivan that he didn't understand why he'd do it again this minute if he were asked. Conflicted, they called it, Minogue remembered. Herlighy, the psychiatrist that saw the most Guards, used that word a lot until Minogue asked him to drop it for something else.

The epiphany, that recall of Herlighy, brought to Minogue caused him to sit up and put the cup back on the saucer. Why hadn't he thought of something that simple. That would do it: talk to Herlighy, for the love of God. Herlighy could map it out, the guilt, the duty thing, the unconscious, all that stuff.

"What," said Sullivan.

"I just thought of something."

Minogue pencilled Herlighy into Number 1 on the list. When he looked up again, Sullivan had eased off his desk. It was Moriarty standing by the partition now.

C.I. Dan Moriarty hadn't wanted Minogue, or any other Garda officer on a skite, coming through his section. He hadn't told Minogue straight out, no hard feelings, etc. Minogue had soon pegged Fiona Hegarty's I'll-do-it-if-I-have-to on Moriarty's lead. Moriarty ate, drank, slept, and dreamed Fraud, Kilmartin had heard. Like a badger, he was, but well thought of. No fan of Garda Commissioner Tynan, was Moriarty. How discreetly he had let it be known too that he believed Tynan feathered nests for officers he favoured, i.e., Minogue, an Inspector with a past and a way of making you smile, but who put you on edge somehow too.

"A word will you, Matt?" from Moriarty.

Sullivan winked and made an O with his mouth.

Fiona Hegarty was sitting in Moriarty's office. Minogue felt himself holding his breath. He cursed himself for being dopey. But you couldn't tell with Moriarty. He always looked grave as though it was a way to get more done or something.

Fiona Hegarty gave Minogue a weak how-do. There was something different about her, he knew, but he didn't want to stare. Moriarty invited him to sit. He heard Moriarty draw in his breath. He watched him scan a page before he looked at him.

"Fiona here got a call," Moriarty said. "We have a problem here now."

Moriarty's eyes flicked over to her but she remained staring at the edge of his desk. He leaned forward and rested his elbows on his desk.

"Jennifer Halloran," he said to Minogue.

Minogue nodded.

"She left here," Moriarty said. "After she spoke with counsel."

Fiona Hegarty shifted in her chair.

"She spoke to him for . . . maybe half an hour, was it, Fiona?"

Fiona Hegarty nodded. She had a paper handkerchief in her fist, Minogue saw. She would not look up from the desktop. The crease on Moriarty's forehead deepened.

"She left in his company," Moriarty went on. "There was no bail sought, right?"

"That's right," Minogue said.

"A young fella," said Moriarty. "Still articling, by the look of him. The release was routine. He took a copy of the statement with him. Didn't make a fuss, but he did register with Fiona here that he believed the statement was improperly obtained. Said he'd need to wait before filing that because well, Miss Halloran, she needed a bit of time to recover."

"Recover from what," Minogue said.

Moriarty opened his hands and shook his head once. So Fiona Hegarty had been right, Minogue thought. Duress would be big. They'd probably go for inadmissible. Well, now might be a good time to take a turn at sliding off the chair himself.

"Well, the tapes will show we're in good order," he said.

"Yes, she waived," said Moriarty. "We're sound on that. That's not it, no."

Minogue couldn't be sure it was not a little sarcastic. He waited.

"He went to a restaurant with her," Moriarty went on. "He thought she could use a cup of tea, a bit of grub, to compose herself."

The swoon, Minogue thought. Maybe she had some

terrible condition, cancer or something. How would that look in a deposition? But she hadn't said a word about anything like that.

"Well, she left the café when your man went to the jacks," Moriarty said.

Why was he pausing, Minogue wondered.

"She went to Tara Street station. He had phoned her ma at this stage. They had a peculiar conversation. The ma got frantic. She phoned us. She said she thought her daughter was drunk. Anyway. Miss Halloran showed up at the station about a half-hour later, it appears."

Moriarty ran his tongue along his upper lip. He rubbed at his eyebrows.

"She, er, put herself in front of a train."

The room was engulfed in some kind of light, like a flash Minogue somehow couldn't see. The tremor ran up to his scalp, seized it. Moriarty was looking down at the same desktop as Fiona Hegarty. Minogue wanted to say something. Moriarty glanced up and his eyes were set in a bleak gaze.

But we did everything right, Minogue wanted to say. Even calling off Fiona Hegarty from putting her through the wringer again. Why would she . . . ?

"So that's what's happened," Moriarty murmured. "God love her."

An Eye-Opener

Quinn spotted Canning talking to a crony on a forklift near a door into the Markets. The place wasn't as mad busy as he remembered it. The smell of rotting fruit hanging in the air was a comfort to him.

Canning noticed him and he pushed off from the wall. The sun had come back out on this side of the street. They stood by the locked door of a fruit wholesaler.

"I don't know the other fella," Canning said.

"Who did the talking?"

"The other one, the older one."

"Tall, you said."

"Maybe, yeah. A culchie. Easy going look to him, until he got to business."

"Are you sure he didn't identify himself?"

"Well, he flashed the badge a second. But I didn't see. And I didn't want to ask, you know, look like I gave a shite."

Quinn stared at the metalwork over the entrance to the Market. Canning held out his packet of Majors.

"Malone used to be in that crowd," he said to Quinn. "What do you call them?"

"The Murder Squad."

"That's right. Jasus Bobby, you're an encyclopedia so you are."

Quinn drew the smoke deep. He'd have to phone Grogan.

"Well," Canning said. "That's Doyle for you. What a total, fucking iijit."

Quinn thought about the van, the drums being rolled out.

Canning drew back and spat far out onto the cobblestones.

"Tell you one thing," he said. "Malone's got some bottle. I don't see his crowd telling him to go in there and act like a hooligan. Officially, like. That's not how they work. Anyone could tell you that."

It just couldn't be, Quinn decided, it couldn't. Doyle had only driven into the garage the same time as the two cops had marched into the office.

"Where is Doyle anyway," Canning said. "We should sort him out."

Quinn shrugged.

"The bollocks," said Canning. "I mean, he's not just a dawbrain, is he. He's a dangerous dawbrain. Didn't I tell you that before, didn't I?"

Quinn watched Canning work himself up.

"Speaking for myself personally like, I'd give Doyle a good hiding, so I would. Straighten him out for good. You know? Want me to get things going there?"

Quinn shook his head.

"What, you think he's onside or something?"

"No, I just need to think things over."

Canning looked at him.

"I have to say this, Bobby, I do. Don't get me wrong now, okay?"

"About what, are you talking about?"

"About this. Listen, if you said to me, 'Beans, head out with Doyle and get us into, say, a factory,' I'd say to you take a running fucking jump. I would, Bobby."

To Quinn the clouds in the panel of sky over the street were like cotton balls. He'd spent a happy, surprising morning by the hotel pool in Portugal looking at them not that long ago. Catherine laughing at him because of it, but he liked it.

"I'll tell you what I heard too," Canning went on. "About Doyle. I heard he's on the needle, is what he is."

He waited for a reaction, but Quinn's face had set into a foggy stare at a forklift buzzing around.

"I heard it on good authority, so I did."

"Did you."

"Delusions, I'm telling you, that goes with it. It's no joke. He thinks he's the Godfather or something, I don't know. I mean to say, how long can that go on? If he's taking your name in vain . . . ? You know?"

"Working his way through all the Commandments, is he."

"And I heard he was dealing, Bobby. What's worse, he was getting it off those Russian fellas, the Bohemians or whatever."

"Where'd you hear that one? Same fella you heard he was a user, is it?"

"I'm only saying, Bobby. Okay, the fella told me, he's in the life himself. But it wouldn't surprise me. Not one bit. What about what happened this morning, those two refugee fellas, as if that's all they were . . . ?"

Quinn frowned.

"Ah come on, the racket. It's all over town! The place went mad with cops and everything. The two fellas shot down there in Mount Street?"

"I heard, yes. They said they were Albanians."

"That's it—Albanians. That crowd. Oh Jesus, a right mess I heard. Shotguns, everything. Just what we need, isn't it, for them fellas to be fighting it out here."

Canning shook his head and spat again.

"In Dublin," Quinn said.

"Yeah in Dublin. Get with it baby. We're in the ha'penny place compared to some of them. We need to wake up. Soon they'll be in on our end of the game here, doing whatever they want. In our country, can you imagine that?"

Canning lit another cigarette from the butt of the one he was finishing. Quinn turned down another.

"Fancy a pint, do you, Bobby?"

Quinn looked up at the clouds again. The ones coming in from behind the hills were the colour of sand now. He'd had to stop the car near Christchurch with the woozy feeling that just hit him. It was like he couldn't breathe or something.

"My twist," Canning said.

Quinn eyed him. Always wondering where he stood, Beans, and still saying and doing stupid stuff to annoy you. Like a child, he was.

That was it, Quinn thought then, and for a moment he felt he was coming back to something familiar and manageable. Beans had learned this when he was a kid, to annoy people so's they'd pay attention to him. And then later trying to undo the damage.

"No," he said to Canning. "Just go over what they said about Doyle though again."

SAVE CHANGES?

It was gone four when Minogue opened the file and typed in today's date. Now his fingers weren't working properly. He fixed the date and read it over on the screen once. Then he saved it and he opened the print menu.

Pages were dropping into the printer tray already. He'd have to wait.

Work, he decided. Try anything. He had another go at the Bala Mineral Water file but he lost it after a few words. Wasn't all that mineral water the biggest con already anyway? He should phone Kilmartin, get him to warm up his contacts in the security firms. The new microchip plants were always looking for people in security.

He pushed the keyboard away. He was completely addled. Maybe Jennifer Halloran might have been on some kind of medication, that was it. But she would have said so, wouldn't she? Not if she had her mind made up, she wouldn't.

He saw Moriarty coming his way. There was the solemn face and adolescent gait, the well-trimmed silver hair that stayed so neat all day, the wire-rims he let hang from those string things on his chest. A banker, a bookkeeper, more than a Guard.

"You know, Matt, you needn't hang around."

Minogue couldn't tell. Still he gave Moriarty the benefit of the doubt. God love her, he'd said, didn't he.

"Thanks," he said. "I'll head out so."

Moriarty nodded and studied the pages issuing slowly out of the printer.

"Fiona's very upset. Very. We had a long chat. I don't know if it helped."

He paused as though waiting for Minogue to offer something. The quiet hung around them, even over the lisping of pages settling in the tray.

"So there we have it," Moriarty said then. "Leave any loose ends to me."

Minogue wanted, didn't want, to argue.

Moriarty cleared his throat.

"I heard you were sound, Matt," he said. "But that you weren't a fella to put the boot in. Hard to imagine in that job you were holding down, the Squad."

"Well, I don't know," Minogue managed. "We got the job done. Most times."

Moriarty sighed.

"I'm telling you now what I told Fiona. There's no way of knowing what would have happened. Hold her for bail, even overnight. That was not on the cards, no. We took into account the home situation and all. She wasn't a flight risk. No."

Minogue had found out that Jennifer Halloran hadn't phoned her mother. He thought of her swooning, sliding to the floor. He couldn't get the picture of some saint in an ecstasy of torment, supplicating eyes on the sky or wherever heaven was back then, as a soldier or someone prepared to finish the martyrdom thing.

"She had her own thoughts," Moriarty said. "We had our

job to do. That's all we know. That's all we have to work with."

He held out a hand. The heave-ho, Minogue realized. He banged his knee on the desk as he stood up.

"Good luck now, Matt."

Minogue watched him go. The ache still gripped him somewhere in the hollow below his chest. It wasn't eight hours since he had sat across from Jennifer Halloran.

The pages had stopped falling into the tray. He sat down again and went to the print menu. He clicked an okay button and then the x in the top corner of the file. Save changes, it asked him? Her mother would go to bits. He should have said something earlier, God damn it to hell. She would have had a chance then.

Yes, save the changes, okay, whatever.

He stared at the desktop and the icons for a while and he thought about refugees who had come to Ireland only to be murdered. He thought about the heather in Sallygap, how the clouds met the endless horizons all about the boggy plateau. The staring and the wondering did not stop the image of Jennifer Halloran's fall, her first fall, maybe. Minogue winced and swore and uttered something that was prayer and threat together to a deity he did not recognize.

Then he ejected the diskette and slid it into his pocket. He took his letter of resignation and let it drop into his very offical-looking briefcase that he hated.

THERE'S NO CHANCE . . . ?

Grogan said little, as per usual, but Quinn knew he was taking it all in. He tried to form a picture of Grogan sitting in a pokey room in his terraced house in Belfast. Grogan had been refusing to leave for years.

"Tell me the place this happened again?"

Hop-penned. The way he said it. Quinn looked down the road from where he'd pulled in. They were building new apartments behind the SPAR.

"In a fish and chip shop," he said. "It's been there for years."

He still was leery about mobiles, even after all the persuading Canning had tried that having them in other people's names was all it took. Grogan talked freely on his.

"The name of the place?"

"Cafolla's."

"Well, do you go there at all, Bobby?"

"No. Before I used to, years ago, the odd time."

"Your name would be known there."

"I suppose. Yes, it's Tony the son running it now."

Quinn was impatient to be home, to be in the kitchen having a cup of tea with Catherine. Anything: just to be normal for a while. To see Brittney combing the hair on a doll or one of those million ponies, even. Watch a bit of telly with her, buy her an ice cream. Imagine that, he thought again: It had only been just lately that he'd been able to get his own daughter to relax a bit around him. Maybe she wasn't old enough to remember some of the things that happened before, but growing up visiting your oul lad in jail, could a kid get over that?

"Look," he said to Grogan. "Maybe I'll talk to that cop, Malone."

"You're sure you should do that?"

"They'd be expecting some reaction, the Guards."

Grogan said nothing.

"Let them know I'm pissed off. That I haven't a clue what they're on about."

"Right, right."

"I'm going to tell them that he was an addict. Out of his tree, that kind of thing."

"There's always that."

Without warning, a shudder ran up Quinn's chest. He must be reacting now, he thought. Doyle, as he pulled him out of the Renault, the small hole that told you nothing about what the bullet did when it came out his face. But it was Roe he'd been thinking about, he realized, and trying not to think about. Whatever they did to one another up there, either in jail or in those kippy little terraces where they cooked up their spite and their hatred.

"Well," Grogan said. "We should know what he said, Bobby."

Quinn wasn't sure what Grogan wanted now.

"But you knew him, didn't you," Grogan said. "There's no chance . . . ?"

"Wait a minute," Quinn said. "I only knew him on account he was always asking for jobs, trying to get on."

"You'd know who he could have talked to, what he knew about the job?"

"I told him what I told him, nothing more. What I told you before. That it'd be just a small thing, just a contract I was passing on to him from other people. Take it or leave it type of thing."

Quinn jammed his eyes shut tight and rubbed hard at them. Layer upon layer, he thought: Beans Canning because he was none too smart, and he had to have some front for the law. Doyle brought in with a yarn about a subcontract that even Quinn himself knew nothing about.

"Case closed, you're saying then?"

"I'm telling you."

"Okay. There are people here who are, well, their comfort level is low. Concerning what goes on down there at your end. You know what I mean, now?"

"Yeah."

"They like reassurance."

"I'll find out what I can."

Grogan would have registered the tone.

"You did rightly phoning," he said.

Quinn pushed the End button hard and he held it. Then he powered off the phone and put it on the floor. He started the engine before he realized that he didn't know what to do. He watched his knuckles go white on the steering wheel. At least it was better than watching your hands shaking. He looked at the cement lorry pouring a load down the chute. Where was he again? So much had changed here even in the three years. Phibsboro, right, the Cross Guns. The Finglas Road, home.

REYNARDINE

Minogue almost made it through the hard part of the drive home, the first ten minutes when he was sure he'd blurt out something to Kathleen. It was the traffic that did it in the end, probably. Kathleen had run out of newspaper. She'd folded it and thrown it in the back. They had talked—she had talked—about where Albania really was, how would this look abroad, was this the start of something. She had caught his mood however, the tiredness, and didn't expect answers. She went back to talking about the article on the foxes that had been spotted near the canal.

"Well, I don't know what I'd do if I saw one in the garden," she said.

The Citroën coasted to the end of a long line snaking into Ranelagh. The brake pads are definitely worn through, he decided.

"They're mostly shy," he said. "As I remember them."

"They're scavengers," she said. "Aren't they? I mean, all the stories."

"I suppose."

"Wouldn't they bite? What about rabies?"

He shrugged.

"Oh, the moving statue crowd will get in on the act," she said. "Wait'll you see."

"How do you mean?"

"Sure I read it already. They say it's a sign, you know. A *sign*."

He didn't ask. He thought about Jennifer Halloran's hands clasping, opening, clasping again on the table between them. Was that her way of praying maybe. The subconscious and all that, again.

The traffic moved on another fifty feet. Minogue retreated to his imaginary smallholding, his Five Acres. A goat definitely, for all the trouble they could be. Call it Jim, of course. A donkey, like they had growing up. Kathleen'd go mad probably. For a while, anyway.

"Come on, Matt. Your crowd'd know. All the country stuff?"

Two cyclists raced by inches from his door handle. He was taking tomorrow off and shag them. And Friday. As long as it took.

"Oh yes," Kathleen said. "'The foxes are telling us something.' I heard this oul fella saying that on the radio yesterday, that's right."

Minogue watched the blue smoke from his car's exhaust diffuse behind.

"Would foxes attack a child?"

"I doubt it," he said.

"They'll eat from bins, won't they? I blame it all on the fast-food thing. Sure there's bits of burgers and things lying around the road every day. Fellas in cars get the take-outs and then they fire the bags out the window. That's the half of it right there."

An ambulance came up behind them on the wrong side of the road. Minogue switched off the engine.

Kathleen looked over at him.

"You're not the best, love, are you."

"I'm okay," he said.

"You look, well, I don't know."

Minogue studied her eyebrows. He put his hand over hers.

"Trouble?"

"Later on," he said. "Later on, I'll tell you."

DUKE OF YORKS, IDAHO REDS

Minogue had half-expected the call. He'd held off as long as he could out in the garden. He'd tied up the berry fence and moved half the stones to the side of the wall where Kathleen said she wanted the fountain. Twenty minutes weeding even.

The dark was in under the trees now. Some yellow held on, he saw, by the hedge, but things had lost their edges now. There was no more than a quarter of an hour left really. Once he had found himself staring into the hedge for minutes. The midges had left him alone. Kathleen had left him alone, but he knew she'd be waiting.

He'd heard it ringing and guessed. Kathleen opened the window, her hand over the phone. She mouthed something to him before she'd let him have the phone.

Minogue headed up the garden with the phone. It wasn't Malone.

Garda Commissioner Tynan sounded tired. Was it Moriarty had phoned him, Minogue wondered.

"I'm down the garden here feeling my way around," he said.

"Hiding out, are you."

"In a manner of speaking."

"What from?"

Minogue had nothing to lose really.

"Phone calls, for one."

"I'd phone you on your mobile if you'd only turn the damned thing on."

Minogue turned to face the house. Not for the first time he remembered he shouldn't be using an old wireless for job calls. He didn't care.

"The way it works is that I have to be phoned in such a situation," Tynan said. "Remember I set that up? So's we wouldn't be tried and convicted in the papers again?"

Minogue stared into the gloom where the pear trees were supposed to be. He wanted to ask how Tynan's wife was. Maybe you weren't supposed to ask. It was one of the more curable ones, wasn't it?

"I thought I'd hear things from your end," Tynan said.

"All right so. We screwed up in the worst way."

Tynan spoke after a pause.

"Miss Halloran wasn't in custody when she did it."

"I should have come in earlier. A mess."

"It wasn't your case. You were just shadowing her."

For a moment Minogue did not understand. The job, he realized then, the learning on the job, that's what they called it now.

"I'm a big boy. I know what's fair and what's not. I let it go by."

"You know that Hegarty is taking it all on? That she's in bits?"

"I'd heard she was upset."

"'Upset'? I'd say PTSD."

"Is that to do with kids who can't sit still or something?"

"Post Traumatic Stress Disorder. As if you didn't know."

Minogue said nothing. Tynan would know he wasn't for humouring.

"You didn't exactly hit it off with her, did you," Tynan said.

"Do I have to answer that one?"

"She told Moriarty about the woman fainting or something. That you called off the interview. So stop beating yourself up."

"I don't know what her family's going to do. But I can't stop thinking about them. I was thinking of getting in touch with them, with the mother—"

"—Don't. Any contact will play into the hands of a nest of barristers swarming around this. They'll take it for a tell."

Why and how did we ever start using gambling words, Minogue wondered. The "tells" that any cop looked for, the way a poker player would: a tic, too much eye-to-eye contact, the dependable wet palms, the casual remarks that weren't casual. There had been no tell that involved a fainting, praying thing in his career before. Or in any Garda's career either, he'd bet. So why, then, could he not believe that himself when it mattered?

His thumb was on the button. He thought about the letter, signed and sealed, waiting on the hall table. The anger gathered around his chest.

"Am I in line for a talking-to? What, guilt, maybe?"

"Don't play that one," said Tynan. "This is something you're getting guidance on right now. In a little while you'll get a reminder of the oath you signed a thousand years ago when you lined up on the parade ground in Templemore. If you can't listen to guidance here, then you'd better hear it as an order."

Cabbages, Minogue started thinking. That's the only answer to this apartment thing. Curly kale. Brussels sprouts. Cauliflower. Spuds, more of them. Take over the whole garden with them next year.

"Are you there?"

Minogue let it hang a few moments.

"I am."

"Kathleen might have forgotten to mention my name there a minute ago. It's Garda Commissioner Tynan."

For spuds he'd go to the Kerr's Pinks, of course.

"I had phoned to tell you that you could never have known."

"That's what Moriarty said. I half-believed him."

"I'm going to repeat myself: You did right, letting her go."

"What good did it do her? She's after killing herself. Over a few lousy thousand quid. The one mistake she made in her life, the one."

"Your duty is to uphold the law. That includes fraud."

"Talk to me about tax cheats or money launderers. The offshore moneymen swarming about Foxrock in their Mercedes, laughing at us."

"That's fraud too," Tynan said.

"But those fellas aren't under the wheels of a train, are they."

He watched Kathleen walk to the window and look out.

"Listen," Tynan said. "Take time to go over it, Have you anyone to talk to?"

Minogue thought about Herlighy again. A fuss high up in the beech tree behind drew his eyes up. Two or three birds scattered, complaining, into the dark. He heard something, leaves brushing together in the long grass by the compost.

"Don't try hiding," Tynan went on. "You're going to move on sooner than was planned. How's your foreign language quotient lately?"

Minogue registered the feint. It was the best Tynan could do for consoling. It was then that Minogue remembered: that's right, Tynan's wife had gone back in for tests. The radiation wasn't enough, apparently. Remorse flooded through him.

"Look, John—"

"—We'll work up something then. Think Vienna. Think Brussels. Think Interpol and international effort. Think joint operations. Now more than ever. Keep your eye on the ball, is what I'm saying."

Minogue watched Kathleen press her face closer to the window.

"Look," he said. "I might as well tell you. I'm thinking of walking."

Tynan said nothing.

"It wasn't just today."

"I'm listening."

"I won't go on. I have no speech ready."

"You've thought about it then for a while."

"I have."

"Take a few days to think about it again."

Kathleen drew back, walked toward the hall. Minogue hesitated.

"What do you actually want to do?" Tynan asked.

"I don't know. I heard there might be something in security."

"Something in security."

"That's about it, yes."

"I hear there's not bad money in it. Company car too. Cushy number, yes."

Minogue didn't return the sarcasm.

"You want to go around protecting some multinational's assets eight hours a day."

Minogue tried to see what was moving in behind the rhubarb now. There had been cat shit there for a while in the spring.

"All right," Tynan said. "But if you decide to walk, tell me first."

The sky was still brown to the west. He couldn't hear the rustling anymore.

"You were due to head over to, where was it, after Fraud?"

"Drugs Central was the plan from October first on."

"Well, it'll be earlier then," Tynan said. "There's work waiting."

It was Tynan who hung up first.

A dog started barking furiously in a garden up the road. Minogue made his way down to the kitchen door. He'd leave the windows open tonight for sure.

Kathleen had the telly on already.

"Well," she said. "You're important tonight."

He watched the main character in the series, an overweight British actor whose name he could never remember, interview a suspect. Stupid, he decided, not for the first time. Kilmartin would have eaten him alive by now.

"I'm taking tomorrow off," he said. "Friday too."

She looked up at him.

"Do you want to run away with me for a few days?"

She muted the volume.

"What's after happening? What did he say to you?"

SHOULD HAVE KNOWN

Minogue woke up with a start at ten after three. It wasn't a dog chasing him in a dream anymore. There were two of them howling now, real dogs.

"I'll go down and strangle that fecker, so I will," Kathleen groaned.

He didn't want to shake clear of the foggy head, the dull ache from the whiskey. He lay still, listening.

"Close the windows, can't you," she muttered. She turned back to her side.

He rolled out and closed the bedroom windows. He perched on the edge of the bed. Kathleen pushed up on her elbows.

"Do you want to talk, love?"

"I don't."

"A cup of something then?"

"Go back to sleep yourself. I have a book below."

He left the lights off downstairs for a few minutes. The dogs' howling had died down. The foliage had kept most of the street light from coming over the garage roof into the garden. He thought about going out, just mooching about.

He picked up the short stories from where he had left them near the couch and he pushed up some cushions before he put on the reading lamp. There'd be no sleep for a while. But he'd gotten almost three hours.

He thought about the bottle he'd put back under the sink, the duty-free Jameson's that Kathleen pretended she'd hidden. If there were a shop open he'd have gone out for a packet of fags. Maybe that was all going to happen again.

He found his page but the words evaporated on him. He kept seeing Jennifer Halloran, kneeling pretty well, her head on the table. What else could it have been except praying. He should have known. That had to be when she decided.

He fell asleep at six, right after he concluded he wouldn't.

QUE SERA SERA AND ALL THAT

Bobby Quinn wasn't sure if he'd actually had forty winks. He reached for his watch on the bedside table. Catherine's breathing changed. He must have slept, then. There were the beginnings of light behind the curtains. Thank God it was the summer at least. He thought about the nights in jail, the early morning hours. A lot of fellas couldn't sleep. There were the junkies, of course, but even ordinary inmates didn't sleep right. The ones who topped themselves usually did it early in the morning.

He'd thought about that very early in his sentence. It happened when Catherine had stuck with what she'd said about not wanting Brittney to see him there. A routine had set in of course, and it had deadened him to a lot of things. It was a way of shutting things down so's you just got through doing your time. Grogan and his crowd knew it all. It was like they used the place as a school, or a business.

The sound of that gun in the garage yesterday—just a thump. He'd realized how tight he was wound up when he got in the door, finally, last night. Catherine trying to let on she wasn't suspicious, annoyed at him, and him trying to be level, but his mind going like mad. Barely able to sit down, to even have a conversation, for God's sake.

They'd sat through the news together, with Brittney play-ing that boy band crap on her Walkman. Why did it irritate him so much, Catherine wanted to know. Just another thing, a setback of sorts. For a while he thought Catherine wanted to say something when they showed the place with the cop cars everywhere on the news. Like what? Like: *Do you know anything about that, Bobby?*

Still he felt her keeping her distance. The nightie he'd bought for her at that lacy place there in Duke Street had stayed away in a drawer somewhere. She was back to those long T-shirt things he hated. She hadn't talked about more kids in a long while now. That was her mother behind that, he knew. She'd always have it in for him.

He stared at the lampshade, wondered what time Cafolla's opened. He remembered thinking just before he fell asleep that he could just let it drop. Malone he could proba-bly figure, but the other fella, the veteran, had serious back-ground.

He couldn't decide.

He squeezed his eyes shut tight. The lampshade was still there when he opened his eyes again. So was the thought and he might as well say it to himself at least: nothing good was going to come out of this. But still, what was done was done, que sera sera and all that. There was no use in speculating.

He slid out of bed and found his way on the parts of the floor that didn't creak. He looked back toward Catherine. She was faking being asleep. He might never be able to avoid seeing it in her eyes, the holding back. Fear, he should call it, to be honest. He didn't blame her. She was waiting, the way anyone would, for it all to come back, to go wrong. Eight months now. It'd take a lot longer than that to persuade her.

He had oiled the door hinges. He made it down to the hall with only one creak. He put on the jacket and found his cigarettes by the telly. A shaft of yellow light lit up the roof opposite. He studied it, tried to notice it creep down the chimney breast with the movement of the sun. Everything was so fresh in the morning, only for people to wake up and mess everything up and wreck things.

He finished his cigarette, lit another. His stomach made one of those grinding kind of moves, like it was shrinking or turning over or something. He hadn't been able to manage anything beyond some crisps and a few biscuits last night. Roe was a meat cutter, Jesus, how much sicker could it get than that.

Quinn studied the burning edge of the paper, the twin trails of smoke curling up from the tip. He held up his arm and watched. The shake was gone for sure. He drew on the cigarette, and in the steady volley of smoke he breathed into the sunlit kitchen he realized that he had to know what Doyle had said to the cop at the chipper last night.

And now that the daylight was here, he didn't need to try to keep that feeling at bay anymore, that feeling that something had started, and that it had nothing to do with plans or being smart or even timing. It was chance or luck, or something like that, probably they had a name for it in India or someplace. Like something was waiting for him out there. The thing was to just get on with it.

He looked at his reflection in the kettle. A cup of tea, a shower, he thought, and then get things going. There was no harm going over to Irene today. It'd give him confidence, settle him. Things would click into place.

LAY YOUR CARDS ON THE TABLE, YOU CONTRARY HOOR

Minogue left the breakfast stuff until the middle of the day. He had felt more than peculiar driving home from town, after dropping Kathleen off. Managing Kilmartin during the phone call had taken a lot.

"Now, is it?" Kilmartin had wanted to know. "This very minute, like?"

"Soon."

"Why now?"

"Soon, I said."

Kilmartin wasn't going to waste a chance to needle his friend.

Why would anyone who's got a brain want to consider walking away from the easiest stroke to come along in the history of the Garda Siochana? The Glamour Job of the Century? Didn't Minogue know a single Guard who wouldn't give his or her right ball for what was lined up for him? What, exactly, was his problem?

"Jim, give me the contact or I'll come over to the Park and tell the nabobs there you're so pally with how you fart at work."

But Kilmartin wasn't about to let go.

"This is some mental thing with you, is my guess. Lost the head a bit?"

"Just take it as a what-if then, is all I'm asking."

"A contrary hoor is what you are. Come on, lay your cards on the table."

No cards were laid. For a few moments Minogue had been ready to tell Kilmartin how he had woken up with a start, terrified of something: trains, shouts, people running in his dreams.

Kilmartin would look around and get back to him tomorrow, then. The talk got on to old times. Minogue couldn't bring himself to tell Kilmartin to give over. He looked out at the garden, at the stones he had planned to move around to a new rockery site. He studied the garden for the full ten minutes it took Kilmartin to tell what had actually happened in the dead doctor's case back fifteen years ago, and a steady silence from Minogue, to get the idea.

"Look," Kilmartin had said then in a tone Minogue hadn't expected. "Don't cod yourself, Matt."

"Cod meself how?"

"You're bored out of your mind in Fraud. You can't work with the likes of whoever they put you with. Right? But I'm going to tell you something now, about what can happen. Are you listening to me at all there?"

Five Acres came back into Minogue's mind, the goat, the donkey. How hard would it be to go down to his brother's farm, to sit by him at the window where he sat most of the day now that the arthritis had stopped him even walking the fields, and to tell him to find a spot he could build. Lots of huge boulders desired, pile them in, high ground against the damp; a look down at the sea, and not to worry about the road in.

"My lovely wife," Kilmartin went on, "God be good to her, is going around like a gamog—don't even whisper to her I ever talked to you, do you hear? With the very best of intentions I hasten to add, perfectly convinced that her hubbie is as happy as Larry here in the Park. Have you heard the like already?"

"A bit, I think."

"Oh right. 'Kathleen says that Maura says that Jim is in great form since he got out of the murder business.' Am I right or am I right?"

Minogue began to listen now. He had forgotten how he missed working around the Mayoman, like a loose boulder in a field. It had taken him years to understand that behind the slagging and the fierceness and the bullying schoolboy in Kilmartin was something of the disappointed child.

"The nail on the head, James. You have the makings of a detective, I'm thinking."

"Shut up a minute, and listen. If you're wondering how I got this Oscar style of carrying on, with the missus and that, think for a minute. I learned all this letting-on, this what you might call disguise, domestic play-acting, from, well, guess who?"

Minogue wouldn't answer.

"I'm onto you, you whore," Kilmartin said, his voice still gentle. "You can't cod me one bit. So keep the flag flying there. No let up. Are you with me, are you?"

Minogue allowed that for now he was, sort of.

No Big Thing

Canning had waited outside Irene's for Quinn. It had been three-quarters of an hour.

"You wait in the car when I go into Cafolla's," Quinn said to him.

"Wait outside? What, am I a waiter this morning?"

"I want to talk to the young fella on me own. Tony."

"What, two of us would frighten him?"

"That's about it."

Canning drove. Quinn felt the resentment hanging in the air. He thought about what Irene had told him about entering a new phase. New conjunctions were becoming closer, that was how she put it, something to do with Saturn and Venus. That was supposed to make you pay attention to your love life or something?

"There's fuck-all sign of Doyle at his place," Canning said then. "He knows we're looking for him, I'm telling you."

Quinn kept his eye on the slowing traffic in Fairview. The Star had turned up in the cards the last time at Irene's, he remembered, and she'd made a big thing out of it. He wanted to tell her to just shut up basically, and not make a performance out of it, trying to make it sound so rosy—just to give him the basics. But she had tried to work around the one that had turned up last week. He hadn't been fooled. The

Tower had lightning on it for God's sake, it was more than just "unexpected."

"I phoned his place four times last night," Canning said. "Then I got a hold of the owner, the landlord or whatever you call him, this morning, did I tell you?"

"No."

"The landlord says he's getting Doyle evicted. He has the place destroyed, says he—Doyle does. And what's more, he's going to get the cops to look the place over for drugs. That's what he told me. So there."

Quinn's eyes still burned from lack of sleep. He watched an old man walk crookedly by some shops. The middle of summer, and he was wearing a cap and a jumper and a jacket. He thought about Roe again, dressed in that schoolteacher gear. The perfect disguise, or was it some kind of a creepy thing he had going on in the back of his mind?

"That's how it has to be, Bobby. You know?"

"What?"

"Doyle. He'll go off the deep end on something. Then where are we? Get the law nosing around . . . ?"

"I'll take care of it."

"I can do for him, you know. Take him out behind the docks there, give him a good hiding, and then—"

"I'll take care of it."

Canning opened his hands over the wheel. He didn't look over at Quinn.

"I'm only saying, Bobby."

"Keep an eye out for your allies today," Irene had said. Well, what the hell use was that to him? All those glass things hanging in the windows, incense as per usual. Still, though. Maybe he should have taken the crystals thing more seriously. No, no, it was rubbish plain and simple. The cards, the Tarot, were the main thing.

"Living like an animal, Doyle was," Canning said. "Says the landlord."

Quinn realized he'd have to make a bigger effort. He looked over.

"Really."

"Wouldn't surprise me if he, you know, had business coming through."

Know who to trust, was Irene's other bit of advice today. Whatever that could mean. Twenty quid a session, that's all it meant maybe.

"So," said Canning. "Are we going to get a drop of rain or not?"

"I don't know."

"Ah, come on."

"I don't listen to the weather forecast, do I."

"I meant the other thing. The Availing thing."

Quinn drew in his breath.

"It's Avalon. And it's none of your business."

"Well, what did she tell you today?"

"Did you hear what I just said?"

"Oh, so that's what she said, is it."

"Park down by the shop there."

Quinn looked through the glare on the window of the chipper.

"That's the da in there," Canning said. "Will you look, the state of him, Jesus."

"We'll wait a while here."

Canning lit a cigarette. He began talking about electronics, how you could watch a DVD on a thing that you could put in your pocket. Then he got onto computers, how someone told him that you could listen in on credit card numbers going by if you had the right equipment, and did he know that?

It was twenty minutes before Quinn spotted Tony Junior's Alfa pulling in.

"Keep an eye out," Quinn said. He waited for Canning to look over. "I mean really keep an eye out."

Tony Junior had begun unloading boxes from the boot. He was heading laden to the door of the chipper when he saw Quinn coming down the footpath.

"Tony," Quinn called out. "How's it going?"

"Not so bad. Not so bad, Mr. Quinn."

"Here, I'll get the door for you."

Tony looked over at the car, Canning watching them.

"You need a hand lifting them, Tony?"

"I'm grand, thanks."

"Need to have a word with you."

Tony Senior had come to the door now. Must be eighteen or twenty stone now, Quinn thought.

"There's only me and the da," Tony said. "Getting ready for the school crowd and all, you know?"

Quinn tried to smile.

"Just a couple of minutes, Tony. No big thing."

Quinn got to the door before Tony Senior, and he pushed it open. Tony Senior said something to his son in Italian. Tony Junior put the boxes on the counter, and said something back to his da. Quinn stared back into Tony Senior's glare.

"Show me that nice new car of yours, will you?"

Quinn nodded at Tony Senior as they left. Tony Junior used a remote. Quinn eyed Canning as he made his way across to the Alfa and he sat in. Tony Junior played with the controls in a half-hearted way. Then he took a paper hankie from the glove compartment and slowly ran it over the instrument panel.

Quinn watched him. A bit of a daw, he remembered. He'd had something wrong with him at school.

"Nice car, Tony."

"Making a living, Mr. Quinn. You know."

"Your da's car, is it?"

"Yeah. Maybe you should talk to me da, Mr. Quinn."

"About what, Tony?"

"Well, I don't know, but like, whatever it is."

Quinn studied the dark brown patches under Tony Junior's eyes. Gone pale then, was Tony. It was one of the Egans ran the insurance here. Quinn wondered how much the Cafollas were paying.

"How's your memory these days, Tony?"

"Well, I suppose it's not bad really."

"You do the evenings, right?"

Cafolla nodded. He began to run his hands along the steering wheel. Quinn looked back at the father standing there at the glass, the big arms folded.

"Well, most evenings," Cafolla said. "Yes."

"Tuesday night, around closing time?"

"The pub crowd, do you mean, Mr. Quinn?"

"That's right. You know, call me Bobby, will you. So you remember a bit of a commotion then of the Tuesday? You remember?"

Tony Junior swallowed. The eyelids going on him, Quinn noted. You could nearly hear the poor iijit trying to calculate here.

"Just what happened, Tony. There's no problem from my end. Do you know what I'm saying?"

"Yes, Mr. Quinn."

"Go on, then."

"There was a fella came in. With a Chinese girl. Actually she spoke English."

"A Chinese girl?"

"I think she was his girlfriend."

"Him being . . . ?"

"Well, he was one of the Malones, wasn't he," Tony Junior said. "We sort of know his family. They used to be fairly regular a few years ago. He has a brother."

"Which one of them was it Tuesday?"

"The cop, the Guard, I mean."

"And who else, aside from the girl?"

"I never seen the other fella before, or at least I don't remember ever seeing him."

"Never?"

"No."

"Who else was here?"

"The young fella works the grill. He's a local lad, a student. But I do the counter and all in the evenings. You never know with people, especially that time of night. You know what I mean?"

"I know what you mean, Tony. Definitely, I do."

Quinn watched Tony Junior's eyes dart around, the faster rub on the Alfa symbol on the steering wheel.

"So," he said. "What happened?"

Quinn nodded and smiled while Tony talked. He had a bit of a stutter on his *s*, he realized.

"Did he say any names, during the thing?"

"Well, I wasn't paying much attention to what he was saying, Mr. Quinn. I mean, I was worrying things might get out of hand entirely."

"Well, did he mention my name, say?"

Tony Junior nodded.

"Tell me what he said."

"Well, like I said, I don't remember exactly every word."

"Do the best you can, Tony."

"Well, he said, I don't know if I got it right, he said something like 'Bobby Quinn can take care of this.'

Something like that, I don't know if I got the words exact there."

"And did he say what that meant?"

"Mr. Quinn, me da wants me in, it's getting late for the dinnertime crowd—"

"—Tony. You need to listen to me. To what I'm asking you."

Tony stopped rubbing. He looked over at the father scowling and tapping on the glass by the door to the chipper. The father held up his watch and pointed at it. Quinn gave him a hard look and held up three fingers.

"Did he get specific, Tony?"

"What?"

"Did he say what he meant, Tony?"

"No, I mean I don't think so."

"You're a bit too quick there, Tony, for my liking."

"How do you mean, Mr. Quinn?"

"This 'no' thing. I think you have a good enough memory, so I do."

"True's God. I was just trying to think what to do."

"Like what? Like call the Guards?"

"No, no. I didn't. No, I wouldn't do that, Mr. Quinn."

"Why not?"

"Well, the fella there, he was a Guard, wasn't he?"

Quinn looked at him. He was nervous enough. This was Tony Cafolla Junior's logic, then, was it.

"This was after the Guard hit him, Mr. Quinn. When he said your name."

"After."

"That's right. He was on the floor, picking himself up, that's what he was doing. You know he wasn't as mad as you'd think, so he wasn't. I remember that."

"How do you mean?"

"Well, up he gets, and I see him, and he's, well he's almost smiling. Yes."

That fits, Quinn decided. Doyle got his way by provoking people, annoying them.

"But he'd started talking about the brother then, right?"

"Right."

"'Your brother's on his way out and you're here buying cod and chips'?"

"That's right. That's what he said. I think."

"And 'you're going to let your brother go down the effing drain'?"

"That's right."

"Just him, and the girl, along with Malone, then."

"Right."

"But the fella doing the grill back in the kitchen? Did you forget him, Tony?"

"Yes—I mean, no. It all started so fast that he didn't know anything, Mr. Quinn. He only came out later when the fella left, when he heard him shouting. 'What's happening, Tony' he says to me, and I says, 'Nothing, go back in the kitchen, it's just a fella with a few jars on him.'"

"No shouting during this dust-up?"

"No. It was weird, like it was a conversation. Like I was saying. That's why it was such a surprise, like. The whole thing. And it was over in a minute."

There was a pleading look on Tony Junior's face now, Quinn saw. His lips were gone dry, and he had been clearing his throat a lot. Quinn looked back at the father, still staring at them.

"Do yous have cameras in the shop, Tony?"

"God no, Mr. Quinn. No, no. We don't use them."

"Is everything so quiet around here then?"

"Well, things are better all around, Mr. Quinn. We don't

have the problems we used to have a while back."

Quinn looked for any irony but there was none. How could there be, he decided. Tony Junior probably believed everything he was told by his oul lad. Who paid his insurance, and was hardly happy about it.

Quinn nodded and he shifted in his seat.

"This is a very nice set of wheels here, Tony. Very nice."

"Thanks, Mr. Quinn."

"You'd be the happy man driving this around, I bet, wouldn't you?"

"That's a fact, oh I'm not complaining there."

Quinn mustered a smile. He held out his hand.

"Thanks, Mr. Quinn. Thanks."

A small enough notch above handicapped, Quinn thought. All to the good.

"For what, Tony?"

He watched the confusion spread over Tony Junior's face.

"It's me should be saying that to you, Tony. Thank *you*."

He grasped the door handle. Sometime soon he could move out of the crap car the cops could laugh about and get into some half-decent car like this.

"Don't be booting it, now, you hear me, Tony?"

"Okay, Mr. Quinn."

"The Guards'd love to get you. Oh yes they would, in a nice flash car like this. Mad jealous, they'd be."

The smile of relief had changed Tony Junior's face completely. The poor dope had that pretty-boy film-star look, all right. Any gold-digger would have to get by his oul fella though.

"Before I go now, Tony, tell me something. I nearly forgot. What was the fella's name there, the fella caused the trouble?"

Tony Junior's face told him all he needed to know. "Never seen him before, Mr. Quinn": bloody sure he knew Doyle. Still he waited a few moments while Junior worked something through his mind.

"Ah it's okay, Tony. Just wondering, that's all."

A Folley-Up

Minogue put the bags of groceries on the kitchen floor and picked up the phone. Malone sounded cagey.

"I just thought I'd tell you," he said. "As a folley-up."

"Fire away, so."

"I'm going to pay Bobby Quinn a little visit—and I'm going on me own."

Minogue watched something sliding slowly in one of the plastic bags. It moved under the *Irish Times* he had draped over the bag, the headlines swelling and receding, it seemed, the photos of the Albanians and the scene by Mount Street.

"Oh, this is your plan then, is it."

"I just don't want this getting by me."

"You'll get it all over you, is what I'm thinking, Tommy."

"Look, I'm going ahead with it."

The sliding stopped. Minogue leaned in to look: the courgette.

"You're that sure there's something to it, are you."

Malone took his time answering.

"It'd be on me mind if I didn't do something. I mean to say, someone's supplying Terry in there, aren't they. And if Doyle says Bobby Quinn has a hold on that?"

"But no one's come out in the open to you about it."

"I'm saying that this prick Doyle is the first hint. That's why I want to follow up."

"Does your mob know you're going to meet him?"

"No."

"You're doing the Mission Impossible effort now, are you."

"I seem to remember a certain person telling me to go with me gut, when we were chasing a killer. That all changes when you're on the fast track to being a Eurocop?"

"Think how it'll look," Minogue said. "If you're spotted with Quinn."

"I've thought about it. It's time to pay him a visit. That's all."

"And you're going on your own."

Malone said nothing.

Just Forget You Ever
Heard About It

Canning put rubber bands around the twenties and he began packing them into the envelopes. At least he wasn't still holding some of them up, looking for the security lines and saying how Euros would always be stupid-looking.

"I'm telling you," he said to Quinn. "Doyle knows what he done. He knows."

Quinn looked down the street. Even the newsagents here had shiny new fronts. A Jag there, a high-end Renault, a Volvo. Farther on was a silver Mercedes.

"What are you looking at?" Canning asked. "Is there law there?"

"No," Quinn said.

"Did you hear me about Doyle?"

"I did."

"He's done a bunk. I bet you he's in England now."

Canning closed the envelope and slid it under the seat. He narrowed his eyes and elbowed Quinn.

"Or maybe something else, Bobby. You know?"

"Like what."

"Like maybe the fellas who did that job out there yesterday, the two foreigners that got shot. Our friends from the North and all that? Know what I'm saying?"

"What friends are you talking about?"

"Ah come on, Bobby. Do you take me for a complete gobshite?"

Quinn watched a Garda car go by.

"I'm only saying. You know?"

Quinn looked across at him.

"What," said Canning. "What are you looking at me like that for?"

Quinn shook his head once and looked away.

"Like, say he has pissed off some of that crowd, that's all I'm saying. They're around, Bobby, don't try to cod me they're not down here now. You've heard the stories yourself. There's the fella disappeared, the Moloney fella, the tough guy they used, the Egans? Then those dealers who were done in last November?"

Quinn started the car. They had two more calls to do, and Coady's later on. Kevin Stacey there wanted a chinwag about getting more to the dealers he was running out of Sligo or something. It was going too well, maybe. Then there was that story he'd heard about a lab starting up somewhere in Cavan—in Cavan, for God's sakes. Tomorrow was Bray, Wonderland, for the big pick-up there.

The numbness, that floaty feeling where he didn't know if he was going to be able to breathe for a few seconds, that must be the reaction, he decided. It was like he was wrapped in something that kept him separated from the world. How everything looked dull and empty and far-off. He'd seen worse, and he'd been prepared, sort of.

"We're going to meet with this cop now," he said to Canning.

"What about the take here, all the cash?"

"Stick it in your pocket."

"You're joking, Bobby."

"I'm not joking. Just do it, will you."

"What if Malone has a set-up and we get snookered? I mean it was him phoned you to set this up, this little get-together. Aren't you in the least—"

"Don't be worrying. It'll work out."

"How are you so sure?"

"Shut up, will you. Just sit in and learn from what you hear."

Quinn turned down Parnell Street. He moved to the curb lane for the turn into the car park.

"Well, you know what you're doing, I suppose," Canning said. "I was only saying."

Quinn let it go. He turned off the ramp onto Level 3. There was no space: they'd have to walk back down.

He parked next to a pillar and checked his watch.

"What, are you going to make him an offer or something?"

"Offer what?"

"His brother? You know, fix him up?"

"What's with you this morning? Where did you get the idea that I deal with cops?"

"Don't give me that, Bobby. I'm not a gobshite. You know—get Malone on board a bit, make the odd call, thanks very much, I'll look after the brother for you . . . ? I mean, what ever happened to that?"

"That was just pub talk."

"No it wasn't."

He turned to Canning.

"Just forget you ever heard about that, will you."

Canning gave him the eye. He heard him mutter as he stepped out of the car too. Well, why wouldn't he feel left out. Everything had changed.

HELL TO PAY

Malone put the ticket on the dashboard and he drove up the ramp into the gloom. Every spot was taken today, then, was it. He caught a shopper leaving on the fifth level.

"So Quinn's kept a low profile since he got out," Minogue said.

"He did four and a half of a seven," Malone said. "Plenty of time to think."

"Is there surveillance on him?"

"Not from us. I checked this morning."

"He has his lorry-driving business."

"'Mighty Quinn,' yeah."

"But he's not living the high life."

"No. Lives in the same house, the Corpo, up in Finglas. The missus took him back in, name is Catherine. She has a job. They have only the one kid. Brittney."

"Mighty convenient that he'd have lorries and drivers, I'd be thinking."

"That's how it looks, doesn't it? The story is that it's legit, but it's a front. He runs lorries of, are you ready, bananas and fruit down the country, for the smaller shops."

"Bananas only."

"Jasus, how would I know? He could have something

running on the side. Fellas with their own transport, contracting. There's a fierce lot of that goes on under the table in that business. Border stuff even."

"There was the landfill thing too, I'd be guessing?"

Malone nodded.

"They're only finding out now what got dumped out in Wicklow and Meath and that. It's been going on for years. And a lot of them were covered up too, you know, the fellas leasing the land sent in JCBs and Caterpillars to run over the stuff."

"Waste-trafficking," Minogue murmured.

Malone glanced over at him.

"Is there no word for it?" Minogue asked.

"Maybe I'll try that one at work one day."

"Well, what about his cronies, then."

"Well, Canning is one. Beans Canning. Nothing special. He was a robber too. A veteran, pretty well an old-timer by now. There's no sign that he's in the drug trade himself either. As a matter of fact, Canning is just a thick. People said to me they don't know why Quinn'd be tight still with a gobshite like Canning. My take on it is that Canning is only in the shop window for us to look at, sort of a cover. Like: this fella's so thick that we couldn't be up to any blags."

"A right nest of rogues, it seems."

"Well maybe, and maybe not. Who knows nowadays, the way things are going."

"You'd know, Tommy. I hope. Drugs Central?'

"If you only knew. That's the whole other thing."

Ting, Minogue heard. *De ho-al udder ting.* He watched Malone lock the Nissan, check the doors.

"Look," Malone said to him at the door to the stairs. "I just want to hear what Quinn has to say. He has to react, doesn't he. I'd be expecting a bit of a performance from him.

I mean the way we marched in to his gaff there yesterday. Show the flag, right?"

Canning was smoking a cigarette by the door on Level 3. There was a faint smell of urine from the stairwell mixed in with a diesel tang and what Minogue had taken to be a dull smell of cement that never left. He took in Quinn's eyes moving around Malone and then to him. Early thirties, he thought, well preserved, an innocuous look to him.

"So," Malone said. "You couldn't get hold of the Complaints Department or what."

"Better to go to the source, I find," Quinn said. "Isn't that why you set this up?"

Canning nodded at Minogue.

"You're the fella with the bug, right? Make sure you switch it on now."

"Thanks," Minogue said. "I'm actually the SWAT team today."

"You need to sort out a few things," Malone said to Quinn.

"Me?" Quinn asked. "You've got that arseways. You're the one needs to do that."

"Like, what?"

"Like what you said at my place the other day."

"What was that?"

"You know what you said. Don't pretend you don't. Those allegations."

"Where is that little go-for of yours anyhow," Malone said. "Is that what the whinge is about?"

"Who are you talking about?"

"Doyle. Who do you think I'm talking about?"

"He's nothing to me."

"That's not what he says."

"I don't know what he says, and I don't care. Far as I'm concerned, he's a header."

"Oh? Well, he says he's passing on a message from you."

"Well, anyone can play Postman fucking Pat, I suppose."

"Oh no," said Malone. "According to him he's your right-hand man."

"When did he come up with that one?"

"Over in Cafolla's the other night, that's when."

Minogue was watching Canning smoking. How he plucked it from his lips, how he fired out the smoke. Rubbing his lips with the back of his hand. The head stuck out on him, like a bull.

"Sancho Panza," Minogue said.

"What?" snapped Canning.

"A fella, a sidekick of a famous—"

"I don't know any Sanch O fucking anybody. And I don't care who he is. Matter of fact, you can stuff—"

Quinn held up his hand.

"He's a gobshite," he said. "Doyle is. I told you."

Quinn eyed Minogue.

"Do I know you," he said.

"Don't you and your crowd know everyone?"

"There is no 'our crowd,'" Quinn said. "That's part of why you need to sort yourself out over these allegations. Harassment and that."

"Oh right," said Minogue. "'I resemble those remarks.' Grand, so. Now I get it."

Quinn gave him a blank look. He gets it, Minogue believed. Knows enough not to take the bait here. Well, fine and well.

"No crowd, is it," Malone said. "Well, what about arse-face standing beside you, there? Could it really be the real Beans Canning, mastermind, break-in and armed robber of the year 1989 or so?"

"You're off your head, you fucking iijit," Canning said.

Malone stepped forward. Canning drew himself up, shook his bracelet free.

"Here," Malone said to him. "Let me see that arm there—routine check."

"Fuck off."

"What have you got to hide there?"

"If you weren't hiding behind the uniform I'd show you more than me fucking arm, so I would."

"Bet you Doyle knows some things though," Malone said. "Wouldn't you say? He's overdue a visit—yeah, we should bring him in and get a serious chat session going."

"Wouldn't be anything new for yous to stitch a fella up," Canning said. "Would it."

"We could give him a few days to think things over," Malone went on. "Amazing what a few days' hold-over will do."

"That works both ways," Quinn said. "If you think about it."

"Meaning what?"

"Meaning a fella can get himself into a bad patch if he can't get what he's used to."

Minogue shifted and leaned against a new spot of concrete. Canning let the smoke out slowly now.

"Tell me about that little concept there, why don't you," Malone said.

"I agreed to meet you for one thing and one thing only," Quinn said. "That's to tell you that I don't appreciate people spreading rumours. Especially cops."

"I'm here to dare you to tell me that there's nothing to them."

"Just because you decide to take something from a drug addict seriously—"

"—Oh a 'drug addict' now, is it? You're selling him down the river pretty frigging fast there, aren't you."

"If this is the best yous can do then it's pitiful," Canning said.

"Shut up you," Malone said.

"I'm a witness to this harassment and all."

"It's the fella owns the circus I'm talking to," Malone said. "Not the fucking clown."

"You're getting hysterical," Canning said.

Malone's hands were out of his pockets now. Minogue pushed away from the wall. He kept his eyes on Canning.

"Doyle didn't make all that up," Malone said. "So forget the citizen act here."

"I told you," Quinn said. "Doyle's nothing to me."

"Wasn't he driving one of your vans a while back?"

"He nearly wrecked it. I got rid of him. After I saw that he was a user."

"What was he delivering for you, bananas?"

"As a matter of fact he was—delivering fruit to the shops down the country. What did you think, they grew the bananas down in Sligo and that?"

"What, you're going to tell me that Doyle's just spreading rumours about you to get back at you for letting him go?"

"I'm telling you that the man has problems."

"Oh, we know what problems all right. Problems in the banana trade, right?"

Quinn looked over at Minogue.

"I hope you got that part on the tape," Canning said to Minogue. "'Cause he's bananas himself, you know, your pal here."

"Okay," Malone said. "Here's what: lodge a complaint, why don't you. Go ahead. 'Two Guards came the heavy at my place yesterday.' Yeah, go ahead. 'And they said not nice things about me. Hurt my feelings. My self-image.'"

"You couldn't say anything decent about your own mother," Canning said.

"Oh it talked again," Malone said.

"Fuck you, Malone," said Canning. "And your junkie brother."

Malone was by Quinn too before Minogue had even managed a step. He had Canning backed to the wall with two shoves. Quinn stepped out of Minogue's way.

"That's the kind of thing I'm talking about," Quinn said. "Out of control. Mad."

Malone let Minogue steer him away.

"Add that to your whinge," Malone called over to Quinn.

"I think your personal problems are getting in the way of your job," said Quinn.

"But you won't, will you," Malone went on. "You won't be complaining at all, because you want to just get on with your banana delivering, don't you. And that's why Doyle skipped, because you told him to get the hell away from here because he had a big mouth, because he knows things, right?"

Minogue stepped back from Malone.

"Look," Malone said. "If I find one speck about you or any of your crowd doing anything in Mountjoy, anything to do with my brother, you'll know all about it."

Quinn seemed to be considering saying something. Then he shook his head.

Minogue watched Canning catch up with him on the stairs.

"I'm not codding," Malone muttered. "There'll be hell to pay."

"Are you finished," Minogue asked him.

Malone turned. For a minute Minogue wondered if Malone was going to apologize or something.

"Okay," Malone murmured. "Not exactly according to plan there, was it."

"What plan," Minogue said.

WAS THERE SOMETHING ELSE?

Grogan arrived in Newry just before five. The check-points were gone for eighteen months now. He had no trouble spotting the towers and the antennae along the way. It was almost a puzzle, a game. There was an RUC Land Rover in a side street as he came in the Belfast Road.

More than an hour in the car would have him in rough shape for a day afterward, not to speak of a lousy night. His hip, where the bullet had shattered, had more of the bone growth on it since the last x-ray. The nerves were never going to get right there. He didn't want to go near the hospital for a while anymore. As a matter of fact, he hadn't much interest in driving either.

He let the engine do the braking on the way down Hill Street. The car park was only half full, to the side near the bank. He checked his mobile and slipped it in his pocket. It was the usual hurry-up-and-wait getting out of the car.

There was always plenty of life on Hill Street. This time of day it was people getting their shopping in before teatime. There wasn't a uniform in sight the whole length of the street. He wondered where the police cameras were. Newry, he thought, how well it looked lately, this the biggest Catholic town outside of Derry.

He concentrated on where his stick was landing on the

footpath. He didn't look back into the faces that came his way on the street. He rested for a count of ten, and watched two girls looking in a window and whispering to one another. He made it to McNaughton's in his next effort, and he stopped just short of the window. The smell of sawdust and suet and fresh, cold meat brought him back to his childhood. He heard the chop of a cleaver from inside the shop. There was no sound like it, if you thought about it, he decided.

When he was ready, he moved to the window and looked in. Artie McNaughton was wrapping up something for an old woman. He looked over and he nodded. Roe was working at a table, wrapping something in plastic, but he was watching him in a mirror. Grogan continued to the doorway.

"How's the form, Liam?" McNaughton said.

"Could be worse, I suppose."

Roe nodded at the door to the freezer. He waited for Grogan to get by him. There was a chair there for him next to the cupboard.

Grogan held out the envelope. He studied Roe's hat, watched him slide it behind his apron. The hats they all wore now, but like some Brit from an oldie film set in the tropics; EU health regulations, no doubt.

"Well, that's that," Grogan said.

Roe's eyes narrowed a little. He looked sideways at Grogan with what might have been a smile.

"For the time being," he said.

Grogan's hip had loosened a bit from the drive, but still the ache was getting stronger. Roe settled his hat over his forehead.

"That fella is organized," he said. "Quinn. I'll give him that. And I don't think he has any bad habits. No."

"You could work with him again," Grogan said. "Is that what you're saying?"

Roe shook his head.

"That I doubt, that I doubt."

"It didn't turn out?"

"Oh no, I really couldn't say that, now could I. Oh no, quite professional, in actual fact."

Grogan waited.

"Well," said Roe. "One gets a certain sense of something, I don't know now. An instinct, you might say, but that word doesn't do it justice. No, it doesn't."

"You don't like him."

"That would be close, yes it would. But he might be a very nice fella. He certainly showed no lack of consideration in the whole business."

"Consideration."

"I mean he had the details right. Can't fault him for that."

"You don't trust them down there."

"Well now," Roe said, and allowed himself a slight smile. "Does anyone?"

Grogan looked around at the tubs and hooks, the white coats and aprons hung by the door. He wondered if Roe had ever used the freezers here for any of his jobs. The next generation, he thought, would they turn out like this too? Would his own Ciaran have, or would he have had the nerve to push Ciaran into a plane for a new life somewhere else? Twenty-eight last May. He had talked once of going to Germany.

He had to move.

"I'm away then," he said.

Roe nodded slowly as though he had been considering something. Grogan wanted to tell him that he wasn't one bit fooled by the slow talk and the way he looked at you. A person couldn't hide that dislike. Contempt, more like it.

He got the heel of his hand onto the stick and readied to

push off. He felt Roe's eyes on him as he levered himself up and got his balance. He looked up.

"Was there something?"

"Ah no," said Roe. Grogan almost told him it'd be no bother for him to wipe that expression off his face for him, permanently. He stared at him for a few moments.

"We're grand now," Roe murmured.

A Cushy Number, Is It?

There were three messages on the machine for Minogue. A dud, then one from his daughter asking if there was a handcart or a trolley or something she could borrow. She sounded a bit frazzled. He debated getting another money order. He didn't want her crying on him, and he didn't want her to think she had to tell him everything either.

The third was from Sergeant Brendan O'Leary. Minogue liked O'Leary, Commissioner Tynan's factotum, aide-de-camp, and quietly stubborn minder. O'Leary wasn't in the business of phoning you to speculate about the price of a pint nowadays.

Minogue wiped the messages and made strong, filtered coffee to mix with the milk he zapped in the microwave. He thought about O'Leary's passion for golf, the course he had built in a desert when he had done a stint with the UN out in Africa. Kids had flocked to him, he'd heard. He'd heard only lately that O'Leary was rumoured to have knocked a tribesman, a chief of some kind, flat when there was some argument about a bride who was fourteen.

Minogue had rewritten his List. He took it out and he read it while he waited for the kettle to finish. Go was staying at the top of the list, then. Number 5, Herlighy, the only shrink a Guard would go to: maybe it's exactly Herlighy he should be asking about Jennifer Halloran. And her mother. And her brother. He felt that falling in his chest again, and remembered that he had to stay busy. There was three-quarters of a bottle of Jameson's in the cupboard too, of course.

He stared out at the pile of rocks that he had started gathering closer to the back of the coalhouse. There had been a dozen slug trails on the drive this morning. Something was at the peas again this year. Did any of this matter anymore. His eyes lost their focus along with his straying thoughts.

Trains. It was seldom enough he took the DART, but the platform was always a place that made him a bit jittery even. It was something about the imminence of the trains that felt threatening, as if he could feel them long before he heard the ticks from the rails that told him one was coming around the curve and over the bridge from the Amiens Street station. What a godawful sound it must have made, when she—

He pushed off from the counter.

And he had probably misread Fiona Hegarty too, hadn't he. PSTD. RIP. PMS. AWOL.

He swore once, quietly, and remembered: that he hadn't slept well; that that made a big difference; that he always had options; that Iseult and her husband would work it out like any other couple did; that lots of couples didn't work things out; that he wouldn't last long back down a boreen in Clare after all these years in Dublin.

"Clearly," he murmured. What every stupid iijit who got a microphone shoved under his nose, or a camera shoved in his face, said these days: *clearly.*

Nothing worked anymore. Clearly.

He turned back to the warming kettle when the phone began to ring. He'd let the answering machine tackle it. He concentrated on trying to figure what the reflections on the side of the kettle were.

He chickened out after three rings.

It wasn't Kathleen or Iseult or the Lotto to say he had become a millionaire.

"The Commissioner'll take your call now, Matt," O'Leary said.

"I don't have a call in to him, Brendan."

"He doesn't mind you being a bit late with the call back."

Then Tynan's swivel chair was squeaking in the background.

"I was in touch with Moriarty," Tynan said. "He knows I'm talking to you now."

Minogue pushed his fingertips harder onto the windowsill, watched the nails whiten.

"Are you there?"

"I am."

"You should know that Garda Hegarty made a statement exonerating you."

For what, Minogue almost asked.

She says she realizes she should have given a bit more weight to things. Her mental state.

"Whose mental state?"

"The suspect's. She's very upset. She's going on a week's leave."

"A week's leave, is she."

Tynan waited. Minogue began to think about Jennifer Halloran's brother, would he understand. Probably not, except that Jennifer wasn't going to be there anymore.

"There'll be the inquest," Tynan said.

"Yes, of course. Yes."

"So, does what I said change anything your end?"

"I don't know."

"Well, it's out there now, you can be sure."

He meant the rumour mill, Minogue realized.

"But the story will come out," Tynan added. "Especially her being so open about it."

Words skittered around again in Minogue's mind. Open. Share with you. Dialogue. Clearly. Maybe he was going mad.

"Yes," he managed. "I suppose there's that, isn't there."

"There's your training course to consider now," Tynan said.

"Hardly now."

"Oh?"

"I need time to sort things out a bit."

"A few days," Tynan said. "It'll come around, it will."

"We'll see."

"Are you maybe thinking you might be less than welcome in the sections where you're supposed to go?"

"I'd expect that, yes."

"Let me think on that then," Tynan said.

Minogue watched a young fella hurtle around the corner on his bike, reckless, gleeful that school was over no doubt, and the summer ahead of him. It came to Minogue then how stupid this was to be here, looking out the window of a house now empty of kids, half-pretending that he was seriously mulling over a job he didn't want, courtesy of Jim Kilmartin. Kathleen and her apartment brochures; the lunches they now had together in restaurants; the money he could spend on a new car now; the long trip to the States. All these possibilities had crept up on him. They didn't feel like freedom at all.

"How's herself?" Tynan asked. "I meant to ask."

"Kathleen? She's going full tilt. Leaves the likes of me in the ha'penny place with the wheeling and dealing she does be at."

"Rachel said she saw her there in Vincent's."

Minogue wanted and didn't want to ask Tynan how the chemo was working.

"Oh right. Yes. Kathleen has an aunt in there after a fall, yes she has."

Minogue thought he heard papers being moved around.

"Before I go. You mentioned a letter there in our last conversation."

The boy on the bike had disappeared now. The hedge needed doing again. His Citroën looked like it had collapsed on the driveway and wouldn't get up again.

"Well, I still think it's time," he said. "Now more than ever."

"You know where you're heading if you stay the course, don't you?"

"Who'd have me in their section after what happened the other day?"

"Didn't I just tell you that Garda Hegarty said you were right?"

"Being right didn't have much effect."

"You did your best."

"I didn't. I should have had my say earlier on. Or stayed the hell out of it entirely. Maybe it was me gave her the chance to do what she did."

"Haven't we had this conversation before? Look: you'd no way of knowing."

Kilmartin's mocking murmur, half-heartedly carrying the air badly between his teeth:

'Tis true that the women are worse than the men
Right fol tight fol ditty eye day . . .

"Then again, maybe I should have kept me nose out of Fraud in the first place."

Tynan was letting it replay, he knew, waiting. He fingered the terra cotta thing that Iseult had made years ago, the thing that looked like a frog but wasn't. Burren, she'd called it, then Carranooska. He thought back to when he had first met Tynan, over the Fine murder. Tynan then, the Deputy Comm, the cool, even aloof, operator with the surprise wit.

"I hope it strikes you how peculiar this conversation is," Tynan said.

"It's getting on for odd, to be sure."

"The Commissioner of the Gardai telephoning an Inspector to see if he can humour him into not resigning?"

"Retiring. I have the time in."

"Well, maybe you do. But after said Commissioner has hand-built a career path because he sees that the state and its citizens badly need the co-operation of police across the continent to help with our problems here?"

"I told you, you should be rooting around for an MBA type, John—"

"—I asked you if you could help me make a dent in what's come to our door, remember? Such as what happened yesterday in a Dublin street. Are you with me?"

"Serious Crime turf."

"Is this going to be like Palermo or something, people are asking. There is a street war started since last year, and it's going to intensify."

And you want to drop me in the middle of all that, Minogue wanted to say.

"Do you really want a cushy number then where you can put your feet up while you wait for the big day, the watch and the retirement cake?"

"It's like you said—we had this conversation before."

"We did indeed, when you signed on."

"I said thank you very much, I'd be honoured to assist in the establishment of this department."

Tynan moved papers around.

"Look," he said. "What are you aiming for, really?"

"As a matter of fact I want a house, with a goat and an ass. Maybe a bike to go in and out of the village for a pint every night."

"Every night?"

"Every night, John."

"You wouldn't stand a chance. You're a Dub now, and you know it."

Minogue picked up Carranooska and felt the weight of it. Lucky Iseult didn't feck it at Pat during a row.

"Listen," said Tynan. "Here's what I want you to do. I want you to move sideways for a short little while. Take a pause to reconsider. Are you listening?"

"I am, a bit."

"What do you know about raves or rave drugs?"

"Nothing. Not a thing."

"Did that daughter of yours ever give you reason to worry about the likes?"

"I'll take the Fifth on that. Thanks for asking, though."

"Well, there's a girl dead. It was out your way."

The low wall, the entry to the park by the Dodder, Minogue remembered. How much the trees had grown there by the river over the years.

"Heard about it?"

"A bit, I think."

"Donnybrook's handling it. I'll give you a name."

Behind the lines operation, he could only think after he hung up. Tynan's specialty. He hadn't even had a chance, no doubt falling in line with Tynan's plan. He looked at the phone, imagined calling the Commissioner back.

Kenny was the girl's name. They thought it might have been a suicide at first. Tynan had surely chosen his words before he'd landed it too, Minogue knew. Of course he had spoken to Moriarty, of course an ex-Jesuit seminarian would understand how to lever guilt.

"The poor girl," Tynan had said.

Minogue folded the piece of paper, slapped the counter, and swore very loudly, once.

EIGHT HUNDRED YEARS
AND MORE

Grogan spent most of the drive back to Belfast thinking about Bobby Quinn, about Gerry Adams on television last week, about why he didn't care much about phoning the doctor to be told about the operation.

The traffic slowed coming into Banbridge, but it was only for gawking. He saw soldiers in the ditch as he drove by two RUC Land Rovers. Beyond them was a car on its side, but no ambulances. He decided to take the M1 into the city from Lisburn then, stay off the Lisburn Road itself, the route he preferred.

Quinn. What more could they want of Quinn after yesterday?

Your friend in Dublin, was how Gallagher still referred to Quinn. Their man in "that crowd." As though to remind everyone to keep that crowd at a distance, because they might contaminate them, infect them. Not even "The Free State" or "The South" anymore: just "that crowd."

Quinn had never given him pause to think. You couldn't fool someone that easily when you did time together. Quinn had said nothing at the meeting, when he told him what had to be done. But the next day, Quinn had phoned and asked him if they'd give it a rethink. That showed that he had thought about it himself, but that he hadn't just reacted.

Doing for the two men would put heat on everyone down here, Quinn had reasoned. Would it be worth that? Why not just put them in hospital a few weeks? Grogan listened and, as he had guessed, Quinn picked up from his lack of comment that there was no going back. It had been decided and it was final. You couldn't say no to the job. If anything less than was planned happened, that would only make them more suspicious here.

There were smudges to the clouds coming in from over the Glens now. A helicopter passed over the fields far to his left. A few of the observation posts had been taken down after the Agreement, he knew, but the sensors and the cameras had only increased. It was useless to keep thinking how much had changed, or how fast. In the early days it had always been him trying to see signs that they were getting somewhere, that they were going to win. Then it was the steady course, the long view, the politicals.

They weren't lost years, those eleven years. Four bullets he'd taken, and twice in jail, the first in the Maze, and the second in the South, in Portlaoise. None of it had been worse than the night they'd sent in the chaplain to tell him about Kieran. He'd been told later that it had been planned for months, that the army was actually hoping it'd be a shoot-out. Target practice, you might say. PR.

He got behind an articulated truck getting onto the M1. The traffic into Belfast was heavy now, and there was no quarter given for a car waiting to get a break from behind a truck that would take miles to get up to any decent speed.

It had been Gallagher who came to him just after that Christmas, when the Peace Process thing was really gathering steam. There were seven of them around that table that morning. He remembered thinking something about seven being a lucky number, and if Gallagher had planned it like that. The prisoner release had every one of them out by Easter. By the end of that year they had every dealer in West Belfast sorted out, and he had brought Quinn in.

That first visit to Dublin had been a real eye-opener for the others. The new money, the building going on, the crowds in the streets.

Gallagher had summed it up that time all right: Had the men in this room served time so's these people down here can forget about everything that's gone on here in this country for eight hundred years, and more? The sacrifices made? Living under siege these decades? Watching their families be arrested, worse . . . ?

Grogan caught his first sight of Black Hill high over the city. Seeing it somehow dispelled the thoughts that seemed to have come with him in the car since Newry. He got out at Grosvenor Road, passed the hospital and made it through the lights up on to the Springfield Road. They were meeting in The Pipers tonight. It was getting closer to the big decisions now. Tonight Gallagher wanted a decision as to whether they'd put out offers to some of the Dublin mobs right away, the ones who were smart enough to read the writing on the wall after yesterday.

Clonard Gardens then, the church, the mural for the prisoners. Oglach Anthony Murphy, 22, Long Kesh, July 3, 1974. A nephew of Tony Murphy had played with Ciaran. Grogan did some subtraction as he made the final turn into Waterbrook Street. Twenty-eight, four months and two and a half weeks.

DIVERSIONS COMMENCE

Minogue heard the first drops on the roof just before he started the Citroën. He left the wipers off until the car ahead had pretty well dissolved. It was only a shower, he decided, it wasn't down for the day.

Kathleen was waiting for him just inside the doorway. She had two bags now, where she had only had the one leaving home this morning.

"Homework, they give you?"

"Just some stuff I didn't get a chance to finish. God, we were busy. Run off me feet, so I was."

Minogue decided on Northumberland Road: he'd go up Trimelston and be flying up Fosters Avenue in no time.

"Me too," he said to her.

"Me eye, you were. The cut of you. But I'm glad to see you relaxing. Were you digging all day?"

"A bit. I was given homework of my own."

"You're back in the swing of things already?"

He told her about Tynan's call, how he'd pulled it on him.

"Wasn't that decent of him to phone you," she said.

Minogue let that go. Ahead he saw the police van and a squad car. There were two Guards on the footpath by the tape. The rain hadn't pooled yet in the gutters.

"That's where it happened," Kathleen murmured. "Those two men."

The traffic slowed by the Asylum office. A tall man slipped in the door. Ethiopia, he thought.

"What?" Kathleen asked. He had said it aloud, then.

"I was making a guess."

"Ethiopia, did you say? It was from Albania they were. They said they were."

"Yes."

She turned in the seat as they passed, and she blessed herself. Minogue began to remember how Jennifer Halloran had gone quiet. They were at the American embassy in Ballsbridge before Kathleen spoke again.

"That poor woman's solicitor was in the paper today, you know."

"I saw."

"She says the system let her down."

"Abused her," she said, "I read."

"Well, I didn't want to say that."

"You won't be upsetting me," Minogue said. "I think she's right."

He knew she was eyeing him as he accelerated through the lights by the RDS.

"So you're back tomorrow," she said. "It's not too soon for you?"

"It'll be different."

"What will?"

"It's a temporary thing John Tynan cooked up to keep me out of trouble."

She waited for him to get around a taxi.

"But you're still going back to the whatever you call the other thing?"

"I told him I had to think about that."

Her voice took on a different one now.

"I hope he gave you some pointers then," she said. "To keep things going."

"Actually, Kathleen, I told him I'd had enough. That I wanted out."

She was staring at him now, he knew.

"I got a bit of a chastising, so I did."

"Well, I'm bloody glad somebody got through to you."

"And new duties."

"What are they, then."

"You remember when we go by that place at the top of Beaver Row there, the Ranelagh Road?"

"That pub there, what, are you going back behind the bar and pull pints?"

"Where they found the girl."

"What are you saying?"

"That's what I'm about for the next little while. Until things get a bit clearer."

She shifted in her seat and she looked away. Bristling, he supposed, but she wouldn't say much until later on. He got into the outside lane after Merrion Gates. Dublin Bay was magenta, getting darker yet, and Howth sulked, blurred behind the rain. Maybe she'd seen herself going with him on meetings to Brussels or something. Maybe she had found his List. He reached over and squeezed her knee. She kept her gaze on the passing traffic.

"That rain won't be down for the evening," he said. "I'm telling you."

"What in the name of God goes on inside that head of yours," she said.

"I moved half the rocks. I'll move them back, if you want."

Oh diversions commence.

"And I made a sort of a stew. I have it in the oven ready."

"A stew," she said, and shifted in her seat. She stared out her window at the bus shelter across the road. He hoped she wouldn't ask if he had been in touch with Pat, had plans to meet his supposedly troubled son-in-law.

"A glash of wayne," he said. "Two, if you'd like."

"It's your life, I suppose," she said.

CÉAD MÍLE FÁILTE

Minogue hadn't been expecting Kilmartin this early. He had dropped Kathleen off, the city grey and humid still with the leftovers of the rain. The rain had kept them indoors last night. He had watched her from the couch while he read, her making notes and muttering to herself until finally she got up from the table and came over. She had fallen asleep against him. That's how tiring, how absorbing, property management, etc., was then. Iseult hadn't phoned.

Minogue had woken up surprised that he had slept. The traffic out on Leeson Street was light. He changed the phone to his other hand as he slowed for the bend by Dwyer's Pub.

"Dimitri is a Greek name," Kilmartin said. "Anyone could tell you that. As for the surnames, sure who could say them?"

"Idrizi is one," said Minogue. "A first name Bekim."

"Well, listen to you. Suddenly you're an expert?"

"It was on the news last night. It stuck in my head, I don't know why."

"No wonder you're headed for the Brussels patch soon."

"It's not a sure thing, Jim."

"Pull the other one. Listen, those two fellas spoke some dialect. That's what I heard from a fella knows a girl working down at the Asylum place. They had their doubts down there, you know. A wake-up call, I'm telling you. This place is a soft touch."

Minogue had heard two people arguing on *Morning Ireland* about the crime committed, that it was just the tip of the iceberg about racism. One of them, a woman sociologist he'd head a fair bit about recently, said "heinous" and, later, "national shame."

"The know-it-alls are already loading up on you-know-what," Kilmartin snorted. "We're bigots. Racists. We don't care. We're not Christians at all, at all. Etcetera. I mean, the place is gone mad."

Donnybrook station had a tiny parking yard under the wall to the cemetery behind. The worst traffic bottleneck in the country, Minogue had heard, where the N11 was wrung and choked down to a street. He pulled in next to a wine shop and looked across at the station. Kilmartin was in full spate.

"Wouldn't surprise me if we're not on every frigging runner's list of places to head for."

Runner: Minogue had to think. Right: he called immigrants and asylum-seekers runners.

"'Come to Ireland, land of a 1000 welcomes' is written on every wall over there. 'We'll pay you to come and sit on your arse—and give you bed and board too.' The state of things, I'm telling you . . . ! What do you think?"

"I'll find out for you."

"Look, I'm making a point here. It has to do with a stupid refugee UN law or something, they made back in old God's time in 1951."

Donnybrook Garda station always looked grim. There had been no changes to the outside in all the years Minogue had driven by.

"Is this going to be about having enough poor of our own," he asked Kilmartin.

"Well, as a matter of fact, it may very well be. You think everyone in Ireland is a millionaire with this Celtic Tiger shite, do you?"

"I know that I don't have to grow spuds if I don't want to."

"Oh I know what we're going to hear now, by Jesus. 'It's our turn now,' that kind of a stunt?"

"It's our turn, Jim. Right."

"You don't get it, do you? This isn't some Famine thing all over again. This is about the doors being wide open to seasoned criminals. They're laughing themselves off the boat here. Tell me this: Did you ever expect to be handed money, to be given a place to live when you came up to Dublin? To be taught a new language—and then, for Christ's sake actually encouraged to go out and have it off so's you could get pregnant in time to have the baby here so, bingo, instant citizen—and the ma gets to stay forever?"

Minogue turned off the engine. He thought about the years he'd gone walking up the green roads and the tracks with Iseult down in the Burren. The tumbled walls of the deserted clacháns where hundreds had fled from the Famine were everywhere amongst the willows. How many drawings Iseult had done of the ivy that had invaded the drystone walls?

"So this is not about the mighty spud. Or the Famine. Do you hear me?"

"Jim, I'm late to meet someone."

"Fine, fine. But don't talk to me about spuds or the like. I think I must be the only man east of the River Shannon growing spuds of my own, or cabbage—sure, Lamb of Jasus, it's in a theme park they'll put me in the finish-up."

"There'll be a pair of us so. Have you the names, the security firms?"

Minogue wrote down four. One of them he remembered meeting several times, Tony Ahearne, a retired Super.

"Says anytime, Ahearne does. First name of Kevin. Go first with him, will you."

"Thanks, Jim. I owe you."

"Before you go—but I don't want to be agitating you. About that woman the other day. You're in the clear, now, are you?"

"By law, I suppose."

"What do you mean by that, 'by law'?"

"I don't want to talk about it, at the moment."

"It was a Bean Garda went in for the hard questions, I heard."

Minogue said nothing.

"The one you were shadowing. Right?"

"She had it rough, Jim—look, I have to—"

"—Well, I'll leave you now, but don't forget, with that 'shadow' of yours. I hope you've copped on already yourself. Thick and all as you are the best of times, don't let anyone sell you down the river over this."

Minogue had his thumb on the End button already.

"And don't you forget it," he heard Kilmartin as he broke the call. He checked his hair in the rearview mirror and he stepped out.

IT'LL BE LIKE
OLD TIMES FOR YOU

The Guard in the public office glanced at the photocard and nodded at the stairs.

"They're above there at the top of the stairs," he said. "Next to the toilets."

"Tunney," Minogue asked. "A Sergeant?"

"Big long glass of water," the Guard said. "You'll spot him handy enough so you will."

There was a smell of adhesive and paint coming from the upper floors. A drill started and then stopped somewhere in the building.

Slouched in an old swivel chair at the far end of a narrow room lined with cabinets, themselves loaded with cardboard boxes, Sergeant Lorcan Tunney issued a slow nod in Minogue's direction.

Minogue made his way around other boxes, took in the long legs Tunney had stretched out to perch on a shelf, the tilt of the head where he held the phone jammed against his ear. Tunney was peeling an orange while he listened. He looked up at Minogue again and nodded at two chairs next to a chipped table.

"Kenny, Niamh," Minogue saw on the file folder. Some of the papers were photocopies of snapshots.

"Okay," Tunney said in a way that Minogue was sure meant the opposite, and he hung up.

Tunney slid back upright in the chair and reached out.

"Matt," said Minogue.

"Lorcan," said Tunney and he sat back. He tore off the last piece of peel.

"The book is here in the drawer," Tunney said. "If you'd like to see it."

"Well, thanks."

Tunney held out a piece of orange.

"Thanks. There's a Tunney over in CDU, is he maybe related?"

"He is bedad," said Tunney. "I've a brother Fintan. We're our own crime family, the ma used to say. My da was in Kilkenny for twenty-two years too."

"No time off for good behaviour?"

"He stayed for the hurling, he used to tell people. 'The clash of the ash.'"

"How well he didn't ask for a transfer to County Clare, so."

"You go west of the Shannon at your own peril, is the approach on that, I'd say."

"Well, the Kilkenny team would know that."

"That was the only game they lost," said Tunney, the one in Tulla. "Sure it was knee-deep in muck there, you might as well be skiing."

"A true test, all the same."

"Ah, that's sour grapes now on account of your crowd not measuring up in the end."

"Next year," Minogue said.

"Next year my arse," said Tunney. "Unless the Clare crowd

invent jet packs or something. Maybe jet-powered hurleys."

"Who let the cat out of the bag on that?"

"Go away with you."

Minogue returned the slow smile spreading across Tunney's face. Still he couldn't get the idea out of his mind that this man really, really did have the face of a horse. But the eyes were flat; maybe a fella who'd go at you in a row without warning.

"I'm Carlow, in actual fact," Tunney said.

"I'll settle for a truce then."

"You will, will you."

The wry smile meant less this time, Minogue knew. He wondered how long it would take before Tunney began to drop hints about this character parachuted in on him.

"Well," Tunney said.

Minogue was suddenly and unaccountably sure that Tunney had made some decision based on the past thirty seconds. Tunney yanked open a drawer to his right and held out the book to Minogue.

"Feast yourself on it," he said. "It'll be like old times for you."

Minogue took the familiar, ribbed hardcover they had used for years on the Squad.

"Wasn't there talk of gizmos a while back?" Tunney asked. "Electronic yokes that could beam things around so's everyone would be up to date and all the rest of it?"

"No doubt."

"They never showed up, did they, those organizers?"

Minogue shook his head. Tunney folded his arms and waited for something from his visitor. Minogue took in the times, the sketches. Marie Kinsella, the new assistant State Pathologist, had attended on the scene. A C.I. Healy was the nominal C.O. for the case.

"Yourself, was it, in the notes from the scene?" he asked Tunney.

"It was. Mickey Collins is the artist."

"Great stuff," said Minogue, surprised only that the lie sliding out of him had such little effect. "A fair bit of foot traffic by the place, was there?"

"We sealed it, and kept control of the site."

Minogue looked up.

"The copies of the Technicals' reports are stuck in there later on too," said Tunney.

Minogue turned the pages. Murphy. John Hynes, Kelleher from the Technical Bureau. They'd been there until after midnight.

"Like old times, then," said Tunney.

"Well, I don't know, Lorcan."

"Lar, they call me."

"Well, Lar, and thanks. I'm only here to assist."

"You're C.I. though still, right?"

"I parked the rank outside."

Tunney didn't blink.

"I suppose someone phoned?" Minogue tried.

"Oh yes, someone did indeed phone. Cig Healy passed it on to us."

Minogue met his eyes for a moment. Passed it on to us, indeed. He realized that he had already written Tunney up as Garda detective number 1,001 in his list of hard, smart and mocking policemen he had met. He went back to the Technicals' drafts.

"Grand, so," he said. "Fit me in anywhere. I'm not one for standing around."

"On the team, like."

"Now you have it, Lar."

"Do you know why you were sent over?"

Minogue was still willing to ignore the tone.

"There was a spot of bother with the parents, I believe. They weren't happy with something."

"Well, that's a fact. You were in Fraud, were you."

"In a manner of speaking. I'm on a training thing."

Tunney stretched and yawned.

"Me and Collins do street crime usually," he said. "We're used to dealing with your basic gouger, like. The handbag men and the street dealers. On a slow shift, we've even been known to apprehend drunk teenagers puking in the street."

"Plenty to be going on with, is there?"

"Oh stop, don't be talking. But Cig put us on this on account of it was us did the beating death above in Rathmines there last year. You might remember it?"

"The rugger-bugger thing?"

"That's the one, the young fella got beaten up. Less the Red Bull than the roid-rage type of thing. The stupidest thing you ever heard. Brats, basically."

Minogue remembered bits of it now. A crowd of teenagers, underage drinking, some lads who were big in their rugby thing and took steroids and daddy's car and girls and dares, all in one big mix on regular occasions. The boy had been seventeen, a star forward, drunk and then clinically dead on the curb.

"A real eye-opener," said Tunney. "All around. But for the Dublin 4 crowd most of all. I'll never forget the parents. All they could say was 'But how could this happen?'"

Minogue closed the book.

"Is this one with the girl more of the same, do you think?"

"Well, Jesus," said Tunney. "There's a question."

Minogue returned the smile. Tunney looked to the frosted window.

"The girl's folks are well connected, let me say. They

know where to push. I'm not saying they don't have a right though."

"Right," said Minogue.

"But we're already getting the same oul stuff, you know, the 'where were the Guards when this happened?'"

"The parents?"

"No. The in-laws and out-laws there though, some of the neighbours even."

Minogue ran his fingers up the spine of the book.

"Feel like telling them we were out chasing Junior who took the da's Jag for a spin, looking for trouble. That tune, you know yourself."

"The words might be new," Minogue said. "But I certainly know the air."

"Well, I'll tell you something now," said Tunney. "You ain't seen nothing yet."

Minogue studied the hawk nose and the stylish cut that always reminded him of Caesar or a gladiator or someone from an epic film of bygone years. He wondered how Tunney acted out on the street.

"Her da is a big thing. He organizes these big dos, concerts even. The house is like, I don't know, Malibu or something maybe?"

"Mr. Kenny."

"Yeah. Colm Kenny. The mother is a basket case. She has basically collapsed, she can't get by without tranqs or something since. It's pretty bad, I don't mind telling you, just awful—"

The face in the opened door put Minogue in mind of a friendly mouse, with whiskers thickened to a moustache.

"Mickey," said Tunney. "A fella here is coming on board a while. The Kenny thing. C.I. Minogue."

Something about Collins' face made Minogue want to

laugh. A stricken, hapless look, like a mime, but enough of a hint of a shy kid who'd gone underground years ago.

"Matt," he said, and caught a limp handshake from Collins.

"Anyway," said Tunney. "The father's talking murder, and where's the expertise we're supposed to have to deal with this, and why is no one accepting the facts as he sees them, and . . . All the rest of it."

Collins took up station against a cabinet. He leaned on his elbow, studied his shoe, and nodded.

"Murder," Minogue said.

"Well, I mean fair enough," said Tunney. "I mean the man is in bits, and of course he'd be angry and that. You can't reason with a fella in that state. Goes without saying. But he won't back off. I do believe . . ."

Tunney waited for Collins to look over.

". . . I do believe that he got the Commissioner in on it."

Collins nodded again.

"Do we have cause yet?" Minogue asked.

"No. But we had a preliminary, and when do they get that wrong, I'd like to know. It was pills."

"Suicide?"

"No. What it looks like is that this girl took something at a club, a rave type of thing. And it was bad. She was with another girl. She got bothered and confused and she felt sick."

"Disoriented," said Collins, without looking up.

"This was about one o'clock," Tunney went on. "She went off, to see someone the far side of the club, the friend thought. But no, she tried to get home, it looks like."

"Alone?"

"Well, there you go," said Tunney. "That's where we are."

Collins stroked his moustache and cleared his throat.

"The club is in Earlsfort Terrace," he said. "It's new. It was her first time there, as far as we know. It looks like so far that she started walking. It's do-able, two maybe three miles."

"Isn't there a late bus?"

"There is. We're trying to track her there, or a taxi. But I think she walked. Maybe she thought—well, it'd clear up or something."

"Walk it off, that kind of thing?"

"Yeah. And then, whatever she was thinking then later on as she got a bit closer to home, she decides to lie down and have a rest or something."

"Was there anything at the scene that said that, and only that?"

"My first thought when I got there was, well you can imagine," said Tunney. "Sexual assault, that sort of a thing."

"Do you know much about rave drugs?" Collins asked.

"Not a thing," said Minogue. "Only what I read in the papers. They can make you overheat and that?"

"That's right," said Tunney. "There's dehydration and the like too."

"You think maybe she overdosed then?"

Tunney shrugged.

"I can't back up what I'm thinking, with the lab, I mean. Yet, anyway. I say she got hold of bad drugs. I'd be guessing Ecstasy, or what was supposed to be Ecstasy."

"I know the name, but that's all."

"Well, it's up and down the country," Collins said. "It's part of a whole scene. There's been a big number of hospital admissions this past while because of contaminated stuff. There are people setting up labs of their own now even, but a lot of them are wild. They don't know what they're doing."

"Isn't it supposed to make you relax or something?"

"Well sure," said Tunney. "Peace and love and that. That's what you see with the soothers and the glow-bands at the all-nighters. There's a lot of horsepower in them. You'd be dancing away all night."

"With the way the clothes were," said Collins, "you'd think she was trying to cool off, you see?"

"Ecstasy," said Minogue. "'E,' right?"

"Oh you're quick," said Tunney. "Do you want my edumacated guess?"

"Fire away."

"I've seen the trade on the streets, and talked to fellas who know about it. The pills have little designs on them, little symbols. It's MDMA. That's the name of the chemical. Don't ask me to remember what the words are. That's the basic Ecstasy pill, see, and you can get one in any pub in town, any night of the week. Really."

"MDMA," said Minogue. "I'd better look it up."

"No—my guess is that it was something else. This other stuff showed up a few years back. A variant, and it's mad. PMA is what it's called."

"The same effect, a bit more of it?"

"They were sold as Ecstasy then, down in Cork City, I remember. Two lads died from them. The PMA is bad because it takes a bit of a while to get going, you see? So a user, a novice, let's call it, might take one, think it wasn't working, and then go and pop another one. That's when things'd go haywire."

"How long would that take?"

"A couple of hours. Longer, even."

Minogue imagined the girl heading home. Was she too addled, too guilty to phone home? But that would mean she was lucid and had some judgement, so why would she walk . . . ? Yes, she thought she could walk it off then.

"Well, what kind of shape would she be in, mentally," he asked Tunney.

"Patchy. Look at where she ended up."

"That wasn't the most direct way home," said Collins.

"What girl in her right mind would take a short cut through a park in the dead of night?"

Minogue opened the book again. He went to the map of the scene.

"So the da is saying she was either brought up there, in a panic maybe, by someone who was with her."

"That's murder, according to him, is it."

"He says that that would be the same person who gave her the pill in all likelihood. So either way, leaving her to die unattended, or giving her the pill, that's it."

"What does he say about this murder thing then?"

About fifty yards to the banks of the River Dodder, Minogue saw. Ten, twelve yards maybe in off the path through the park.

"So there's a certain logic to what he says," he murmured.

"But fuck-all sense," Tunney said. "When you think about it, is there, now."

Minogue exchanged a glance with him. Add a possible cruel to the hard, smart, and mocking. Collins was back to his shoe study.

"Kenny knows better than everyone," Tunney added. "Already."

"Plenty of people go like that, Lar. In my experience."

"That a fact? And off they go right away, phoning the Garda Commissioner?"

Minogue said nothing. Better the mask slip on Tunney now than later anyway. He watched Collins testing his other shoe for toe-room now. Collins would stay in Minogue's quiet, shrewd, and reticent list. A very short list indeed. Maybe a shy kid still in hiding, he thought, and there was something of the adolescent too about Collins that made Minogue want to protect him, engage him. Hardly a pose. Promotion chances lousy.

"Telling him what to do," Tunney added. "And how he wants it done. Rent-a-cop."

Minogue saw only the eyebrows move as Collins shifted his feet. The joint trials and convictions of Mr. Kenny as a well-to-do-operator pain in the arse, and Inspector Minogue as the white-haired-boy pain in the arse parachuted in by Tynan had been conducted in his absence. And Tunney was going to keep lobbing them.

Enough, Minogue decided then. He offered Tunney a smile, but kept the stare.

"Well, Lar. Mr. Kenny didn't phone me. That I can tell you."

"Why would he need to," Tunney said, a thin smile of displeased triumph around his mouth now. "When Tynan did the phoning for him?"

PUSH COMES TO SHOVE

Quinn braked for the Shankill roundabout and accelerated out onto the N11 again. The shower had only started a minute ago but the wipers had to go full blast already. A BMW swept by with barely a sound.

"Bastard," said Canning. "Tax-dodger. Chancer. Child molester. Whatever your name is."

"You know him, do you."

"I know a lot like him, don't I."

Quinn's headache had been coming on for a while now. He hoped it wasn't one of the killer ones. He might have to take a pill to sleep tonight.

"Look," said Canning. "They're all the same. They're called white-collar thieves. Playing the stock market and that sort of thing."

Quinn leaned in closer to the windscreen. The wiper on the passenger side was missing a piece of the flap near the bottom. Canning rubbed his hands.

"Well, I wouldn't mind a go of one all the same," he said.

"Who wouldn't?"

"Oh soon enough, I say."

"Don't get ideas."

"What do you mean, don't get ideas?"

"You know what I'm saying. Keep away from stupid stuff that'll get us attention. Like I said at the beginning."

"You never said we were going to run a charity, did you."

"Just get the idea of robbing cars out of your head, will you?"

"I'm—"

"Will you just shut up, for fuck's sakes?"

Again the hands up, like a priest at Mass or something, Quinn thought. Like, I don't deserve this.

"I'm only saying, Bobby."

"Well don't."

Canning shifted in his seat, slumped against the door and looked out the window.

"Yeah yeah yeah," he murmured. "But listen."

"What."

"What do they drive up there, I'd like to know. It isn't a shitbox like this."

"I don't know what they drive."

"Didn't you get driven around at all?"

"Why is this car thing so fucking big for you today? What exactly is your problem anyway? Jasus you're like a big child or something."

Canning gave him a few moments.

"No need to be jumping all over me there. What has you so touchy anyway?"

"You're getting on my nerves with these stupid questions, is what."

"Why is it stupid, when I see that we're making a good stack here, that we have a good stroke going, but we're driving around in this yoke, like knackers?"

"Okay then," Quinn said. "Go out and rob yourself one. Go ahead."

"Maybe I'll buy one, so I will."

"With what?"

"I manage. Or at least I will, according to what you keep telling me."

"Even if you did have the dough, I'd set me watch and give you about ten minutes before the Revenue shower are in the door on you wanting to see the bills."

"Okay, it's back to Plan A, then, isn't it?"

"Spare me, will you?"

The curve on the cut-off to Bray nearly had the Opel aquaplaning.

"Christ," said Canning, and took out his cigarettes. "It always rains in Bray. Nowhere else. I hate it."

"Everyone hates Bray."

"Except them what know what they want here and can get it," said Canning. "Right?"

Bray had always had the name, Quinn remembered. IRA and INLA fellas went to ground here too, back in the early days.

"Right."

"Hey, Bobby."

"What."

"Are you sort of expecting something new today, maybe?"

"How do you mean? Why are you asking me that?"

"Is conversation illegal today or something? You're like a bear with a sore head, aren't you."

"Look. I just didn't get a good night out of it, that's all."

He steered down the hill by the old Wexford Road onto Main Street. The shower was dying out.

"Okay, tell you something now, Bobby. You listening?"

"I'm listening."

"If you're worrying about them fellas up you know where. Well don't be."

"What the hell is wrong with you? You woke up and

dreamed you were a shrink or something? What do you know what I'm thinking about?"

"Maybe I do. But I know what I know."

"You know fuck-all then, about this in anyhow."

"What's the good in biting my head off? I'm trying to tell you something and you don't want to hear it."

"Well, what are you telling me then?"

"I'm telling you that when the chips are down, down here in Dublin, which is where I'm from and you're from, and where we've lived all our shagging lives—I'm telling you that those fellas don't count."

Quinn turned before the Royal and headed down toward the seafront.

"They're different from us, Bobby. I'm telling you. Different."

Quinn pulled in before they got to the Harbour Bar. He rolled down his window for fresh air. Raindrops fell quivering onto his arm. He looked over at Canning.

"What," said Canning. Quinn kept up his stare.

"They don't impress me, Bobby. That's all's I'm saying. They look down their noses at us. Just 'cause we haven't been shooting one another for thirty years. Forget the politics, that's all crap. Nobody cares. But I've been thinking. And I hope you have too, Bobby. I do."

The feeling of being trapped had left Quinn now. He felt his heartbeat slow. He watched the next part of Canning's performance, the long drag on the cigarette.

"Those two fellas getting shot there the other day, the two foreigners. That didn't just happen out of the blue, did it?"

"Like, how?"

"Well, I asked around, didn't I? And guess what: the word is that no one here did it. The Egans? Nothing. Nailer Keogh and them, the Neilstown crowd? Nope."

"Is that a fact."

"Oh go ahead. Be sarcastic, if you want. What I'm telling you is what everyone else knows, Bobby. They might as well have been waving a flag when they did for those two . . ."

Four in the morning, lying there in his own bed, thinking about Roe: how calm he was getting the body out of the way. The look he'd given him as he'd driven out the door of the garage.

". . . You have the flu," Canning said. "That's what it is."

He was really here in Bray. In the car, with Canning as usual yapping away. There was a gurgle from a drainpipe nearby. He could smell the sea.

"What flu?"

"Look at you shivering there. That's what it is. Plus you look like shite."

Quinn shook his head. The stunned feeling, like you'd hit your head and everything seemed to be far off out there. He could think of nothing to say.

"But like I said, Bobby, if push comes to shove . . .You know?"

"No. What?"

Canning turned away from the window to face him.

"You haven't heard a fucking word I said, have you?"

The sun was coming out again now, so suddenly. It caught the drops still clinging to the top of his window. He stared at one, then another.

"Okay, I'll tell you," Canning said. "I'd put them away long before they'd try something on me, Bobby. That's what. I'm not afraid of a few headers with Northern accents."

Quinn looked over at him.

"Okay," he said.

He let the wipers run three times and he took the Opel down to the seafront. The sea was milky grey, but the sun blazed on the cross at the top of Bray head.

"But business is business," he heard Canning say. "Isn't it."

Quinn didn't like the crowd at Wonderland, the thick culchie accents off most of them that came by, up from Wexford and Kilkenny and even Waterford some of them. He couldn't tell if they were slagging him for being a Dub off his turf. They probably were. They were jackals, and he had no illusions about that. Cocky too, too young really. Too much of the video gangster thing going on there somewhere in their brains. If they'd only think beyond the next ten minutes, stuffing twenties in their pockets, going on skites and making a nuisance of themselves. And one of them was bound to get it into his head to go his own way soon enough, already had maybe, and he'd have to deal with that. A visit with Canning and a baseball bat to get the message out.

The seafront was sharp and drenched in colour, the grass almost glowing, the road black and clean from the rain.

So he was coming out of it then. Maybe it had been one of those you're-asleep-and-you-don't-know-it things he'd seen on the telly last week. Narco something. Quinn thought over the numbers. This week there was twenty-eight and a bit thousand quid to pick up and to move. This time six months, there'd be ten times that, according to what Grogan had told him. He remembered that expression that annoyed him so much, about getting all your ducks lined up in a row. It put him in mind of the shooting galleries they used to have in Bray when he was a kid and came out with the parish group.

Quinn gave him a nudge.

"Know what'd make my day here today?"

"A few pints and a game of snooker."

Canning chortled and gave him another nudge.

"Ah, you're on the ball there, Bobby. Jasus I was a bit

concerned there for a minute. Ah you were close! Yeah, I wouldn't mind that, but wouldn't it be just grand now if we bumped into that gobshite here? And him thinking he'd be okay out here laying low for a while here in sunny fucking Bray?"

It took Quinn a few moments.

"Be gas, wouldn't it? Doyle walking around and suddenly he's off his feet and in the back here, singing like a canary. I'd give him a good hiding, so I would, that little bollocksing troublemaker. A free ticket to Wonderland, for real, know what I'm saying?"

Quinn found a spot next to a building site. New apartments, flats? What did Bountiful mean? Ahead of them the amusement arcades looked mostly empty. Even in the brilliant sunshine some of the arcade's lights glowed and smeared on the road that stopped under the hill.

NIAMH

Minogue half-listened to an expert on fox behaviour while he looked down through his notes. He had walked through the park twice now, and returned to the Citroën back on Whitebeam Road. An old woman was eyeing him, surreptitiously, she believed—until he winked at her—from the top window of a terraced house.

According to Professor Donal O Connor there was no rabies in Ireland, no need for concern. Foxes were very adaptable; they were not put off by busy streets and traffic. Minogue stopped reading and looked at the radio: this O Connor wildlife biologist fella sounds like a fan of the animal. No, there was no consensus on why they were showing up this year in the city. I suppose we'd have to ask the foxes themselves, said the host, a man whom Minogue had initially liked some years back, but now regarded as a gobshite. Put lids on your bins, said O Connor. Minogue went back to his notes.

Bronagh, the "best friend," had been in the dead girl's class. Class in school, as well as social class, going by her address. Katie, another friend, had been the one who'd gone clubbing with her that night though. He tapped his notebook with his Biro hard and he looked out at the dripping hedges.

Why was he having trouble remembering the dead girl's name? Niamh, Niamh. *Niamh. NEEVE.* Not naïve?

Irish names had come back in for a while now, even before parents had started trying to get their kids into all-Irish schools. He still didn't quite understand it, but he had a shifting theory that it had something to do with people reacting to being full Europeans now. It wasn't a relapse into the maw of a walled, Catholic Ireland though: no way were no-guilt sex, laptops, and BMWs going to be renounced.

Bronagh—that surely couldn't have the same root as bró-nach, the Irish for sorrow, though. The Bronaghs and the Niamhs and the Ciaras and the Maedhbhes didn't walk primly down the halls cowed by watching thin-lipped nuns anymore: these girls went to Honora Park, the bastion of Irish Protestant families in bygone years. The speed of things more than the actual shifts had still not become real yet.

He checked his timeline again. The parents had phoned the Guards first thing in the morning. The mother had gone into the girl's—*Niamh's*—room at three, saw she wasn't there. Resolved to clip her wings severely, decided to wait until the morning. It had happened before but Niamh had phoned to say she was going to sleep in Bronagh's to save the taxi fare and . . . The retired nurse, Eileen Magee, who'd found the girl. Steady, a tough bird, she was; details, times. Training never left you, of course.

"Will a fox attack a person," from the interviewer. "A child, say?" There was a pause and a considered answer from Professor O Connor.

"Rare circumstances. They're scavengers more than hunters in an urban setting."

He flipped to his notes from the preliminary. There were no bite marks. But creepy, to be sure, the sighting from the Magee woman.

He turned off the radio and stepped out onto the footpath. He turned his head to see if the watcher was still there. The curtain flickered.

Hedges seemed to be the rule on this street. He passed gates and driveways, under laburnums and chestnuts and heavy, dripping willows. The sun came through dappled and flaring in spots on the spores and the minute blossoms and seeds that the rain had dashed to the pavement. A lot of thought had gone into the landscaping here he believed, to make it look so normal. Big houses these were now at this end of the road, built before the war, and all within a few miles of the middle of Dublin city. A million easy, some of them these days.

There were three cars in the Kennys' driveway as well as two others parked tight to the gate outside. Minogue took in the Galway registrations on two almost identical Meganes; a Lexus with a Dublin plate, an older diesel Mercedes, Galway registered, with a tow-bar that said rural use to him.

There was a face in the small window by the door. Minogue nodded. The woman had her hair pulled back tight, and there were baggy shadows under her eyes. He continued around the boulders and the swelling shrubs to the door.

A lemony smell went by him from the open door. Skylights, high ceilings, and a floor with huge earth-coloured terra cotta tiles were his first sight as he stepped in.

"I phoned a while ago," he said to her and held his photo-card up higher.

"I'm Colm's sister, the woman said. Una Fahy."

He smiled at her. He heard tones more than words from the voices behind a door to the left. Maybe South Galway he thought. He had relations in Gort himself.

"You're over from Donnybrook, is it?"

"That's it. I was asked in to assist."

She made no move to continue, but waited. He guessed solicitor. Those plain clothes that cost a damn sight more than you'd imagine.

"So it's Colm you'd be wanting then."

"If you please. Is he okay to . . . ?"

She looked at him. That's what they mean, arrested by a gaze, he thought.

"He is. But Nuala's not. You may find it takes time to get used to Colm."

"Spoken as an older sister then, I take it?"

She raised an eyebrow. He fended off his annoyance.

"I have a ton of sisters myself," he said instead. "They never give up."

She looked him up and down.

"You're not Galway yourself, by any chance?"

"Near enough."

Her face gave way a little. She put her hands in her pockets.

"Minogue," she said. "Nothing to Minogue's Pub there in Tulla?"

"Not quite," he said. "My crowd are up above Ballyvaughan."

"Ah," she said. "Now there's a spot."

He held back on telling her that the village didn't always sell scampi or witness kayaks being deftly slid off the roofs of Saabs.

"Safe from civilization yet," he said instead.

Her jaw moved around as she looked into a dining room.

"Colm can't sleep, is what I meant. He won't take anything."

Wrong about the solicitor bit, Minogue thought. A doctor, a pharmacist maybe.

"Okay."

"He didn't get a good impression of the others, I must tell you. The other Guards."

Minogue nodded.

"He said that the Commissioner would be sending out someone though."

He examined a painting that had no frame, something with sea in it.

"Colm knows him socially, you know. Commissioner Tynan."

He gave her a quick glance.

"Do you think you could let your brother know that I'm here?"

There was a pause before she turned toward the door, but he didn't take his eyes off the painting. A bit of the actress then too, he decided.

"Do you drink tea, Guard," she said then, leaving.

"Only coffee," he said. "But thank you."

She closed the door behind her.

Would it always be like this, he wondered. Even with the changes, would he always be the mucker standing in the ditch, and the likes of Una Fahy, MD or LLB or whatever, be the townie. His Ireland was still improbably small scrubby fields you fought with to rear a family, only to watch them leave; theirs, music lessons and boarding school, future solicitors and doctors and pharmacists. The very ones that Iseult scorned, but hoped would show up at her exhibitions to buy her work. No, no, no: this couldn't be, he decided. Silly to still think like this. That was all gone by the board; it had to be.

He looked over when the door of the kitchen was yanked firmly open. Here was Mr. Colm Kenny then, angry, half-mad, demanding, stricken father. But the same Kenny had felt it kick in by now, Minogue knew as he took in the ravaged face of Niamh Kenny's father. She wouldn't be coming home; this really had happened, it was still happening; this couldn't be stopped.

So this was it, Minogue knew, and the glam Euro job and the nine to five and the rest of it wouldn't measure up. What mattered was going with this man and his wife, people he would never have met otherwise, strangers almost, and trying to do something that he had never been able to put words on—certainly not help—but a settling of some kind, with an unspoken promise that made no sense really at all, to somehow fix things.

Kenny looked like he was wavering a bit on his feet. The voice was a whisper.

"Are you the one they said they'd send?"

"I am," Minogue said. "I suppose."

FOREMOST IN OUR MINDS

It was the way Kenny spoke too. He must lecture or some-thing, as well as the architect thing, Minogue decided.

"You have to understand," Kenny said again. "This is not some *accident*. It's not *misadventure*."

Minogue came up with a thoughtful nod. He continued his leisurely, covert inventory of the room. Paintings he thought he recognized, the style or artist at any rate. A startling metalwork thing that looked like a Famine thing. High up were the skylights filled with branches and leaves.

"We need to keep that foremost in our minds, right?"

Minogue nodded again.

"Because I know, I *know*, just how expectations shape a thing, right from the start. Yes? And if you, I mean we, go in to something with preconceived notions, well you know what happens then."

"That's in your line of work, is it, Mr. Kenny?"

"In any line of work that requires thinking."

Minogue had discovered a spider web in the corner of the ceiling.

"You know what I mean don't you, about the power of the subconscious?"

"To be sure," Minogue said. "Could we talk a bit about

Niamh's mates?"

Kenny blinked several times. In a trance, Minogue thought. He'd noted the twitch in his eyelid earlier, wondered when it'd be back. Kenny let his stare sink slowly down to his hands.

"I know the last fellas here, the other Guards, didn't have much time for this. No doubt you know that already."

Minogue waited for him to look up before he replied.

"It's okay, Mr. Kenny."

"What's okay? What do you mean, it's okay?"

"There's no one can tell anyone else what it's like, that's what I mean. You can say what you want. I don't keep score, or anything."

Something changed around Kenny's bloodshot eyes but Minogue couldn't decide. He wondered what it was like to grow up around a father like this, the intensity of him.

"I could tell right away," Kenny said. "The Guards, when they came in. The very first time. What they expected, what they assumed. People notice, you know. They might not be aware of it, but people take in stuff."

"Ah," said Minogue. "Now you're talking my job description."

He took out his Biro, hoping Kenny would get the hint.

"They saw well-to-do people," Kenny went on. "Busy career parents. Kids who got overlooked. Spoiled, I bet they thought."

"Oh, I don't know now."

"Rich people getting their comeuppance. I could feel that coming from them."

Minogue wrote today's date carefully. That seemed to be working, he understood: Kenny's eyes were following the movement of the Biro now.

"Like we deserved this, somehow."

"That's an effect of the shock, Mr. Kenny. That feeling—"

"—There's a word for it, if I can remember it. I really have to rest, I know. I don't think I can though. I can't stop, you know."

"*Schadenfreude*," Minogue murmured.

"That's the word," Kenny whispered. Minogue smacked himself for the vanity.

"You said that all the stuff from Niamh's locker was delivered here this morning?"

Kenny didn't seem to have heard him.

"I'd like to have a look at those items, please."

He waited for Kenny's eyes to focus, to find his. The man's eyes turned toward Minogue eventually, and even returned the contact, but to Minogue the empty look remained.

BACK TO CIVILIZATION

Quinn let the phone ring six times before he gave up. Catherine was gone out to the shop or something. Tonight he just wanted to sit with her, just like the old days. Whatever she wanted, well that'd be fine, even if it was a curry thing out of a package. His stomach hadn't been completely right since his time inside; it was the only thing that had given out on him, and he had never talked about it even to Catherine.

Or they could go into town, one of those places down the Temple Bar. Then they'd go for a few jars in that place she had talked about last week. Maybe even Brittney could go over to Catherine's sister for the night, stay with her cousin Samantha. Yes, he thought: Mammy and Daddy are going out on a date.

The clouds had come back, swiped the sun that had cheered him only a half an hour ago. From the mouth of the alleyway he watched a lone van coming along the seafront, dipping the odd time to slough water from the puddles. The place here actually felt greasy: the air, the wet roadway, the leftovers of the rain still darkening the gables on the older houses along the promenade. Light ragged surf broke beyond the railings. The pinks and baby-blues on some of the walls made the place look like a big toy, like melted ice cream dropped in the gutter.

Quinn didn't like standing around here, but he was damned if he was going to stand inside the arcade at Wonderland while Canning shovelled money into his stupid shooting-game things in there. He watched seagulls circling over the beach.

He could just go ahead and book tickets to Portugal and surprise her. And if she came up with the what-will-I-say-at-me-job, or I-hope-you're-going-to-include-Brittney? Ah, she wouldn't, things weren't that bad. He'd tell her that this trip was very important for them as a couple. He wondered if she'd read the horoscopes lately too, if she had seen what he had seen as a common thread behind them: reconnect with your loved ones, get back in touch. The one in yesterday's *Sun* said it all, actually: Get your priorities right, Cancer, you'll always have a career, but you might get laid off by your family. A bit harsh, what?

It was going to rain again.

The weariness came down on him again. He headed back to the arcade. The same fella with the dog he'd seen on his other trips was still hanging around. He gave him a nod. Quinn ignored him, tried to peer into the arcade instead. The noise was actually getting into his teeth. It took ages for his eyes to adjust. There was no sign of Canning here where he'd last spotted him. Quinn made his way through the arcade, by the motorbike games to the shooters that Canning liked.

Then he spotted him, the shape of him at least, in silhouette, yapping to someone over near the dodgems. The other fella was showing Canning something, moving it around, pointing to it. He stood facing them but Canning didn't notice him.

Quinn sized up the other man as he made his way over. A

ring in the ear, a tattoo, the hair almost shaved. Hundred-quid sneakers, but he smokes. Another one of the local stars, right.

"Come on," he called out to Canning. "Let's go."

"H-h-here," said the other man. "Let me s-s-show you then."

Quinn looked at the small box, the wire that looked like on the mobiles.

"I was just s-s-showing your mate this thing, it's brilliant, it's a camera."

"Get lost," Quinn said.

"But you don't even kn-n-now what I'm going to show you."

Quinn flicked his head toward the door.

"They're all u-u-using these now, did you kn-n-now that?"

Quinn headed for the door. The man came with him and tapped him on the arm.

"Don't do that," Quinn said.

"What? I can't hear."

"I said don't fucking do that. I'm not interested."

"What, you don't want to kn-n-now what this beauty can do?"

"Shove it, pal. Are you deaf?"

"Oh, ignore a p-p-perfectly good suggestion. Tells you who's serious then, doesn't it."

The cheek made Quinn stop. He turned. Canning had caught up with them.

"What are you on about? Do you want to get yourself a going-over here?"

The man glanced over at Canning.

"You, you bollocks, why'd you tell me he was interested, you—"

Quinn shoved him in the chest and stepped after him. The girl in the booth looked over. Canning's hand was on his arm now, pulling.

"Do you know who you're talking to?"

"Yeah, I do. Bobby Quinn, right."

The man hadn't tried to move Quinn's hands off his shirt.

"Show a bit of respect there," Canning said. Quinn wanted to tell him it was a bit late to put on this act now.

"Do you see me arguing," he said, "do you? Alls I'm saying is have a l-l-look at this. This is what the Russians and them use, you know."

"What Russians," Quinn said. "Are you on drugs or something?"

"Ah come on now, do I need to t-t-tell yous, really?"

"What did I just tell you a minute ago," Canning said.

"But this is so easy!"

He held up the camera by its antenna. Quinn let go of his shirt.

"No wires, see? You can w-w-watch from across the street and you can tape it all too. PIN numbers. Yeah? Garages, cash points, shops—anywhere. It's b-b-brilliant!"

Quinn looked down at the man's lips where he had wrung out the words that were choked by his stammers. Maybe he was high.

"It's magic, you know, m-m-magic! And I can get them for you and set them up."

"You can sell the numbers you get on the camera, I mean you d-d-don't have to do anything else."

"Who are you?"

"Gannon, Bren Gannon. There's lots I do, you know, this isn't the only s-s-stroke, you know. Oh yes, I always have me eye out for b-b-business, and opportunities."

Quinn looked at Canning. Canning shrugged.

"Matter of fact," the man said. "Maybe you'd know me, or me n-n-name, from a mate of mine, you know him."

"What mate?"

"Doyler."

"What or who is Doyler?"

"Come on, you know Doyler."

"You're dreaming," Quinn said. "What are you on exactly?"

"What, he does be out here n-n-now and then. See the sights and all—Sunny Bray and all that."

"Why is it always pissing rain in Sunny Bray then?" Canning asked. "Ha ha."

"Oh that's a g-g-good one. But Bray's very popular spot, let me t-t-tell you. It can't be all that bad here if yous are out for a v-v-visit, can it?"

Quinn took a step back. The wink, the shuffling feet, the bad teeth, he thought.

"Gannon, are you?"

"That's me, Mr. Quinn. Bren."

"Okay," Quinn said. "Maybe you can help us out a bit here. Bren."

"You want the c-c-camera for a few days, try it out? No bother—"

"Shut up and listen. Here's your job. You tell Doyle that when I catch up to him, I'm going to break his arms, and his legs, in a door."

Quinn held the man's eye with his stare.

"Tell him it takes time to do it that way, but I want it that way because they don't usually pass out until later on. Got that, have you?"

Gannon said nothing.

"Tell him it's on account of him being a stupid, big-mouth, gobshite. Can you do that for me?"

Gannon looked over at Canning now.

"And when you're finished that little job, I want you to get on your bike and get to hell out of here. Out of Bray, for that matter, and stay out. 'Cause if I ever see you, or if you ever try to walk up to me like you just did once more, or even nod my way, you won't be using your legs for a long, long time."

He heard Canning breathing hard to catch up to him on his way back to the car.

"Lost the rag there a bit, Bobby, don't you think?"

"Don't you ever try to get me involved with a little shite like that again."

"Don't you think he might be on to something though?" Canning asked him across the roof of the car. "I mean, I'm only saying, Bobby."

"Don't talk to me. I told you about stuff like that, didn't I? Don't fucking talk to me."

Canning sat in after him.

"What," said Quinn, "we have every wannabe in Bray thinking they can walk up to us like that, nudge-nudge, wink-wink?"

"Opportunities, Bobby—"

"—Did it strike you for one minute that that stuttering bastard could be a set-up?"

Canning rolled down his window.

"No need to lose your rag over it," he said. "Is there."

Quinn started up the Opel. He listened to the exhaust. Yes, there was a hole in it somewhere.

"We should be keeping an open .mind though, right," Canning said. "I mean, there's no harm, is there?"

"Keep your eye on the ball, will you. That's all I want to see, or hear."

"What ball, Bobby? Can't I do a bit of me own thing?"

"Do what you like, but don't get me dragged into it. In any way."

"Well Jesus, I mean, what's gotten into you? You're biting me head off every chance you get. Ease off, will you?"

"I'll ease off when I know you're not some magnet for gobshites like that, fellas that'd bring you down as quick as anything—would bring me down with you."

"Ah, it's harmless enough."

"It isn't—nothing's *harmless*."

He drove hard back down the seafront and turned under the railway bridge and up toward the centre of town. What a difference a patch of blue sky made. The jitteriness came to him as a kind of breathlessness now. Canning lit a cigarette. He said nothing until they came to the stop sign by the Royal Hotel and the sign to get back out on the N11.

"Back to civilization then," Canning said.

They had a good run after the roundabout in Loughlinstown, and got green lights all the way to Stillorgan. Quinn braked and rolled down the window more. Canning was humming along with a tune on the radio. In one ear and out the other, Quinn thought. At least the ache in his neck hadn't turned into a headache—yet. Yes, he had decided not long after getting out of Bray, he could go to the travel agent before they closed today.

Canning realized that Quinn was looking at him. He stopped humming.

"What?"

"You're a bollocks, Beans," Quinn said. "Do you know that?"

"Takes one to know one, I say."

"Keep away from the video games. They'll only make you dizzy."

"Fuck off. You're only jealous cause you're crap at them."

The tiredness hit Quinn like a wave now. His eyes slipped out of focus.

"What are you thinking about?" Canning asked.

"Oh, nothing. I could use a bit of a holiday, maybe. A bit of the beach and that."

"Well, I got that idea pretty quick, didn't I. All over your man back there."

"That type of a chancer, what's his name, Gannon—"

"Gaga they call him."

"Well, he is ga-ga. He'd only drag us down. The cops would play the likes of him like a fiddle."

"Well, maybe. Maybe."

"I'm telling you," Quinn said.

"But don't you think he's onto something, with that stuff? You know, getting those card numbers and selling them?"

"Look. If he's a mate of Doyle, that says it all. Am I right or what?"

"You got a point. All right. But a camera like that?"

"Forget that shite, will you? You're driving me mad with it."

Canning looked out at the cars using the filter light to turn off up to Stillorgan.

Quinn stifled a yawn, waited for the words he expected but Canning remained silent.

SALVAGE

Minogue got through to Malone after three. Collins had come and gone in that quiet molelike way of his. Tunney was somewhere in the building. He hadn't been too interested after Minogue had told him that the dead girl's father hadn't clawed his eyes out. Minogue didn't feel a need to tell him that he had come away from the Kennys too aware that he was working hard to fight off that feeling leaking steadily into his mind, that Tunney had been right from the start. Misadventure, salvage, had been circling in his brain, driving him bonkers.

The rain had kept off. Collins had told him earlier that a new coffee place had opened up just beside the pseudo-Italian delicatessen. He had been half-reading the *Irish Times* again. The size of the headlines was indeed rare, he believed, something for big bombings or constitutional referendum votes. He'd kept away from the high-voltage stuff about the murder of refugees, and the editorial about what this crime said about modern times in Dublin and Ireland generally. The Garda spokesman had been Cooney out of CDU. Minogue didn't understand how the case had gone to them.

He heard Malone yawn in the middle of saying something about this may be wrapping up for now at least.

"Well, you still have a job," he said to Malone.

"If you can call it that. A day of meetings with fellas in from the city centre units."

Minogue let his eyes drift over the newspaper again: a car leaving the scene at speed, thought to be a Renault; two men in it.

"What's this new gig like then," Malone asked him. Minogue stretched and looked around the room.

"Well, it seems to be either an overdose, or this girl took bad drugs."

"Was she in the trade?"

"She was a schoolgirl, Tommy."

"Sorry. Tell you the truth I'm surprised we don't have more of that."

"The line here is she had bad luck. Her parents are connected though."

"So you got dropped in?"

"That's it. I'm just going through her school stuff. You know the way they write things, diaries."

"I don't have good memories of when I was a schoolgirl. Sorry."

"Ah, come on. Bits of songs. Drawings."

"Really? I fecking-sure remember being bored out of me skull a lot of the time."

"I want you to do something for me. Get me dealers and suppliers in the South City."

"Where are you talking about?"

"This girl went to Honora Park. In Milltown."

"Isn't that a fancy school?"

"Indeed it is."

"Milltown's still got rough patches. Better than it was though. A fair number of gougers there and down the way in the flats in Donnybrook, though."

"That's a start. Names, though."

"Dealing at a school, though?"

"Well, find out, will you? Whoever would know people, right down to the street."

"Give me a day or two."

Minogue risked a question to Malone about his brother.

"He's getting some treatment. But the thing the other day is on me mind still."

"So it should be."

"I just want to know for sure if the bastard was spoofing or if Quinn really has something going there. Yeah. I'd like to get a hold of him, Doyle."

"When you do, you're going to take someone with you. Am I right?"

"Yeah, yeah. What gets to me is that I know that they know it's working."

"What's working?"

"This is how they do it. They're never direct, like, out straight: 'Make a call to so-and-so and tell them so-and-so, and we'll look after you.' They like to just, you know, insinuate. It's a head game. And it works, doesn't it?"

Minogue thought about Terry Malone, the face the same as his brother's but then in subtle ways different. Of course, it was the way he wouldn't look you in the eye, but there was a lack of solidity to him the time he had met him last year, of something about his shoulders or his way of standing that Malone had. But it had been years since Terry had done any ring training, Malone had told him.

"Don't go losing it now, Tommy. Are you with me, now?"

"Huh," said Malone.

Minogue was finished with Niamh Kenny's copybooks when Tunney showed up. Tunney had his roll half-eaten coming in. He planted an unopened tin of Fanta orange on the table. He finished the roll and stood again, plucking, shaking, and patting the crumbs and pieces of crust from his shirt and lap.

"That's how the Mullingar men dance," Tunney said.

"Mullingar?"

The wife told me that years ago. They don't move their feet, says she.

"Is she from Mullingar?" Minogue asked.

"Edenderry. I met her and I was stationed in Mullingar. In my salad days."

"Great."

"There's nothing great about it," Tunney said. "Except maybe the bypass."

Minogue wondered if this was a thaw, or Tunney winding up something.

"I've heard that said about the Midlands, all right," he tried. "But I don't know."

"That's right you don't know," said Tunney. "But I do. That rain that's held off since the showers earlier on? Well, in Mullingar it doesn't hold off. It just stays."

"Where did you get that roll?"

Tunney sat down in a swivel chair and hoisted his feet on to the desk that Collins had been writing at earlier.

"Delaney's below," he said. "It's a tuna fish thing. Where'd you get the girl's school stuff?"

There were things in her locker got sent home. Her father gave it to me. I sent a jumper and two T-shirts for testing.

"I bet you left that place with your ears burning, but."

Minogue looked over his list. Lyrics from Nirvana, wasn't that a bit dated now?

"It'll dawn on him," Tunney said. "Sooner or later. Hard not to feel bad for him, all the same."

How hard would that be for you, Minogue didn't ask.

"But by Christ he is a royal pain in the hole. He was to me and Collins anyway."

Minogue heard the Fanta wash down his gullet.

"Have we set up talk-time with her friends yet, Niamh's friends?"

Tunney took another swig from the can.

"No. Not yet."

"Well, we know who went with her to the club. We can start with her, if that's okay then."

"Grand," said Tunney and he drained the can.

"If Mick Collins was still here I'd be asking for a hand, so I would."

"He'll be in in the morning," Tunney said.

Minogue watched Tunney's slow method of crushing the can. He made a dent with his thumb and then worked the two ends together over the buckle. It was almost noiseless.

"Is he working another end of it?"

"No," said Tunney. "Not today."

Minogue waited.

"I told him to go back to the car thefts. We were doing a lot of that before."

"Who else can I get in with? There's a lot to hear before things go stale."

"Well," Tunney said. "It'll be plenty busy here then."

Minogue looked down his list again. Collins had made himself scarce. He might have known Tunney was going to go on him for manpower.

Niamh had spelled her friend's name Brona without the -*gh* at the end, he remembered.

"A few questions," he said to Tunney.

"Fire away there. Fire away."

"What do we know about her behaviour prior? Niamh's . . . ?

"Well, what I have is from her da. I had a short enough session with her ma before she, well before she went under, you might say."

"Was she a bit wild maybe?"

"The girl? Not according to the da. But that's not to say there weren't issues, now. The da gave her a dressing down at Christmas about coming home a bit off."

"How off was she?"

"She was half-cut, said the da. Not falling-down drunk now."

"Late hours, friends they weren't sure of?"

"She was 'headstrong.'"

"Did she run with a rowdy crowd at all?"

"Her mates don't seem that wild, no. She only started in that Honora place there in secondary. There are the usual pecking orders, is that the word?"

Minogue vaguely remembered Iseult's tribulations in the middle years of seco, a particularly tireless pair of bitches, the names of Deirdre someone and Emer someone else. They'd been like a tag-team, he remembered Iseult saying.

"I'd be keen to get some names," he said. "How was she doing in school anyway?"

"She wasn't top of the class. They put markers down for her, the parents did, a while back. Marks in exams, study times and that."

"She had a social life though?"

"Steady enough, says her da, yes."

"Fellas?"

Tunney shook his head. "She went to hops, dancing."

"Clubbing?"

"You know, I didn't get into that part. But don't you have to be eighteen or something?"

"No," Minogue said. Tunney looked around the top of the walls.

"She'd been on an exchange thing in Germany last year, if that's socializing."

Tunney adjusted his slouch more. Over size twelve, Minogue had decided.

"Thing is," he went on, "he says the wife and himself did-n't want to go too far with laying down the law. Like telling her what to do and that. He reckoned she could manage her-self well enough."

"Any idea what that meant?"

Tunney gave him the eye. Minogue didn't care now that Tunney was on to him, maybe even keeping a count of the questions that were being fired at him.

"She wasn't off the wall, is what he meant. That's what I concluded, Cig."

Minogue registered the dig.

"Well, did they know where she was when she was out?"

Tunney finished his Fanta, said "aaahhhh." He mimicked a phone held to his ear.

"A mobile?"

Tunney shrugged.

"I know," he said. "But what am I going to say to them that they don't know already about mobile phones?"

"They knew about the place she went to that night?"

"No. But it was new, that was the draw too. 'Planet Nine.'"

Tunney sat forward and laid his forearms on his knees.

"Let me ask you something."

"Yes," Minogue said and added "Planet Nine" to his to-do list.

"What exactly are you aiming for here with this, like what do you think has to be done to close this?"

"Well, I don't know."

"You don't know?"

Minogue looked up from his notebook and shook his head.

"You were 2-I-C in the Murder Squad though."

"I was."

"So is this a murder case?"

"If I had more manpower I'd have an answer quicker."

"Well, I sort of missed the bus maybe on this then," said Tunney.

"You're ahead of me now."

"I mean, let's say you get to find out where the girl got the stuff, I can see that. You might even nail a dealer too, fair play to you. But I'm sort of thinking you end up with a little creeping Jesus, a nothing who unloaded them from someone else up the line. You know how hard it is to go back up the line? They don't talk. You saw what happened there the other day, the foreigners?"

Minogue didn't say Albanians.

"So, like, it's taken ten years or so, new laws, a few million quid—just to get started on the whole drugs racket here. I'm not telling tales on anyone here, am I?"

"No."

"So you know how tough it is to get a little pisser off the street to put the hand on his dealer, his high-up dealer—the jackrats."

"I'd heard."

"Well, they won't do it. They'll take the three years or whatever they get." Minogue could still smell the bread from Tunney's sandwich.

"The PCP thing is all over," Tunney said. "It's kids now, it's fellas at work, it's housewives, it's anyone really. They buy a bag, the clubbers do. Order 'em in over the phone. It's cheaper than trying to get into a pub underage, isn't it? Off they go, dancing their little feet off for ten hours straight. I'm telling you, parents don't know the half of it."

Minogue let the quiet drag on for a minute.

"The woman who found her, the nurse," he said then. "She said she saw some young lads there."

"Right," Tunney said.

"The two kids haven't shown up in the door-to-door?"

"No. But look at the reports yourself. Nearly every one of the fellas doing the door-to-door are from here. Downstairs, where they're always short-staffed."

Minogue closed his notebook and felt for his phone. Then he began putting Niamh Kenny's belongings back in the bags. Shorthand, scribbled notes to friends, jokes, old projects. *History of the Land War;* study notes he supposed, on French irregular verbs. Calculus had driven her mad, it looked from the welter of lines and crossings out, Mr. or Mrs. Kenny had kept her clothes it looked like. He'd forgotten to phone and tell them he needed tests on the clothes. One of her hair things had fallen on the floor. He slid it into the bag.

"It's tough," Tunney said. "There's nothing you can say that isn't going to hurt them, is there?"

"That's about it."

"But we can't give them false hopes. I mean what use is that?"

Minogue closed the drawer. He didn't recall seeing Tunney thoughtful before.

"She got lost though, somewhere. Didn't she? One bad move was all it took."

"They want to know," Minogue said. "Bad or good. I'd want to know too."

"I'm willing to bet you something," Tunney said. "And it's this: There'll be no end to what they'll want or expect or demand, will there?"

Minogue had no answer.

"But Kenny will tear into us, into you, and poke and prod whenever he can. And phone his friends and his connections and all that. Isn't that all part of the denial thing?"

"But in the heel of the hunt, he'll be smart enough to realize that it's not the Murder Squad he's wanting. By the way, does he know we don't have one anymore?"

"He was certainly told," Minogue managed. "But I don't know if he believes us."

A WEE CHAT

Grogan was trying not to watch David Frost doing something about celebrity homes when the phone rang. He
waited, and at the third ring it stopped.

He levered himself up, made his way to the kitchen and
took out the mobile. He'd kept it in the cardboard box that
the pay-as-you-go phone had come in. By rights he should
have dumped this one a fortnight ago. Maureen had messed
up the other one, grabbing it without thinking one day back
in May sometime.

He switched it on and waited for the signal.

Gallagher sounded like he'd just finished a yawn.

"You'll remember what we talked about the other night,
the business we had to get done there recently?"

"Go ahead."

"Well, there's something's come up. Something else."

Grogan leaned against the closed door and shifted to his
good foot. It had only struck him how small a kitchen it was
after going on holidays last year. It was the first holiday he'd
had in twenty years. Maureen had gotten the idea after she'd
heard him slagging the Dublin crowd going to Portugal.
Except for the heat, he hadn't minded the week in Portugal,
as long as he didn't have to move around too much.

"I'm listening."

"It's got to do with your friend. Well, the word is that a mate of his is gone bad."

Grogan looked at the tealeaves in the drainer. The shelf had he'd built all those years ago when he'd had the tools. Kieran like a bag of weasels every damned morning, always banging into something, hated school. The battle dress and sunglasses and flag hadn't meant much to him at the gravesite. He was back in his cell that night anyway.

"He's talking to the wrong people," Gallagher said.

"To do with that business?"

"Well, we don't know. But he's talking, that we know."

"But it was all kept tight," Grogan said. "He handled it himself there, all of it."

"The other fella is with him on a daily basis now," Gallagher said. "You know who I'm talking about better than I do now."

"I know who you're talking about, sure I do. But he's nothing really. Nothing."

"A daily basis," Gallagher said again. "They go back a lot of years, the two of them."

Grogan held back.

"Well, we didn't want you hearing about this problem from someone else first."

We, Grogan thought. Why did it sound peculiar now?

"Do you have time for cup of tea then," Gallagher said. "A wee chat?"

Grogan said okay to four o' clock and he switched off the phone. He didn't bother to plug it back into the charger.

He leaned against the sink, his back still prickling with the feeling of being here near the window, exposed. They had broken all these windows during the hunger strikes. Maybe that was what had done Kieran in, that kind of terror staying in his head from then on. It was Paras coming through, chasing fellas over walls, any excuse to knock out windows, especially a known man like Grogan. They'd known he wasn't home that night too, so's he wasn't even there to protect his own family. And just as dependably as they sent in Paras to harass and taunt him, they'd sent in repairmen with new windows. Just as they put him in hospital for six months and made him limp every day of his life, they paid him dole and medical. An odd world indeed, the future had turned out to be.

Quinn and the Dublin crowd, he thought, that's what the "chat" would be about. He didn't feel up to persuading them again though.

He heard the ads through the wall, and remembered watching Maureen after she'd fallen asleep in front of the telly last night. He was quite a cook now, and he had time if he wanted to go back to doing the joinery and the furniture. People would always want things fixed, heirlooms, things they became attached to.

He went into the hall and took a piece of paper to write Maureen a note.

Do What You Have to Do

Minogue entered Honora Park thinking of pheromones, later of his own foolishness. They must hover in the air—they must—he was sure. But how thick was he, how misdirected his fossilized mind, to be imagining that a girls' school emptied of its students for the summer could still be so alien, so charged, even in the absence of an overwhelming number of almost exclusively young female persons in the one place.

Mrs. Tovey, the headmistress, had given perfect directions. He was ten minutes early. Plenty of time to gawk at the framed photos in the hall lined by doors to one side and windows to the other. A staff room, he noted; a supply room; a room with two photocopiers; a huge cleaner's cupboard it looked; the headmistress' office.

Before the eighties, there were no Murphys, O'Connors, or Doyles inscribed on the nameplates of former staff and headmistresses going back over the years in Honora School.

"Everything's changed, of course," he heard himself muttering. And then a door flew open behind him.

Mrs. Tovey—an early middle-aged woman with the gait of an athlete and flat shoes which told a confused Minogue he was definitely right about something—did wear the glasses he half-expected, along with an intense expression he put to the cause of his visit. She also had a fierce country accent. She held her hand out.

"Thanks for arranging this," he said.

"Oh I hardly need to be checking an identity thing now, do I? A Chief Inspector . . . ?"

Minogue offered a smile and put away his card. Since when were teachers—a headmistress of a private school—allowed to wear jeans?

"I'm in here all July," she said. "It's nothing, I mean, to meet with you. Whatever I can—we can—do."

"Paperwork is a divil, to be sure."

"Don't talk to me," she said. "It doubles every year."

She pushed open the door to her office. Awkwardly he got by her, waited for her to park her briefcase.

"Sit down, sit down," she said. "I just have to forage around here a minute."

She covered up what looked like some printout of a timetable and closed a drawer.

"You work with the other Guards then, I imagine?"

"I was asked in just yesterday to help."

She pulled two bulging folders from the briefcase, then a laptop, and she stacked the folders at the outer edge of a table behind her. She swivelled back.

"We're all very upset here. Very. It's been very difficult."

He nodded.

"I have to tell you," she went on, "that when you first suggested this, I wasn't keen. It took me a while."

He thought about Kathleen slagging him while he put on the good suit, wondered if that too had set up some primeval reflex that had him here, a countryman in front of the head-mistress of probably the most exclusive girls' school in the country.

"Like I said, it'll help us all."

The gently raised eyebrows were a signal to make his case again, maybe.

"The way it is, it'd be hard enough if I were to be visiting them at home. Not to speak of the time I'd need to be going around."

"Well, it took some persuading the parents, er . . ."

"Matt."

"But they surprised me. They'll all come. They didn't utter one word of protest."

"That's great."

"They're worried sick," she said.

"I suppose they would be, yes."

The phone went off.

He listened to her, let his eyes wander the room. "Yes," she said. There was a younger smiling Mrs. Tovey on a horse somewhere. He began to invent a past for her: country house, West Cork, Anglo Irish, huntin and shootin, dogs in the kitchen, long windows, cashmere jumpers. "They're here," she said. "I mean he is here, an Inspector, ready." She listened, nodded. "And thank you for doing this, it means so much. Yes."

She replaced the receiver and looked over at him.

"They're here, the O'Neills. Bronagh."

"Mrs. Tovey, before I have a chat with any of them might I ask you a few questions?"

"Go ahead."

"It's about Niamh. What you might know or not know of her and her friends."

She sat back and gathered herself. Then she spoke. She had expected him to ask, Minogue realized, had prepared in detail for this. *Formidable.* He couldn't shake the word from his mind. She told him the limits several times; how protecting those in her charge was a sacred trust; how she would hand onto the school counsel any questions or points she didn't believe were hers to answer.

Then she looked down at her watch.

"I have a question for you now," she said. "Before I show you the room where you can talk to them."

"If you find out that this tragedy was a result of something going on in our school . . . ?"

For a few moments he wondered if he had misread her: the firm handshake, the accent he guessed as Cork. Would it be the honour of the school or some guff like that, he thought, or maybe even some effort at coming the heavy with confidentiality stuff.

"Well," he said, "you can imagine that we have to go at every angle."

She blinked, kept up her earnest stare.

"Do you mean, say, if we found out there had been some illegal activity here in the school?"

"Something like that, yes. I'll be honest with you. Talk of drugs would do a lot of damage to our community."

The fact that she had uttered one of the words that had been driving him around the twist for a good number of years shouldn't be counted.

"I'm not here to cause damage," he managed. "I just need to find out what happened to this girl."

She had glanced down at her desktop, he thought as he followed her down the hall, stared at it for several moments in the way that told him she had made a decision that was hard for her. Sized him up probably, knew that it was better not to keep on that line. The brisk manner when she stood, the all-business smile, had registered with him.

The room she guided him to had décor strikingly mod enough for him to start at the sight of it. A pot of coffee, biscuits, even pens and paper. The oval table was high German boardroom style, the chairs themselves works of art.

"You've gone to a lot of trouble," he said. "Thank you."

Mrs. Tovey glanced at him before she moved an overhead projector off a chair.

"It's still Ireland," she said, tucking two chairs in and turning back, her hands on her hips. Minogue had been studying the halogen lighting, the plasterwork.

"Rachel Tynan was a neighbour of mine growing up," she said.

"Was she now."

"She's like me. She digs with the other foot."

"Oh, I see."

"Jesuit John, yes."

Minogue didn't want to mistake the raised eyebrow. He wondered if Mrs. Tovey had phoned Tynan or vice versa. He returned her smile.

"I believe that maybe that particular name is used on occasion at their house, he said."

"She says hello. She hopes to see you and yours soon enough."

She means Iseult, Minogue thought, the artsy stuff. Who had told him that the treatments left your immune system shagged, so's you couldn't meet people, you'd get any little bug floating around?

The hint of mischief left Mrs. Tovey's features before the smile did.

"Do what you have to do," she said to him. "Whatever comes of it. We'll manage."

A FELLA

Bronagh O'Neill was in a terrible state. A lot of times she was unable to say a word between bouts of crying and being held by her mother. Her father, a man considerably younger than Minogue and whom Minogue suspected of being that John O'Neill stockbroker he'd seen plastered all over the financial section not long back, did a not bad job of hiding his impatience.

"Come on now, love," he'd say every now and then, to little effect.

Mrs. O'Neill looked French, elegant, tired, worried. She had that accent, the one they called the DART accent, that he had stopped trying to figure out long ago.

Bronagh gave a shudder like a hiccup every now and then. She spoke in a raspy whisper, sometimes squeezing out the words. He heard her pulling at her nails under the table. Her freckles went right to her hairline.

He took Niamh's bits of paper and placed them on the table next to her. She stared at them for several moments and then burst into tears again.

"Quite the artist," he said to her when she was able to sit up again. "A great eye there. The same with clothes and that?"

"Yes. She could pick something exactly right."

"Did you sometimes do shopping expeditions together?"

Bronagh nodded. Her face began to go again. This time she was able to fight it off. Minogue pointed at the stylized letters and words.

"I'm embarrassed to tell you something now, Bronagh."

She returned his gaze, and her face eased a little.

"Ninety-nine percent of this means nothing to me. Except maybe Ireland's Greatest Band there. But the rest . . . I'm prehistoric."

She half smiled and wiped her face. Her mother held out another tissue.

"Those are bands, too," she whispered. "And that one there. Words to songs."

"The logos there?"

"I think that one's for PINK. There's a designer called that. And that's OAM. One a.m. A band."

Minogue sighed.

"I'm truly lost," he said. "Bad enough that I'm a culchie, but I think I must have been living on another planet this last while."

He waited for another smile from her. Then he decided it was time.

"Did you take Ecstasy pills yourself, Bronagh?"

Completely still, her eyes locked onto the edge of the table. Minogue thought of Jennifer Halloran again, the blunders.

Mr. O'Neill crossed and uncrossed his legs.

Mrs. O'Neill's darting eyes, and she put her hand on her daughter's shoulder, flickered from her daughter to Minogue and back.

"We talked," she said, hoarsely, and swallowed. "Bronagh will tell you. Won't you, love?"

Minogue hardly heard her.

"It's not a crime," he said. "You'll be getting no lectures from me."

"Yes," she whispered.

She was moving her jaw from side to side but wouldn't look up.

"I didn't see her go," she said, and began to shudder. "I didn't see her. I would have gone with her."

She fell sideways toward her mother, and put her arms around her.

"Bronagh has a summer job now," Mr. O'Neill said. "She'll be busy. And then we're all going over to my sister. She's outside Washington. It's going to be all right."

He leaned in, patted her shoulder. Minogue heard her wail smothered in her mother's shoulders.

He let his thoughts run to the clearing in the woods over Shankill, that patch between the gorse that opened out over the sea. It'd be soggy enough there now. He didn't care. He'd give it until eight or even half eight, when the light would begin to change in earnest, and he'd head up.

"Bronagh," he said in a gap between her sobs, and he waited.

"Bronagh, is it going on with others here in school?"

She nodded.

"It was Niamh had them," she whispered. "She showed them to us back before exams. But I wouldn't."

"Did you take one that night?"

She nodded. Minogue thought it was the mother's breath going in that he'd heard now. Mr. O'Neill was staring at the wall.

"You're lucky to be alive."

The girl became very still. Minogue saw that her eyes had lost their focus. Was she going to keel over, he wondered.

The mother broke the spell, slowly rubbing the girl's fore-arm.

"You say she had several. How many?"

"Maybe seven or eight. They had different marks on them," she said then. "And she said, Niamh said, that she had her own one. A special one, a present."

"A present from whom?"

"I don't know, I don't know any name."

"Another girl maybe?"

"No. But she slagged him."

"Not a boyfriend?"

The quick twist, the nose wrinkling might be a sign she was coming around, Minogue thought.

"God no. 'A lad' she called him. That's sarcastic, like."

"Not a term of respect, is it?"

She shook her head.

"A scruff, is another word. I didn't hear her say that, but it means the same."

"Was there anything about where or when she met this fella then?"

"No—wait. No. But she just said she'd been bored out of her skull some days, down at her parents' place, somewhere in Wicklow. They have this place, I don't know what you'd call it. Mom?"

"The Links, it's called," said Mrs. O'Neill. "It's a resort down in Kilcoole."

Minogue remembered coming across the place a few years ago on a jaunt with Kathleen down the backroads from Wicklow town. A hotel and spa thing, chalets, with lots of landscaping and golfey things. Pricey, he recalled Kathleen telling him, a country club type of a thing that had sold quickly. A weekend place you could turn the key on, a view of the sea, all organized and only thirty miles or so from Dublin.

"Kilcoole," he said.

"She used to go into town, but there was nothing to do, Bronagh said. I think that's what she said. She didn't want to go there on those weekends, but her parents used to go. It's golf, I think."

"Into town, do you mean back into Dublin?"

"No. Sometimes her parents, well her mother, might go back in as far as Bray with her. Some shopping, I think, you know."

Exhausted, she looked, already. Minogue let the quiet work on the parents too.

"Some fella then, we think," he said finally.

Bronagh nodded.

"Maybe someone she met in, where is it again, Kilcoole? Bray maybe?"

"That's all I know, honestly."

Minogue felt the father's eyes on him now. Testy. Well fine, he thought, let them wait. There had to be something better than "a fella."

He began to rearrange Niamh Kenny's copybooks and scraps around the table. His mobile sounded.

Tunney said it was about the girl.

"Wait a minute, will you," Minogue said. He looked at Mrs. O'Neill.

"I'm just going out to take this call outside. I'll only be a minute."

He saw the can't-we-go-glance the girl threw at her mother.

"Bronagh," he said getting up. "I want you to do something now, if you please, while I'm taking this call."

There was wariness as much as the shock on her face now. Friends were everything at this age, weren't they. It wouldn't be at this session she'd be willing to tell him everything. And the parents know, he thought, they do.

"I want you to look over these," he said to her. "See if you can spot anything on these—doodling, drawing, letters, words, anything that strikes a chord with you. Anything that might tell us about this fella."

He closed the door and rested his elbows on the windowsill at the end of the hall. The clouds had shapes to them now, he saw, not the blanket of grey that had dumped tons of rain on them. This was promising.

"Okay," he said. "Sorry about that. I was interviewing her friend there, the O'Neill girl."

"Well, what's the story with her?"

"I don't know. I can't really push it today. Tell me yours, why don't you."

"Okay," said Tunney. "There's a woman just come in to the station here, with a phone her young fella found the other day. A mobile phone."

"Niamh Kenny's?"

"Looks like it," Tunney said, on account of where he found it. Up in the park is where. Him and his mate. It was the mate told his ma, and that ma went over to the other ma. She found it in the boy's room.

"I'm going back to the house with this woman and have a chat with the young fella. He's ten, only."

Minogue ended the call. He let his gaze rest on the yard and the fields beyond. Was there ever a lonelier place than a school during the summer.

Bronagh had to know more than this. He thought about putting the heavy word on the O'Neills. He didn't doubt but that they could bite back: a Garda intimidating a minor, a distraught minor—he sensed the presence in the hall behind. Mrs. Tovey had materialized in a doorway.

"I heard the voice," she said. "Didn't quite remember you were here."

He held up his mobile. He made sure he had locked the keypad and slid it into his pocket.

"How's it going inside?"

"Well, we're working through things," was all he could think to say.

"It'll take a long, long time for them to process this at all," she said. "To really get back on an even keel."

He nodded.

"They're still kids," she said. "Even with the mobiles and the skiing and the travels. They're not half as worldly wise as they might try to have us believe."

He looked at the door, where Bronagh O'Neill and her parents were waiting.

"You won't mind me asking now," he said, "but do you ever wonder if there are things going on in these girls' lives now, well some of them anyway, that are kind of invisible to other people?"

"Like me? Like their parents?"

"That's what I mean."

"You hardly mean the secrets and schemes and romance stuff."

"Something else I was thinking," he said.

Mrs. Tovey looked beyond him to the window out onto the playing fields.

"I do," she said, "and it worries me as much as it worries their parents, I think."

She made a half smile that reminded him of the expressions he thought he'd only seen in court, when a verdict or a stay had gone against the State.

"It's very different nowadays," she said, "isn't it."

A Rat, Surely

Grogan actually didn't appreciate the door of the restaurant being held open for him. Still he nodded. How could he growl at the young man who was decent enough to know that doors should be held open for the likes of him? It wasn't just to impress the girl with him. There was a strong whiff of cologne as he got by him. So this was it then, he thought. When Catholic kids can go out and buy perfume or leather jackets or cars for themselves, that's when we know when we've won. Or maybe not.

Kelly was at the counter already; Gallagher had a table. Was it tea, Kelly wanted to know. Grogan said that it was, and he made his way around the oul wans and their shopping bags clustered around them. Someone—Gallagher, he guessed—had already tucked in the chairs to give him room to manoeuvre.

Gallagher knew better than to ask if he wanted a hand. But still he lifted a chair with one hand and placed it by the table ahead of him.

"How's the man," he said.

"Not so bad."

Grogan wondered as he slid down into the chair if Gallagher was still proud of any chance to show how strong his arms were. A vanity no one could argue with, to be sure, though. He had watched Gallagher propel that wheelchair of his down the road like a bloody ladder, the biceps and the gloves, the chest huge on him leaning forward, hell-bent on doing all the Belfast marathon in a record time.

Never one for blather, Grogan remembered, even before the shooting that had done him in. Still Gallagher had told him a few years ago that the one thing that scared him now, the only thing, was if he couldn't move when he had to, when they came for him. Not if but when, and the them being, Grogan guessed, the Red Hand or someone hired by the Brits to finally top him. It had cost them nearly half a million quid so far, Gallagher had also told him: grants for fixing the house, the dole and disability, chairs, mobility, job training. He'd heard that Gallagher had started carrying an automatic any time he left his house now. Nothing to lose now, apparently.

The teapot was one of those spill-it models. Kelly swore, but didn't stop pouring. Grogan watched the young fella, the door holder, and his girl. Cappuccinos, the both of them. Maybe he worked in computers, maybe she did. For a moment he wondered if these were the people who bought all the weekend drugs, or cocaine.

Kelly had been eyeing them too. He flicked his eyes to Gallagher and back for Gallagher's take on the couple. Gallagher shrugged. Kelly turned to Grogan.

"Sorry to take you away from the gardening now," he said. "But we need to get ahead of this, this thing."

"You better say what," Grogan said. "And back it up."

Kelly gave him a look and then he poured milk.

"It's the fella he works with," Gallagher said. "Tight with him, so he is. The name of Canning."

"I know his name," Grogan said. "He's just window-dressing. Doesn't get the goods at all."

"Well, how would we ever be sure of that?" Kelly asked.

Grogan stirred his tea.

"We're always back to Quinn," Kelly went on. "Taking Quinn's word for it. You standing in for him."

"You know something," Grogan said after a pause, "you never got over the fact that he's not political, did you."

"It's not that," Gallagher said.

"Well, it fucking is," Grogan said, calmly. "As much as it is that you don't trust any of them down there."

"It's not Quinn we're talking about, Liam," Kelly said. "Okay?"

Grogan shrugged and tasted the tea.

"The fella's been talking," Kelly went on. "He's a rat surely."

"Who is?"

Kelly leaned in.

"This Canning. How much do you know him?"

"I saw him the once, met him down at that place in Kells that time."

"And what did you think of him then?"

"I didn't think much. But he was only in for show, so I didn't give him much time."

"He goes back a way with Quinn."

"If Quinn brought him on board, that was his call. I don't question him on that."

"That was then," Kelly said. "But when Canning saw some of the money coming through, where this was going . . . ?"

Grogan put down his cup. Gallagher was looking from face to face in the restaurant. Grogan watched the couple leave the restaurant with their coffee in those take-out cups. Right, he thought, they drink it while they're walking around these days.

"Okay," he said. "Let's hear it."

"Canning gets paid by the Guards there," said Kelly. "They think Quinn has something going, but they can't see it. So they got his mate. And from what I hear, this mate wasn't very hard to get on the payroll."

Grogan tried to remember what Canning looked like. He couldn't get beyond short, strong-looking; a lout, though. He watched Gallagher flex his fingers in his gloves.

"You know we have someone in their place there, what do you call it—"

"—CDU," said Gallagher.

"That's it, but our source says that this Canning is putting his leg over the wall with them."

"How much?"

"Not a big thing, but I hear he slips the odd word out, the odd time. The man is definitely touting, Liam."

"How long?" Grogan asked.

"Only found out yesterday. Says it can't be that long, on account he'd have heard before, or at least a hint."

Grogan waited for Gallagher to look up from flexing his fingers.

"The way it looks," Kelly said, "is that Canning was always in with them, some bit. From before."

Gallagher's eyebrows went up, and then he pretended to be interested in the creamy thing Kelly had brought over with the tea. Grogan looked away to the oul wans. They were gathering themselves to go. He wondered if their husbands were off together in a pub, or a bookie's maybe. Women lived longer because they were better connected, didn't they.

"Well we have it so that we all decide," Grogan said. "That hasn't changed, right?"

"Course we do," said Kelly. "This doesn't affect anything about that. Not a thing."

Grogan knew that it was probably peculiar that he felt nothing now that he had decided. A nod of his head would do it, and he didn't have to get involved after this meeting. Meeting, he thought; this cup of tea, Earl Grey, and a gawk at some cream buns or something that only Kelly would end up eating. Yes, meetings. He'd dealt with all kinds of life at meetings. Prison guards who thought they could squeeze them for more all the while pretending they were onside. Dutchmen and Libyans and Yanks who considered Ireland to be a backward hole, the most of them, where they could turn money into more money or use it for leverage or points or pressure elsewhere. The so-called intellectuals who wanted to rub shoulders with them, meet what they called "active service" people, to get their jollies from the smell of cordite and the solidarity forever crap. That was over half his life, those meetings.

"I'll talk to Quinn then."

"No, Liam," Kelly said. "No dice."

Grogan looked to Gallagher. The eyebrows did the talking again.

"Has to go, Liam," Kelly said. "And if Quinn knows ahead of time, it'll go bad."

"This is too quick," Grogan said. "There's too much happening there, after the operation the other day. He needs time to evaluate."

"It can't wait," Gallagher said. "It can't."

Grogan moved his cup and saucer to a new spot. He licked his fingertip and pressed it to the spilled granules of sugar.

"We wouldn't expect him to take care of it himself," Kelly said. "No way."

"Very decent of you."

"Nothing's easy, Liam. But we need to keep our eye on the ball."

"Let me ask you something," Grogan said. "The both of you. You believe me when I tell you that he said nothing to Canning about the business, the Albanians?"

Kelly nodded. Gallagher looked toward the windows again.

"I spent nearly three years with him," Grogan said. "I know what sort of a man he is. What he would or wouldn't do."

"Okay," Kelly said.

"If he gave me his word that it's only him knows about the job with those two, that's good enough for me."

Gallagher pulled at the fingers of his gloves. Grogan's eye lingered on them. Like a racing driver, he thought. Gallagher went through them pretty quickly, he'd heard.

"Which two," Gallagher said. "There were four altogether, am I right?"

"I can count," Grogan said. "I meant the first two."

Kelly met his eyes, and Grogan understood that it was more than just Canning now. He looked at Gallagher. Gallagher pulled at his wheels every now and then, and let the chair rock back. Kelly lit a cigarette. Would it be Roe again, Grogan wondered. The expert.

THE BOHEMIAN AMBASSADOR

Minogue walked around still puddles by the side of the school. He imagined what Kathleen's reaction would be. How'd it go for you today? A trying day. I was interviewing crying schoolgirls half the day.

The Citroën was down on its haunches completely now, of course. He sat in and settled his notebook on the steering wheel. He had marked and numbered the corroborations with his red Biro. There were no expressions that jumped out to say they had rehearsed what they'd tell the Guards. The times matched, their recollections of what they said to one another. All the girls were upset they hadn't seen Niamh leaving. Fair enough.

He stared at the wreck he wouldn't sell, his conglomeration of French mechanical flair. Maybe it did look like a water buffalo or a shot rhino, like Kilmartin said. The weather-stripping by the back window could hardly be glued again. Rotating the tires wouldn't make the one he studied any less bald. A company car, in private security?

He looked back up at the school. "And what did you learn at school today," he murmured.

(A) That these girls' parents wanted to put as much distance between their kids, their lives, their futures, and a dead Niamh Kenny. One parent, the Fanning girl's mother, had done a lousy job of masking the fact that they wished this was forgotten about. Imagine: she'd had to actually allow her daughter to be interviewed by the Guards over this.

(B) That headmistress, Mrs. Tovey, turned out to be game ball. He took no satisfaction in telling her after the last interview that there were probably a half-dozen girls who'd taken Ecstasy or the like from that group. He remembered watching her frown, the distracted look, then the resolution in her voice. "We need to know these things," she'd said. "We can't be quiet about this."

(C) That he was losing the battle to keep words out of his head: "unfortunate," "accidental," even "misadventure."

The rubber seal around the edge of the sunroof was pinched again. He pushed at the offending part, itself frayed from the same treatment over the years. He stopped.

The man eyeing him was half into a battered Lancia, one of the old ones. A salt-and-pepper beard not far gone beyond heavy stubble, and sunglasses; a ponytail. A whitish linen style of jacket over a cobalt blue shirt telegraphed artsy to Minogue. The ambassador from Bohemia.

He nodded at him.

The man seemed to decide something. He uncurled himself from the car seat and headed over. Minogue took in the slow rangy walk of him. The insouciant ambassador, he guessed. He turned on the ignition, the electric window grunted and squeaked by the rubber seals.

"You're a Guard, right."

"I'm the Archbishop of Dublin," Minogue said.

"Undercover?"

"And you're?"

"Marc Chagall, Your Worship."

Minogue gave him the once-over and he fetched up his icy smile.

"Ah sure, Marc, I wouldn't recognize you. How have you been, since they buried you."

"That's the idea."

"I'm so used to seeing you fly by, overhead."

"Are you, now. Well for a culchie, you know a bit."

"For a broken-down hippie, you still have some interesting prejudices."

"East or west Clare?"

"You tell me. Mr. Shag-All."

"I'd go with the West. Rocky. Contrary."

"Okay then. I'll give you five points for that."

"You should give me a damn sight more than that. I spend three months a year in Fanore."

"I didn't think they had cappuccino there."

"There's a time of day, up a road there when the stones move."

"You should steer clear of the local poteen. A fella was blinded not so long ago."

"I don't mean move, I mean *move*. It's the light."

"It's probably German tourists rooting about there somewhere. They're heavy."

"I figure there's a few more years in the place before Starbucks."

"Not so long," Minogue said. "It's been gone that way this past long while."

"You don't go anymore?"

"I do. I was born and reared above the Pass."

"I might have seen you then over the times. Greene's?"

"I might risk a pint late in O'Lochin's. For old-time's sake."

"The father is still in it."

Minogue nodded. The quiet, the taciturnity he liked almost as much as sitting at the counter in the quiet.

"Well, I never saw you there."

"How well you wouldn't. I like to be out of the way during the daytime."

Ponytail Bohemian ambassador looked across at the playing fields.

"I'm Tom Anderson," he said to the grass, it seemed to Minogue. "I teach art here."

"I'm Garda Minogue."

"Niamh Kenny?"

Minogue stared at him.

"Have you a minute? Come over to the car and I'll show you something."

BUSINESS AS USUAL

Bobby Quinn drew on his cigarette again. Grogan had said five minutes. He had switched phones, and walked out to the car for the call. He looked at his watch again. Ten minutes had gone by.

He looked out the passenger window at Canning helping the driver load the boxes for the pound shop run. Everything from fecking replacement stoppers for your sink to bars of chocolate that had stuff like cherry peanut crap in them that no one wanted to buy. To think that he had enjoyed doing the runs himself when he first got started. But there had been the few pints on the way back to Dublin, a laugh at the culchies. There had been the brassers doing their trade next door to the place in the Newbridge too. Ages ago, it seemed.

He drew hard on his cigarette, counted what was left in the box. Yes, smoking like a frigging chimney. He couldn't get much more jumpy than he was. A half an hour ago, had jumped at the sound of tape ripping on the boxes. It had taken a few minutes for him to realize that it was from Roe taping plastic yesterday.

Canning had stopped helping with the boxes. He stood smoking by the back of the lorry, eyeing him. He didn't want to lose it, to snap at Canning, but it had come close. Earlier on he'd been whinging how opening all the boxes was stupid, that they'd have to repackage them again. To Catherine: Well are you going to be home for tea or not? He should get sleeping pills or something. The phone rang.

"I shouldn't be talking to you right now," Grogan said.

Quinn felt his chest go tight.

"You better tell me what you mean."

"Well, I can only go so far with that."

The quiet way Grogan was speaking brought him out of the dull tension he'd felt growing, smothering him.

"I met with some people," Grogan said. "You know them. It wasn't what you might say a routine meeting."

Quinn concentrated on the smoke coming from the tip of his cigarette. Grogan had always had that way with words, making one ordinary word sound important. Some way he had of seeming to slow things down a bit so's you knew you understood what he was saying.

"There was a decision taken," he said. "It concerns you, but not directly."

"Tell me, then."

"It's awkward. The decision is in the nature of a general thing. I don't know exactly what's going to be done."

He was waiting for him, Quinn realized.

"They don't know I'm contacting you."

Something began to move together for Quinn now. He turned in his seat to take in all around him.

"You have to tell me something," he said to Grogan. "Some clue, you know."

"You're at your place, are you?"

"Well, I'm at work. Packing lorries. Look, what is it?"

Grogan didn't reply immediately.

"There's a leak," he said then. "And it's not here. That's all I'm telling you."

Quinn felt it as a pulse that reached down to the pads on his fingertips. The quiet on the phone, the resigned way that Grogan spoke, drove it home worse.

"It's three now," Grogan said. "You remember that place we did the meetings, back there at the start? You know the place."

"Today, you mean?"

"Today. And you're coming on your own."

Quinn looked out at Canning. Now he had the driver standing around smoking too.

"It'll just be me," Grogan said. "I'll be there from six on. If I get any flak at the border, I'll give you two rings and hang up."

"Liam," Quinn said. "I don't know about this."

"Like I said, Bobby, I shouldn't even be phoning."

Quinn kept his cigarette to the very end, until the filter began to scorch. Canning sauntering over broke the spell.

"What are you so happy about," Canning said.

The lorry driver glanced over and grinned. Quinn did a quick count of the boxes still on the ground.

"Is that stuff ready to go," he said.

"Near enough," said Canning. "Are we in a huge rush or something?"

Quinn looked up into Canning's face, but he said nothing.

"Okay, okay, Bobby. I hear and obey. Business as usual."

He watched Canning's jaunty walk back to the lorry. He didn't hear whatever comment he made to the driver, who grinned and threw his head back before flicking his cigarette away. He switched off the phone and checked the battery. He'd be needing it tonight.

A Bit of Chaos

Minogue left Niamh Kenny's watercolours on top and he laid the sheaf back on the seat. Anderson was resting against the door, one arm over the wheel, his left arm along the top of the driver's seat. What kind of a gobshite takes off the headrests on a car, Minogue had wondered. Smoke from a Gauloise curled to the roof, flattened, and eddied toward the window.

Hairy arms like an ape, Minogue was thinking. He'd decided that Mr. Anderson must go to some trouble each day to arrange his hair so that his widow's peak was minimal.

There's a lot in there, Anderson said. Bold with colour there—the bit of the mountain or hill there—not confidence, or real skill now. But look at what she did with the textures.

All of which meant nothing to Minogue. He remembered the time he used to smoke Gauloises himself.

"You were going to bring those over to her parents?"

"I was thinking of it but I probably would have waited a few days at least."

"Why didn't you just hand these into the office and let them take care of it?"

Anderson's jaw set and then his face gave way with a thin smile.

"Well? Why didn't you?"

"I'll tell you why. It's because of Niamh's imagination, and her vision, and the things she loved. I didn't want them processed through the office."

"Processed," said Minogue.

Anderson raised his eyebrows.

"They call me Picasso, did you know?"

"I didn't."

"And the studio is Guernica. Clever, isn't it?"

"I don't have an agenda in that regard."

"Maybe you should try."

Minogue searched his face. The smile had changed to a sour grin.

"I feel a speech coming on."

Anderson turned to him.

"You probably know that Niamh wasn't exactly the prize student here. But she sure liked art. I'm not saying she was good at it, or would be. But this is what she did best here."

"You liked Niamh."

"Yeah, I liked Niamh."

"Did she know that?"

"She did. I think she did. It showed in her work. I hope."

Minogue watched him roll the cigarette around between his thumb and forefinger.

"Did you meet with her much," he murmured.

Anderson stopped rolling the cigarette.

"You should be ashamed of yourself," he said.

Minogue weighed, wondered, waited, watched.

There was the usual, of course, the emotional jackals who wanted in on someone's calamity to rubber neck, to dip their toes a bit and then to scurry back to safety of their world. *Schadenfreude*, a cliché by now.

He watched Anderson smoke, and wondered if he could be that rare one. The one who wanted the icing after the crime, the one who wanted, or was even driven to, tease, to dare. Mind games. The one who showed up for the funeral; the one anxious to help, the one who sought out the cops to chat to and get in on the game.

"Why did you wait here to talk to me?"

Anderson shrugged.

"How'd you know I'd be here?"

"Well, herself mentioned it. Sandra."

He nodded in the direction of the main building. Mrs. Tovey, Minogue realized.

"It takes me a few days to clean up at the end of term."

He turned back to Minogue and fixed him with a glance.

"You know," he said. "I should have expected that from you. You get to hear it all eventually. But you forget."

"I don't get it."

"What a non-teacher would think. Especially a cop."

Minogue studied the receding hair, the wrinkles.

"You must have enjoyed the sixties a lot, did you."

"You're thinking crushes, admit it."

"Tell me it doesn't happen, so."

"You think I teach here for all this while and not know that?"

"Look," Minogue said. "I got the idea. You're not so keen on administration. You're a rebel. How far does that go?"

Anderson's eyebrows shot up.

"Ask around," he said. "Check me out."

Minogue gave a slow nod.

"They do care here," Anderson said. "Really they do. But they miss things."

"Who," Minogue said. "Teachers, is it? Miss what?"

Anderson moved a cheap digital watch off his wristbone.

"Adults," he said. "In general. Not noticing. They're numb, don't you find."

He looked away again. Minogue waited until the quiet registered with Anderson.

"Sounds to me that you knew her very well."

"I'll take that as a compliment."

"Do you take the same interest in all of your students?"

"Since I started here, just after the Ice Age, I have taught over 4,000 students."

Minogue let him believe his point had been made.

"You didn't get around to telling me what keeps you in it."

"Well, it's none of your business, actually."

"I say it is," Minogue said. "I'm trying to find out how and why a schoolgirl is dead. And one of her teachers is talking to me, and seems to know the girl quite well. That'd definitely be my business."

Anderson cleared something Minogue didn't want to see from the tip of his tongue, looked at it, and flicked it out onto the tarmacadam.

"Is there something that you're forgetting to tell me here, about Niamh? Her friends?"

Anderson looked up at the spreading branches nearby.

"But I think that she might have had something. And I won't forget her. Her boldness, I suppose. Limits, edges. Frontiers. Boundaries being explored."

Impulsive, Minogue translated within. Niamh Kenny, risk-taker. A turn-on for this superannuated hepcat?

"She didn't turn away," Anderson went on. "When there were mistakes, or stuff broken, she kept at it. I think she knew that it's the broken stuff, the false starts, all that messy starting over, that's the way important stuff gets done—and that it ain't pretty."

Artsy talk was a sure flag of surrender, Minogue had been told by Iseult; like track pants, slippers, diet beer. Well, someone had to teach Art, didn't they. Maybe it was the glibness, or Minogue's growing certainty that Anderson had delivered the likes of these weighty insights into artistic creativity many a time before, and would again. But his antennae were no longer humming on this fella.

"How can I reach you?"

"Pardon?"

Minogue looked in at the leather upholstery in the Lancia again. A crap car after the first few years, he remembered. Temperamental, dear crap.

"I'm a Garda, Mr. Anderson. I'm investigating the death of a young woman, a schoolgirl, maybe I should say. I might call on you to help in our inquiries."

He thought he heard a soft sigh of disbelief. Maybe it was anger, he thought as he drove away. Contempt, probably.

MOOD CHANGES, THAT
SORT OF THING?

About of listlessness, along with the too-familiar strangeness he got, or that got him, in the late afternoons, had Minogue by the window gawking at nothing. Clouds ran low over the south city, in patches and torn fleece and shovelled-up clumps. They were impossible to turn to any shape or figure. Still he tried.

He listened to the noises below him in the Garda station, felt too the low hum of the place, and wondered if it was talk or electricity or computer fans or water or gutters still draining rain off the roof. Noticing things, was Anderson's gig then.

He had the place to himself. Once, a boisterous Guard had barged in. Laughing with a cannonading bellow in the hall outside, full of taunts and a fluency in cursing that Minogue hadn't heard for a long while, he called for Tunney, "You fucker come out where I can get hold of you, you fucking whore's get, come out, you fecking Carlow buff, come out, let you."

He hadn't seemed overly embarrassed to find Minogue looking up from his perch by the window. Tunney was out, could he give him a message. "He could," said the Guard, "bring in the fucking tools I loaned him, the wife wants the kitchen finished this weekend bejasus or there'll be blood and snots flying around my house."

Then a sly but lively chat, a laugh Minogue hadn't expected when this Guard, Dan Moynihan, agreed that Mayo were dreaming when they thought they could come home with a win in Limerick on Sunday. Thicks, to think that. But you had to hand it to them for believing in themselves. Up Cork, was Moynihan's approach. Still, he hated them for the concussion they'd handed the Tipperary captain a fortnight ago. The bastards would rue the day they sank to that. A handshake like a blacksmith, see ya again, er.

And back to thinking. Moynihan's cynical benevolence, his savage cheer, had energized him. He pulled the big watercolour up to the top again. "Well, okay then," he murmured. Why couldn't that be Bray Head. Maybe that was supposed to be the seafront and the lights. "Wonderland," she'd called it.

Anderson: his notions. The colossal arrogance. The one-eyed king. Easy to be top dog with impressionable kids around. How could he verify what Anderson had told him? No how.

Niamh had told him it wasn't the Alice in Wonderland idea. Well, what? The assignment was to think up the place where you are happy, that place you go to in your imagination. It could be anywhere. When you were bored out of your skull in class and you took your mind off somewhere. Your escape from the normal, a magic place.

Anderson hadn't pressed her on it, he'd said. To talk about too much would ruin it, or block it, fair enough. Plus he had a class to run, other kids to help. He remembered trying her again afterwards too, when she was finished, where it was.

Niamh didn't like what she had done but had to leave it—she'd be getting marked on it. He'd told her not to worry, that it was more than acceptable. That she had tried hard, that it could be a theme, a motif she could return to again and again to work out in later life.

Minogue looked up from the paper.

Is that the way teachers talked to kids these days?

He had to talk to the Kennys tonight about what Anderson had told him. And, what's more, he wouldn't be waiting for Mrs. Tovey anymore. He dialled her office number. She answered it herself.

"It's Inspector Minogue again," he said.

"I was getting ready to phone you. I had to double-check."

He waited. She turned a page, moved the phone around.

"A total of six school days," she said. "The last was a day in the first week of June."

"Explanations?"

"Two don't have any notation. We put an N or a P, note from parent or phone call. We expect a note."

"The June one."

"That's one of them, and the one the last week of May. So, they're only a week apart, when you look at them like that."

"No ideas then, where she was? At home, or sick?"

"No," she said. "I'd need time to follow up on that, yes. There would have been some communication with parents."

"Who does that?"

"I do some. Then we have a vice-principal, Mrs. McCutcheon, who's away in Germany, unfortunately. I don't recall dealing with this . . . so should I be getting in touch with Mrs. McCutcheon about it? Will that be necessary?"

Minogue turned the picture sideways. Why would there be a dragon wrapped around a peace sign? Maybe connected to the yin-yang thing she did.

"Well," he said. "It'd be grand if you'd locate her, have a phone number for her in case we need to get a hold of her."

"Done."

Magritte, he thought. Had Niamh seen any of his? Was that the effect she was after with this picture?

"I'm obliged to you. I'll be in touch."

"Before you go," she said. "Excuse me now. I have a sense that you are following something a bit more definite in regards to Niamh's school life."

"Now, Mrs. Tovey. I'm trying to fill in more of a picture of Niamh. To get a sense of what she was like."

"Mr. Anderson, then, was a help. I told him he should talk to you."

"He seems to pick up on a lot," Minogue said. "Mr. Picasso."

She smiled.

"We do value Stephen here, yes we do. He's an institution among us."

He stopped marshalling the paperclips he'd been deploying around the desktop without knowing it.

"Have you ever had cause to worry about him?"

There was a pause before she spoke.

"If I said to you this was a matter of professional confidentiality, I think you'd get the wrong idea."

"Well, how wrong?"

"He's a dedicated teacher. The very best. There's never been the slightest trace of, well, what can I say. You know what I mean, now, don't you?"

He pushed one paperclip to get the stray wire end back in line.

"I know I asked you this already. It's about drugs. You might have remembered something more, now?"

"I have been thinking, and I'd still go by what I said this

morning. Did I mention that our teachers are inserviced about symptoms and behaviours to look for?"

"Mood changes, that sort of thing?"

He didn't mistake the hint of drollery in her voice.

"We could have a long, long conversation about that," she said. "But I'm not sure you'd be any the wiser. I'm not sure I'd be any the wiser either."

IT'S ABOUT TRUST

It had been months since Quinn had been in Drogheda. The town had caught plenty of the good times, and the new estates on the Dublin side were still being built. He'd never really found out for sure whether it was true that the real go-boys stayed in Dundalk still up on the border. There had been an accident near the new by-pass, but RTE didn't tell anyone on the radio until the jam was good and thick. The tail backs went half a mile anyway that he could see.

Two Garda cars had gone by him, heading for the accident, then an ambulance. He wondered, as the second squad car went by him on the inside, if it was only about ten feet from where that Guard sat, to the gun he had put under the passenger seat. Things you think about.

He thought about phoning Grogan after a few minutes of complete standstill. He decided not to bother. If it was important, Grogan could wait. The car was on its roof in a field, down a gradual embankment, the other, with its driver side torn to shit all down to the back bumper—a nice new Jag too—was in the ditch across the road. The rain, Quinn thought, the gusts of wind. There was a crew of men from the County Council it looked like, putting up a new sign in the ditch "Welcome to the Land of Legends."

It was ten after when he saw Grogan's Fiat parked at a meter along Shop Street. He went by the car, turned the corner, and found a spot by the café: Bridie's Traditional Irish Food. No, it wasn't a joke. The blustery wind and on-and-off rain had emptied the footpaths. He felt for the grip of the pistol under the piece of carpeting and drew it over the hump by the seat front. He checked the street up and down again and he picked up the pistol. He thumbed the safety again and slid it into his pocket.

The pub had a new coat of paint, striped awnings, and a sign flapping and cracking in the wind. The umbrellas were tied and beads shuddered and slid on the iron tables no one was using.

He headed straight through toward the toilets. Grogan had found a spot along the wall and was reading a paper. Quinn stopped at the door to the toilets and looked back. He hadn't missed anyone in his walk through. The white-haired oul fella up near the window was sitting across from a chair with a woman's coat draped over the back.

He washed his hands and headed back. The woman, as old as her husband, was back. The waitress, cashier, and general bottlewasher for a slow day said hello to him.

Grogan put down the paper when he sat across from him.

Poxy weather was all Quinn could think of to say.

The waitress was over already. Grogan didn't order more tea for himself. He watched the waitress head back to the counter, the old couple begin to get ready to head out into the weather.

"Okay, Robert," Grogan said. Quinn watched him do his twist thing to adjust something so he could put his elbows on the table.

"You remember back when we got started, do you? When you started your sentence."

Quinn nodded.

"How we used to talk about things, in the groups? The future?"

"I remember."

"You know then what we're dealing with here now."

Grogan winced as he moved in his seat.

"It's the trust thing again," he murmured, and breathed out.

"Not politics then," Quinn said.

Grogan shook his head.

"Well, that's a fucking relief then, sort of."

"I can tell you're annoyed," Grogan said. "You don't have to advertise it."

Quinn returned the look for a few moments.

"There's been a lot happening," he said. "Anybody would be a little touchy, for Christ's sake. Don't you think?"

Grogan pursed his lips and pushed his thumbs together.

"Okay," Quinn said. "Let's hear it."

Grogan concentrated on his thumbs as the colour drained from them.

"Is this about the job, the other day?"

"Partly. Where's your mate at the moment? Canning."

"I didn't bring him. Like you told me not to."

Grogan ignored the tone.

"Would you have? If I hadn't told you."

"I don't know. I'm used to him. Anything comes up, he can handle it."

Grogan breathed out as he relaxed his hands.

"He goes out with you, on business? And I don't mean driving boxes of plastic Chinese toys up and down the country to those pound shops."

"He does that too. Sometimes a driver won't show up. They're only paid by the run. That's why he's handy."

"How much does Canning know, then?"

Quinn pushed his shoulders back and found a spot against the rim of the chair back.

"Only what he needs to know. Like I'm always saying, when this comes up."

"You're sure."

"Yeah, I'm sure."

"He gets a fair cut."

"Too fucking right he does."

"Does he know the cash though, overall?"

"He might. He's not thick. He sees it coming in, more of it now."

Grogan sat back, seemed to gather himself. Quinn began to think of Catherine again, the mood she'd be in when he got home. She'd never get over that time she found out about the sessions down the Blessington Road those times with those women.

"Look," he said to Grogan. "Didn't we go through all this, but, like a dozen times?"

"We did."

"You always knew that Beansie's no politician any more than I am. He just does a job. It's good to have him there in the window, that's my attitude. Isn't that good enough anymore? I mean, what do you want me to do? What do *they* want?"

"They?"

"Come on. You know. 'It's about trust,' you said. Didn't you?"

The waitress slid the plate of scones onto the near side of the table. They were to give her a shout if they wanted more jam. Quinn looked into the pot to see if the tea was ready.

"That's right," he said. "We all have our limitations. I mean, we're talking about two very different places still."

Quinn looked up from the pot.

"Well, I don't know when they're going to get it. Do you? I mean what does it take? I've done everything according to cocker here, you know. Everything. Don't they get that yet?"

"It's 'we,' Bobby. Give over with the 'they want this' and the 'they don't know.'"

Quinn pushed the tea bag against the side of the pot with the back of his spoon.

"Look," he said. "Did I drive all the way here, get in shite with the missus, get stuck in the rain and a traffic jam, just to get a speech? It must be slow times you're having up there if that's all that's on the agenda."

Grogan looked across at the old photographs of the town, the dried flowers, the local artists' drawings next to the windows.

"This isn't like you," he said. "You need to calm down. Get your wits about you. Now, more than ever."

"You better spell it out, Liam."

"I asked you where this man was tonight, Canning. And I didn't hear your answer, did I?"

Quinn put down the spoon. Something had changed here but he didn't know what. Grogan was staring at the tea bag now.

"You don't know, do you."

"No. Should I?"

"I think you should."

He edged forward.

"'Cause the word today is, your mate's a tout, Robert."

Quinn kept his eyes on the waitress wiping the table, lifting the cup and saucer.

"Yous are all paranoid up there," he whispered. "Fucking paranoid, the lot of you."

"Maybe so, maybe so. But that's how it goes there. And you can't change that."

"You can take it from me—"

"—Listen to me."

Quinn looked down at the knuckles, Grogan's grip on his forearm.

"I don't think you're listening," Grogan whispered. He let go slowly.

"Have you forgotten everything, how we talked, how we said it would be?"

"No."

"It doesn't matter there."

"I've done everything they wanted, I'm doing my bit. The proof is there for Christ's sake, the job . . ."

Quinn stopped then.

"It's that fucking psycho trying to cause trouble. Isn't it? What's his name, the one they sent. Roe. He's an out and out nutter, I don't care what you say. It's him, isn't it?"

"I can't do everything, Robert."

"What's that supposed to mean? Are you gone like them, is that it?"

"It's us, I told you, not them."

"Fuck that, no way. It'll always be them and me. Them and other people. Them and the rest of the world. They'll never get over it—what, should I have been pretending to be the real politico there for them, a provo or something, so's they might begin to excuse the fact I'm a Dublinman, that I wasn't born and beat up and thrown in jail like they were, for oul Ireland? No way. They wanted a man knows his way around, had connections. Someone who could look after things down here. And that's what they got. Now they're still asking questions? They're nuts, that's what they are."

Quinn didn't want any of the scones. Still he plastered them with jam and went at them fiercely. He eyed Grogan occasionally while he ate, watched the fingers close on one another, the stupid things he did with his hands for exercise.

"So?" Quinn said finally and lifted the teapot again.

"It's not going to be people conducting interviews or asking your opinion, you know," Grogan said. "Or mine. Remember that."

"Opinion about what?"

"About what to do."

"I'll tell you what they should do. They should get their facts straight, that's what they should do. Let me talk to them."

Grogan shook his head.

"If they heard you just now," he said, "that'd be enough for them."

"It's not we anymore, I'm hearing. Look. I'm going to do a bit of checking up on my own, so I am. I'll see if there's anything about Beans that looks a bit off."

"Don't."

"Why not? What they need is a wake up, a bit of reality. This paranoid attitude is going to end up wrecking things, that's what."

"Leave Canning. Keep away from him. You have to."

The aftertaste of lukewarm tea soured at the back of Quinn's throat.

"You can't be saying that. You can't."

"You have to, Robert."

"How can I do that? I can't."

Quinn waited for Grogan to say something else, to explain.

Grogan slid an English fiver under the plate. Quinn was slow himself to get up. He knew better than to offer Grogan a hand manoeuvering around the table. There was something about the way Grogan's jaw had set, the way he wouldn't look at him as he put on his coat.

"Is that it then? All the way here?"

Grogan glanced around the restaurant.

"Can't you persuade them? Jesus. It's just stupid what they're saying."

"Think about what I said," Grogan murmured.

Quinn grabbed his arm. Grogan kept pushing the button through at the top of his coat.

"A break," he murmured. "You need a holiday. Get out of Dublin for a few days. A week."

Quinn watched him leave, followed the half sideways walk as Grogan headed out in the blustery street. The scones and jam on top of the crisps he'd eaten on the way weren't going to do his guts any good. The waitress hadn't seen the money yet, and she was sizing him up for paying the bill. The annoyance had gone and Quinn didn't want to think at all about what the slowly falling ache that seemed to start at his ribs might mean.

REFUGE

Minogue had given up on Tunney about ten minutes before the same Tunney finally phoned.

"The young lad, the older one, did fine," Tunney said. "But the little fella kept bawling. I let it go. The parents were ready to rear up on me in anyhow."

They wouldn't be the only ones, Minogue might tell him when this case was put away.

"How was the older lad on his times that day?"

"Not great. He doesn't have a watch."

"Did he say what he thought was going on when he saw her?"

"He said he thought she must be sleeping. Said too that he felt creepy, like he was being watched."

"He said nothing to his ma, or anyone at home?"

"Well," said Tunney, "maybe you know more about what goes on in a kid's head. It was only when the sidekick, the little fella, started getting the willies that it all came out. The little fella had dreams, and he was crying. It was his ma who put two and two together. That's how it got going."

Minogue listened to Tunney's half-hearted walk through his interview notes. There was nothing there really. He looked down at the notes Tunney had made of a session with

Eileen Magee over a cup of tea in the Murphy woman's house. Foxes weren't completely nocturnal, were they.

Tunney said he wouldn't be stopping off at the station. He had an appointment. Minogue almost asked him if Collins had the same kind of appointment.

Ten to five on the clock, a few minutes short of the symmetry which said to him that he need not feel too guilty about heading home. Marooned, he sat back and dithered. He fished out the *Irish Times* where he had reread the page and a half reporting on the murder of the Albanians. He looked again at the official line from the Garda press office: There is no evidence yet that the murders are related to their status as refugees in Ireland. Then the paragraph quoting a Special Branch statement that there was reason to doubt the identities were as stated in the asylum claim. A right frigging mess, he could hear Kilmartin declare. Gangsters popping up all over the kip like jackrats in a demo skip. Im-fecking-possible, the mess dumped on the Guards.

Then the drawing of a fox in the sidebar: "Reynard's return? P. 8."

Hardly. He half-remembered some pointers from an interview with a Dutch-sounding biologist: composting, stress, traffic patterns had driven foxes into urban patterns. Fast-food waste. Had he mentioned that? At least he hadn't tried to say it was a message from the Little People.

Minogue thought then about having those two girls, and their parents, show up at the station for a second interview, and let things happen that way. See if they were so keen to jettison Niamh Kenny, to get on with their lives then. See if their memories improved, about drugs and parties and clubs and everything bloody else that their goms of parents wanted to believe wasn't going on. How much had they kept from their parents, how much had the parents kept from him? Did they think he was an iijit entirely?

Yes, he thought: keep them waiting awhile in the public office here below, under the posters and the notices and the wanted signs. That'd warm them up. And let the parents freak out as much as they'd want. Kilmartin's Way, yes.

He missed Kilmartin, the way he could park people in the system, to let the place get to them. How often Kilmartin had sat back, too often lighting another cigarillo, easing himself occasionally with a light sigh Minogue could bet was a fart, while a narky interview candidate cooled his heels outside. Not quite ripe, Kilmartin would say, and settle back into his chair. Leave them hanging awhile yet.

Whoever had drawn the fox for the newspaper knew how to make it so's the eyes were always on yours, like looking into the camera.

It struck him only then how much he'd strayed. Maybe it was Tunney's take on the Kennys that had coloured it for him from the start. Or was it how the O'Neills had looked at him during the interview with their daughter? The feeling that they were holding their noses, having to deal with policemen and ugly events. There was the slowly building anger he was still trying to ignore when he heard Tynan's name cropping up everywhere. Kenny knew Tynan socially, said Kenny's sister, a substantial pain in the arse, Minogue had concluded, like her brother. Then Mrs. Tovey as much as telling him straight out that Tynan had phoned her to let her know he'd sent Minogue. Minogue, some sort of gillie, an ambassador from Commissioner Tynan sent to calm the waters.

He thought how Kenny talked, like he was issuing directives half the time. The house, the money they must have. Who was the snob now?

He swore and slapped the desktop once and stood. He folded the paper, hurriedly, tried again to rein in his skittery mind. Then he closed the casebook, locked it in the cabinet and pocketed the key that Tunney had given him.

He had already decided and he hadn't realized it: he was homing in on that half hour of the day, the long grasses and the light behind the hills where he'd hide, a bit of refuge— Kathleen or not.

He stopped by Niamh Kenny's second to last work of art. The place where you go to even in your imagination, Anderson had assigned a secret place, if you like, where you feel best. Niamh liked to dance, the parents had told him. He found a phone book under the table on top of a stack of "Stay Safe" pamphlets for handing out to schools. The yellow pages had a section on nightclubs. There was no Wonderland club. Nor in dancing schools even.

How Much Is That
Doggie in the Window?

Quinn's back was at him now. He shifted a few times, once nearly falling off the rickety fold-up chairs they had at the Academy. It was nerves, of course it was, he knew, there was no getting around it.

He didn't remember bits of the drive back down from Drogheda. But he hadn't forgotten the weird bits, the games his mind had started playing on him. For a while, he'd actually felt something was in the car beside him. He was able to mostly fight off thinking about Doyle and what Roe had done, but the car wheels slapping the cracks on the shite piece of road near Balbriggan sounded for a minute like what he'd heard coming from the tool room at the garage yesterday.

He had only admitted later, when the city filled up around his car again, that he'd gone blank because it was a kind of panic. That helpless, what-have-I-done thing that had been part of growing up, with his father and the drink and the treatment he'd given his ma—like the accelerator was jammed and the steering wheel wasn't working.

Catherine didn't help much. Oh, she knew there was

something wrong, fair play to her, and she knew not to ask him. But still, there was a coldness about her that was worse than just being plain pissed-off for being late for the recital.

"This one's Jessica," she whispered to him.

He looked up at the fat little one going at it with the tap shoes.

"Her best friend," he whispered to Catherine.

"No," she said quickly. "Tara's her best friend."

Without looking at him either, he saw. She didn't really expect him to know. He tried to stretch his back again. The chair leg scraped. Catherine gave him a quick look.

He had to get some sleep, that was it. The systems were slowing down on him and he had to get the message. He should get Beans tonight and sort this out, good and proper. Do what needed doing.

The music accompaniment started. Catherine sat forward, began to smile at last.

"How much is that doggie in the window . . ."

Yes, there was no doubt. He was going mad.

BE FAIR TO BRAY TIME
HAS COME

Kathleen Minogue walked across the strip of grass to the promenade proper. She stood with her back to the railing, and studied the apartments beside where Minogue had parked. He stepped out warily, the smell of candy floss and decaying seaweed drifting, took in the salt air.

He had to admit it: they had done a lot here over the years. The lawns, the flowerbeds, the bandstand were in good order. The lights along the promenade were new. Nearly all the old hotels and B&Bs had serious facelifts or been replaced entirely.

A steady stream of cars processed by him toward the lights of the arcades at the far end of the seafront glowing and flashing under the steep rise of Bray Head heaped in the twilight above. There was a lemon sky behind the buildings, a sliver of a new moon to the north. Dublin glowed behind Dalkey Hill there, civilization.

And to be fair, he had forgotten how beautiful the view could be here. It had been years since he had been down the seafront here. He had chosen only to remember the saucy English seaside postcards where all the men had those shiny, sausage noses and leers, the buxom women half-bursting out of their bathing suits, with fingers perpetually at their mouths feigning surprise. Greasy chips, dogshit, Honda 50s. Even the hordes of louts staging bottle fights might be long gone.

The sea was silver. Be Fair to Bray Time has come. He followed a darkening coast by Shankhill up to Killiney. The sweep of the bay had never dulled for him.

"There's a lot you didn't notice here now, isn't there," Kathleen said.

He put his arm around her, saw how pleased she was at his defection.

"It's a family town now, more than ever," she said. "And there's the DART, look—you're in town in a half-hour."

She began to stroll toward the busy end, near the ice-cream shop.

"God," she said, "remember Daithi here with the sand-castles? Fighting to keep them and crying all night?"

Hardy Canute, Minogue called him for a week afterward. He didn't want to spoil things by reminding Kathleen of the spectacular vomiting and diarrhea both Daithi and Iseult had had after a long day here.

Smiling, Kathleen stopped and turned toward the apartment building.

"They certainly pay attention to detail," she said.

It was expert, he had to agree. Landscaping, railings, big windows.

"Sort of a nautical theme, isn't it," she said. "What you might call maritime."

Minogue looked along the façade, noted the Mercs and high-end Volvos. He thought about broken drystone walls, heather under the bank, the strange pleasures he'd had lately listening for curlews.

Then he heard the clacking from the train station. The

gloom from which he had escaped a few hours today, ran back at him. What were Jennifer Halloran's family doing tonight, except having their hearts ripped out every second probably.

"You could revisit the process in five years," she said. "And you'd do well out of it—I'm not saying we have to call this home."

He didn't know what revisit the process meant. It came from the same vague space that he knew dimly about and kept at bay, the kind of talk he heard on chat shows, the brash verbosity of the entitled: feeling comfortable, relationships, concerns. Issues.

He squeezed her shoulder without knowing it. There was nothing wrong with wanting things, she was right, and she shouldn't have to put up with a man who didn't seem to know what century he was in. *I wouldn't mind an odd visit one of those times when you land on our bloody planet again!:* her words. Not so much angry as hurt, expecting more, that they could agree a bit more after all these. *Wandering off on me again, hiding, so you are!*

She looked up at him. They stepped aside to let a family get dragged along by a spirited purebred collie.

"Look," she said. "Dublin—eight miles away. The best of both worlds here."

Somewhere near that blinking column that was the RTE mast in Donnybrook were the Kennys and their dead daughter, a niagara of grief and pain and unknowing. And he didn't like those people. The shame pierced him, again.

Her smile became rueful. He took his arm from inside hers.

"Go ahead," she said, but he believed she wasn't annoyed. "Spoil it here now."

Yes, it was his mobile, he knew. He was forgetting to switch it off.

ANOTHER DAY

Grogan went back to finishing the letter to his daughter.
He didn't like leaving space at the end of the page. Over
the years he had become good at the wrap-up paragraph. He
avoided weather always. It wasn't as if the weather in
London or outside his daughter's house there was radically
different from Belfast's, was it.

London, he thought so often lately, where Siobhan had
ended up. Of all places.

He only put in reminders about things like anniversaries
very occasionally. He usually put in one or two general questions to give Siobhan an idea for beginning a letter in return.
He never asked her when she'd be coming home again.

"Who was that?" Maureen asked.

He didn't look up from the table.

"Something I have to take care of later on."

Maureen dropped the tea bags in the drainer.

"You're not going out tonight, are you?"

"A short while," he said. He finished the sentence asking
about how David's promotion was working out. A banker, for
a son-in-law. A nice fella, he could never like.

He put down the Biro and looked over at Maureen running
the cold tap slowly into the cups. The air in the kitchen was

close in these summer evenings. Global warming? He still wondered the odd time about unscrewing the metal clamps and the security bars that ran down deep into the metal frames. The coating on the glass was stuff they used in Jerusalem they'd told him when they were putting it on. Holy glass. The upstairs windows didn't let in much of a draft here.

"She told me the other day they'd get a flight for the Bank Holiday weekend," Maureen said.

"Start buying the nappies then," he said.

"Well, they were thinking of staying with David's folks this time so they were."

He looked up at her.

"They'd be coming around during the day," she says. "And we'd be hitting the shops there. No way would we miss that, says she. And wee Gavin tagging along."

Gavin he thought, a television name. Once, watching a documentary about the start of The Troubles, when a seventeen-year-old Liam Grogan had been tossing stones and Molotov cocktails half the length of the Falls Road, he had calculated that David, his son-in-law, had six more years to wait until he was born.

"That'll be a sight," he said. "Gavin."

"David's folks have a grand local too," she says.

"Well, good for them then."

"We're invited up there for a dinner for sure."

He determined to finish the letter. He began a sentence that he hadn't planned, one where he told his daughter about remembering the time she had stood up to her teacher, arguing about Irish history—at the age of eight. He didn't know what to do with the half-begun sentence.

"I wouldn't mind being waited on," Maureen said. "A big dinner."

"I'm sure they'll be a good influence on us," he said.

He went back to rescuing the sentence. He could ask if Gavin was showing signs of that streak of independence— and he could make up something about Gavin, at the age of four, maybe showing him how to use a computer.

"Liam."

"Yes, love."

"Liam, how about a bit of a skite?"

He kept going.

"A skite," he said.

"You know," she said.

"What do you have in mind, love?"

"I don't know, do I? But the time of year that's in it. For God's sake, the Orangemen tramping around. Loads of people head out, down to the South and that."

"Before or after Siobhan comes over, is it?"

She didn't catch the edge in it, he realized.

"Before. I mean, at last we can do it. Joan McStravick told me that she and Paul had the best time in Dublin. Not a bother getting a nice place, and being able to walk around."

"We can walk around here, love."

She waited a few moments, and drew in a breath. He finished the sentence about Gavin.

"Joan says the place is full of all kinds of people. Dublin. She says she heard a half-dozen languages spoken, so she did. Can you imagine?"

He tried to smile, but his eyes fell out of focus. Gallagher would be here in a few minutes to pick him up. They had to talk about this Quinn's sidekick, something else had come up about him. More proof.

"Dublin," he said. "Didn't you hear about the shootings there?"

"I saw something on the news. But that's a crime thing, wait until you see. Or something like that."

He looked at her.

Dublin, London. Anywhere but Waterbrook Street.

There was more anger in her voice than impatience now.

"Oh come on, Liam. Things *change*. They do."

He watched her light her cigarette, fold her arms again.

"They do," he said. "How right you are."

"You're not listening," she said.

"I'll tell you one thing," he said. "I know more about London, or England, from Siobhan, than I ever learned in my life before that."

"Liam, she has to follow David, the career thing. She has to."

Siobhan's accent had slipped a few times on their last visit home. He'd pretended not to notice. He suddenly remembered hearing Gavin speak on the phone last year, the English accent. And the boy's hair wasn't cut, it was styled.

"David's solid, he is. We can't complain."

"Oh, a good catch," he said.

"Well, he is. The education, the travel. It makes such a difference."

"We'd better catch up then, I suppose."

She made a faint smile.

"We're not doddering now, are we," she said, and she came over.

She pushed his stray hair over his crown to cover the bit they used to laugh about. He looked down at the letter, the bit of Irish he always put at the end. Some day he might stop doing that, he realized. Not today.

He folded the letter and slid it into the envelope. There were a few stamps left in the drawer. He heard the theme for one of Maureen's favourites, and then the ads as he wrote in Siobhan's address.

He took a twenty from the press and made sure he had his

keys. The metal walker he'd used in rehab was behind the door still. Gallagher couldn't drive down the street to pick him up at the door, and make it easy for them to track how they moved.

He paused as he pulled the hall door behind him and set the second lock. The street lamps were always fixed promptly, bright enough for the young fellas to kick ball all night if they wanted to. There were a few hall doors open even, a pram out near the end of the street. Everyone watched, he knew, in one way or another. The last time he counted—that was before the Dohertys moved out, of course—there were fourteen families on the road who'd had fathers or sons involved. The McAndrews of course had their daughter Sheila killed eight years ago in an ambush.

He got a howdo from Paddy Smyth sitting by the window in number 15. Paddy was as grey as a badger now but he still went to the clubs and got taken in by the RUC for questioning. He said it was almost a hobby now, and he enjoyed meeting the new crop of detectives every few years. The Brits had pulled back completely, and the RUC patrols hardly came by more than twice a day during the daylight hours. You'd only see them normally near the peace walls or if something had happened earlier on.

Three streets, Grogan thought. His life had been contained in three streets from the day he was born. That was except the time in the South, the time on remand, and then in maximum in Portlaoise.

He thought of Quinn, the times they spent talking about being parents, what they'd go back to on release, what the future would be in twenty years. Quinn had told him he wouldn't have had kids if he had known, or at least waited. It was his missus had wanted one. A daughter, and Quinn had hinted she was happy with that.

That was a different Bobby Quinn from this afternoon in Drogheda. Well, what if he hadn't been rattled by the operation there the other day, with the shooting, and then having to deal with the other fella? No, he couldn't fault him for that. The others could, and they would, that Quinn wasn't like the others. You could still have a conscience, of course you could. He remembered the time he'd told Quinn, after a long talk in the yard, that he must have good parents, whatever else. Quinn had laughed. It was unusual for him to laugh outright like that. His ma, okay, he told Grogan, maybe. But his oul fella was a write-off. He was living in England somewhere for the last twenty years, somewhere in the Midlands he believed.

He didn't want to be standing on the corner watching traffic. Gallagher would no doubt go the Antrim Road from the Ardoyne, down into Millfield and onto Divis Street. He crossed at the corner of Lismore Street and looked for Gallagher's red Vauxhall in the cars approaching, the glasses Kelly only wore driving. An RUC Land Rover went by, the antenna waving lazily on the turn, a face turned to his through the mesh on the passenger side. Smile for the camera, they used to shout at them.

They could go anywhere, Siobhan had told him once. Canada, the US—but Australia was too far. David was useless with money she'd told him a long time ago—working with the bank! It was computers he was hired for, of course, yes. He'd brought one of those laptops with him the last time. Grogan had been puzzled why he was angry to see wee Gavin sitting with the dad playing on the stupid machine. He hadn't let on. The games were so different now. With Ciaran it had been the racing games, in the arcades. He had never taken to the shooting ones.

Grogan moved down the footpath, his leg already beginning to nag at the side of his mind. Soon it'd be: sit down, lie down, wait. He looked at the Peace Through Justice mural that had gone up just after Christmas. Now there was an artist. Surely to God a talent like that shouldn't just be taken up with these murals. He stopped and did the exercises with his toes pressed down against the cement. Ciaran, he thought, he'd tried with murals, but he had no eye for it. That night he came running in, the smell of tear gas off him, and petrol, excited and scared. He was supposed to be out with his mates, down at one of those arcades. The row he'd had with Maureen afterwards; slapping her hard, twice. The shame later, the letters he'd written her every second day from Portlaoise.

He'd walk up a bit of the road so's not to be standing there like an iijit. Maybe Kelly had been pulled over, the usual effort keeping him there waiting in his car while it took a quarter of an hour to check his licence.

Not good. He took out his mobile and turned away from the traffic. The memory hadn't gone at all on him; in fact it was getting better. The more you couldn't leave on paper or in your phone directory, the more exercise your brain got.

Gallagher answered on the second ring.

"I can't talk," he said. "They're giving me the treatment here going through the car."

"RUC?"

"That's it. Another day."

Gallagher hung up. Grogan switched off the phone and headed back.

The driver of the sporty Japanese thing that squealed to a stop at the curb wasn't making any effort to be sneaky. Grogan knew it the moment he heard the light, lasting squeak of the brakes, even before the tires began to howl. He knew this was for him too, or, about him, and he began to run. His arms clawed at the air and the pain he expected from across his hip as he landed on his bad leg twice, three times, was somehow far off, happening to someone else that he needn't concern himself with. How strange, he thought, almost amused, to be able to run like this at last.

And his thoughts had suddenly cleared. They thought it all went back to him—Canning was bent, Quinn must be, then surely Liam Grogan must be too. Gallagher's way—cover every angle. He wondered if Gallagher had planned this all along, if it was just another chess move for him. Words flew through his head, the tone he should have recognized when Gallagher asked about his health, the leg. Yes, maybe those had been hints he missed.

Someone was shouting. Soft shoes, he heard, a grunt or a sigh and heavy breath out of someone's nose behind him. A car skidded to a stop across the road and he glimpsed the open mouth. Ireland, he thought, I've lived and fought for Ireland, and done my time for it, and I would do it all again. Maureen's face when he got out that day, raining in Portlaoise, the enormous muzzle flashes off the M50 he'd used in the ambushes in Fermanagh. A shadow collided with his in front. He put his arms up around his head as he turned and thought that now he was afraid. He had a moment to glimpse the running shoes, almost time say something to Roe before the shotgun lit up and he was thrown to the wall.

FLUFFY

Tommy Malone was in a pub somewhere. "Yeah," he said to Minogue. "I meant to phone you earlier on. I was heading out and I saw them sticking it on the board here. His ma's looking for him, and says she's worried."

"Doyle'd be of interest to your crowd, is that it?"

"That's it. We have the rogue's gallery here. We look it over all the time so we can make them on the street."

"If his mother wants the Guards' help finding him, well what is that saying?"

"Not much, so far as I know. I went back in and talked with a fella knows Doyle a bit, a uniform out in Clondalkin. He says the mother's all right, it's just Doyle went over the wall with a bad crowd years back. Matter of fact she phoned him personally, she knew him from before 'cause he nailed Doyle a few years back. Fluffy, he goes by."

"Fluffy," Minogue repeated. "Fluffy Doyle."

Minogue looked out at the surface of the sea, the yellow halogen lights he hated flickering gold on the water before the darkness took over beyond.

"So that's how it goes," Malone said. "If you're interested, that's all."

For a moment, Minogue wondered. Guilt did strange things.

Malone, a twin, would surely go to the wall for his brother.

"Tommy," he said. "Is there something else you're forgetting?"

"What? What do you mean?"

"I mean, what have you not told me."

Minogue heard some guffaws somewhere in the pub, the clinking of glasses.

"With Doyle? No. Actually, I'm not sure why I phoned you. I just thought, you know."

"Doyle was nothing to you?"

"He was a fu—. Wait a minute. What are you getting at?"

"I think you know."

Minogue turned to the railings, away from Kathleen.

"Are you there, Tommy."

"Yeah, I'm fucking here."

"Well?"

"Well, yourself. What are you thinking, for Jasus' sake? Are you totally off your rocker here?"

"No more than usual, I'm thinking. How about yourself?"

"What? Is it because I'm in a pub, is that what you're trying to get at? What's the matter with you?"

Minogue said nothing, waited. It didn't take long. Malone's voice was just above a whisper now.

"You can't be serious, boss. You can't."

"I'm too long in the business not to wonder, Tommy."

"You think I'd try to fit you up too, going around looking for Doyle or Quinn the other day, to make it look like . . . ? Ah for the love of Jasus, you're mental. Mental, is what you are. And I'm being charitable."

"He's on your mind."

"You'd never say what you're saying face to face with me. Never."

"I might have to. And there wouldn't be just the two of us."

Malone spoke slowly.

"If you weren't who you are, if I hadn't a worked with you . . . I just can't believe you'd say something like that. Even think it."

Buh-leeeve, Minogue repeated several times in his head while he waited. *Tink*.

"Answer me, Tommy. Doyle keeps cropping up."

"Well yeah, he was on my mind then. Okay? Along with a hell of a lot of other stuff. So what? This was a courtesy call, how's-it-going, and thanks very much for the other day and all. I didn't expect to be talking to the fucking FBI here. Here, what are you doing, are you knocking back bottles of Paddy?"

Minogue wasn't ready for conciliation yet.

"Jameson's, if I was."

"Same difference, the way you're talking, in anyhow. I can't believe I'm hearing this."

"Tommy, he knew the buttons to press, didn't he though. Your brother."

"Don't," said Malone. "Don't start again. I'm warning you."

He wanted to get you going.

"I told you, don't start that."

"You lost it in the chipper, that's a fact. Was there more to it, later on?"

"You're lost in the head. I can't believe it. Here I am, phoning you, keeping in touch, like Kath—. Look. Just forget it. I'm going to hang up now."

"Wait."

"—Wait for what? This is fucking madness—"

"—What about Kathleen? Who said what to you?"

"I'm going to phone you tomorrow, okay. You can dry out by then, okay?"

"What did Kathleen say to you?"

"Forget it. I shouldn't have said what I said. Good luck."

Minogue redialled. Malone's phone rang once before the robot came on.

Kathleen was halfway down the path looking up at the lighted windows in the new block of apartments.

"You're right," she said. "The phone's a curse."

She read something of his mood and looked away. He was ready to say something but he didn't know how to start. The anger raced through him and he tried to keep his breathing quieter.

"Well," he managed to say. "That was Tommy Malone."

"And how is he?" she said in a quiet voice.

"If I knew I'd tell you," he said. "But according to him, I'm a head case."

Kathleen walked on, touching the leaves through the railings.

I'll Take Care of It

Quinn was suffering now, by Jesus. Three cups of tea, Anadin, and as much water as he could drink. He didn't want to risk eating much more than a bit of toast. He was surprised that he'd slept through Catherine going because she was always tough on the hall door. He'd been out like a light but the dreams had come back, and there was a new one. He didn't even know if it was supposed to be Grogan, but some voice, no accent, telling him to do something or not to do something, but it had to be soon.

He went back over last night. Canning wasn't home even by midnight. Quinn didn't want to phone his missus again. That was it, then: right then and there he'd decided to bloody well drive out to Canning's and wait for him, even if he was waiting all night. He'd made it to South Circular Road, he remembered, before he pulled over and gave in. He was shagged.

Canning would have been jarred anyway. Why would he have heard a word he'd tell him. He'd gone home with Catherine and Brittney earlier, tried Canning's number a few times, and then headed out. Catherine hadn't been too thrilled.

He'd started in Murphy's, where Canning used to call his

local. He'd ended up in Hedigan's, too well aware that he'd spent nearly forty quid trying to find Canning, at the same time as forget the shitty day he'd had, and that weird talk with Grogan. Grogan wasn't one for mind games either. Maybe the others up there were just winding him up. But why?

The crowd in Hedigan's had been okay for the first while. He'd almost put Grogan and his weird conversation out of his mind at last. Even that look from Catherine, after him going to all that trouble to show up for the stupid dancing thing. Sitting there in a crowd of gobshites, with those iijity grins on their faces. Looking up at kids doing their little dances, the half of them hardly able to put one foot in front of the other. Dressed up like dolls, some of them with make-up. There was something not right about this stuff, for sure.

He'd thought things were going well all the same, especially with the rushing back from Drogheda and all that had been going on. And there was Catherine, almost hovering on her fecking chair at the recital, looking like she'd been hit by fecking lightning or hypnotized or something. Brittney up there tapping away. For Christ's sakes, he'd been driven to say afterward at home, she's a kid not a doll, Catherine. And you wonder, says she and her eyes scrunched up like a cat's, why we don't have more kids, and you wonder.

He shouldn't have said it. But she shouldn't have said what she said, should she.

It had been a warm night, and there had been crowds still around the take-outs, a small crowd of lads drinking and sort of carrying on down the lane near The Barge. He'd driven down the road once without stopping. Nothing strange that he'd noticed anyway. The lights had been off, upstairs too. He remembered sitting in the car awhile, having a smoke and a think. Decided at some point that they wouldn't go around him to Canning. They had too much invested in things going smooth here, especially after the other day.

As knackered as he was, as late as it was, he'd known even when he came in the door that he still wouldn't be able to sleep. He was kind of proud of the fact that he had enough self-control even with all the drink, not to bang into things, not to bother her. He'd watched television with a bottle of duty-free and finally headed to bed when the fags ran out. It must have been about three. Catherine had stayed well over on her side. He was sure she had woken up when he came in.

He rewrote the note to Brittney, signed it "Love, Your Biggest Fan," and wrapped it around the tenner. That'd make up for things a bit, so it would. He phoned Julie again. Canning hadn't shown up yet. By Christ he was going to have it out with the bollocks, hangover or not. No wonder they'd think he was touting the way he carried on. He stared at the phone as the light on the display went out. He let the question finally come to the front of his mind. OK: what if Grogan's mob were right about him?

He got up quickly from the table, tried to shove the question back somewhere, thought about the godawful ache all over his face and his sinuses and the empty, wormy feeling running through his guts. He washed the breakfast things quickly—see, Catherine?—and headed for the jacks.

The phone in the hall stopped him.

"Bobby?"

It was Julie's voice.

He stared at the photos of Brittney in her ballerina outfit from last year. This year it was tap, right. The studio pictures had been a hundred and something quid.

"Bobby, someone just phoned looking for him."

Beans, Quinn had to think.

"Who was it?"

"They didn't say. A man. Just now."

"What did they say?"

"It was a man, and I didn't recognize him. I thought maybe it was Larry, the new driver, or the other lads."

"No, *what* did he say, Julie, not who, okay?"

"He didn't say anything. He just said, is Mr. Canning about."

"That's it?"

"He was kind of, I don't know how you'd say it."

"Just fucking tell me, Julie, will you?"

"Well, I don't know, I don't know how to say it . . ."

Quinn held his breath.

"I'm sorry, Julie. Sorry, I'm just kind of, you know, a bit screwed up. Go on."

"He wasn't trying to be funny or that, Bobby. But he had this kind of sing-song voice, like he was trying to be pleasant or cheerful. Oh, and super polite. 'Good morning to you, I wonder if I might be able to speak with Mr. Canning, if you please.'"

The tea or something was moving around somewhere in his intestines.

"Is that how he talked?" was all he could say.

"Well, yeah. But it was a bit weird, like, 'cause for a while you couldn't help but wonder was he being sarcastic like. Like it was some kind of joke, but it wasn't, like? Like he was trying to explain something to a kid, or an iijit maybe?"

Quinn had to get to the toilet. He pulled up his leg to try to stop the pain.

"Was he Dub?"

"God no, he wasn't, Bobby. He was sort of a culchie, for sure. But I think he might have been from up there, you know, except it wasn't the usual kind of whinge you hear when they do be talking on the telly, you know the North."

He imagined Julie sitting in the office, the glass door with Mighty Quinn Haulage letters backward, the corridor, the steps down.

"What did you tell him, Julie."

"I told him nothing. Nothing."

"I mean, what way did you tell him. Like what did you say?"

"'Mr. Canning is not in the office,'" I says. "'May I take a message.' And he says, 'Ah, a shame I missed him.' But then that was it. He didn't say goodbye or good luck or anything at all. Just hung up."

"Julie. Are you listening to me?"

"I am."

"Don't bother trying to reach Beans anymore. His missus does be out most mornings, right?"

"There's no answering machine there, Bobby. She just mightn't be picking up the phone—"

"Don't worry about that. Listen, now. I want you to close up shop there. Did you hear me?"

"Close up?"

"Yes, close. I want you to lock up like it's the end of the day."

"What about Larry and the other lad, they're due to pick up the baby food and the other stuff?"

"No, no, Julie. They'll be grand. I'll take care of it."

"Are you sure, Bobby?"

The pain in his gut moved around like a snake. He'd have to go, but quick.

"Go, Julie. Really. Right away—look, I have to go meself, I'm in a hurry. I'll be in touch."

"Is everything okay?"

"It's grand," he managed to say between his teeth. "Now, go."

He messed up with the phone trying to get it back on the knobs. He let it dangle and doubled up. He made it up the stairs. He paused a moment and thought about reaching in for the gun, but it'd be too late by then.

He yanked at his belt, and backed up over the bowl.

"All fucked up," he groaned, as he let go. "The whole fucking lot of you."

And as for you, Beans, he thought, sensing this relief would not last the morning, after all I done for you.

He didn't finish the sentence. He shifted on the toilet seat and pushed his knuckles hard into his tightly clenched eyes.

YOU'RE LOST. AREN'T YOU?

Minogue stayed away from Donnybrook, of course, and headed instead to the Ranelagh Road, on his way to Harcourt Terrace. Malone said he'd buy. Minogue had protested a bit, but Malone had said he had a head on him so he'd be eating two breakfasts and a bucket of tea. He wouldn't even notice the price of a fancy coffee on top of that.

Minogue and Kathleen had sat in the kitchen for a long while after they'd come home from Bray last night. Quite a row, it had been, the Bray episode, and whiskey or not, he remembered everything. She had taken out the quarantined Jameson's from behind the Ajax under the sink and poured herself a small one after his. A big gesture, he knew.

"Just a tincture for me," she said. "Or do you want to be on your own?"

"I don't mind."

The sea air has me knackered.

"You'd do well to avoid it so."

She didn't fire back. He knew she wouldn't finish even the small amount she'd poured. He found the brochure for one of Iseult's early exhibits and went through it. That was back when she believed she could make a living as an artist.

"Pat took a few days off," she said. "He came back up last night."

Minogue wondered if it was an effort to save their marriage.

"Iseult phoned. I forgot to tell you. She said they were probably going to go away a few days, the three of them. The B&B down in Wexford they like, the child friendly one."

Through the open window came the sounds of cats fighting somewhere. Birds twittered, squawked, and hit leaves as they left their perches. Minogue tilted the glass, watched the whiskey curl and level as he turned it.

"Declare to God those feckers are gone wild entirely," she said. "Did you hear them the other night?"

"It was dogs I heard the other night. Costigan's old gamog, I think."

He finished the drink.

"Go on," she said. "Have another."

He gave her the eye. These truces brought out odd things. The making up after a fight thing they talked about was overrated. He knew somewhere that he'd be angry for a few days at what she had done. It was manipulating, he'd argued, and was not ashamed to remember raising his voice for all to hear on the seafront in Bray. Goddamned Bray. Going about like that, the best of intentions or not, worried about him or not, soliciting Malone to phone his old boss, to keep him in the picture on account of how Minogue was off his game ever since the Squad had been closed. Pity, he read it as.

He had been close to furious when she'd told him about Kilmartin a few weeks back, retailing confidences from Kilmartin's wife, Maura. Harpies, he'd said, unfairly. Couldn't they just leave their husbands alone? Couldn't they stop interfering? Stage managing things and playing frigging amateur psychologists? It was like having some damned

Mother Superiors or something, who always knew better.

Well, we wouldn't damned well have to, was Kathleen's fair shot back, if you and Jim knew how to fecking well express your feelings, in the name of God. Or had the good sense to use some bloody psychology, or talk to a psychologist or something. Where was the shame trying that, in this day and age, especially seeing as how well he himself had done by Herlighy in the bad days after the bombing? Well?!

The image of Kilmartin marooned in that big living room he was proud of, with the big television whose technological features he had detailed to Minogue several times, watching the satellite programs of bighorn sheep charging head first at one another could be comical. Except that Maura Kilmartin, damn her, had told Kathleen Minogue something. And same Kathleen Minogue didn't know better, it seems, even after all these years of being married to a fella who held some strange pact with aloneness that he never asked for and barely even understood himself . . . and Kathleen Minogue had passed on to him that Maura had discovered Kilmartin crying one evening. Kilmartin crying was something impossible. To turn the knife, Jim Kilmartin wasn't aware that his wife had noticed. So now, it was Minogue's secret too. He hated it.

"No more, thanks. I'm actually going to hit the sack."

"You're not sleeping the best, are you love."

"It does be warm at night I find," he tried. That'd do it.

"Will you have a talk with Dr. Herlighy, you know?"

"I won't. And I don't want—"

"—Can I tell you something? Can I? You're not supposed to know this."

Minogue fixed an eye on her.

"If it's about Jim Kilmartin, I don't want to hear it. No way."

"It's not really," she said. "I can't help worrying. Don't

give me that look. If it's about Tommy, I'm sorry. I said I was already. He was the only one. I was worried."

"And you're not worried now."

"I am. That's why I was asking you if you'd see Herlighy. Because Maura Kilmartin let slip—well, you know what I'm going to say."

He looked at how she had wrapped both hands around her glass. He was sure she'd have poured it down the sink if he weren't here.

"This is an ambush," he said. "I thought we had a lay-down-your-arms thing after that spat below in Bray tonight."

"Listen, Matt. Maura has persuaded him, telling him that you got such value out of it. Now remember—you're not supposed to know."

She looked up.

"I actually feel bad telling you. But there's nothing I won't do, to get you back up again."

"I'm not down," he said, his voice rising. "And if I am, well that's okay."

"You're in denial."

"Blue or white?"

"What?"

"I'm feeling good about myself," he said.

"Oh, what's the use."

The whiskey's fire glowed near his ribs yet. Oh for a smoke.

Who was he codding here? He remembered bits of one of Kilmartin's rants not long back, about someone's inner child, some rock celebrity in the Sunday papers. How if that little fecker of an inner child ever turned up, someone should do this gobshite a favour and beat the ears off it and teach it manners.

The slow, deep-throated cry of the cat was closer now.

Minogue waited to hear its combatant's cry next. Territorial, no doubt. Again, he thought of Kilmartin, carving out his fiefdom in supply and services, cultivating his vassals, showing his colours. It must be innate in him, staking out his kingdom, he thought. And Minogue had been more than content to be some kind of an agent in Kilmartin's vanished realm, The Murder Squad. Like Camelot or something.

So now, what had he to look forward to? Bottles of mineral water and shiny tables, meetings in exotic places like Vienna? Air miles, maybe, right. Hotels and suits on a clothing allowance. Regaling people about The Big Picture on crime across the continent. EUnuchs, had been Kilmartin's fifth-hand term for the Euroland apparatchiks.

He looked over at Kathleen. She had a cautious smile. He clasped her hand.

"I'm not afraid to tell you something else," she said.

For a moment he felt the anger surge in, the disloyalty he had been dragged into with Jim Kilmartin. Then it just fell away. He stared at his wife now, wondering: is this what they meant by zen or things like that. How everything counts and nothing matters?

"I think you should meet her," Kathleen murmured.

"Who, Maura Kilmartin? I'm already married, love. So's she."

"The guard that did the interview, the one you were with in Fraud."

He waited for Kathleen to look up from her glass but she didn't.

"Well," he said. "You don't give up on this mental health issue, do you."

She said nothing.

"Bray was just to soften me up?"

"I'm sure she needs it too."

"Wrong. She already knows everything, Kathleen. She has everything she needs."

"That's maybe how it looks to you. I'll tell you one thing, you won't get anywhere on your own with this."

He got up slowly. At least he could sit below in Dwyer's Pub in peace. Tonight he'd smoke, yes. He thought of Kilmartin singing over the phone: *'Tis true that the women are worse than the men. . . .* His eyes stayed on the empty glass.

"No," he said. "I did something terrible, so I did."

"Stop," she said. "You're beating yourself up for no good reason."

"There's a woman dead under a train, is what."

"You didn't put her there."

"I didn't stop someone else putting her there."

"She did it to herself, Matt! You didn't push her, and even that Guard, what's her name, didn't push her."

"Fiona Hegarty," he said and forgot what he was going to say next. Hearing her name had derailed him. He felt a recoil somewhere in his chest.

"You're worried about the inquest."

"I am not," he said. "It's she should be worried. I don't care a damn. The woman is dead, Kathleen, that's all that matters. I should have stepped in earlier, taken over—"

"How could you? For the love of God, you said yourself you were only a tourist! How could you see a lot of them resenting what you were about! How you were just trying to keep your head down and get through it!"

"Well, we won't have to be worrying about that anymore, I can tell you."

"And what does that mean?"

"It means I have my resignation typed up and signed— and divil damn the waiting I'll do for Kilmartin or anyone to offer me a soft spot to land. 'Security' or the like."

Kathleen sat back and folded her arms. He heard his own laboured breathing.

"What are you planning to do so?" she asked in a tight voice.

"I'm going to buy a goat and a donkey. And go down to that nephew of mine, tell him to cut out an acre of land off the farm for me so's I can rule the goddamned world."

"From your palace on a heap of rocks in the Burren. Is that it?"

"That's the style. I'll build a beehive hut with them. Like the monks."

"With the goat and the donkey helping out."

"They'll keep people away. I'll train them to be a bit mad. The goat'll keep his horns and I'll remind the donkey how to kick."

"You won't have far to look for a bloody goat, I can tell you."

"I'm going to call the goat Jim."

"And what'll you call the donkey?"

"I'm not sure. I was leaning toward some fancy name. One that'd show how dangerous it could be if you went again it. But to show it had a good nature too, as long as it was treated with respect."

"Matt, then."

"That would probably be best. Yes."

"And when'll this be happening."

"Tomorrow morning, first thing."

Kathleen was the first to break away, her smile giving way suddenly to laughter. She turned and covered her face with her hands. He reached for the bottle, thought about the smokes, decided that would be asking too much.

He screwed the top back on the Jameson's and reached for her glass. She trapped his hands around it.

"You'll only waste it," he complained. "Only pretending to like it. With your Florence Nightingale goings-on here. 'Denial.' 'Share your feelings.' All that."

"Oh yes, you have the donkey already," she said. "You're well on the way."

"Yous Dublin crowd are all the same," he said. "Ganging up, then hitting below the belt. A million and a half in the GPO Easter Sunday, was it, again?"

"Will you phone Tommy tomorrow then? He only wanted to help."

He nodded, finally. She let go the glass.

"You're lost, Matt," she said, softly. "Aren't you."

He let the small mouthful under his tongue before swallowing it. Another day gone by, won't come back.

"I am," he said.

The cat's yowl came from close by now. Minogue tilted his head to hear the scratching better.

"They must be up on the bloody shed," said Kathleen, rising. "Honest to God, I'll shoot them."

Well, she hadn't, had she. She'd gone in to the news. As if that hadn't been an eventful enough evening already, he thought.

He had changed his mind about going down to Dwyer's and stood by the window instead, half-listening to the news about the economy and the peace process. He'd finished Kathleen's glass just when he spotted the dog move by the shrubs near the apple trees. It had stepped back then out of the light cast from the kitchen, its pupils reflecting the ghostly clarity of two rings. He remembered putting the glass down on the windowsill, knowing. He'd thought about calling Kathleen but had decided not to. He opened the door to the extension and found the short spade he kept for the potatoes.

He reached in and switched off the kitchen light and headed out the door to the garden. It might be the whiskey, he thought again, and he wasn't thinking straight if it really was what he thought after he saw the tail.

He closed the back door quietly, waited until his eyes were a little used to the half-light. The shadows by the hedge were completely opaque now. He held the shovel across his chest and headed around by the peas. There was no sign of the mad cats now. The smell of the soil rose up to his nostrils along with the slightly bitter scent off the leaves on the potatoes. He stopped and listened. There was another smell out there. The damned cats, the bastards, doing their business in his garden. How could anyone like cats, it was well known and even allowed they were selfish little creatures.

The fox was watching him from beside the trunk of the Granny Smith. The high ears moved a little and the snout wobbled slightly. Minogue couldn't see the brush. Whiskey aftertaste burning at the back of his throat, his chest thumping.

As though it doesn't care, he had thought, and wants me to know that too.

But what about rabies and distemper, if foxes went mad and just attacked a person for the hell of it. Cats or dogs being eaten, foxes sniffing around the back doors of the houses at night, would a fox come right into the kitchen.

Off it went, turning and stepping out in one smooth curve. Minogue lowered the spade and stared into the gloom. He thought he heard a last soft scratch.

Kathleen wondering if they shouldn't phone somebody, some outfit to tell them about the fox. Minogue with another glass of whiskey he knew he shouldn't take, sat watching the telly while Kathleen phoned Costigans and O'Hares farther down the road. Someone arguing stridently about child-centred curriculum and a man with glasses and a tic talking about how boys were different.

Minogue had listened and followed none of it really, thought about the fox, how it seemed to be nonplussed. He kept up a half-hearted watch on the host, a man he had thought had recently died but hadn't apparently, trying to hold back the child-centred woman. She continued with the bought-into and process and issues. Then he knew the whiskey had gotten ahead of him. He'd be sorry and stupid half the day tomorrow.

But no. That tomorrow was now, and here he was in unexpectedly good order, getting a good run of it over the canal and down to Camden Street and the city centre. Maybe, as he'd been told for years, the trick to not getting hangovers was to stay drinking, keep it topped up.

It wasn't the remorse he knew from overdoing the gargle last night, or Kathleen's quiet this morning. It was something else that he didn't understand or even remember had changed him. Sitting at the edge of the bed, eyeing the pattern on the curtains for probably the hundred thousandth time, Minogue realized that there was no going back. First, he'd settle with Malone, and then he'd be phoning Fiona Hegarty.

No Hard Feelings

Quinn tried Beans Canning again just before he stepped out of the car by Irene's.

The bastard had turned off his mobile on purpose. He tried to remember where Jacqueline was working now. Beans had said something about a shoe shop down in Henry Street.

He knocked twice. Avalon: Irene was educated, that's why she called it that. She had tons of books all over the kip, but she never came over that way. But those things she had hanging in the windows, well, what could you do. Maybe people probably expected that. He'd had a go at some of the books she'd left lying around in the front room, one on foods, and another on dreams.

Irene opened the door, gave him the business smile, and showed him into the front room. Five minutes she said: she had someone else.

"I left something on the mantelpiece for you," she said. "Go ahead."

He took the stone off the mantelpiece and felt it. It was smooth like all the ones she left out, heavy. There were red, sort of pink bands along it. The sign said it was for courage. Why'd she put that one out? Did he sound that desperate on the bloody phone? The restless feeling was getting worse; he could hardly sit for two minutes.

He tried to remember what she'd told him from a while back.

Closing your eyes while you were holding it was good. Let it warm up, was what she'd told him too before. Think about when it was being made millions and millions of years ago, the fire, the sun, the volcano. Should he think about ape men running around in nip too, he'd asked her, but she wasn't amused.

He leaned on the windowsill and looked down the street. Fancy new apartments or not, Kevin Street and the Coombe could still be dog rough if you didn't know who you were dealing with or where you were going. Tony Smith, McCarthy, Gears Delaney had taken on a lot of the doings here now. Delaney had been done for assault recently he knew, but the orders still came through.

Here was a book: *Angels Every Day*. The angels were not like the angels he'd learned about, these were normal people with a glow around them. He flipped through a few pages with his free hand, let it close again.

He thought about Grogan. Johnnie Roe, a vampire, is what he is. Something had to be done, this was gone out of control. Things were happening around him and he couldn't see them. He couldn't get his head clear, he had no direction.

Another book was *Past Lives*, with hardly any pictures. There was one called *Visits*. He picked up *Past Lives*. Irene was letting someone else out the hall door. He got up and followed her to the room next to the kitchen.

"I wasn't expecting to come, like," he said.

"Oh, that's no bother, Robert."

Robert—how strange the sound of that, he thought. Grogan was the only other person who called him Robert. She had given him the once-over, he knew. Though he'd never admit it to anyone, he believed now that there were people who could see everything right away. People who could pick up on things instantly, like, no talking or anything needed. He wasn't sure if Irene was one.

"Will we try the tarot?"

"I don't know," he said. She'd know he was nervous about a bad one turning up.

"We could have a look at your life map, then."

He didn't understand or remember, but he didn't want to say that.

"The aspects," she said, and sat at the table. "You know, how things are lining up."

"Or not lining up," he said.

She made a brief smile. He knew that he made her a bit nervous. That suited him most of the time. It was his guarantee she wouldn't be trying to reef him, to hook him into the stuff.

"Do you want to take off your jacket," she said.

He did stink then, the stale smell all around him in the car that he tried to ignore.

"No. No thanks."

"You're in a hurry?"

"Why'd you say that?"

She gave him a guarded look. He had put her at forty, not having a clue, and he still didn't know.

"Well, you look like you're in a rush."

He was able to let that go. There was one time he left and he'd given the steering wheel such a whack. It was still confusing and he didn't really trust her. It was more that he didn't trust himself. She wasn't stupid. She'd figured out he wasn't a civil servant, but she'd copped on quick enough. She'd only suggested that other stuff, the staring into his eye and telling him what she saw there, the name he couldn't remember, once. He'd tried to find out more, looking in the bookshop, but it was just a whole lot of bullshit. He had been annoyed at himself for returning, but that was only for the first few times.

He made an effort.

"Ah, you know," he said. "There's never time."

"I have your chart here," she said. "We can do that."

He leaned in as she spread the paper. The weight of the gun pulled his jacket out.

He listened but didn't really pay attention. She knew he wasn't really into the details, but she went through them anyway. He didn't mind. There was some strange comfort in hearing her talking about Venus and Jupiter and that stuff. It was a story, sort of. It was only a while ago that he realized he liked it because it reminded him of the good times he'd had in school, the few good times before things had taken over. The teenage thing, of course, too.

It was that birdlike Miss Heaney who used to tell stories about the constellations. He had actually loved it, and if he pushed himself and was honest, he loved her. It was because she was old—well, old was anything over thirty then, wasn't it—and didn't mind the kids being half-cracked a lot of them, like, she expected it. It was him knowing that she knew about him, and his family, and his oul lad in and out of jail, and she called him Robert still and expected him to be taken in by her stories. Which he was, because he wanted to.

"Can I ask a few questions there, Irene?"

She nodded.

"Like, I have important things to decide now, but it's like I'm blind. It's like I'm in the dark about what I should be doing."

"Well, you can see that confusion on the map."

"Where?"

She pointed at two pencil lines she'd drawn between

Jupiter and Venus. He wanted to sweep the fucking map off the table. When had she last visited frigging Jupiter?

"You see there," she said, holding her thumb and forefinger on the lines.

"That angle," she went on. "It's nearly one hundred eighty degrees. That's a Jupiter Venus transit. That's what you might be feeling."

"What? I mean, what does that tell you?"

She looked up. His eyes were burning from the lousy sleep. He didn't want to eat. He wanted Canning to be waiting for him to prove that what Grogan had said was a load of bullshit. He wanted Grogan to tell him that they'd just been screwing around, or got it wrong, or were pulling stunts for spite. He wanted Julie to be wrong about the fella who had phoned looking for Canning.

"I'm not asking for fucking guarantees. Just make sense, you know. Okay?"

She blinked slowly, stared down at the map, and sat back. No way was he sorry. He'd paid enough over the last year.

"Have I ever asked you to, you know, get to the point before? Black and white?"

"I told you, like I tell everyone," she murmured. "This is about possibilities. Opportunities. Some people forget that. We don't pretend to be fortune tellers here."

"Well, why'm I paying fifty quid for a fucking hour of whatsit, 'possibilities,' then?"

She looked up again. She was scared all right.

"This isn't working out," she said, and swallowed.

"You think I don't know," he said. "That time you read the cards there. You left bits out, didn't you?"

There was a catch in her voice now.

"We should stop now. It's no good if there's so much stress and an—"

"This isn't a psycho session," he said. "What I'm saying is that I know a bit and I think you can do a damn sight better that talking about 'conflicts' and that. Yeah?"

"The map says you're in a place where there's a lot of opposition to the things you value. Jupiter's for growth and expansion. Travel maybe, I can't say."

He sat forward again. She wouldn't look up from the chart. He wondered if she was going to cry.

"So what do I do," he said.

She shook her head.

"I found out about that Tower card, you know. You kept that out of the picture, didn't you? The last time? Catastrophe, it says."

"It depends on the situation," she said.

"A catastrophe's a fucking catastrophe. Why didn't you tell me, then I wouldn't—"

She wouldn't look at him.

"Do you want to go on with this?"

Quinn wondered, but now didn't care, how mad he looked. Here he was in the middle of all this incense and glass and rocks and books and shite.

He thought about Roe after he'd finished with Doyler; the ironed shirt, the hands scrubbed clean, the faint smile. Face it: they were basically animals up there, that's what they were. Maybe Grogan had something left in him up there, but the others didn't.

"We better finish," he said. "I have to go."

He remembered her saying something about the domestic things. She meant the home. He didn't really think about whether it could be done or not if it mattered now. He kept an eye on her hands over the cards, how they shook, how she tried to hide it.

He didn't ask her any questions. He wondered if he'd be back, after this.

"Thanks," he said. "Thanks, Irene."

She nodded but wouldn't look him in the eye. He sat back, looked at the half-moon thing in the window. He wondered if he'd ever come back.

"The Tower isn't just bad," she said.

"Well, getting hit with a dose of lightning can't be good for you, can it."

"It's a symbol," she said in a soft voice.

He tucked his arm tight over the gun when he went for his wallet.

"There's still time," she said.

"What do you mean?"

"You have a quarter of an hour still."

He'd had the fifty ready anyway. He placed it on the table. She didn't want it?

"You're okay," he said. "Really. No hard feelings."

So It's Nobody's Fault, See?

Malone offered Minogue a pick at his second breakfast. Minogue declined.

"You're still annoyed, are you."

Minogue said nothing.

Malone made short work of it. Minogue watched a couple humouring a man with Down's Syndrome. A man in black, wearing sunglasses, arrived at the cashier. Minogue was sure he was someone famous. Sting? No. Jeremy whatshisname, the actor fella who looked like he'd died: no.

"There was no plan," Malone said then. "I says to her, I says, Kathleen, you just want me to make sure he doesn't run off with a brasser. The midlife crisis routine."

"No need to spare my feelings there."

"So get over it then? Your missus knows coppers. She knows the story."

"Is that it, then?"

"Well, if you're asking . . ."

"Go ahead. Give me your considered opinion."

"My, em, considered opinion is you're holding yourself back. You want to stay a culchie. That you'd be caught being an iijit if you sat down next to them continentals at a meeting in Brussels or Berlin or Rome. My, um, considered opinion is that you're, um, suffering from an inferiority complex. So there."

Minogue raised his eyebrows.

Malone finished the fried potatoes. Minogue returned to his survey. The newspaper fiends, the quiet ones, he saw; the shoppers, the meeters and laughers; the fellas taking a break; the watchers who didn't read, even.

A watcher himself, of course. The city was basically roaring and racing. It paused only to rear up with the latest thrill or trend or happening, then plunge madly down the course at top speed again. What course, had been his question for a good number of years now, and what was waiting around the turn, a clear flat. Or was this a mad steeplechase with the horses spooked, where you daren't even try to slow down or dismount?

But this was his city still. It was a steady gladness he felt when he met with more foreign faces in the streets this past while. The accents and the languages—Arabic the other day in Mary Street—and he walked closer to hear them. The olive and brown and coffee skins he wanted to look at closer; how dark a woman's hair was, how white an eye set in that face. All somehow new, all beautiful, every day. Would they always be that exotic? He'd have to watch himself, too. The trouble he could get himself into for staring, asking questions. People took offence easily this day and age.

"Fact is," Malone said, and wiped his lips. "You see, your missus and me, well we know what's going on. You don't. I mean, you weren't born in Dublin. So it's nobody's fault, see?"

Minogue watched a man he guessed to be, wanted to be, from the Sudan arrive in the room. The height, he thought, the thin frame, a smile lingering somewhere on the face. He wanted to wave at him, to sit by him, to ask him stupid, probably offensive questions about his family, the heat there, goats. Yes, he was definitely losing it.

"Why don't you bring up that topic with Jim Kilmartin at the next veteran's session," he said to Malone. The superior intelligence of the Dubs. The perpetual thickness of us culchies. The inferiority complex thing.

"Don't tempt me. You don't mess with a Dublin man."

Minogue wanted to ask him about his brother.

"So," Malone said. "Are you going to stick it out? The magic carpet route to Brussels, or wherever?"

"I don't know, Minogue said. I just don't."

"I heard what happened, you know," Malone said then.

For a moment, Minogue didn't get it.

"She screwed up," Malone said. "Hegarty, is it? She came the heavy. I don't care what anyone says about women have to be brutes to keep up, all that. She was trying to impress you. Ever think that? The Murder Squad, all that glamour?"

"My arse and Katty Barry," said Minogue, with little feeling.

"All I'm saying is, you shouldn't go round carrying a frigging cross over it. Unless of course there's a part of you likes that sort of thing."

Minogue took a sip of lukewarm coffee and he eyed Malone.

"Suddenly you're Freud today, is it," he muttered.

"What, the chef fella on Sky Channel?"

Malone wiped the corner of his lips again, he crushed the serviette, and sat back. He yawned and stifled a belch.

It was all gone, that life, Minogue knew. He would not admit to anyone how much he missed it. The sessions they'd have after a case, he remembered, maybe the second best part of the job. Yes, closing time in Willie Ryan's in the snug, Kilmartin in top form, the shirttail out on him and the tie half off. Leo the barman listening in, like a child watching giants. Hoey listening, looking like Buster Keaton for all the world. John Murtagh fighting with Kilmartin about how nurses could be more trouble than they were worth on a date. Plateglass Sheehy and Jesus Farrell fighting over how horses were being drugged and passing tests still, and how could a man make a fair bet these days. Tommy Malone, a sideliner, strangely sagacious with the drink, asking the hard questions he'd be embarrassed to ask sober. How do you show people how to really notice things, not to just stagger around in the effing daze they call normal?

"Are you listening to me?"

Minogue's hangover that hadn't happened today might have been a cruel trick. A dullness behind his eyes was turning into the beginnings of a headache. He shifted his gaze from the clientele back to Malone.

"You're not on a leper list, that I know of."

"You checked, did you."

"Yeah, I checked. I found out that what's his face, the Fraud boss, bounced you."

"Moriarty."

"Yeah. He's got cred, he does. He just had to contain the situation, according to his way. No hard feelings, is what it is. No shite on you. That's the story I'm hearing."

Malone began slowly shuffling plates and cups on the table.

"Gas," he said. "Isn't it? One day it's you doing a check on me, see if I'm headed for the dock, and then it's me sorting you out. Oh yes, thing's are going well today."

"Chasing frightened clerks and petty thieves is not what I'd call 'going well.'"

"Oh here we go again," said Malone. "What is it with

you? Does everything have to be life and death, or something? What, on your knees in some ditch, swabbing and
scrubbing and poking?"

"It's not how it looks."

"Yeah, yeah, yeah. Like I haven't heard that from you
ever."

"You mean to tell me that all that while in the Squad you
were actually listening?"

"Who cares? It suits me the same way it suits you, to be
taken for a gobshite sometimes."

"Ah. The Dub, the Hard Man routine. A good performance, Tommy."

A small, thin smile started around Malone's mouth.

"Kilmartin never did get that, did he? He was always
onstage himself, in anyhow. Like nobody knew."

The thought of Kilmartin crying, thinking he could let it
out alone, cut hard into Minogue.

The man from Sudan glanced over. Minogue looked away
quickly. He'd been staring again.

Malone stirred the teapot. Minogue stole another look at
the man from Sudan.

"The source of the Nile," he murmured. Malone stopped
stirring.

"Well yeah, if that's the way you want to put it," he said.

Malone looked at his watch.

"We're squared up then," he said. "I don't have to watch
me back. Right?"

"*Ruoyyggh*," said Minogue.

"Practise that more."

Minogue sat in over the table.

"I want to talk to you about something," he said. "Some
official stuff, about drugs. Party drugs. Drugs going to kids at
dances, that class of idea."

"Is this about that girl they found dead out the south side?"

Minogue nodded.

"It looks like she took some kind of pill that was laced with something else."

"'Cut,'" said Malone. "Like, mixed in."

"Adulterated, is it?"

"That shows up a lot," Malone said. "Especially this last year or so. You're talking about Ecstasy, are you? She was at a club, right?"

"She was. She got confused, panicky maybe. She made it a bit of the way home."

"How'd she do that?"

"It seems like she tried to walk it. She ended up lying down for a rest, it looks like."

"Well," said Malone. "I can see that. Her judgement gone, that's the story there."

"What I'm wondering," Minogue said, "is this. Can we go backwards from what they're saying in the preliminary? The drug she got, if you follow me."

"Yeah. Maybe. Maybe not, though. Look, it's not that easy. Tell me a bit of what they've said so far from a PM."

"Initials MDMA. Flour, would you believe—they think also."

"Ouch. There's nothing there that'll point you to the one source. That I do know."

"Go on."

"Tell you what—you need a bit of background, don't you? Come back up to the Fort a minute with me, I'll give you a package. It's an information thing they give you when you're starting out in Central."

The two detectives made their way up Grafton Street and headed out along by the College of Surgeons. Minogue lis-

tened to Malone talk about amateurs getting into the manu-
facture; a lab started in a place near Kildare town but the
word had gotten out somehow and it turned out a no show,
except for recovery of materials and that; continental connections, of course. Holland was big.

They found no way but to wade through a tribe of Spanish
students coming at them by the traffic lights.

"The ingredients?"

"That's it," Malone said. "A lot of them are explosive,
you know. Being made, I mean. The chemicals, like?"

"Volatile."

"That's right. I saw a video of fellas going into a lab with
bomb shields and suits. Germany, it was. It took them three
days to get the stuff out."

A tour bus now, the older double-deckers with the roof
peeled off, came by. Sardine tins, Minogue always thought of
and knew it wasn't fair. Once he thought of Magritte's people floating, drifting off the bus into the louring sky over
Dublin. There'd be rain before the morning was out.

"It's complicated," Minogue said.

"Well yeah, sure. But it's not Einstein territory, you
know. There are regulars. Well there were."

They waited for the bus to turn onto the Green. A woman
with very big teeth waved shyly from the top deck.
Indianapolis, Minogue thought, for lack of a longer word.
Polyester nation too, by the look of her. He felt ashamed of
his disdain. The guide's voice barely made it over the noise
of the traffic, something about coming up to the College of
Surgeons, site of resistance during the Easter Rising. He
waved back.

They crossed to the Green and sidestepped the crowds
under the memorial arch. There were couples lolling on the
grass everywhere, two with dogs. Malone sniffed the air and

glanced at Minogue. Any one of a dozen couples could be smoking the dope here. The path ahead went arrow straight to the gate out to Harcourt Street. Even with an overcast sky, the thick foliage overhead carved light and shade on the path.

"I'll tell you something now and keep this under your hat," Malone said when the crowds were behind them. "Lately, I'm hearing a rumour that the higher-ups think there's someone on the inside who's feeding out just enough little scraps of info to gougers involved in the trade."

He rubbed his thumb against his fingers, gave Minogue a knowing look.

"In your mob?" Minogue asked.

"Dunno. But it's someone somewhere who has access. Not just in Drug Squad Central, but in other stuff. There's a big undercover thing going on . . . that we're not supposed to know about it. The Internals?"

He glanced over at Minogue.

"Well, there's millions, what am I saying, tens of millions involved. I'm not joking. And there's plenty of sharks and bigger sharks eyeing it."

"Like who?" asked Minogue.

"Well, there you are," Malone said, looking over his shoulder into a dense thicket of holly near the Yeats monument. "What can I say? That's the limit for me."

"Okay," said Minogue. "But the girl, you know. Her family—"

"—Oh listen to you. Look, amn't I telling you? This isn't snakes and ladders. You don't just walk down the path from the pills to the bad guys."

Minogue had thought of Colm Kenny a few times on the drive into town. The people who gave it to her had murdered her.

"Sure who am I talking to?" Malone said, with that flick

of the head that Minogue recognized was Malone's way of closing the show because gobshites had arrived.

"I don't follow you, Tommy. I'm nobody in this. Pure ignorant."

"Not for long, pal. You're headed for Serious Crime sometime, aren't you? Well go to the door that says Drug and Crime Syndicates first. Maybe it says Kingpins and Big Time frigging Mobsters. Seriously, talk it up with Criminal Assets. They're the ones who do a lot of the poking. Remember how they got Al Capone?"

They reached the gate that faced onto Harcourt Street. Minogue thought about stopping in at Kennedy's for a little present for Iseult: a few brushes maybe, or that sort of thing. Daithi, well he'd drop into Conradh na Gaeilge a few doors up and get a few postcards in Irish. Lame, but Katy had bought two bumper stickers in Irish there.

Malone glared at a van driver who ran the amber as it turned red. They gained the far footpath, Minogue searching for telltale drops of rain, thinking of the sunroof, the smoke that came from the exhaust now.

"Come on up for a minute in anyhow," Malone said as they rounded the curve on Harcourt Street and came in sight of CDU. "I'll give you the whatchyoumacallit. Give you a bit of an edumacation in this."

"Tommy."

"What?"

"Who's at the head of all this?"

"The head of what?"

"The drugs business here."

Malone gave him a blank look, and then fixed his eyes on the gateposts and the barrier in front of the checkpoint.

"Like, who'd be at the top?"

Malone faced him.

"Listen to me. You might land a dealer. Fair play to you. I'm willing to bet you a fiver right here and now that he'd be a scut, a small-time shite who's probably on the needle himself. He'll be a let-down because you'll see you're dealing with a stupid little fucker. The problem starts when you realize that he's not that stupid that he wants to cough up anything that would lead you to the big boys. He knows he'd last about one and a half minutes in any jail in Ireland."

"Is there a witness protection thing?"

Malone's frown turned to a pitying look.

"I'll have to get back to you on that," he said. "But remember, there's going to come a time when you're going to have to say something to yourself, and it's this: The girl wasn't forced to swallow them. You know?"

"You said sharks and plenty of them."

Malone looked beyond Minogue at the traffic speeding down toward the Green.

"Well, we know that there's fellas from the North have moved in."

"Weren't they always in there somewhere?"

"Course they were, but the 'movement' didn't like it. Officially. Drugs, especially the hard drugs, was bad juju, according to them. You know about kneecapping dealers and the like as much as I do. But that's changed."

"How?"

"Well. It used to be the thing hereabouts, that some of the gougers here could call in a favour, say, from fellas who were in with the IRA. There was INLA too. They had the hardware and the rep, right? So, they sort of hired fellas on a one-off job basis."

"Just as a threat, you mean? For the protection rackets?"

Malone looked back at the Inspector for a moment.

"Well, what do you call the two Albanians, the two

Albanians who are turning out to be someone else's, the other day?"

Minogue studied the haircut behind Malone's ear for a moment.

"That's part of it?"

"Fucking sure it is. My money is on the fellas from up in the North."

"Can you link them?"

Malone made a frown.

"What do you think."

He cleared his throat and spat an expert, compact gob halfway into the street.

"Sorry about that," he said. "Like I was saying, it's complicated."

Malone had his card out now. Minogue didn't know what he wanted to ask yet. The Guard at the barrier gave him the nod but looked closer at Minogue's photocard.

"He's game ball, Larry," Malone called out, already making for the door. He's the coach for the ladies' snooker team here.

"A right go-boy you're teamed up with," the Guard said to Minogue. "The language I do hear out of him. Fierce."

"They shouldn't be giving jobs to the Dublin crowd," said Minogue.

"Only the dacent farmers' sons. A good Corkonian is all we need."

He returned the wink and hurried after Malone, all the while wondering why his heart had suddenly lightened. He wondered also how he knew that today—and soon—he'd be tearing up the latest version of his letter of resignation.

CREDIT CARDS ON THE BRAIN

Quinn was sweating even more by the time he got through Smithfield. He'd gone to all the vegetable and fruit dealers he knew that Canning liked to hang around. It was from the old days, Canning had told him. He'd shifted stuff off the containers and the boats there, done his driving lorries all over the country half-locked and mostly enjoying it. The slap and tickle shops down near the Four Courts, knocking shops where he'd seen a High Court judge sneaking in one day—and had turned that into a bent court case that nobody knew about.

Quinn's armpits prickled with the heat. He felt another bead roll down the small of his back. He had started to take off the jacket once, but had changed his mind. He couldn't get the picture out of his head of the damned gun falling onto the footpath and going off. He sat on the cement block near a closed loading dock and watched the entrance to the market. The smell of rotting fruit he didn't mind at all. Some faces he still knew. He returned some howiyas with nods.

There was no sign of Canning anywhere. He took out his phone and tried Canning's number again. Same. Quinn didn't let himself think any further than what he thought when he started out this morning: Beans Canning was just giving him grief, rubbing his nose in it. Like a child, he was, annoyed he wasn't getting what he wanted so the bastard sulks. More than once Quinn thought of Canning sitting in a pub all day or playing cards like they used to down at Kelly's in the North Strand.

He stood up and headed back toward Capel Street. The doors of the pubs were open. He still remembered the first times he'd gone into the pubs here, way underage, nod-and-wink then. The cool, dim inside, the malty smell of spilled stout.

There was nothing he could do. No-thing. He had to sit tight and wait and get straightened out. Change the message on the answering machine at the office and phone Canning every once in a while. Have a shower. God knows, even a snooze. He could phone Grogan, that's what he could do. Maybe it was time to back away from things a bit, let things settle here. He was getting infected, that was it, he thought suddenly. They were mad, and they'd make him mad too— the paranoid carry-on, the need they had for violence.

He stopped in the shade of a cloth wholesaler that he'd never seen open, and studied the grime built up behind the mesh on the windows. Now why couldn't he do that; buy and sell places like this and make money that way, instead of trying to keep it together here with Beans and that gang from Belfast. Grogan could see daylight up there, he'd be able to understand things from this end. He thought about the way Grogan had talked about his son those times. Everyone had feelings, for God's sakes.

He found the new number and dialled. He counted five rings. Today was the day nobody was at home then. He slid his thumb over End, but the click stopped him.

"Hello?"

The voice was all wrong.

"Hello?"

"Who is this?"

Maybe Grogan hadn't cleared the recall list. Maybe they had a way of seeing his number there.

"You're looking for Liam, is it?"

"Who are you?"

The hesitation again.

"I'm a friend of his. He said you might be calling so he asked me to take the call here. He's in the toilet."

All wrong. The back of Quinn's neck crawled.

"Give me the message and he'll get back to you."

Quinn took the phone from his ear.

"Hello," he heard again. He'd have to do something, he knew.

"If you give me your name there—"

He held his thumb over the button and switched the mobile off. This wasn't panic yet, he said to himself.

He looked up and down the street. Everything looked different now. He knew he couldn't delay, but he didn't know what he needed to do. He thought about Catherine, going to her place and telling her everything. Getting the money out of the pipe he'd dug in the woods up near Ticknock.

Someone was calling his name. He put his hand up under the jacket but didn't look around.

"What's the story, Bobby, are you looking for a job?"

The mocking sounded familiar and he glanced over his shoulder. He couldn't remember the name. The fella worked in the markets somewhere. A bit of a head, he remembered from not too long ago, something to do with car parts. O'Hare? O'Hara?

"Are you lost then, Mr. Quinn?"

"No. No, I'm not."

"Well, you look it, I'm telling you. Aren't you boiling there?"

"I'm all right."

The man's smile faded a little.

"Are you sure . . . ?"

Quinn stared at him.

"Okay, well," he said. "It's just—well, I seen you with Beans, the odd time. You know?"

Quinn said nothing. The man took a step back, cleared his throat.

"Okay well," he said. "See you around then?"

Quinn watched him kick gently at the curbstone.

"How'd you know Beans," he said to him.

"Well, who doesn't. The brother and him used to have schemes going inside in Smithfield."

"That's back a while."

"You're telling me, it was."

Quinn studied the glaze of mockery over the man's eyes. Hughes, he was. "You're Aidan Hughes aren't you."

"Ah no, Mr. Quinn. That's the brother."

He drew on the cigarette and squinted at Quinn. Cheeky, Quinn saw, and with drink on him.

"I do me own thing," he said. "I'm Barry. The smart one. Ha ha."

"The smart one, are you."

"I have me own doings. And I think you might be someone who might be interested."

Quinn looked up and down the street as a van passed them.

"I'd be interested," he said.

"That'd be great, Mr. Quinn, do you want—"

"—interested in seeing Beans real soon."

"Beans? Isn't he here with you?"

"Does it look like it?"

"Let me tell you something."

He moved in close to Quinn and looked down at the curb as he spoke.

"Don't get me wrong," Hughes said. "But by the sounds of things he needs to be on his own awhile."

Quinn looked at him.

"You were talking to him? When, today?"

"Wait a minute. Do you know what I'm saying here?"

"Where did you see him?"

"Whoa there now. Everyone has their fallings out and all and I'm not saying it should stay that way. All I'm saying is that I'm good, you know—I mean, I can fill in for him until it gets sorted—"

"Listen you fucking git. Before I brain you."

"I didn't mean to cause any—"

"—Tell me where you talked to him."

"Right here. Connaughton's Pub, right there. That's where."

"When?"

"Jasus. Half an hour back? Three-quarters maybe."

Quinn headed for the door of the pub.

"But he left," Hughes said. "He left."

"Where'd he go?"

"I don't know. He came in, had a pint, was talking to the barman, Mick what's his name. So I sort of knew Beans, well I'd met him hadn't I, when he did jobs with me brother."

"Did he say where he'd be?"

Hughes shrugged.

"He was talking to Mick about credit cards or something, if a lot of people used them in pubs."

"Credit cards?"

"Yeah. And then I says, how's it going there, Beans. And he's not in the best of humour, I can tell right off the bat. He didn't know who I was until I told him. So he's asking about

Barry, what's his line nowadays, dah dah dah. So I says, well you can phone the Governor up at Mountjoy now, he could tell you, ha ha."

Hughes looked to him for effect.

"Barry broke his fucking leg trying to do a drive off of an artic down the Naas Road or somewhere. They gave him three years."

"Did he say anything else, like where he'd be in a while?"

"God, no. But he was grouchy, I'm telling you. Credit cards on the brain. Even started asking me about them, did I know anyone knew a lot about them."

Hughes flicked his cigarette into the street.

"I knew he was with you—I mean, the way people would talk, you know?"

Quinn eyed him.

"It's just talk, I'm telling you. So I says, well any chance of putting in a good word for me with Bobby—you, like. You know? 'Cause like I was saying, I been around and—"

"What's he want to know about credit cards, did he say?"

"Fucked if I know. He was off on his own angles there. But he gave me the brush off, see. Says he, you don't need to go astray for that. It'll only hold you back, like it's doing to me. Now that's all he said, honest to God. Didn't say 'Bobby Quinn's holding me back,' no, it was 'it's holding me back.' It, like."

Maybe he'd do a quick look through the markets again then. Canning might be still around.

"It didn't make any sense to me. I mean to say you do what you like, as long as you do right by your mates. Right? That's what I do, that's why I'm here."

"Okay," Quinn said. He turned back down the footpath.

"So what do you think," Hughes said. Quinn looked over his shoulder.

"I'll think about it."

"He told me you were holding him back, you know."

Quinn stopped, half-turned. He watched the eyes slide around, a stupid cautious smile play around his lips. For a moment he saw himself shoving the gun into his face.

"Is that a fact," he said.

"Swear to God, Mr. Quinn. Do you have my number?"

"I'll be able to find you," he said.

A REAL WORK OF ART

Minogue perched on the edge of a desk while Malone went in search of the folder on street drugs. It had been produced for teachers and social workers mainly. It had been written by someone in the Department of Health.

Minogue had had a walk-through of Drugs Central before. A crony of Kilmartin's, a Super McKeon had done a tour for them. Minogue didn't remember the batteries of walkie talkies, phone rechargers, the computers everywhere. The armoury door was new, of course. He got the once-over from more than a few of the Guards going by. They looked like soccer players in a post-game conference, he thought.

He fell to thinking about numbers again. Where had the 15,000 heroin addicts in Dublin figure come from anyway? He should ask Malone. And a fiver for a pill of 'E'? Was it really true people took them at work even? Some people had a daily thing with them. What was the difference between that and a packet of fags each day anyway?

Malone returned with a badly bound photocopied booklet, "Guidelines for Health and Education Staff on Ecstasy and 'Rave' Drugs," by Dr. P. Crosby, Department of Health.

"That comes from a nurses' training thing," Malone said.

"There's a chapter 'Symptoms' you might want to look at. An overdose bit in the middle. This other one here is kind of technical, 'Supply and Purity Issues,' I think."

Minogue leafed through it while Malone checked his voice mail.

"I owe you a pint then," he said finally, and stood to go.

"At the very least," Malone said. "Here, before you head off. You might as well have a gawk at something. The bollocks who nearly did me in there, in the chipper?"

Malone led him out toward the lift. The corkboard was close to full. Minogue recognized two of the faces from a while ago in the newspapers. He read the details under a blurry photo of a man who looked Arabic, one Imir Zoldi.

"This is him," Malone said and tapped on the photocopy of Doyle's face with his knuckle. The pinched look had to be after arrest but there was a sneer too, Minogue thought. Doyle had sideburns, for God's sake.

"The little bollocks," Malone murmured. "Look at the sheet on him, will you. Assault, with a weapon, procuring, theft, B&E, assault of a police officer."

"Quite a career he has going."

He looked down the Distinguishing Features.

"Procuring," Malone said. "Battering girls into it, I found out. Real class."

Minogue reread the features part. A career criminal with a peace sign on his arm. He stopped and turned to Malone.

"A tattoo," he said. "On his arm. Did you see one?"

Malone gave him a look.

"No. I was mainly interested in taking his head off, remember I told you?"

"You didn't see the tattoo? It goes right down . . . ?"

Malone shook his head.

Minogue ran his finger along the text again. With a snake

wrapped in it. For several moments, he had to stop, to wait now, to think. It was possible, he thought.

"Tommy," he said. "I want to know all about this fella."

"You do? What for?"

"I'll tell you later."

"What do you want to know about him?"

"If you have a file on him here. Photos."

"I can tell you everything in one sentence if you like. Save you the bother."

"Pictures, I want."

"Huh. How about the summary? Doyle-Is-A-Fucking-Low-Life-Gouger. Get the picture now?"

Minogue gave him the look.

"Okay," Malone said. "If that's the way with you. But we'll have to find a spot where nobody'll see you."

Minogue returned to Malone's desk. A passing detective took a pad of paper off Malone's desk and winked at Minogue.

Minogue told him that he wouldn't tell. He spotted the edges of the photos on Malone's desk where the pad had lain. He pushed aside the sheet of perspex over the map of Dublin that Malone always liked to keep on his desk. A picture of Malone and his brother at their Holy Communion, the mother and father standing next to them. How much Malone was getting to be like his oul lad. Another photo was further back. A lousy photo of Squad staff at a piss-up last year. Éilis with the worst of the red-eyed demon look and her lopsided smile. Kilmartin like a bear, grabbing Sean Murtagh around the neck, a pint in his other hand. Minogue himself with a fair flush from the drink. Malone with a rare smile.

"Shea Hoey," Malone said. "It was, who took that."

"Excuse me."

"Ah, you're all right. I forgot about them."

He kept the file under his arm.

"Come on down next to the photocopier. There's a cubbyhole there for the cleaners and that."

Malone stood in the open doorway whistling low.

Minogue turned the pages, trying to find more than the mugs.

The photo was stapled to the back of the file folder. It was sideways but Minogue had seen enough.

"Now we're talking," he said. Malone turned and looked at the folder.

"Oh, a real work of art," he said.

"Is that a prison one?"

"I don't know. To me, it looks like he paid for that one."

"Is it a common one, this? A gang thing?"

Malone frowned and looked at Minogue.

"I don't know," he said.

Minogue found the Associates. One was from Bray. He held it out to Malone.

"Know any of these heads?"

Malone hesitated.

"Only the one in the middle, I think. I think that's Gannon. Gaga, he goes by, I think. He's not much. The fella I trained with mentioned him once, that's how I know. That's how I remember."

"Is this file on Doyle a match for what's on the computer?"

Malone gave him a disparaging look.

"What do you think?"

"I'm taking that for a no, then."

"Yeah, I mean no. A confidential no."

"Is it still a bit of the old school here, then?"

"Sure is. Jasus, half of them here don't let on who their touts are. They'd never file it. And you know what, who'd blame them? The access to files isn't half as tight as they pretend anyway. You know that, even."

"So who can I talk to more about Doyle then?"

"What do you want to know more about Doyle for? You never told me."

"Research."

"It isn't about the thing with him and me the other night is it?"

"No. It's just a very odd coincidence."

"Why aren't you going official on this?"

"I thought Kathleen told you to humour me."

"Oh, thanks. Thanks very much. My neck is out to here already, showing you internal files, and now you want the whole shop."

"Which are no different than what I'd get off the computer. Isn't that so?"

"Oh look, now you're using that on me?"

"Come on, Tommy, don't push throwing triplicate at me."

"I'm not going to be your friend anymore, so I'm not."

Minogue closed the file and handed it to him.

"Come on then," said Malone. "Culchies. They'd take the eye out of your head."

"Come on where?"

"See if Carroll's in. Tony Carroll. He's the one made the last entries there."

PICTURE-IN-PICTURE

Quinn sat back into his car and rolled down his window. The thumping from the jukebox or whatever they had up there was still loud even out here. Up by the tables it just about set your fillings rattling. How could Canning stand it?

It was all for a younger crowd now of course. Over thirty was banned.

Frames was open until 3 a.m. now. Cappuccino, fancy lights. Still he bet there was plenty more going through here. There had to be. Nobody played snooker these days, did they?

It was still Chalky White though, complete with the designer duds and tan job and the dyed hair. Only trouble was the duds were seventies. Plus, he looked like Elvis, more and more, the Elvis who stayed at home eating cheeseburgers and pills. Chalky hadn't seen Canning for ages; well, he said he hadn't seen him, for at least a few weeks. Quinn had had a hard enough time hearing what White had said. He left White with a look that he hoped said "wonder why?"

A traffic warden was eyeing him. He started the engine and headed back down Amiens Street. So here he was, doing what his brain was telling him to stay away from. On the way here he had heard himself even saying it aloud, "If they don't break your legs, Beans, then by Jesus, I will."

Canning didn't have the brains to know how to get ahead. Wasn't that the trouble, that the people who didn't know their arse from their elbow didn't know that they didn't know? Of course it was, for Christ's sake: so simple—if the likes of Beans knew anything at all, he wouldn't be the way he was, would he? "To The South," the stupid road sign said. Like "The North." What use was that to anyone? Why couldn't they just say "Road to Bray"?

Quinn began to think about destiny and fate. He once thought of buying some goldfish and calling them that. Irene thought that was quite amusing. That was earlier on when she didn't know him that much. He hadn't told her how he made a living, and she hadn't asked. He knew that she knew something of it after a few sessions. For a while it made him feel good, knowing she was on edge. It was only today that he'd finally admitted to himself he didn't trust her anymore, that it was all bullshit.

Now, what was funny, but actually not so funny, was that he felt sort of cut off, like he was on his own. Going around blind, with no idea where he was headed, as if she had the map or something.

"Jesus," he said aloud. Maybe this is what it's like when you go mental.

He stopped at the lights by the Custom House. A huge ad for a phone you could watch a video on—that was Beans, right there. He'd be in there trying to get his hands on it. Like a kid with the latest toy. Maybe he'd been spoiled too when he was a young fella. Always getting his head turned by anything new, any shiny new stuff. Right, Quinn remembered, like the load of televisions that had got him his last stretch. He had still been going on about them even after he'd done his time: Bobby, they were the best, they were picture-in-picture. The best! Never stopped, until he got on to the next thing, of course. Like a jackdaw or a magpie or something.

A black Mercedes ran the light coming out of the financial services place. Quinn caught a glimpse of the two men behind the glass. Well, they could laugh. The fancy motor, the air conditioning, the buying and selling or whatever they did for a living in there along with the rest of them. Using a keyboard to make millions, no doubt. Was there a time when everything changed, not one day, but, say one year, when all the electronic things happened? Himself, he wasn't stupid. He'd noticed right away how much had happened since he'd gotten back out, and had known what to do. Grogan and them weren't thick either. They'd know the writing was on the wall and it was catch on or lose it all. He looked up at the ad again. You could buy things on a mobile now, even a tin of Coke out of a machine.

The light went green just as Quinn felt the idea slam into his brain. He began trying to figure out which lane he had to get to so's he could turn down the south quays. He could be there in a half-hour, even less maybe.

Maybe Beans wasn't that thick after all, he thought. Maybe he had the right idea in general, but he was just too out of it or even impatient greedy, more like it—to get it working right. Maybe he thought it was as easy as that gobshite had told him. But he'd want to see it in action, a bit anyway. He wasn't that thick.

He got in ahead of a lorry and made it around onto the quay. He thought ahead to the turns he'd make to get him up through Ballsbridge and out by Donnybrook. No, he remembered as he got the Astra into third and gave it a heavy foot, he'd never heard the fella's name. But he was a regular there in Wonderland it looked like. He'd find him soon enough. The fella with the stammer—Video Boy would do for a name for now. Beans Canning, genius, would be sitting right next to him. Not even a clue that the maniacs up North were out for him.

He was up to the lights in Ballsbridge before the tightness came back into his chest. He hadn't been breathing right, he realized. He didn't mind admitting it was either fear or something too close to it. He stared at the sign by the bridge pointing to the N7 and tried to blot out Grogan's face, that expression he'd seen on him in that restaurant in Drogheda. It could be the RUC had picked him up for something, just to keep him on his toes. But that had stopped a couple of years ago with the Peace thing.

If it were true, what Grogan had said, he thought. Canning didn't deserve all this running around and bullshit, that was a fact. But no one was going to talk down a phone from Belfast and decide what Canning did or didn't deserve.

WONDERLAND

Detective Carroll was a taciturn mesomorph from Galway. His tiny hands, which Minogue had to fight himself to stop gawking at, just didn't go with an air of combativeness. Minogue doubted he could work around this man for long. Obviously busy, obviously not in a humour of passing on information to an Inspector outside the Holy of Holies that was Drugs Central. No invite to sit either.

Minogue and Malone stood by Carroll's desk. Carroll nodded and chewed occasionally at moustache hairs that curled in to the edges of his mouth. Minogue wondered if Carroll would have words with Malone about this later.

"That's right," Carroll said. "It was them filed this. They'd know Gannon too."

"In Bray."

Carroll nodded.

No need to be so bloody talkative, Minogue wanted to say.

"So," he began again. "There'd be an in there with this fella, for Doyle, I mean. Sort of mates, confederates?"

"That'd be a reasonable assumption," Carroll said.

"You weren't out there yourself?"

"In Bray?"

"Yes, in Bray."

"No, no. I wouldn't be going out there. No."

Minogue had to think another way to crowbar anything out of this Galwegian.

"Not my cup of tea at all, no. Drug Squad in Bray would be well versed in that."

"You just know *of* this associate, the Gannon head, by the way, is that it?"

"That'd be it now."

"The way you'd be hearing a name mentioned."

"Now you have it," Carroll said.

Minogue looked up from the file.

"Well, Dermot," he said. "You're like the rest of the Galway team."

"What makes you think that now?"

"We can't get the ball off you at all."

"Well, that's how the game is played, isn't it?"

"You'd nearly be tempted to use the stick just to get the game going, but."

"Would you now."

"And take the penalty," Minogue added. "Whatever it is."

"You're well known for overuse of the hurley in Clare," he said. "But there are no cups for that, are there."

Minogue summoned up a smile. It wasn't easy.

Sometimes the satisfaction of a good clout is better value.

Carroll chewed on his moustache once, and gave Malone a lingering look.

"He has a tough case," Malone said. "There's nothing to go on. Right?"

Minogue nodded.

"He *is* a tough case, you mean," Carroll said. "Along with Kilmartin and the rest of them in that outfit. Don't think we lead a sheltered life here."

Malone shuffled his feet. Minogue heard him crack his

knuckles. Yes, he had to concede, Jim Kilmartin's chariot had spattered many a department over the years. He wondered if Carroll had heard about the mess with Fiona Hegarty too.

"So it's likely that Doyle could have been there in Bray then," he said. "If he's a crony of this Gannon fella."

"Possible," said Carroll.

Minogue gave up. He rolled his eyes as they returned down the hall.

"I know," said Malone. "Everyone guards their patch."

Minogue phoned Donnybrook station. Tunney wasn't around, but Detective Collins was. He didn't want to phone Tunney's mobile, no.

"Just to let him know I won't be by until, well maybe the morning," he said.

"All right," Collins said. "And you'll talk to him about the two girls, the friends of hers in the morning."

"That's grand."

He heard Collins turning a page.

"Me pen's gone," Collins said. "Give me a minute. . . . So you think they know a bit more than they let on then, the pair of them?"

Minogue didn't answer. He hated being prompted to keep a conversation going. It was like turning on a television or a radio for background.

". . . and you're following up a lead in Bray, is it?"

"I am. There might be a go on where Niamh Kenny got those things, those pills."

". . . pills . . ."

"Did you get all that?"

". . . in Bray . . . I did."

"If he wants to know, it's a place called Wonderland I'm heading to."

"... Wonderland ... Can you believe it, this fecking Biro is banjaxed too?"

Malone looked over when Minogue sighed.

"... Wonderland ... you're going to."

"That's it. I'm going to Wonderland."

"I'll leave a note for him, so I will."

LEAVE THE FIGHTS IN THE RING

Minogue put the mobile on the dash of the Nissan. The sun had made an appearance, and the traffic was flying by on the N7 toward Bray. His hangover ache had disappeared. There was also that lightness in his chest that he hadn't felt since they'd put through the last case in the Squad. Seven, eight months already, he couldn't stop thinking.

Inland, the hump of Katty Gallagher and the hills behind were almost glowing with colour. The wind rushed across the two policemen, scattered some papers on the back seat.

"I'm going to tell you something now," Malone said. "And you're going to keep it under your hat. Right?"

"Royh-at."

"Are you slagging me again?"

"I am. A bit, only."

"It's not like you can enunciate your fucking words any better, you know."

The seaside, Minogue thought, that's what had him a bit giddy. Out of the city, imagining that Daithi and Iseult were infants again, that there'd be Fanta and sandwiches and mullocking around on the beach in Greystones, safely beyond Bray.

"What were you going to tell me?"

"Nothing. It's all right."

"Was it about how what's his face, Carroll, is going to be very put out, about giving away a precious morsel, is it?"

"No. Carroll's an iijit. A lot of them are like that still. They want to keep everything in the shop. No."

"Go on then."

"No. It's okay. I'll tell you later maybe. Just to get your reaction, like."

Minogue let his hand run along the rubber seal where the window had slid down. He had rolled up his sleeves. He lifted his watch to see what the sun had done this past while. He thought of father Ted's housekeeper, whatever her name was.

"Ah go on," he said to Malone. "Go on, go on, go on."

"Feck off, why don't you."

"Feck off, Inspector, I think you mean?"

"Okay. Feck off, *Inspector*. Now, you happy? What has you so bleeding chipper then? Are you taking something?"

"Maybe I am. Are you?"

Malone looked over, and then pulled out to pass a minibus.

"Okay then, I will," Malone said. "The thing is, it was no big deal when I thought about it."

Minogue waited.

"I mean, you did it," Malone went on. "So it couldn't be a big deal."

Minogue glanced over.

"What are you trying to say?"

"I'm booked to see a shrink. That's what."

Minogue watched the road lines slide over as Malone took the exit to Bray.

"So there," Malone said. "What do you think about that, huh."

"Whose idea was it?"

"Mine."

Minogue looked up at the chestnut trees as they passed through Little Bray. He wanted to ask Malone questions about Sonia Chang, about her accent and her family and the Chinese restaurant her family had started up in Whitehall, and her studies to become an accountant. He wanted Malone to tell him how they had started dating.

"It'll help me to, you know, evolve."

Minogue looked back at a kebab restaurant.

"Leave the fights in the ring, is that the idea?"

"That's about it," said Malone.

He turned in off the Main Street by the hotel and waited while a lorry backed out of a lane. There were cars parked everywhere. A group of foreign-looking teenagers came around the corner. Minogue waited to hear them better. The freckly ones, the girls with sunburned noses and shoulders, were the Irish ones for sure, the hangers-on. One of the boys, a very cool customer with wraparound sunglasses, started singing and two of his friends joined in, waving their depleted cones. Spanish it was he was hearing. Minogue saw that a lot of them had jumpers around their waists. No, señor, we do not trust this Irish weather, no way José. The girls were in regulation pop starlet skimpy. No doubt the beachfront was crawling with kids now the sun was out.

Malone made it around the lorry at last. Soon they were by the terrace of houses that looked south down the beachfront.

"The bit of sun brings everyone out, bejasus," Malone said. "Like lab rats."

Minogue looked down at the traffic, stopped the most of it, and the people in groups along the grass and the promenade. Malone grunted and turned the Nissan up on a patch of curb. Minogue heard a metallic clink during the manoeuvre.

"Might as well walk, I'm telling you," he said.

It took Minogue a moment to figure out why Malone had put on his jacket. Drug Squad detectives almost always stayed armed on duty now. He reached in and took his own jacket and slung it over his shoulder.

The hotels and pubs had put out their umbrellas. There was tinkling music from farther down the arcades. They walked on the roadway, between the parked cars and the idling traffic, toward the end of the promenade. The malty smell of a pub filtered out to Minogue more than once. It was too much to leave Bray later on without helping out the local economy a bit then, he decided.

A motorist with a family in the car was half out his door. He was angry with another one who had taken a parking spot. Minogue's eyes met the wife's, a woman with a flushed face and a jaded look.

Bray Head grew higher as they threaded their way down through the crowds. He spotted a family entertainment arcade with screens flashing and people hanging around near the doors. The racket coming out of the place was fanned out on a hot breeze of candy floss and vinegary chips. Young fellas not more than nine or ten were shooting bad guys with startling realism. Oodles of blood, jumping figures, and a wild racket of noise. He paused to look in at bumper cars sparking and crashing at the back of an arcade.

Malone stopped and stepped into the shade.

"We're coming up to the place now, I think. How do you want to work it?"

"I'll wander in on me own for starters. Give me a few seconds and then you mosey in and keep your distance," Minogue said.

"All right so."

"It's Doyle we want to get to. If he's lying low, I don't want to set him off again. And go for Gannon if we see him too?"

"Fair enough."

Minogue didn't want to take out the folded paper with the printout from Gannon's record.

"So," he said. "Brendan Gannon. He has a bit of speech impediment thing going on there, it says."

"A bit like yourself."

"You can talk, you're a Dub."

"I don't mean the accent, man. So maybe you'll tell me what you're bursting to talk to him about? This mysterious long shot you're talking about?"

A LITTLE TALKING-TO
ABOUT LOYALTY

Quinn thought about turning back when he saw the traffic already building up before it was even close to the
seafront. This wasn't his caper at all, he thought while he
followed traffic on its stop-start way up the hill toward the
Royal Hotel. It was really none of his business if Canning
wanted to dig himself into a hole.

The sun had come out, and it began to heat the interior of
the car quickly. Groups of people, teenagers mostly, were
headed down the footpaths toward the seafront. That's how
desperate we were here, he thought. In Portugal, you could
get up in the morning and know you were going to have blue
skies all day long.

He imagined turning around and just cruising back into
town, going home, and . . . taking Catherine out for a jar.
He'd pick his time to tell her. Tell her what? Well, a fortnight
in Portugal, that's what. Tell her he had to stay out of the
way until something got settled. Or tell her he was going to
find out if his old mate Beans Canning had judassed him?

He found an opening and he turned down toward the
seafront. It was jammed solid at the far end. He pulled in at

a gate, and he looked at his phone. This was not smart, what he was doing. Not smart at all: he was losing it, basically. He should keep trying to reach Beans or his missus. He had to go with what he knew. It was one of those types of things happening that looked bad but turned out to be just weird, coincidence, fate. He could ask Irene, right. As if.

He dialled Canning's home number. It was answered right after the first ring.

"Jacqueline?"

"Yeah?"

"It's Bobby. I'm glad I got you. Look it, I've been looking for Beans all day. Where is he? Why's he not answering his phone?"

"Well, I only got home there a minute ago, didn't I, Bobby . . ."

There was something in her voice he wasn't used to. She was always kind of, well, not exactly cheerful, but up.

". . . The phone never stops ringing here today, for God's sake. I do Friday nights so I get this afternoon off, so I don't know, you know . . ."

"Is he around then?"

"Well actually, like, he's not. No."

It was the way she finished what she was saying, a sort of a down note, like that was final.

"Is there something wrong, Jacqueline."

"I don't know," she said. "Is there?"

"I don't know," he said. "But I'd like to get a hold of him. You know?"

She said nothing. He thought he heard her sigh.

"I don't have a problem," he said to her.

"Well, you know," she began, but stopped.

"Go on. What are you getting at?"

"Didn't he talk to you though?"

"No he didn't. I wish he had."

"This is awkward Bobby, you know. He wouldn't want me talking."

"Talking about what?"

"Look. I'll tell him you phoned, that's the best."

"No, it fucking isn't, Jacqueline! Sorry, sorry. Listen. Sorry—really. But I have to talk to him. It's really, really important."

She said nothing. He wondered if she was going to hang up.

"Jacqueline?"

"Yeah, Bobby."

"You have to tell him. I don't know what his problem is, but it's going to get out of hand if he doesn't get in touch."

Still she had nothing to say. He watched two skinheads carrying a plastic bag with bottles in it.

"So will you do that for me? Will you, Jacqueline? To phone me right away?"

"Okay. I'll tell him."

"Thanks, look I'll be waiting on him now. Tell him that."

"Fine."

Quinn waited. She was still on the line.

"Is everything okay there, Jacqueline? I mean, is there someone there, you can't talk?"

"No, I'm okay. It's just, well, it's between you and him. I better leave it at that."

"Jacqueline, listen. You have to believe me here. Trust me now. Okay? We all want what's best, right?"

"Okay."

"Well, where is he? You know I've got a feeling maybe you know and all . . . do you know?"

"No."

"He didn't tell you anything?"

"No. He's started drinking, that's all. I hope he's not going to, you know."

"I'll talk to him, Jacqueline. I will. I'll straighten him out—but nice. Really."

"I don't know if he wants that, Bobby. From you, like."

The car was beginning to bake now in the sun. He pulled at the visor to get a bit of shade on his neck.

"Jackie, listen to me. You're worried, I can tell. We're on the same side here. Come on."

"Well," she began.

"Was he talking to you?"

"Jesus, we're married, Bobby, you know."

"I mean, about work. Only that."

"I'm going to tell you something, Bobby. Maybe I shouldn't though."

"No—Jackie, you can tell me anything. Really. I don't mind."

"Okay. . . . He's kind of, fidgety. A bit jittery lately, like restless? He gets like that—you probably know better than me."

"But that's easy fixed, Jacq—"

"Well, maybe. But I don't know. He's not happy in himself. Things aren't going his way, like. And he wants his own thing. That's what it comes down to, Bobby. I mean, don't get me wrong."

"Right," he said. A coiling, like acid, was going on in his guts now.

"He doesn't have the patience maybe he had, Bobby. It all catches up on us, doesn't it?"

"You're right there."

"So that's the drinking too, that's a sign. He went off early, and I smelled it off him before he left."

"He just needs a chat, Jackie."

"Well, I don't know, Bobby. It's very personal with him, you know?"

"He wouldn't want you worried, Jackie. It's between me and you here."

Quinn wondered if it was a sob or a sigh he heard then. Her voice was more pinched now, higher.

"He doesn't like the other people involved, Bobby. Doesn't trust them. In work, like. He's not comfortable with them."

"We can work on that, Jackie. I know we can. It takes time, right."

"I suppose."

"Tell him if he asks, okay? Tell him that you think Bobby's forgetting to do things right by him. To include him? Everyone takes their mate for granted at some point, right?"

She swallowed and he knew she was trying not to cry now.

"It'll work out," he said. "But Jackie, you have some idea where he goes when he's out of sorts. Right?"

"Maybe," she said. "He just said, well he said he was going to see a fella. Some idea, some new idea he could work with, his own thing."

"Did he say who?"

"No, no. He just said he'd be glad to get out of the city for a bit anyway."

"He didn't mean going on the lorries again, did he, you know the fruit limo down to the culchies?"

He could tell she was trying to rally now.

"Ah, no. But he did enjoy that, I remember, back at the start anyway. He did. No, he didn't say that. He just headed out, hardly said a word. I says will you be home for the tea and he says nothing. Then he says . . . what did he say again? Something to do with bumper cars. 'I'm going on the bumper cars today,' he says. What bumper cars, I says."

"The dodgems?"

"That's what they call them isn't it? Where you go around crashing into other fellas?"

Quinn's thumb was beginning to cramp. He changed hands on the phone.

"Where would he go for that, Jackie?"

"God, I don't know. Don't they have them here in town?"

"You said he'd be aiming for getting out of town for a bit."

"Well, I suppose. You know something? I meant to tell you, but I had this same conversation already today. Another fella. Well, sort of like this one."

Her laugh was fake.

"What," he said. "What other fella?"

"Ah, I'm addled here. No, it's just funny, sort of. I sort of just assumed it was whatever fella he said he was going to meet."

Quinn was holding his breath. He turned the mouthpiece up, away so she wouldn't hear his breathing. A cop, he thought, maybe even a few of them, like Grogan said. On the payroll. No wonder the bastard was coming apart at the seams.

"I just told your man the first thing that came into me head," she said. "Just something in his voice so irritating, you know? I was in a bit of a rush, the phone's ringing, I'm late, the kitchen's like a bomb hit it and I'm heading out the door, see?"

"Who was it Jackie, who phoned?"

"I don't know, I'm telling you. He said he was supposed to meet Beans today, but Beans hadn't said where exactly. He asked me where he'd be, 'cause he didn't go to work, right?"

"He didn't say what it was about, did he?"

"Well, I wasn't in a humour of dealing with him, especially seeing as he was so, well, sarcastic—"

"How'd you mean sarcastic?"

"Like, sarcastic."

"What was he cursing or slagging you?"

"No, no. It was just the tone. Says he, 'Would I be correct in assuming then that Larry will be absent from the office today?' 'The office,' Jesus. You know."

"It is an office, Jackie. It is."

"Sorry, yes, but you know what I mean, right."

"Sort of Northern?"

"Yeah. Probably. Well spoken, but in a weird way."

Quinn's scalp began to crawl now. The heat wasn't registering with him anymore, it was something else.

"What'd you tell him?" he said.

"Ah, I fobbed him off—I actually put down the phone on him."

"But what did you say?"

"I said, 'For all I know he's off on the bumper cars in Bray or somewhere like—'"

"Bray? Why did you say Bray?"

"God, I don't know, Bobby. It just popped into my mind. Larry mentioned he was out there a few times, you know, work."

Quinn shivered once. He wiped his forehead and looked at the moisture on his hand. He thought of Doyle, cursing as he slid across into the passenger seat to get out that moment before he heard the shot. Doyle's foot kicking up at the door as he was thrown back. He turned and looked at the people walking along the promenade, the cars that had begun to move.

"It was just to get rid of him, Bobby."

He got back into the traffic and took the first turn back into the town that he could. Why was he on the lookout for a van? That's how his head had gone, just stupid.

He found a car leaving a spot near the DART station. He probably wouldn't get closer than this with the car. He turned off the ignition and rolled up the window. Roe wouldn't have the neck to do it in broad daylight here with crowds around.

He might.

He felt for the bag under the seat and tugged at it, thinking of the soft pressure from the magazine spring as he had loaded the clip with ten rounds. He pulled up the bag and wrapped it in his Adidas jacket and laid the bundle on his lap.

The car felt like an oven now. He was pouring sweat, his face swollen with the heat. He should just turn the key, drive back into Dublin, and do the smart thing: get Catherine and Brittney, go to the airport, and leave. He could do some things by phone from there. It didn't matter if things fell apart for a week, or a fortnight, or forever, for that matter. Grogan and them weren't going to just walk all over them here.

The bundle felt a lot heavier than it should. He remembered when he'd first picked up the gun off in that pub out in what do you call the place, Enfield. CZ, what was that, why wasn't there proper stuff being sent down to him, he'd asked. The guy who'd showed up was from up there, of course, with a serious sneer. *Liam says to take his word for it, it's a good one.*

His hand went to the door opener but he stopped. Drop the matter, Grogan would tell him. Start the engine and just get out of here.

He opened the door instead, felt the dread drop into his chest. He stepped out onto the road, the bundle held tight to him. He tried again in his head to talk the panic away. He'd find Beans first thing, just grab him, shove him in the car, and go. Pull off the road in a quiet spot somewhere and give Beans fucking Canning the going over of his life, see if there was even an atom of truth in what Grogan had told him. Give him a little talking-to about loyalty.

He smelled candy floss somewhere, seaweed or sewage maybe. He checked the doors were locked. He knew he couldn't panic now; a cool head, keep the lid on this. He looked up and down the promenade. Packed, like he'd expected. But why did everything look so weird, so dangerous here now?

GAGA

Minogue felt in his pocket for the photocopy. What was it about tattoos, he wondered. Was it really as pat as self-mutilation? It couldn't be. He looked around the arcade. The fella with the mohawk and the dog had pegged them going in, he knew, but he'd stayed put. He squinted back into the glare. Mohawk still hadn't moved off. No doubt there'd be lookouts somewhere else.

He saw Malone edging his way around clusters of teenagers by a machine that had something to do with dancing. There was a wicket of sorts next to a counter, and next to that a display of gewgaws you could win. The woman behind the counter was half-occupied with a Pepsi and a Hello! She dipped her cigarette in an ashtray hidden below the counter. The bass beat of the music was going right through Minogue's jawbone now.

The bumper car arena had a garage-sized doorway on to the lane at the side of the building. It looked like there were two fellas supervising. Malone too had started eyeing the goings-on the floor here. He caught Minogue's eye and nodded at one of the two men moving between the bumper cars. That was Gannon then—Gaga: tank top, a wispy goatee, the sunglasses up over his head.

Gaga had a grace to him that reminded Minogue of a monkey. The swings from the bars, the fluid landings, bounds and even springs as he moved between the cars were like a ballet routine. Gannon then swung up onto a platform and his mate, a young fella with an almost bald head and the same wraparound sunglasses, slapped a button.

Gaga had spotted Malone. Minogue stared at him until Gaga turned and made him out too. He raised his eyebrows and nodded. Gannon turned and said something to his mate, and then he skipped over a partition. Malone stepped in front of him. Minogue took his time getting over, pausing to watch two boys blasting people in some American city.

"A word with you," Mr. Gannon, he said.

"What," said Gannon.

Minogue had seen the lips seize to quell a stammer. He nodded toward the lane.

"Yu-yuh-yuh."

Gannon stopped and sighed, and then he shook out the words.

"Your man here already asked, answer's no."

"I can't hear you."

"Leave me alone, is wah-wah-what I said."

"What's the rush here," Malone said. "Where are you going?"

"I have nothing to say to yous. So yous can sh-sh-shag off. It's a free country."

Minogue looked around Gannon's face. A boy really. No violent stuff on his sheet.

"It's only free if you have the money," he said.

"What?"

"We're trying to get in touch with a fella. You know him."

"Don't talk to me. I'm out of here."

"Okay," Minogue said. "I'll leave the money with the dog fella over there, then."

"What moh-moh-money?"

"Don't be worrying," Minogue said and reached into his pocket. "It's square."

"What are you doing?"

"I'm giving you your wages, is what I'm doing."

"Are you m-m-m-mental?"

Minogue took out two tenners and folded them carefully. The woman at the wicket had caught on now.

"Should I leave it with the woman over there for you instead?"

"Fuck off the b-b-b-both of you, I know my rights."

"I hope she gives it to you later on," Minogue said." People these days, you know?"

Gannon's face twisted up.

"Don't you try that, you f-f-fu-fuh— you bastard."

"You have the idea now, do you."

"That's the lowest I ever seen, even from a cop. The l-l-l-lowest."

Minogue kept up his gaze at the man at the controls. "How could you see anything in those sunglasses."

"Who do you think they'll believe," he said. "I mean to say, are there people who believe that a Guard's going to just walk up and fork over twenty quid, for nothing?"

Gannon shifted his eyes from Minogue to the woman at the counter.

"You're a fucking low-down bastard, is what you are."

"I'll meet you over there by the door," Minogue said. "A couple of minutes, just so's you can go and explain yourself and look tough with your mates there."

Gannon's eyes narrowed. Minogue wondered if he was going to spit.

"Go on with you," Malone said. "Give us a few more hard ones with the bad language too. Play to the gallery. You fucking git, you."

"Fuck you too," Gannon said and he walked away. "B-b-b-bollocks."

Minogue did some head-shaking. Malone shouted a parting curse at Gannon.

"Okay," Malone said then. "I have to go to the jacks. I'll be out in a sec."

A bumper car hit another hard and hopped. The two girls inside screamed and Gannon swung out to push the car back onto the grid.

Minogue headed back toward the counter. Malone had stopped next to a bank of video games. He caught Minogue's eye and flicked his head toward a gaggle of students playing racing cars.

They were Italian or Spanish, Minogue didn't know yet, around the three car-racing games. Aftershave galore, olive skin, beautiful eyes. He moved around them and saw the man that Malone meant him to look at. The man was holding a gun at the end of a wire. For a moment Minogue couldn't remember him. The man shifted into a shooting stance.

Canning, it was, Bobby Quinn's fella.

He edged his way around to see the screen. "LA COPS": a few cars overturned on a city street, and bad guys leaping up at random from behind things.

"And you," Canning said. "You're a goner too. You bastard."

Minogue leaned against the side of a Race Team 2000 pretend motorbike. There were sweat patches down Canning's shirt. Minogue smelled whiskey breath.

A warning came on the screen, a timer counting down. Canning shifted on his feet and shot faster. He was drunk, or close enough, Minogue decided. On a bender. Maybe he'd gotten a payout for something.

The game ended with bullet holes on the screen, and red paint flowing down. Continue, it said. Canning tried to jam the gun back into a plastic holder. He missed once, a second time, and then threw it at the console.

For a few moments when he turned, Minogue wondered if Canning would just gawk and walk. Maybe he was in the DTs and think he was seeing things.

"Well," Canning said. "Well, well, well."

Minogue nodded.

Canning took a step back and tucked a shirttail into his trousers. Minogue heard his breath whistling in his nose. Canning straightened up, but his eyes seemed to still wander.

"You getting paid for standing there?"

Minogue nodded again. Canning belched and rearranged his feet.

"Robbing the taxpayers. That's what. You're all the same, you are."

Minogue kept up his study. Canning was trying too hard to keep still, but he swayed again and had to move his feet again.

"What are you looking at?"

"I'm waiting for my laundry," Minogue said. "I hear it's the place to go. When you need to launder things."

A sneer spread across Canning's face and he sniffed loudly.

"Oh, very funny. Very fucking funny is what you are. I don't think."

"Are you part of the cast here then?"

"Cast? What are you saying cast?"

"Do you scrub the collars, is it, or iron the sleeves here? The laundry, like."

"You're a gobshite, is what you are."

Minogue glanced at the LA COPS screen.

"Did you always want to be an LA cop?"

"A comedian, bejasus," Canning said, louder. "He thinks he's a comedian. Go and fuck off and leave me alone. And not be harassing me. You culchie fuck, you. And your side-kick, what's his name, Tonto. The Dub."

"Muhammad Ali, you mean."

"Just fuck off. You're in me light."

Canning pushed by Minogue and shouldered some students out of his way. Minogue considered trying a Drunk and Disorderly on Canning.

"Out of the way yous fucking, yous . . . *budgies!*" he heard Canning shout over the din. "With yis'r babbling—out of me way!"

One of the students made a stand and said something but Canning didn't stop.

Then Minogue saw the bag left under LA COPS. He picked it up and looked down into it. A cardboard box had been hurriedly repackaged. He slid back the tab and pulled out a bubble-wrapped package. Some kind of electronics, a heavy enough box, a thing with a lens. Initials CCD.

Canning came back barging through the students. He grabbed the bag. Minogue let go of the straps.

"You thief, you! Look at you. Robbing stuff."

He headed back through the group. This time the students made way. One of them caught Minogue's eye. Minogue tapped his forehead.

"Loco," he thought he heard the student say.

"What was the Spanish, or Italian, or whatever, for drunk and stupid?"

Minogue left by the promenade entrance. He saluted the fella with the dog.

"Grand weather now at last."

Dogman looked away.

Minogue headed around the corner to the lane. Malone was already there. There was no sign of Gaga Gannon.

"Guess who or what nearly ran me over coming out of the jacks," Malone said.

Minogue didn't want to spoil it.

"Canning," Malone said. "You know, Quinn's go-for? And he's arseholes drunk."

I KNOW WHAT I SEEN

Bobby Quinn's headache came on so fast. It had started just after he had stepped out of the car. Right away he knew it would be a bastard, one of the ones he'd started to get in prison. Two doctors told him it was migraine. Another doctor told him it probably wasn't.

The pain had started in his left eye. In no time at all it was in both eyes, like nails, and the whole thing topped off with one of those ice-cream headaches. It's the sun, he thought through the fog of pain starting. The lousy sleep he was trying to get by on. This unholy mess he was in.

He began to forget that he looked stupid and conspicuous, and probably a bit mental, with the jacket over his arm. He narrowed his eyes against the sunlight, but that didn't slow the pain. It just gave a yellow cast to much of what was around him, a sort of worn-out look to everything. The sun off a passing windscreen went through his eye like a blade.

And nobody knows, he couldn't stop thinking. Nobody here knows except Roe and himself. There was no one to turn to; there was no help. Grogan had left him swinging now. Somewhere around here Beans Canning was lolling about, on the piss maybe. Playing bloody video games, probably trying out this spy camera stunt that that bollocks had been trying to palm off on them the last time they were out.

Quinn stopped. He massaged his eyes, pushed them gently back in their sockets. It brought him no relief. He couldn't keep thinking like this. It was more of those bastards and their scheming up there again, Grogan's mob. That's how they operated, setting people against one another. He thought about trying Grogan's number again. Maybe someone had robbed his mobile. Right—Grogan had left it somewhere by mistake.

Foreign students, the place was full of them. They didn't talk, they babbled and they shouted and they screamed while they barrelled down the footpaths and out on to the roads even. He grasped the rolled-up jacket tighter, imagined it going off. But no way was he going to check the safety again.

The place was packed, just packed. Teenagers everywhere, a few oul wans on the bandits, a family there annoying the mother and father for money for The Claw machine. The racket from the arcade began to separate from the noise of the music in the shops nearby. He recognized the thump and squeal of bumper cars drifting over the video games every now and then.

The lookout with the Doberman was here again, complete with shades. His head turned toward Quinn, and then down to the dog. He wrapped the leash, secured it, and said something to the dog, who sat. He started to head over to where Quinn had stopped to suss out the place.

"The Law's here," said the man with the dog. "Plainclothes. They went out again."

"When?"

"Only a minute ago."

"Anyone with them, coming or going?"

"Well, I seen them talking to a fella."

"What fella?"

The man hesitated. He looked back to his dog leashed to a lamp pole. People were giving the dog a wide berth.

"You'd be doing me a favour here," Quinn said.

"Well, it was Bren they were talking to."

"Bren, who's Bren?"

"Bren Gannon. The bumpers and that stuff. He does them."

"Gaga?"

"Yeah. People call him that."

Quinn examined the man's face, tried to see through the tint in the glasses.

"So you're a friend of his, are you?"

"Not really."

"Not really," Quinn repeated to himself. No, why would you be. It was every man for himself out here, everywhere now, wasn't it.

The man with the dog was waiting.

"Does Gannon have his own thing on the side here?"

"I don't know."

"Sure you do. Tries to fence, to move stuff?"

"Maybe."

Quinn looked over at the dog. The bugger was watching everything they did. Very protective, Quinn half-remembered. He reached up quickly and plucked the shades off the man's nose.

"Are you on the make here," he said. "Are you a two-faced lying bastard, strung out on something, would sell his mother down the river for a hit? Are you?"

The eyes were a bit bloodshot. He said nothing, but didn't look away. The dog had stood up, Quinn saw now, and was scratching at the cement.

"Well then. Do you know everyone here then?"

"A fair few. A fair few."

"Do you know me?"

He nodded. The eyes were moist and red-rimmed. He needed more than a few nights' sleep for whatever got him this way, Quinn decided.

"How?"

"The day before yesterday, you were here. With another fella."

Quinn stared at him.

"A short fella, gold bracelet. Likes to play on the games here sometimes."

"What time of day was that, then?"

"A quarter after two."

He made a signal to the dog, which cocked its head to the side. He signalled again, and the dog backed to the pole and sat. The man was slow to bring his eyes back to Quinn's.

"You're a nosy fuck," Quinn said. "Do you know that?"

He shrugged.

"That could get you into a lot of trouble. You hear?"

"More for you, I'd say."

"What? What did you say?"

Quinn grabbed his collar. The man seemed to have expected it. He kept his eyes on the crowds.

"You have some mouth on you."

He glanced at Quinn for several moments. Quinn let go of the collar slowly.

"If I find out you're trying to wind me up, I'll do for you. You hear? Today—right here. You hearing me?"

"I know what I seen. Why would I make up stuff? I gets paid to keep me eyes open."

"Who pays you?"

"Management."

"What, are you running a thing here? Who are you with?"

"No. It's legit. I know everybody. They don't want hooligans or knackers ruining the place."

"Just you?"

"Me and the dog. That's all."

The ache rolled relentlessly back into Quinn's forehead.

"Okay," he said. "The cops are gone, you said?"

"One of them came out this way. He says how-do to me. He knows, right? Then he went up the lane there, the lane leads up to the shops."

Quinn watched a young couple leaving Wonderland. The girl was arguing with the boy. He reached up to hit her it looked, but stopped. He shouted at her, but she didn't back off. She called him a name, and he stormed off.

"So I'll keep an eye out then, will I, Mr. Quinn?"

Quinn stared at him. Brazen.

"Okay. Are you going to try and charge me for that?"

"I'll take what you give me."

"You'll get a damn sight more than you expect if what you told me turns out to be wrong too, let me tell you. You and your dog here."

"Mr. Quinn."

Quinn turned back.

"The fella who was with you the other day."

"What about him?"

"The cops weren't talking just to Bren."

Quinn thought about just swinging the gun up and clobbering him.

"Don't say that," he said. "I don't want to hear another fucking word out of you, you lying bastard. I'll deal with you later for that. You know who I am, what I— What? What are you looking at me like that for?"

"He's here."

"You're sure? Where?"

He nodded toward the bank of consoles.

"In there?"

"I didn't see him coming out either, not this way, in any-how."

"You're sure? I swear to God, if you're playing games . . ."

"I'm sure. I don't make mistakes like that."

Quinn looked into the gloom.

"That should be worth something, maybe," the man said.

Quinn jabbed him in the chest twice, slowly.

"You be here when I come out. Don't move an inch. We'll see what it's worth."

He brushed against a trio of teenagers hanging off the back of the seats for Grand Prix. The engine sounds were so loud here they were coming up through his shoes. The woman at the counter, Valerie or whatever she called herself, had spotted him. She'd have seen Beans too, she was no dope, he decided. He headed her way, trying to blot out the racket and the heat and the pain like a bar pressed in over his eyes. He was a couple of steps away from her, and she was waiting for him to speak, when he saw the man stepping out of the jacks.

What he knew now didn't have to do with the man's face, which he didn't see anyway, or the fact that he wasn't a kid. It wasn't even the way he walked, the familiar stride that he couldn't place, the way he was in a hurry but trying to not let on that he was in a hurry. The Adidas bag was in the left hand, like before, like he was going to a game, or to the gym. It wasn't just the way the man moved. It wasn't even the fact that he wasn't one of the million teenagers here. Not even the moustache, although there was something about it, or the hair. What it was, was a few things together. Mostly it was a tiny thing going on in Quinn's mind, like why is a bloke that age carrying a rucksack here, he's not a kid coming home from school, is he, and there's no school anyway. And why is he in a hurry but trying to not let on that he's in a hurry. Why is the packsack new anyway; a warm summer's afternoon; an arcade full of kids. It was something else yet scratching at his mind, and he couldn't ignore it. What was it about the guy that felt familiar?

"Roe," he yelled through the noise, and he pushed away from the counter and headed down the other side of the consoles toward the front door. In a space between two games he saw the man brush by a kid, the kid calling after him. Quinn pushed a girl aside, ignored a teenager's "hey, watch it you gobshite," and made it to the end of the row. The man with the rucksack had been slowed by a bunch of kids, but he was nearly out. Quinn moved to the middle of the passageway, shouted again. The man glanced over this time. He turned and began making his way back.

Quinn felt his arms go weak, a tremor in his legs. He took a step down the passageway, knew he might be hurting kids as he pushed them hard to the side. He clutched his jacket tighter. The man with the packsack had skipped beyond the crowd.

Quinn cleared the end of the passageway and hurdled the wooden barrier for the bumper car arena. Gannon, the thick who'd gotten Canning out here, was out on the floor fiddling with one of the cars. A guy at the controls had jumped out on the floor, shouting. He got close to the running man, and made a grab at him. Quinn got around three stalled cars, and saw the dodgem fella take a step back, with his arms up at his shoulders. Gannon stood with his mouth open. The man with the moustache was pointing something. Then he lowered his arm, and the gun, and ran.

Someone was screaming now, a girl. Quinn felt in his jacket for the pistol, thought how stupid this was. His legs were almost cramping as he stood rooted to the floor, unable to decide. He studied Gannon's open mouth, tried to guess what words he was struggling to say. All this might not be actually happening, he thought. A nightmare, or he'd been in some accident. A heart attack or a stroke or something?

A girl fell as she tried to get out of one of the stalled bumper cars. People were rushing around him. Gannon was coming over his way. The other fella who ran the bumpers was half-walking, half-skipping back toward him too, looking over at the door out into the laneway. Quinn thought of Canning, the man with the bag leaving the toilet. He knew in some part of his mind that wasn't working right now that he had to get out of here. They'd do anyone, they would. Maybe it was too late.

JUST LET ME SEE HIM

Minogue watched Malone biting his nails. He thought that Malone had broken the habit a while back. The turning hand reminded him of someone sewing. The air in the laneway seemed to be holding a smell of chips and vinegar and sugary flavouring in front of his face.

A young man and a girl with the sideways look and freckled, ruddy faces came up the lane, arguing. The jaunty "How's it going boss" from the man as he passed, the wink that told Minogue he'd been made as a Guard, said tinkers to Minogue. Traveller, he should say. Whatever, as they said on the telly now. Whatever. Iseult had lit into him a fair bit not long back about that. The girl resumed swearing at the man over money before they were gone ten feet farther down the lane.

A new disco racket began pouring out of the speakers now. Abba was back, again, again? Minogue examined the speaker set down by the door to the arcade to see if it was actually vibrating on the cement. He could kick the wire loose handy enough without electrocuting himself. He went back to the photocopy of Doyle's tattoo again. He tried to remember more from Niamh Kenny's painting.

"This is stupid," he heard Malone call out over the music.

"I'm going in and pull him out. I'll fucking Gaga him, I can tell you, if and he's done a bunk on us."

There was a shriek from somewhere close by. Minogue looked down the lane. Malone looked over at him, and turned toward the door to the arcade. The man running out had one of those sports bags in his hands. Not a young fella, Minogue saw. But pickpockets come in all shapes and sizes, didn't they? And tinkers worked in gangs, didn't they? This one was a butty of one of the pair that had just gone up the lane?

"Oi there," he heard Malone call out. "Oi you, stop it right there."

The man was breathing hard. He looked up and down the laneway. He was holding something in the bag. "Red-handed," Minogue muttered. Malone stepped out to block the laneway now. Right at two Guards. And the odd-looking hair had to be the crappiest disguise. A true pro, by God.

"What's your hurry there pal," he said.

Minogue saw the man pull something up from the bag. Ditching whatever he'd robbed, was his first thought. Then he waved something at Malone.

The panic that grabbed Minogue seemed to be noise, a great roar about his ears. Malone had gone into a crouch and he was backing across the laneway, pulling at his own jacket. Minogue let himself fall sideways toward the wall across from the door to the arcade, heard his own knee crack as he went down. The cement was uneven under his hands, greasy, and luke warm. He kept his eye on the barrel of the pistol as it wavered, and he saw the man's hand snap as he let off a shot. Kilmartin was right, he realized again: a suppressor made a sound like a mallet.

He knew it was Malone shouting now but he didn't know what Malone was saying. He pulled up his knees and wrapped his arms around his head, felt the wall at his back. Malone let another roar out of him again. He heard an automatic going off again and again, counting five, then six. There was a sound of a shoe scuffing nearby, the jarring slap of a bone on cement. How often he had heard it when kids fell, the shocked second before they began to wail with the pain and upset.

He moved his elbow and saw the man with the moustache stir once on the ground. Malone was sitting, his back to the wall across from him.

"I'm hit," Malone said. "Boss, are you there? I'm hit, I think . . ."

Minogue felt the cell phone in his pocket grinding into him as he slid across the cement. Wrappers, ancient bits of blackened bubble gum he hadn't noticed before, gritty parts to the cement. He kept his eyes on the fallen man.

"I'm here," he said. "I'm coming."

He wriggled to within arm's reach of the man and rolled up onto one knee. Then he threw himself on him. He heard a breath, he thought, but there was no push back.

"I'm on him," he called out. "I have him."

He got his knee between the man's shoulder blades. He felt the wet soak into the knee of his trousers. He pulled at the right arm that had gone under. Malone was getting up now, his mouth open and his back arched. Minogue looked down at where his knee was lodged. There was red on the man's jacket there.

Malone hopped, fell back against the wall, holding his thigh.

"Give me a line on him, boss, just let me see him."

There were faces in the doorway, a shout. Minogue had the man's right arm at the elbow. The man was slack still. He pulled the arm out, saw the finger jammed, broken even, in the trigger guard from the fall. There were flecks of blood on the man's neck. Minogue stared at the way the head was twisted, saw the edge of the netting where the wig had slipped.

He grasped the wrist now and tugged at the grip of the revolver.

"Hey!" Malone roared then. Minogue looked to where he was now pointing his pistol.

Quinn's mouth was open. He crouched, took a step back.

"On the ground," Malone shouted. "Put that jacket out there in the ground—drop it! *Drop it!*"

Quinn's nostrils seemed to have disappeared. He let the jacket down on the cement. Minogue pushed down again with his knee and worked harder to get the pistol out of the fingers. He pulled the hand back and slid the gun over the finger. The wig had moved up on the man's head. It was probably over his eyes by now.

Minogue was light-headed when he stood. He kept his thumb on the hammer. He heard screaming start up again from somewhere in the arcade. Malone's voice had a ragged hoarseness to it now.

"I want to see your hands," Malone called out to Quinn. "Flat out on the ground. And folley them down, the rest of you. On your face!"

Malone squeezed his eyes shut and shook his head once. He pushed himself away from the wall with a grunt. There was blood on the cement where he'd been.

He dropped plastic restraints on the pavement.

Minogue pushed off from the fallen man, his eyes on Quinn. His knee was burning now, and he let his fingers run over it, felt the rip in the fabric, the torn skin. He watched Quinn's arms go up along the cement. Quinn was saying something. Malone told him to shut up.

"Keep your arms up there," Minogue said to Quinn.

He started at the ankles. He pushed down on Quinn's neck with his left hand.

"Hey," said Quinn, "I'm not going to—"

"Not a word out of you."

Malone was wheezing now. He lurched in closer.

"I have him, boss. Okay. Clip him up, I'm on him."

Minogue thumbed off the gun he had taken from the fallen man. He pulled the lead tight through the restraints, and closed the cinch. He tugged at them, felt the weight of Quinn's arms, and let them down again.

"Christ," he heard Malone say. He turned, saw Malone had unwrapped the jacket. Quinn's pistol was an American .38. Malone slid it out and emptied it, left it open on the cement for Minogue.

"Who else have you here?" Minogue asked.

"I swear to God," Quinn said. "I'm not in this at all, I only came out to stop him."

Minogue drew Quinn's left arm down first. He pulled the retainer tight and secured it. Quinn's cheek pressed harder into the grit on the pavement, but his eyes stayed on the shoes of the fallen man. Minogue tested the nylon tie and stepped back. Malone hadn't been able to bend down to retrieve the pistol. Minogue picked it up again, snapped it closed, and put it in his other pocket. Malone let out a low grunt and sucked in air through his teeth. He began to hobble, he stopped, and he leaned on Minogue. Minogue had his phone out already.

"That bastard shot me," he said. "He *shot* me, I can't believe it."

"Yes, Wonderland," Minogue said louder to the dispatcher. "The seafront, the arcades. And it's a shooting, a Guard, yes."

Malone's left trouser leg was saturated now, he saw. Minogue couldn't see any entry. He looked around for Gannon. Maybe he'd done a bunk.

A movement caught his eye, and he watched a dark line move slowly from under the chest of the fallen man along a fault in the cement.

"I came out to stop him," he heard Quinn say. "I swear to God."

"Shut up," Malone shouted. He clenched his eyes tight and groaned again.

Minogue looked up and down the lane. The shouting had stopped. Bray, teeming with people, was suddenly deserted? He didn't know he had been shaking so much. The noise from the open door of the arcade seemed to be louder now. A movement there: Gannon's face to the side of a console, some kids, open-mouthed.

Malone lurched in on Minogue then, his fingers clawing tighter on his shoulder. His hand, still pointing the automatic at the fallen man was wavering.

"What the hell is keeping them," he heard Malone say. There was panic in the voice. He shouldered harder into Malone when he felt the slide.

"Things are going spacey on me," Malone muttered. "I'm going to sit down."

A million stars burst in the light around Minogue as he got Malone under the arm. He tried to brace himself better, but Malone was going slack on him, muttering, hissing. He fell the last bit to the pavement.

"Ah, me arse," he heard Malone whisper. Then his breath squealed and he clenched his eyes tight.

Malone's face was gone white now, and there was a sheen to it. He opened his eyes wide, stared at Minogue. He spoke in a clear voice.

"Are they here now, boss? Are they?"

Minogue kept pushing on where he thought the entry was. It wasn't an artery, he thought. The colour, the flow.

He saw that Malone's arm was wavering.

"Let me have that, Tommy."

Malone said nothing. His face was relaxed, a hint of a curiosity in his eyes.

"Let go of it, Tommy. Or you'll do me by mistake."

"The other fella," Malone said.

"I'll take care of it."

Malone's grip loosened a little. He looked down at where Minogue was pressing the jacket against his leg.

"Am I okay?"

The dreamy voice had Minogue sure Malone was going to faint.

"You will be, yes."

Malone leaned to the side to look at the fallen man.

"Is that him?"

Minogue took the automatic, realized it had been four years since he'd done training. He let Malone's hand down on his lap.

"Don't take your eye off him, okay?"

It was the drowsy, fearful voice of a child waking, not waking fully, from a nightmare, that Minogue heard.

"Yes, Tommy."

"Can you believe it?" Malone said, the whimsy breaking out in his voice. "He just did it, he pointed a gun at me and he shot me."

Minogue glanced at Malone's face, saw the eyes widen.

"Not long now, Tommy, I hear the cavalry."

More faces, teenagers, began to appear from inside the arcade. Minogue kept trying to wave them off.

"Who's that, boss?"

"Just kids, Tommy, it's okay."

"Someone's shot," he heard a girl say. "Look, a gun over there."

"Oh, where in the name of *fuck* are our lads," Malone groaned.

Minogue watched Quinn's eyes. They moved from the cement by his cheek to the fallen man and back.

Then a white car shot by the top end of the laneway. Minogue heard the tires bite, doors slamming. A Guard ran by the top of the laneway. Minogue saw the gun in his hand. They've missed us, he thought, the thicks.

"What's that," Malone said. "Are they here yet?"

The Guard came back, and looked down the lane. Minogue watched another Guard, then two detectives run along both sides of the laneway now. More people began inching out into the lane from the arcade now.

He got up from his hunkers, waited for the spinny yaw in his head to stop.

"The cops," one of the teenagers shouted.

Minogue had his photocard out. He held it up. The detectives had gone in to run to both sides of the laneway and taken up stances. He didn't want to look their way, to see the guns aimed at him.

"Drug Squad," he called out. "There's two of us, one hurt."

"Get down on the ground there," one of the detectives shouted. "Get down, and put that gun flat out—use your fingers. Get down!"

Minogue looked at the detective now. He studied the line between the eyebrows, the fear in his face. The vest had slid up under the detective's chin. He could barely see the automatic pointing at him. The other detective was saying something. Quinn had bent his neck to watch them.

"Get down, I said! You! Do it!"

The second detective had his hand on the other's shoulder now.

". . . know him . . . ," Minogue heard.

The siren he was beginning to hear had better be an ambulance. The second detective was calling out to him.

"You're what's his name, are you? Kilmartin's old mob?"

"That's me," said Minogue. "Get us an ambulance."

Malone's voice was a reedy wheeze now.

"Me too," he said. "So easy does it there, cowboy."

Welcome to the Real
World There, Pal

Kilmartin showed up on the ward pretending to be surprised to see Minogue and his wife sitting outside the door to Malone's room. Minogue studied his friend's professional stroll down from the lift. Very much the new visitor to the planet, he decided.

Kilmartin issued a big smile at the nursing station.

"Do they still make suits like that," Minogue murmured.

"Now!" Kathleen hissed.

Kilmartin was in debonair mode, to be sure. He leaned in over the counter to share some wit. Up came the right leg of course, Minogue noticed, kicked up like a horse. He had asked him years ago about the mannerism. He couldn't remember Kilmartin's explanation.

"Jim's very dapper, with the get-up," Kathleen whispered. "And he's lost weight."

There was no proper reason why Minogue was thinking of Maurice Chevalier as he eyed Kilmartin's withdrawal from the nurses' station. A crisp click from the leather soles, a shine to beat the band.

"The bookworm himself," Kilmartin called out. "Not your breviary, I take it."

"Oh hardly, Jim," Kathleen said.

"Ah, Kathleen Mavourneen. Why do we need the rain to remind us how lovely the flowers are?"

"A rose among thorns," she said.

"What are you on," Minogue said to him. Kilmartin closed one eye.

"A knocker is what you are. A *professional* knocker. I'd say more, but . . ."

"Tell them to move the patch down your arm a bit," Minogue said.

"Don't mind him, Jim," from Kathleen.

Kilmartin beamed.

"Never fear, Kate. Many's the year since I did that, by God."

He poked at the book Minogue still held.

"Vienna? Is that a sign of something?"

Minogue closed the book. He eyed Kilmartin tugging at his cuffs, rubbing his hands together.

"You oul tart," he murmured. "You should open a book yourself."

"You're like an oul one there. Here, have you been in yet?"

"We're waiting our turn," Kathleen said. "For an audience with him. He has people in there now. We didn't want to be crowding them."

Kilmartin looked at the door to Malone's room.

"Oh, good move there, Kathleen. The crowd in from Tallaght-fornia there—the howiya bags and the Babycham and all that."

"Tommy's crowd are Inchicore," Minogue said.

He looked back down the page to try to remember what the Prater was again. "You big gom," he added.

Kilmartin still had the moves. He tipped the book closed with his right hand, and with his left he pushed at Minogue's arm.

"Come up, let you," he whispered. "Let me take the tough talk out of you, you buff, you. Come up, I say, and not be hiding behind some shagging book!"

Minogue rolled out of the chair and made a grab at Kilmartin's arm.

"Ho, you thick," Kilmartin whispered. "You'll have to get up a damn sight earlier to cod me with that stunt."

Minogue closed on him, but Kilmartin managed to bat him off with a shove.

"None of the tricky stuff, you Mayo hoor, you. Don't make me hurt you."

Kilmartin pretended to roll up his sleeves.

"Well, by God now," he said. "If Molly's after getting himself shot in the arse out in Bray, you're definitely in line to get kicked in the arse here in this place, what-do-you-call-it—"

"Dublin, you iijit. You've only been here for thirty years now."

Minogue made a feint and came around on Kilmartin's left. He caught him wrong-footed from the decoy and he shoved him to the wall.

"Mind the suit, you gobshite," Kilmartin said. "Sorry there, Kathleen. It slipped out."

Minogue poked him in the ribs.

"You leaping hoor's get, you! Sprry, Kathleen! The dirty moves here—"

Minogue let go when he saw the door to Malone's room swing open. He stood back and smiled at Mrs. Malone. Five foot one, Malone had told him. Up and down, not across. Malone's sister Theresa was the spit of her. Kilmartin had been right about the trademark howiya bags of the Dublin-born matrons.

"How's it going," Mrs. Malone said.

"Not so bad, thanks," Minogue replied. "And yourself, Theresa."

"Well, Jeezis, I wasn't one bit well yesterday, I can tell you," said Mrs. Malone.

She looked over at Kilmartin.

"But I suppose I have to believe what I was told in there. Me head is still spinning, so it is."

"We had no idea," Minogue said. "When it happened I mean, out of the blue."

Mrs. Malone sighed and shook her head once. She tilted her head then, and squinted at Minogue.

"Well, are you okay," she said. "Yourself like?"

"God, Missus," Kilmartin said. "He was never all right."

She almost managed a smile.

"Well," she said as though having put down a heavy load. "'Stumbled into it' says smart boy inside. As if that's going to help me get a wink of sleep after that. Am I right, Theresa?"

Malone's sister had her brother's set-in eyes, the laconic Dubliner's now-hold-on-there-just-a-fuckin'-minute way about her. She was married to Larry, an ambitious pipefitter from the north County Dublin. Larry liked to sing, especially after a few jars. Malone had told him that Theresa had recently told her eldest, Malone's favourite niece, that she was going to be a surgeon, so start working on it. Malone had also mentioned that it was Theresa went in twice a week to Mountjoy with stuff for their brother Terry. She was fierce upset even after ten years, on and off, of this.

Mrs. Malone moved her handbag up further on her arm. Minogue spotted a balled-up paper hankie in her fist.

She looked down at her shoes and then straight at Minogue.

"I've been meaning to tell you," she said. "But I couldn't

phone you. I wouldn't a been able to, you know? Thanks, is all I had to say to you. Thanks."

"I did nothing," he said. "Except hit the dirt and roll up in a ball. And pray."

"Ah now," she said. "Go on with you. He says you stayed with him all the way into the operating room."

"He was asleep, Mrs."

"Don't be codding now," Theresa said. "Ma's no thick, are you, Ma?"

Minogue watched her dab at the edges of her eyes.

"He owes me a tenner," he tried. "I didn't want him out of my sight. The Dublin crowd, you know?"

"That's a fact," said Kilmartin and he rubbed his hands together. "I'd have to change sides now and back him on that one."

Mrs. Malone made another effort to smile. She sighed then.

"Nothing personal there," Kilmartin added. "The Dublin crowd, I mean."

"Go away out of that," she said. "A right pair, you two. You're as bad as he says, so yous are."

They watched the two women head down the hall.

"Tough birds," Kilmartin whispered.

"Sure they'd have to be," Kathleen said. "What else could they do?"

"And what's this 'pray' thing?" Kilmartin said. "There's a whopper now."

He reached out and tapped his knuckles on the door, and pushed.

"Get dressed, you Dublin gurrier," he called out, and tapped again. "Cavalry's here. Book him, Danno. Cover your ar—"

Minogue tried to take a step back, but he had been too close. Kilmartin stepped on him as he backed out.

"Sorry," he heard Kilmartin say, and he walked on him again.

Sonia Chang's mother had steel grey hair. There were freckles or something high on her cheeks, sunspots maybe. Her eyes flickered around the hall and then went to her daughter. Only a few words of English, Minogue remembered.

"We're just going," Sonia Chang said.

Goh-ing, Minogue heard. He wondered if he'd ever be able to say to her that he liked how she spoke—how she said *Ih-land*—without offending her, or somebody.

"God, no," Kilmartin said and backed off again. "Honestly. Don't mind us at all, at all. Honestly. Take your time. Really."

He held the smile, nodding all the while, and pulled the door behind them. He looked at Minogue.

"The people in there," he said.

"Right, Jim."

"The two Chinese-looking people in there? The two women. Have they started bringing in nurses from there now?"

"Sonia's his girlfriend."

"You never told me anything about this."

"And her mother."

Kilmartin looked from Minogue to Kathleen and back.

"The mother's old style or something," Minogue said. "She chaperones the daughter."

"A chaperone?"

"The Caucasian thing. It's a bit of a wobbler for the mother."

"Caucasian," Kilmartin said.

"Tommy's a Caucasian."

"He's a Dublinman, is what he is."

"You're one too," Minogue said. "So am I. Caucasians."

Kilmartin's forehead dipped a little. He gave his friend a hard look.

"I have never in all my frigging long and happy life— excuse me, Kathleen, I can't help it—been called that. A . . . *Caucasian?*"

Minogue shrugged, strolled back to the two chairs he had lifted from the waiting area. He found the page on where Freud's office was now a museum. It wasn't some kind of a joke. It looked like everything was walkable in Vienna.

"A takeaway is what I thought," he heard Kilmartin trying to reason with Kathleen. "Your man in there likes his grub, that I know for a fact, yes."

"Maybe I got it all wrong," Minogue said. "Maybe they're in to get the laundry."

Kathleen looked at her watch and she began a slow walk down the hall. Kilmartin flopped down in the chair beside him.

"God almighty," he whispered. "Every day in this town. What next."

He poked Minogue.

"Well. This Quinn character still singing, is he?"

"I believe he is."

Kilmartin stroked his neck slowly and then sighed.

"Jesus. A right wake-up he got. Out of his depth by a long shot."

Minogue nodded. He thought of Sonia Chang's mother again. The things she had seen in her lifetime.

"And his mate shot to bits in the jacks there," Kilmartin said. "Canning, that his name? Well, it's time to reconsider then, isn't it?"

"It's got a lot of things happening in Serious Crimes, I hear."

"Did I hear the RUC had a file on your man as long as a Mass in Lent? What's his face, the fella came down to do them?"

"Roe," Minogue said.

"Yep. A real case. Pure mental, right?"

Minogue nodded.

"A butcher, for the love of God. But the feckers above in the RUC didn't see fit to warn us about him. Bastards."

"They couldn't pin him, I heard."

"Me bollocks. He'd no politics either, is what someone told me. But he was more than just a do-for too. The disguise wasn't just the tools of the trade."

Kilmartin looked down the hall to see if Kathleen was out of earshot. He dropped his voice to a whisper.

"Went around the twist in prison, right?"

"That's what I've been hearing," Minogue replied.

The ring of streets around Vienna would have him dizzy walking maybe. Kilmartin leaned in.

"Tell you something else I heard. He liked to dress up in a certain way. If you take my meaning."

Minogue watched Kilmartin adjusting his tie. Then he turned to wondering how many calls Kilmartin had made. He'd never allow that he was out of any loop.

"Good'll come of it," Kilmartin said. "It's out in the open that the IRA is into drug rackets worse than any of them. Let's see how they wear that one, by God."

Kilmartin stopped when a sedated patient was wheeled down the hall. Minogue stole a glance at Kilmartin's covert study of the sunken face as the attendant pushed the trolley by.

"As if we didn't have enough trouble," Kilmartin went on, his eyes still on the trolley. "Russians and Albanians and Bulgarians and your men the Turks even—and all the other fecking I-don't-know-whats—running their efforts into the country. Baloobas. Christ, Matt, they must think this is heaven here. We're gobshites here, ready and willing to be led down the garden path."

Minogue remembered the curving tarmac path by the banks of the Dodder, the trees ahead, the murmur of the river near where they'd found the girl. What was it her da worked at again, that he couldn't get his head around? Events management, that was it.

"Money laundering," Kilmartin muttered. His eyes still followed the progress of the bed and its gently swaying drip as it continued slowly down the hall.

"Drug labs in industrial estates."

He nudged Minogue.

"Hey. Is it true about that fella Roe, you know? Cutting Doyle up . . . ?"

Minogue nodded. His thoughts had strayed back to Jennifer Halloran now. Moriarty from Fraud had phoned late last night, said Fiona Hegarty wanted to go to the funeral. And could he consider meeting with Fiona, as it might do her some good. She was losing it apparently. It had all fallen apart on her.

"You still say he hadn't a clue?" Kilmartin asked.

"What, Jim?"

"About Doyle, that fella. That he'd palmed off the pills on that girl . . . ?"

"Niamh. Niamh Kenny."

"Well?"

"I don't know."

"Jesus, you're playing your cards very close to your chest there, bucko."

"I really don't. I just know that Quinn started talking after he got the witness protection signed."

"Huh. A bloody record that too—in thirty-six hours. He must have the goods."

The trolley turned the corner where Kathleen was standing reading something on the wall. Kilmartin uncovered his watch.

"Ah come on," he said. "What are they doing in there? You know what I'm thinking, don't you. Chinese mammy or not in there with them."

"Ah now. They're not. You have to be married for that carry-on, Jim."

"Very smucking fart aren't you. But look, back to Quinn. He should be able to clear that up in one second, the business about that unfortunate schoolgirl, the Kelly girl. Right?"

"Kenny," said Minogue.

"Isn't that what I said?"

"Niamh Kenny."

He stared at Kilmartin.

"Yes? Well?"

"Sixteen, she was. Sixteen, Jim. Niamh Kenny. Have you got the name now?"

Kilmartin made to say something but held off.

The faces of the mother and father came back to Minogue. It was gone eleven o'clock when he'd gotten to the Kennys' house. Met the Kenny boy, a huge man actually, a rugger boy no doubt, with an American twang already. They'd talked until one. The mother's head had been almost vibrating—he still couldn't get a better word to describe it. Her hands too, of course, and the eyes on her: sunk in, like a blind woman's, unfocused. Sedated to hell and back, he'd figured. She mightn't even know it's the middle of the night. He had expected her to scream, jump up, do something, but she was like a stroke had hit her.

No let-up from the father until an hour or so into it. Minogue had waited him out. Colm Kenny had burst into tears in the middle of half-shouting, half-whispering something about predators, or jackals, or something Minogue couldn't quite remember exactly. And Una Fahy, the aunt, looking at him with an expression he didn't want to believe was disdain. He had sat in the Citroën for half an hour at the bottom of the road then afterward—smoking, and taking more mouthfuls than he had expected from the bottle of Jameson's he had in the boot.

And that odd conversation with the same Una Fahy yesterday on thephone: could they meet, to discuss some important matters? What matters exactly, had been his first question, of course. Her answer had been as annoying as it was intriguing, the answer that had him deciding to head over to her office in the morning after Quinn's court appearance. The matter related to the death of a suspect recently charged with defrauding a Dublin company of an amount of money. Jennifer Halloran? Ms. Fahy'd rather not say over the phone. Said she. Beyond haughty, it was. A bollicking, she deserved.

"Well?" said Kilmartin. "Are you still with us here? After that little performance?"

"He said he didn't know."

"Ah, my arse to that! He falls into witness protection inside of thirty-six hours and he doesn't know that? Who are you trying to cod? Who is *he* trying to cod?"

Minogue shrugged. He remembered that a vein had stuck out in Colm Kenny's neck when he'd told Kenny, again, that Quinn wasn't connected to their daughter's death. That Niamh had gotten the drugs from Doyle. That there was probably no way any parent could have predicted that such a fella like Doyle or his cronies down at that amusement place in Bray would have been able to get to sixteen-year-old kids.

"He says no, Jim. It's head-the-ball at that arcade. Gannon, was the pal of Doyle's. Gaga. He says that Doyle told him he had an in with the Albanians. That they were giving him freebies."

"'Samplers,'" said Kilmartin. "Christ, like the pharmaceutical crowd give the doctors. Honest to God . . . !"

He uncrossed his legs and plucked at a trouser crease over his knee to restore it.

"Tried to play everyone, didn't he, Doyle. Smart arse— look where it got him. Well, wherever he is now, I mean. Bits of him all up and down the Belfast road maybe? I say the Northern crowd knew all along."

Kilmartin leaned in again.

"Like they knew about Quinn's sidekick all along, the fella out in the jacks there with the lead poisoning."

Canning had been shot at least twice in the head, Minogue had learned.

"Now here's the thing," Kilmartin went on. "The shite hasn't hit the fan yet, has it, I mean really hit the fan. You know what I'm saying."

Minogue raised an eyebrow.

"The insider. Whoever's with our mob that was throwing them bits."

"Uh," Minogue said.

"Quinn knows damn well who the insider is. That's why he got protection in world-record time. They want him something fierce, oh yes. It's his best card. He'll hold out a long while I tell you. They can get anyone and he knows it— in prison, relatives, anywhere."

Kilmartin was the fourth person who had told Minogue this in the past two days. Still, he wasn't sure; he had stopped being surprised at how little he cared now.

"He wants everything, Matt, Quinn does," said

Kilmartin. "The papers, the witness relocation, a lorryload of money. And do you know what?"

"Go ahead."

"He'll get it. He will. The fucker."

Minogue watched Kathleen take her time strolling back down the hall. He didn't return her wink and smile. Kilmartin gave him another nudge.

"He knows how much it's worth to tell us which of ours was on the take for them in Belfast. Our frigging Judas. Whoever fed Quinn's butty—Canning, now I remember his name—to them."

Minogue almost decided to tell Kilmartin then. That Beans Canning had passed nothing on to the Drugs Central detective who was supposed to be cultivating him. That he'd never taken money. That Central had begun to conclude that Canning was trying to string them along and to deflect them from Quinn too.

"Have you heard of disinformation?" he asked.

"Course I have. What the hell are you asking that for?"

"It means that we mightn't ever know. Basically."

Kilmartin sat back in his chair. He gave his friend the crooked smile he offered when it was clear that he was dealing with iijits.

"Well, listen to you," he said. "Up is down, down is up. 'We may never know, Jim.'"

"Well, we won't."

"Well, listen to me now. I'm going to tell you something that you won't like one bit."

Kilmartin seemed to reconsider.

"Ah, never mind," he grunted. He looked at his watch. "Jasus, I can't be sitting here all the day."

"Say it, Jim. Whatever it is."

Kilmartin glanced over at Kathleen.

"Okay. I will then. What if a fella said that you don't *want* to know about this fink we have somewhere in CDU. Or worse."

"What's worse. That I'm in the Nile?"

Kilmartin drew himself up.

"Well ha, bloody ha. No. 'Worse' is this, that you're covering up for . . . ?"

Minogue kept his eyes on Kilmartin's. Kilmartin nodded toward the door to Malone's room.

"He has a brother, doesn't he . . . ?"

Minogue said nothing.

". . . that he, er, cares deeply about?"

Minogue looked around Kilmartin's face. No, it wasn't a joke.

"Are you registering anything I'm saying there?"

Minogue blinked.

"I take that to be a maybe," Kilmartin whispered. "Listen. Try and be objective for once. Our friend is in Drugs Central, isn't he. He knows Quinn and Canning and the others too, I'll bet. He knows, what do they call it, 'The Life.' Well?"

Minogue's eyes had slipped out of focus. Nothing changed, really. Kilmartin had always had it in for Malone. Already he saw himself walking down the hall and out into the car park.

"Here's a word to hold, Matt. To hold and keep. *International*. We're not some frigging oul rainy afterthought on the edge of Europe anymore, are we. Welcome to the real world, pal. Oh yes."

Minogue knew that he had to do something before the anger took him over. Twenty how many years had he known Jim Kilmartin, watched him finesse the bull-necked Mayo culchie act into an almost flawless decoy, seen him sink his teeth into cases and put away what must be scores, hundreds, of murderers.

Minogue narrowed his eyes. Kilmartin sat back.

"I don't hear much out of you, do I? That tells me I'm not far off the mark."

"They'd love to hear you talk like this," Minogue said.

"Who would?"

"People who'd make something out of the Guards tearing away at one another."

"Oh Christ, do you think I get any satisfaction out of thinking like this? I'm not saying he did or he didn't, Matt. I'm just saying that these things happen. Keep your eye on the ball, etcetera."

"They'd be—"

Sonia Chang had yanked open the door. She said something in what Minogue decided must be Chinese. Minogue stood and gave Mrs. Chang a nod.

"Fresh and well you're looking today, Sonia," he said.

"My mother," she said.

"How's it going with yourself, Mrs."

Kilmartin was on his feet by now.

"A big dinner, he wants," Sonia said. "At the restaurant, of course."

"Well, look out when that gets going," Kilmartin said. "We'd all pile in for that if we knew when and where. Wouldn't we, Matt?"

Macau was the name of the place, Minogue remembered now. They had been held there for three years. Malone had told them it had been touch and go until the restaurant got going, that there'd been a lot of tension. Sonia's mother wanted to go to Australia in the first place. She thought the Irish, or more particularly the Dublin people, were nice enough but disorganized, even with all the money here now.

She'd given up on learning English recently. Sonia was not looking forward to a looming showdown between her ma and da, Malone had told him. Her da was pushing harder for Sonia to go into accountancy proper, and get out of payroll software or whatever thing Malone had told him she was doing when she wasn't in the restaurant helping out.

"He's stronger today," she said. "Thomas."

"I suppose," Minogue said. "But I doubt his nose has straightened out."

She smiled.

"You have to be born outside Dublin to be handsome. Maybe you didn't know?"

"Hah," she said in that breathy sigh he'd heard from her before.

"But Thomas said not to believe you if you say such things. You see?"

"Well put," said Kilmartin.

Sonia waved at Kathleen. Minogue watched the six feet of Kilmartin curl a little more as he tried to get the mother's attention away from some point on the floor down the hall. She wouldn't look at him, but he kept shuffling and trying. He began speaking as though to a deaf child.

"I think we're in for rain," he said. "Mrs. Chang?"

She glanced up.

"Rain," he said, and pointed at the ceiling. "Good for the garden, but. Cabbages?"

She nodded, and Minogue saw her eyes sweep over toward her daughter's feet.

"Come on," Kathleen said. "We don't have long."

Kilmartin took his cue, said a loud Good Luck now to Mrs. Chang along with a stiff bow, and pushed open the door. From Malone inside, he heard "Jasus, they've sent in the bouncers to get me out of here." Kilmartin's "Well lookit the hard chaw himself wrapped up with a nappy, my Jasus."

Kathleen rolled her eyes. Minogue paused in the doorway, and put his hand in to get the baby Powers whiskey he had bought at the off-licence. Forgotten it. The head was going on him.

"Well, Kathleen," he heard from Malone, the nasal drone of the Dub accent full-bore now. "They send in the good-looking one last, do they?"

Minogue looked through the closing door, saw Malone's hairy leg stretched out over the sheet, the beginnings of the bandage above his knee. His mobile, yes, in that pocket. Wallet, keys. Notebook. No, no whiskey. List.

He was alone in the hall. Things had taken on that strange cast again, and he was slipping into thought. Dreamy, Kathleen would notice, no doubt.

He heard Kilmartin calling Malone Wyatt Bloody Earp, Kathleen's short laugh. How everything seemed to go on, he thought; particularly, relentlessly. No wonder he was tired. He hadn't slept more than a couple of hours straight in almost a week now.

Meetings. He wondered if he could call off the one Fiona Hegarty asked for. Why outside Clarendon Street church? She wanted to thank him, she said. Was it some kind of a prank? Off her rocker?

And the Kennys would be waiting to hear back from him again. They didn't understand why it took ten days to get results from the pills Gaga Gannon had handed in, the ones Doyle had gotten from the Albanians.

He thought about Jennifer Halloran's brother. About why he wasn't as angry now at Kilmartin's sly digs about Malone. About Tynan, and his talk of expediting the program. An earlier start, was the phrase he'd used yesterday—get that German phrasebook working. Why, he'd asked Tynan twice, with his letter sealed in the envelope under his plate in the restaurant: Haven't I screwed up enough? And he knew that Tyan knew what was in the envelope, the way he wouldn't let on or even look at it. Something he'd said in that tone that a lot of people would surely take as sarcasm about the art of moving from failure to failure with confidence.

His list changed daily, sometimes hourly, these last few days. The goat and the donkey, and the two-room house looking out over the bay from the Burren heights, had moved down. A fool he was surely, a bigger one than he'd been a week ago, and the sleepless small hours of the morning told him that.

"What's keeping you?"

It was Kathleen's voice from the doorway behind him.

He turned.

"Little things," he said, as always.

He'd phone Iseult the minute he got out of here; coax her and Eamonn up to the paths over Shankill, into the deeper woods where few people went.

Kilmartin pulled open the door.

"What the hell is keeping you? Come in and explain yourself—and translate what this fecking Dub is talking about. By God he must have been clocked in the head the way he talks, he hasn't learned the . . ."

Kilmartin stopped, stared at Minogue.

"Are you all right?"

Minogue nodded.

"I'm jacked, in actual fact," he said.

Kilmartin let the door close behind him.

"It wasn't your fault, you know," he said.

"That's Bray for you," Minogue managed. "Full of surprises."

"Ah, it's a kip—I *never* liked it. *Ever*."

"It's improved."

"It was that girl, I meant," said Kilmartin. "The Fraud thing."

Minogue had forgotten that Kilmartin still referred to anyone under ninety as a girl.

"You don't say," was all he could think to say himself.

"I know it," said Kilmartin. "And lookit. That other thing with Malone, that was only a theory. That's all it was. Maybe I'm watching too many of those cop shows."

Minogue looked at Kilmartin's tie. It had come askew from the horsing around.

"What?"

"That's the worst tie they ever made."

Kilmartin was quicker than Minogue remembered. He had him in a headlock and halfway in the door before Minogue decided he wouldn't even try to get free. He heard Kilmartin's shoe on the door to Malone's room.

"Look at what's lurking around these parts bejasus, sorry Kathleen, again—fecking autograph hounds, by God. I'll fire him out the window, so I will."

Minogue was released. He looked over to Malone. The sardonic gaze he expected wasn't there, just a stare. Malone kept his eyes on Minogue's and nodded slowly, once. Minogue could only nod in return.

WHY ISN'T THIS ABOUT NIAMH

Minogue didn't remember the Special Criminal Court looking this much like, well, he wanted to say Sarajevo, since they'd been pulling in the gangs after the murder of the journalist. Was that five years ago already?

It had taken all of four minutes for Quinn's appearance and remand. He watched the soldiers climb into the Toyota Land Cruisers he didn't know the Army had until today, and head out. He'd given up trying to spot the ones on the roofs and the parapets and in the doorways all down the street. And now, even with the barricades down, the street was still strangely quiet and empty. He looked up at the overcast sky and stretched. The helicopter's batting and droning was gone. The air was close, heavy with smells here in the old part of the city.

He nodded at two of the Serious Crimes detectives who had been called by the State. The judge would leave by car, no doubt, under escort.

He should phone Kathleen, he should fix the letter of resignation, he should stop thinking about cigarettes. He should also stay way to hell away from Una Fahy, Niamh Kenny's aunt.

Una Fahy had turned out to be a solicitor all right, and

Minogue remembered that it had taken a few troubles to get the right side of her that day at the Kennys' house. Far too late now, he thought, and didn't much care really. But he hadn't been able to hide his surprise that she had left a message—not about her niece, or how Colm Kenny was going to sue every Guard in Ireland for letting a criminal walk the streets . . . but about Jennifer Halloran.

He looked at his watch: five minutes to get to the Distillery Building, the far side of the Markets where Una Fahy had her office. Full of barristers' and solicitors' offices now since they'd done it up. A shame really.

He made it across Church Street at a trot. How could he whinge about that burning ache in his knee, while Malone had lost more than a litre of blood? He stopped at the SPAR by the Distillery Building, his hand on the change in his pocket.

He didn't have much fight in him this morning. He watched a woman with a bockety leg step out the door, unwrapping the cellophane off a pack of Carrolls. She let it fall to the ground, drew out one hurriedly, and lit up. She noticed Minogue watching. She frowned at him and headed off up the path, her body swinging around the bad leg.

Somehow, Minogue got through the door of the Distillery Building without a packet of cigarettes. There was light overhead in the foyer, a catwalk style of a bridge or corridor crossing to join two parts of the floors upstairs. Fierce mod entirely, the cement and bare brick.

The porter at the desk was on the phone. Two gowned barristers swept out of the lift, passed him. The accent off one of them, the way he marched, as much and more than something about the gown and the suit and the shine on his shoes scraped at Minogue's patience. He took the *Mirror* from the end of the counter.

They'd gotten a picture of Quinn somehow, and put it in the corner, one of him wrapped in a flak-jacket being shoved into a car by two detectives. "I knew my family was next!" was the headline. There had been no pictures of that Grogan fella yet, but old ones of the godfathers in Belfast had been on the television after the arrests. He'd never heard of Roe before.

The fox killed by the van up in Goatstown had been deemed a front-page story for Indo readers too. Some Environment Officer—did they have such things now?—was snapped beside the outstretched body.

The porter put down the phone, but when Minogue looked up to answer him, the woman walking across from a doorway under the catwalk was Una Fahy.

She put away her glasses before ordering coffees. Minogue didn't remember her being so compact in her movements, her eyes so tired-looking.

She chose a table well away from a chattering bunch. Minogue sipped and looked around while she went back to get brown sugar. A swell joint here.

"Thanks for coming in," she said.

"I was in the area."

"Special Criminal Court? Green Street . . . ?"

He didn't answer. She stirred her coffee and scooped off the froth.

"It's still a small town," she said.

He wanted to ask her how he thought she was entitled to say that, being as she was from the country. He watched the man behind the counter instead.

"I wouldn't try to compromise your position," she said.

"Why isn't this about Niamh," he said.

She paused as if to absorb the rudeness. She spoke in a very soft voice then, her eyes focused on the saucer.

"It doesn't need to be. Colm and all the family are very grateful for . . . well, for what was done. They're coming around. Colm is, I should say."

Minogue waited.

"So he won't be launching an action to sue the State, the Garda Siochana, and anyone else he can think of," she said.

"He's not doing anyone any favours there."

"Do you think I don't understand my own brother?"

"Good, so. Then you'd have told him that he wouldn't have a leg to stand on. Being as you're a solicitor and all that?"

She sat back and looked around the room. He thought about the fox in his garden, if it had been the one run over, about why he felt so badly about it.

"I was going to give a speech from the dock here," she said.

"Before sentencing?"

"Just about. It would have to do with denial, and guilt, and anger, and a lot of other stuff."

"The Blue or the White?"

"Pardon?"

"The source of the Nile, Mrs. Fahy."

"Ms."

"That's grand."

"I was Mrs."

"None of my business, excuse me for dragging the matter into our conversation."

She searched the Inspector's face for sarcasm.

"I got rid of him," she said. "He was like Colm."

He kept his eyes on the pattern on the surface of the coffee.

"Jennifer Halloran," she said.

He looked up.

"No," she said. "I'm not acting for her family. I told Mrs. Halloran that too. I mean, I declined."

"A small town, you were saying."

"Our office handles a lot of cases in that line. Compensation. Labour law. That sort of thing."

"Why did you decide to tell me this?"

"I'm not sure now that I should say anything more."

He sat forward in the chair, felt the elastoplasts on his knee. A bruised bone, Malone had, he remembered. The bullet had gone by only two millimetres away. He'd managed to kill Roe outright with the one, the only, shot that had hit him.

"I'll be on my way, so."

"You're not curious about it?"

"I am," he said. "But I wouldn't want to compromise your position, to be sure now."

"Colm," she said and paused. "Colm. You know why he is the way he is?"

"I could guess."

"Guilt?"

"That'd be on the list there, yes."

She nodded slowly.

"I want you to know what I told Mrs. Halloran. That in my opinion, she had no case or cause against the Guards for what happened."

Minogue sat back. He tried to keep his face from showing his anger.

"I've seen what guilt does, Inspector. I know what it does."

He kept up his stare.

"It might destroy Colm yet. And his family. It's why he was so angry at you, at the other Guards."

Minogue began to imagine pulling at the cellophane, the

little tag that released the two parts of the cellophane. The silver foil off his thumb, and crushed quickly against his forefinger. He'd hold the packet up to his nose, of course, to smell the fresh tobacco—the fresh, chemically saturated tobacco, that is. The first drag on a cigarette after years would have him dizzy.

She was still looking at him.

"So here is my chief impertinence now," Una Fahy said. "The point of me chasing you down."

He was having a hard time keeping his eyes in focus now. He looked down at his cup.

"I told you about Mrs. Halloran for a reason. It's because I think that you should not go on with a big weight of guilt around your neck."

He ran his finger along the handle of the cup. How much of a racket it would make if he fecked this across the room, he wondered.

"I did some checking before I gave that advice to Mrs. Halloran."

"Did you, now."

"Let me just say this, that she would have done what she did anyway. She had decided, that if she was caught . . ."

"How do you know that?"

"In her office, in her desk, there was a letter. She had written it, a sort of a diary thing, not long before she went away on a holiday. I haven't shown it to the mother yet."

The last of the coffee was bitter enough. He thought he heard light rain now but the skylight glass was so distorted he couldn't tell. Somebody's mobile went off, an awful piece of Beethoven.

"That's private information," she said.

"I'm going to pass that information on to two people," he said to her. "Two Guards."

"It'll stay private?"

He nodded. She began to fiddle with her teaspoon. There was some grey in her hair he hadn't noticed before.

"Did one John Tynan and you have a conversation recently?"

It wasn't really a smile, he thought again as he headed out onto Church Street that was indeed wet and grey.

There was a line up at the counter in the SPAR. He was late already for something, he'd forgotten what.